# TOKENS OF MY CONFECTION

## D.S. WILLIAMS

# PROLOGUE

C ady knew she was in trouble.

Unlocking the front door, she found Jameson waiting at the dining room table, his rigid figure an indication of how tightly strung his emotions were. His broad shoulders vibrated with tension. With anger.

Taking a deep breath, Cady dropped her purse on the couch and walked further into the room but kept a healthy distance between Jameson and herself. The waves of fury emanating from him had her nerves on edge, a warning to Cady that something was wrong. Very wrong. With a wary eye locked on her husband, she scanned the room for Montgomery. He normally greeted her at the door, his fluffy tail wagging a happy greeting.

"You're home early," she commented quietly, her breath hitching in her throat. She listened anxiously for sounds in the house, some clue to where Montgomery was. She desperately wanted to ask, but Jameson hated the dog with a passion and his mood was already black. Perhaps it was best if she navigated the mess she was in first, searched for Montgomery later.

For a minute, she wasn't sure he was going to answer, and the silence stretched out between them, increasing the tension. Cady glanced uneasily at her purse, wondering if she should turn tail and run.

"You're late."

His words made her jump. There had been a time, a few years ago, when that same voice had filled her with an overwhelming sense of security. Now it had a much different effect and Cady cringed. "Yes. I'm sorry. I had a cake to finish and it took a little longer than I expected."

Jameson's shoulders tensed, and his hands scrunched into fists. "Cakes. It's always the cakes." He held up a page torn from the newspaper. "Fucking cakes," he sneered. "Cady Caldwell. The Queen of Cakes."

He spat her name as if it was a curse and Cady considered her options. Should she admit to knowledge of the newspaper report, or plead ignorance? Which one would work? Jameson's angry stare, his brown eyes penetrating, made it hard to decide. "Why don't we go out for supper?" Cady suggested, deciding avoidance might be best. Perhaps he could be sidetracked – though the whisky bottle and empty glass beside it suggested it was already too late. Jameson had been drinking, and given the nearly empty bottle, he'd been at it for a while. Certainly, long enough to work up into a rage.

He got to his feet, still clutching the newspaper in his fist. "Did you think I wouldn't find out?"

Cady shook her head, her eyes wide. She'd been so careful. When Mario decided to enter her cake in the prestigious Decorators of America competition, he'd promised to keep her name out of it. She didn't need the attention, not when Jameson was so incredibly jealous. When Mario showed her the newspaper this morning, his blue eyes filled with regret, Cady knew it had been a terrible mistake. True to Mario's promise, the newspaper hadn't used her name, but what she'd assumed would take up a few lines in the back pages turned out to be front-page news. 'Mario's Bakery Takes out Prestigious Gold Medal for a Sublime Creation'. It went on to describe the cake and its decoration at length, and the prestige which came from one of San Francisco's favorite bakeries scooping the gold medal out from under the noses of other, more famous bakeries throughout the States. They hadn't mentioned her name, but the subtle hint about the creator being 'the wife of a world-renowned chef' was enough to cause overwhelming damage.

Jameson stepped towards her, his movements slow, measured, his eyes burning with hatred. "You smart ass bitch. You're throwing my failure in my face!"

Cady twisted her head rapidly from side to side, backing away. "No Jameson... that's not true... you aren't a failure..."

"Offering fake sympathy when those bastards over-looked me for the third Michelin star, pretending to care! I bet you were laughing behind my back, the whole time. You're *nothing* without me! You slap a bit of icing on a cake and you win a fucking award for it! Thought you were clever, not giving them your name? You must think I'm a damned fool. It could only be your doing; that idiot you work for is such a dolt, it couldn't possibly have been his work. You're going to wish you were dead by the time I've finished with you!"

Cady panicked, making a dash for the door even knowing it was a useless endeavor. She shouldn't have come inside, should have driven straight to Harry's when she saw Jameson's car in the driveway. She could have come up with some excuse for visiting, even though she hadn't seen Harry for nearly six months. Jameson's jealous rages had isolated her from everyone, using her desperation for his financial help as a counterweight to everything he demanded.

He wrapped one hand around her arm and wrenched Cady backwards. She struggled desperately to escape, but he was stronger. He wrapped his arms around her waist and Cady kicked and struggled when he dragged her through the house, thrusting her down into the basement. She caught her ankle on a step as she fell, and it wrenched painfully. Any hope of escape was gone and when Cady hit the cold concrete floor, she curled into a ball, making herself into as small a target as possible.

The first kick created a wellspring of agony in her lower back, convincing Cady her kidneys had exploded. The second kick cracked a couple of ribs. Jameson resorted to using his fists, punching Cady's face until she was seeing stars. Her screams were reduced to horrified whimpers, and then little moans as her body became a ball of incessant pain. Jameson clutched her shoulders, lifting her head again and again, slamming her against the unforgiving concrete. He stopped abruptly, using a knife to tear her shirt away, his eyes filled with fury. The knife flicked through her bra, catching her skin when he cut through the fragile lace and Cady whimpered. "You're an ungrateful little whore. You used me from the beginning," Jameson muttered, shifting his attention to her jeans.

She tried to see past the stars inhibiting her sight. When Jameson came into focus, she watched anxiously when he lit a cigarette, lowering it from his lips to blow against the smoldering end, to make the ash redden.

He brought the burning cigarette down and pressed the tip of it against her naked breast. Cady screamed and screamed, the lancing pain in her head surpassed by the pain as her skin burned. Her last conscious thought, as the world darkened around her was that Jameson was going to exceed his plan. He'd announced she was going to wish she were dead.

Cady thought she probably was dead.

## 1

M eredith Caldwell paced. A fine figure of a woman, she was still a beauty in her advancing years. Her gray hair was stylishly cut, and she filled out a pair of jeans like a woman who was two decades younger. Yes, indeed; a damn fine-looking woman. Sheriff George Davis watched as she walked back and forth across the living room, pausing on the completion of every lap to peer through the lace curtains, watching anxiously for an approaching car. He idly wondered if she might wear a hole in the carpet before her granddaughter arrived.

George tried – and failed – to keep his eyes off her shapely legs. He sipped from the coffee mug he gripped in one calloused hand then cleared his throat. "Meredith, for Christ's sake – sit down. They'll get here when they get here. You wearin' a hole in the carpet ain't gonna hurry them up."

She stopped pacing and glanced at George with anxious blue eyes, tiny frown lines marring her skin. "Shouldn't they be here by now?"

George glanced at his watch. "It's a couple of hours

drive to Garrison and they could have hit traffic leaving Billings. I'd guess they'll arrive anytime in the next half hour." He watched Meredith resume pacing and drew himself from the chair, placing a hand on her arm. "Meredith. You pacing ain't gonna make a lick of difference. Sit down. Please."

With a heavy sigh, Meredith took his advice and settled on the edge of the couch, but her attention remained focused on the window. She'd waited so long for this day. She'd met her other two grandchildren more than twelve months back, but today was the culmination of a long wait to meet her eldest granddaughter. Even now, it was obvious she couldn't quite believe it was going to happen. If only it was under better circumstances.

George sat back down and picked up his coffee mug. "You haven't told me much about her."

"I don't know much."

George shrugged, determined to keep Meredith talking if it meant she'd relax a smidgeon. "So, tell me what you do know."

Meredith clasped her hands together. "Her name is Arcadia, but she apparently prefers Cady." Her gaze had to be forcefully torn away from the window to face her friend.

"No surprise there." George grinned. "You've got to admit; they gave those kids the worst damn names." He'd never heard such ridiculous names in his life – even with the younger generation's penchant for bestowing God-awful monikers on their kids – Meredith's son had taken the cake.

"I've met Sid and Harry. It's been wonderful having the opportunity to know them after the shock of discovering they existed." Meredith smiled warmly; obviously pleased with the relationship she'd forged with the girls.

George knew that despite the masculine-sounding names, 'Sid' and 'Harry' were women. Sidonia and Hermione. God-only-knew-where their parents had gotten those names. It wasn't much wonder the girls preferred the nicknames they'd bestowed on themselves. It had been an emotional moment for Meredith when she'd discovered her deceased son had fathered three daughters. It had come as quite a revelation, not only to Meredith, but to the entire small community of Garrison.

"You still don't know why Cady wouldn't meet with you before now?" George asked quietly.

Meredith had lost her battle with impatience and was pacing again. She shrugged. "I have no idea. Maybe because she was older, Mark managed to turn her against us. Lord knows, he made his own disdain obvious enough. It wouldn't come as a surprise if he'd told Cady any number of lies."

Everyone in town knew the story of the Caldwell's oldest son – Mark had gone bad as a teenager, rebelling against his parents and descending into a sordid life of drug use and alcoholism. He'd up and left Garrison when he was seventeen, and other than intermittent contact with Meredith, usually begging for money, he'd had no contact with his parents.

Jim Caldwell had passed away just a few short years after Mark's disappearance, the strain of worrying about his son bringing on a heart attack at the age of forty-nine. Meredith had been left to bring up their younger son alone, but she'd done an excellent job. Unlike Mark, David had matured into a good-hearted, responsible man. Meredith was so proud of him; he was caring and considerate, and he'd never given her a lick of trouble in the years since.

Three years ago, George had been the one to bring the

terrible news to Meredith of Mark's death. She'd accepted the news stoically, reassuring George that to all intents and purposes, Mark had been dead to her for years. Despite the heartache, she'd provided her son with a Christian burial, bringing his body back to Garrison and he'd been laid to rest close to his father's grave in the town cemetery.

The few belongings Mark had in his possession when he died were forwarded to Meredith. It had taken a few weeks before she could face going through them and George recalled her excitement when she discovered there were three birth certificates for three baby girls, resulting from a relationship Mark had with a woman named Lisa Drummond.

With David's support, Meredith hired a reputable private investigator to find out more about Mark's family. Over the next few months, she'd received sporadic reports, learning that Mark lived with Lisa Drummond for several years. They'd had the three children together, but the relationship was volatile from all accounts and there'd been more than one occasion when the children were taken by social services. Reports of arrests for drug use, alcoholism – even prostitution – were recorded for both Mark and Lisa. Meredith had been devastated by the knowledge; worried about what the three little girls had dealt with, and so sorry she hadn't been able to help them.

"You think Mark would have fed Cady more bullshit than he did Sid and Harry?" George questioned. There was something strange about the situation, and George had been chewing over the mystery for months, ever since Meredith first contacted her granddaughters. While Sid and Harry embraced their newly-discovered grandmother with open arms, Cady had been reticent, refusing to meet her. Cady's current circumstances could have something to do with it, but George's gut instincts told him there was more to the story than met the eye.

"She's the eldest," Meredith pointed out. "Sid and Harry were maybe too young to influence." She chewed her lip pensively, searching the street outside.

"She's agreed to come now," George offered. "Maybe what was a bad situation for the girl will turn into something good, for both of you."

Meredith frowned, crossing her arms over her chest. "She didn't agree to come. Not without considerable pressure from Sid and Harry. I think it's been an uphill battle to get her here at all."

"She'll be safer." George intended to be certain of it, after hearing what her bastard husband had done. He'd seen the medical reports – the information he'd kept from Meredith. She was anxious enough about Cady coming to stay, without hearing about the beating the young woman had taken; the history of domestic abuse. George soothed his conscience by reminding himself of his legal obligation to suppress the reports. He'd received them as a courtesy from the San Francisco PD and once George read them, he'd taken no chances, going so far as to send Kane to collect the young woman from Billings. Nothing was going to happen to Cady Caldwell on his watch, he respected and cared for her grandmamma too much to let anything go wrong.

Meredith turned to him, offering him a tense smile. "Thank you, George. I appreciate everything you've done."

"It's nothin', Meredith. I know how much you've come to love Sid and Harry and the SFPD agreed it was a good idea to get Cady out of California."

"There's still no word about her husband?" Meredith asked.

George scowled. "No sign of him, he's lying low." The bastard had disappeared after he'd beaten the crap out of his young wife and left her for dead – and George's blood boiled whenever he thought about it. Wife beaters were lower than pond scum and George had seen a few in his time, but this case – where it involved someone he knew, even by association - was stuck in his craw. He wouldn't rest until Jameson Le Batelier was captured.

"They're still searching, aren't they?"

"Yeah. He can't disappear for long. The guy is too well-known. His face is recognizable."

"George, be honest with me." Bright blue eyes sought his and he gave Meredith his full attention. "Do you think he'll try to hurt her again?"

George inhaled sharply; this was a conversation he'd hoped to avoid. "I can't answer that," he said gently. "This asshole doesn't have any prior convictions, but I don't know enough to say what he might do. There's a history of violence with Cady, but it was never enough for the police to press charges, not when Cady wouldn't corroborate. What did Sid and Harry tell you?"

"They had no idea about the physical abuse. But neither of them had seen Cady for nearly six months." Meredith turned back to the window.

George knew what happened with Cady was standard procedure for a wife beater – isolating them from family and friends. He wondered how Cady's sisters were coping with what had happened. Domestic violence never just affected the victim; it had a ripple effect on their families and loved ones too.

George heard a car coming down the street, his years as Sheriff fine-tuning his senses. "Looks like the wait is over. I think that's them."

---

## 2

D eputy Kane Garrison drew to a halt in front of Meredith's house, glancing in the rearview mirror at the young woman sitting behind him. "We're here."

Sid whooped with joy. "Gran's gonna be so excited to meet you, Cades. Let's go!" With a brief smile, Sid pushed the car door open and launched herself onto the front walk towards her grandmother.

Cady watched Sid throw herself into the arms of the older woman who stood near the bottom of the steps. Even from the car, she could hear Sid chattering a mile a minute. When Deputy Garrison picked them up from Billings, Sid had climbed into the car beside him without a hint of shyness and proceeded to talk his ear off for the entire two-hour journey. Typical for Sid, she was exuberant and excitable, her joie de vivre tangible to everyone around her. Through Sid's intensive questioning, Cady knew that Kane Garrison was married with twin sons and was a descendant of the original town founders, who'd travelled across the wilderness to Montana in the mid-eighteenth century and settled in the area.

The Deputy stepped out of the car, reaching down to open the back door for her. "Ms. Caldwell?" He held the door patiently, waiting for her to make a move. She was as skittish as a newborn colt and he watched her take a deep breath, centering herself, but still she didn't attempt to get out of the car. He leaned over and regarded her for a second or two, offering her a warm smile. "Your Grandmamma's excited about meeting you, honey. Come on out, now."

Cady brushed her fingers across Churchill's fur, savoring the comfort she found in patting him. She'd been apprehensive since they set off from Harry's apartment this morning, and the anxiety just kept reaching higher levels as the day wore on. Even now, Cady wished she were back in San Francisco, where she'd built a life for herself and her sisters.

Until it all collapsed in a whirlpool of disaster.

Why she'd even agreed to come to Garrison, she couldn't say. Sid and Harry had repeatedly tried to convince her she'd like her grandmother once she met her, but flash-backs to the past had kept Cady from contacting the woman. It unleashed too much pain, too many memories that she'd spent years suppressing. But circumstances out of her control had brought her to this point, and Sid and Harry had pressured her into agreeing, despite her qualms. Stuck between one nightmare and another, with nowhere to go in San Francisco where she would be safe, Cady found herself agreeing to stay with her grandmother, at least until Jameson was captured. With a sigh, Cady cautiously edged towards the door, Churchill's leash clutched in her fingers.

She eased out of the car, her eyes widening when she caught site of Meredith's handsome Victorian. It was one of the finest homes in Garrison, built in the late nineteenth century; it featured beautifully painted gingerbread features and a turret, which stood to the right of the front door. A wide veranda graced the entire lower floor and the gardens were a treat to behold in mid-summer, filled with flowers in a multitude of colors and shapes. "It's a lovely house, Ms. Caldwell. I'm sure you'll enjoy your stay."

"Thank you, Deputy."

Kane took the leash from Cady's fingers and watched the dog climb down eagerly from the back seat, intent on inspecting a new garden. Kane stifled a grin, reaching for his wide-brimmed hat. The trip had been worth it, if only to get a look at George's face when he discovered Kane had transported the huge dog in a County Sheriff's vehicle. He had no doubt he'd be tasked with cleaning the back seat until every speck of dog fur was eradicated, but it had been a deal breaker if he hadn't agreed. Cady Caldwell had absolutely no intentions of getting in the car if the dog didn't get in with her. Thinking back, it had been the most animated she'd been during the entire trip, eyes flashing with single-minded determination as she'd stood at the curb, her fists clenched, and her jaw set in a stubborn line. Reminded him of his wife when she got a full head of steam up, and that was always fun. Of course, with Hallie, making up was the best fun of all.

Kane strode across the lawn with Churchill, catching George's horror-struck expression from the corner of his eye. Yep, he'd definitely be cleaning out the patrol car in the morning. He might even be forced into doing it tonight if the way George's eyes were bugging out was any indication.

Cady hitched her purse onto her shoulder, taking the first tentative steps towards where Sid stood with the older woman. Meredith Caldwell was attractive, her grey hair curling loosely around a face that was lined, but soft, and she was beautifully styled with subtle make-up. Cady couldn't see much resemblance between this woman and the father she remembered, and she relaxed incrementally. Maybe she could survive this ordeal.

Sid did the introductions, drawing Meredith along by the hand. "Cady, this is our grandmother, Meredith Caldwell. Gran, this is Cady."

"Cady, I can't tell you how much I've been looking forward to meeting you." Meredith was stunned by the beauty of her eldest granddaughter. Sid and Harry had told Meredith a lot about Cady, and they hadn't overstated her uniqueness. They'd told her Cady was enchanted by the fashions of the fifties and she was dressed elegantly and beautifully in a stylish sky-blue suit. The skirt flared softly around her slim legs and the jacket was closely fitted, buttoned up the front with a collar trimmed in navy blue. Her deep red hair was artfully curled until she'd achieved a perfect early-fifties style and her make-up was subtle and stunning.

Cady attempted a smile, but it didn't reach her eyes. "It's a pleasure to meet you. Thank you for letting me stay in your home."

"It's your home now too, Cades. Isn't that right, Gran?" Sid was watching Cady anxiously and Meredith could see how much the younger girl worried about her older sibling.

"Of course it is," Meredith agreed. Cady looked terrified, her eyes brimming with tears and she resisted the urge to wrap the younger woman in her arms and take the hurt away. She reminded herself to give Cady some time, let her get used to things.

"Thank you, but I... I won't be staying long. As soon as the police have captured Jameso— my husband, I'll be heading back."

Meredith frowned, but decided against comment. Cady

was fragile and hurting. There would be plenty of time for talking once she'd gotten used to Garrison and started to relax. No sense in agitating her further now. Meredith eyed the dog Kane was holding, amused to see the young Deputy letting the dog walk around the yard at his own pace, sniffing flowers, the grass, the trees and doing all the things dogs seemed to like to do. He was a mountain of dark brown and reddish fur, his face almost completely concealed, and she hid a smile when she caught sight of George's dismay as he watched the behemoth of canine fluff on her front lawn. "He's a lovely dog, Cady. What's his name?"

"Churchill."

"Harry and I chipped in and bought him, after—" Sid stopped abruptly, rolled her eyes and her cheeks colored. "Damn it, Cades, I'm so sorry."

Cady shook her head, her face expressionless. "They brought him after my husband killed my first dog. He broke Montgomery's legs with a baseball bat and slit his throat."

Meredith had to hold herself very still, fighting to avoid overreacting. She flashed a quick glance towards George; his stiff expression revealed he'd been aware of those details. She made a mental note to interrogate him later, find out exactly what had been done to her granddaughter by the man she'd never met but held a burning fury towards. "I'm so sorry, Cady. That must have been awful for you."

Cady drew herself upright, straightening her shoulders determinedly and Meredith felt a burst of pride in her quietly stoic demeanor.

"Why don't we head inside, I'll make coffee," George suggested. He held his hand out to Cady with a gentle smile. "I'm George Davis, a friend of your grandmamma and Garrison's Sheriff. Welcome to Garrison, Ms. Caldwell."

Cady took his hand and smiled weakly. "Sheriff."

"Yes, let's go inside." Meredith was glad for George's interruption, at a moment when she was struggling to form a coherent thought. "George, if you'll make coffee, I'll take Cady up to show her the room where she'll be staying."

Cady followed Meredith into the house, clinging to Sid's hand like a lifeline. She didn't want to do this, didn't think she could become comfortable in this house, no matter how hard she tried. The house itself was beautiful and decorated with an understated elegance which Cady could appreciate, despite her anxiety. A doorway to the right led to a bright living room, and the door to the left was open, revealing a handsome study. Meredith led the way up the stairs, into a hallway decorated with photographs of what appeared to be local scenery.

"This is your room, Cady. Sid is next door and the bathroom is on the other side of the hall." Meredith pushed open the door and stood back, letting Sid drag Cady into the room.

The room was lovely, and Cady stood in the doorway, taking in the details. Wooden floorboards added a distinct warmth to the room. The walls were painted in the palest shade of blue; the windows on either side of the bed curtained with floral material in muted pinks and blues. A cast iron bed head was uniquely antiqued with white sand wash, and the pink gingham ruffle around the edge of the bed was complimented by matching sheets. Cushions and pillows were plumped up against the bed head, in pink gingham and floral prints which matched the curtains.

"I'll leave you to get comfortable and go help George." Meredith slipped from the room and left the two sisters alone.

Cady rubbed her arms, glancing around the room uncertainly.

"Was this... our father's room?"

Sid lifted Cady's bag onto the bed and unzipped it. "Nah, it was Uncle Dave's but Gran redecorated after he moved out." Sid started taking things out of Cady's bag, and opened drawers, putting the clothes away.

"I can do that." Cady moved to Sid's side, but her younger sister brushed off the offer.

"Nope, I'll do it. You relax."

"I've done nothing but relax for the past six weeks." Cady rubbed her lower back absently, aware of the low-level ache which seemed to develop when she got especially tired. The surgery to remove her ruptured kidney had been successful, but there was still some residual pain to overcome and she hoped it would soon settle down.

"You can just keep relaxing," Sid responded imperiously. "That bastard nearly killed you, Cades. You need time to recover from the injuries." She lifted a pile of Cady's lingerie from the bag and installed it in the top drawer. "You can do that with Gran's help." Sid slumped onto the side of the bed. "Let her in, Cady. She's a wonderful person and she only wants to support you, like she does Harry and me."

"Harry and I," Cady corrected Sid automatically, as she'd been doing for years. She glanced up and found Sid watching her through green eyes so much like her own and filled with unadulterated sympathy.

"I still don't get why you didn't want to meet Gran," Sid began quietly. "She's not like our parents, Cades. She's a wonderful person."

Cady didn't need the reminder and she turned away, staring out of the window at the gardens below while she composed her thoughts. "I know that," she finally admitted.

"So why didn't you want to come?" Sid pressed,

brushing her fingers through her hair. She resembled a little pixie, with her dark auburn locks cut short around her face.

"Because our father lived here. And I didn't want to be reminded of him."

"None of us like those reminders, Cades. But Gran won't talk about him, not unless you decide you want to. She's not like that."

"I don't belong here."

Sid smiled gently at her sister, going to her and wrapping her in an embrace. "You'll learn to love it. I did."

## 3

M eredith was settled at the expansive breakfast bar in Nancy Garrison's kitchen, nursing a mug of coffee and a half-eaten oatmeal cookie. After regaling her best friend with the details of Cady's arrival and the subsequent two weeks, Meredith was at her lowest point. "I don't know what else to do," she admitted. She'd honestly believed she could help Cady and develop a positive relationship with the younger woman. Despite her best intentions, it had been an unmitigated disaster, with no sign of improvement anytime soon. She'd decided on the spur of the moment this morning to drive out to the Silver Peaks Ranch for a visit, see if Nancy could provide her with any ideas on how to proceed.

Cady was monosyllabic at best – answering direct questions with a polite detachment that made Meredith's teeth grind. She wouldn't be drawn into talking about herself or her sisters, the few subjects Meredith had initially thought would be safe topics. Cady would offer no information about herself and showed no interest in developing a relationship with Meredith, nor in seeing anything of Garrison, for that matter. Meredith tapped her fingernails on the black granite counter while she waited for Nancy's reaction.

Nancy sipped her coffee and eyed her friend with sympathy. Meredith was a strong, independent woman who was a pillar of the local community, helping many locals through times both bad and good. To be struggling with her own flesh and blood, particularly after what happened with Mark, was no doubt a bitter pill to swallow. "Nothing is working, huh?"

"Nope. She barely leaves her room, other than to take Churchill for a walk twice a day. Sid's so worried, she's talking about deferring her last semester at SFSU and coming back to stay with Cady until she starts to recover."

"That'd be a shame, she's only got six months to go."

"And I'd hate to see her put her dreams of becoming a doctor on hold, not when she's so close. I don't want to agree to her suggestion, but I don't know what else to do."

"What does Harry think?"

Meredith shrugged gracefully. "Harry's worried too, but she thinks Cady will start to improve when she believes Jameson won't find her in Garrison. Harry's trying to convince Sid she needs to stay at college and finish her degree."

The back door opened, and John Garrison stepped into the kitchen, brushing his boots carefully on the worn mat outside the door. At sixty-two, he was an attractive man and his piercing blue eyes zeroed in on his wife with the seductive look of a man who was as much in love with his wife today as he'd been when he and Nancy met over forty years before. He brushed a soft kiss across his wife's lips before straightening to offer Meredith a warm smile. "Hey Mer, how's things?"

"Terrible."

John exchanged a glance with his wife, resting one fist against his lean hip. "No success with your granddaughter, then?"

Nancy slipped from the stool she was perched on, brushing a hand across John's backside. "I'll get you a coffee; Meredith, would you like a fresh cup?" Meredith nodded agreement and Nancy picked up her mug. "John knows you've had some trouble with Cady; he might have some ideas of how to proceed."

John settled on the stool Nancy had vacated and grabbed a couple of cookies, biting into one and chewing thoughtfully before he spoke. "Mer, she might need more help than you're capable of providing," he announced bluntly. "The girl went through God-knows-what with that prick she married, and we know social services were called in more than once when the girls were kids. That must have left some pretty deep scars on her psyche."

"We know that, honey," Nancy protested quietly. She placed two steaming mugs on the bench and leaned on it, her arms crossed. "Cady's got no real family support network to fall back on, only Sid and Harry and let's face it, for years she's been like a mother to them. All Meredith wants is to provide her with the support she needs, find a way to reach out to her and be accepted."

"It might not be possible." John grabbed another two cookies, levelling Meredith with his direct gaze. "You can't always fix somethin' which is broken."

"I have to fix this," Meredith responded stubbornly. "I'm sure I could help her heal, if she would just let me in. You haven't met her, John. She's a wonderfully unique individual, who deserves so much happiness. She's capable of great affection; she's absolutely devoted to Churchill and showers him with love."

"Churchill?" John raised an eyebrow.

"Cady's dog," Nancy supplied. "Sid and Harry bought him after that crazy bastard son-of-a-bitch husband killed her first dog."

John's lips quirked at his wife's outburst and he didn't miss the flash of anger in her pretty blue eyes. His usually placid Nancy had a head of steam built up over this young woman he hadn't met. He knew, in that moment, it was a lost cause to try and fight them. Nancy had joined Meredith in a mission to help Meredith's granddaughter and no amount of arguing would dissuade either one of them from their goal. He wondered if he should drive into town and speak to the girl himself – give her fair warning that she was about to be tag-teamed into submission by two very deter-mined women. Better still, maybe an invitation to the ranch might draw the young woman out of her funk. "Why don't we invite Meredith and Cady to supper?" If he was going to be shanghaied into any crazy schemes the two women came up with, he figured it'd be best to go on the offensive and make sure anything they planned was something he'd want to be involved in.

"I don't think she'd come," Meredith argued. "I can't get her to leave the house other than to walk Churchill. She's avoiding meeting anyone."

John shrugged. "Okay then. We'll come to your place. Nancy and I, maybe Kane and Hallie. You say she's met Kane already, and Hallie is about her age, which might help them establish a connection."

Nancy and Meredith exchanged a long, silent exchange and John amused himself by trying to figure out if they really did have the ability to talk telepathically to one another. He had his suspicions it was true. Judging by the looks on their faces, there was a lot of silent discussion going on. "It does sound like a reasonable idea," Nancy finally said.

John smirked. "Thanks for the vote of confidence, darlin'."

Meredith was still considering the proposal, examining it from all angles. She feared Cady would veto the suggestion outright and voiced her concerns to John and Nancy.

John stood up, grabbing another couple of cookies. "So, don't tell her. We'll bring everything – that way she won't have a chance to shore up her defenses if she sees you preparing." On those parting words, he pressed another long kiss to his wife's lips, winked at Meredith and headed back out to work.

---

CADY LAY on the bed with a book, although she was struggling to concentrate on the words. She hadn't read much since Jameson had beaten the crap out of her two months ago, continued to struggle with the after-effects of the attack. Having your head smashed repeatedly against concrete tended to mess around with your thought processes. Some of the residual effects had long since disappeared, but others were still making their presence known. Although reading was difficult, she'd found it was the easiest way of staying out of Meredith's way and avoid her attempts to forge a friendship. There was nothing wrong with Meredith, nothing at all, from what Cady could see. She just didn't want to start a relationship with the older woman, not when she intended to get the hell out of Garrison as soon as Jameson was captured and charged. She needed to get back to San Francisco, Mario had promised to keep her job for her and she needed to start working as soon as possible. With the fees for Sid's final semester at college due soon, she needed the income to pay that debt, along with the massive medical bills she'd accumulated after Jameson's attack.

Her attention was captured by Churchill, his ears pricking up in interest as he turned towards the windows. Seconds later, Cady heard car engines, growing louder as they approached Meredith's house.

Excited by a change of routine, Churchill vaulted from his position at Cady's side and leaped straight over her and onto the wooden floor, his claws clattering on the wood as he approached the window. He wagged his enormously fluffy tail in excitement before running to the door and turning back to Cady with expectation in his eyes. At eight months old, the Tibetan Mastiff was highly intelligent and devoted to his new mistress.

With a sigh, Cady stood up and peeked out of the window, careful to remain hidden from view to anyone downstairs. Two late model trucks had parked by the curb near Meredith's white picket fence. An older couple stepped out of the first vehicle; they were about Meredith's age and busied themselves retrieving baskets and hampers from the back of the sleek silver truck. Cady recognized Kane Garrison when he stepped from the second truck and watched as he lifted a little boy from a car seat and set him gently down onto the grass verge. Dressed in faded blue jeans and a white polo shirt, he leaned back into the car, drawing a second little boy into his arms. This boy was identical to the first one and Cady could only assume they were the twin sons he'd mentioned. Setting the little boy down onto the grass beside his brother, Kane exchanged a warm smile and quick exchange with the pretty woman who was exiting the passenger seat. With dark eyes and a smile that lit up her whole face, the woman flicked her long ponytail over her shoulder before picking up her purse.

Cady drew back from the window and slumped onto the bed, a sense of dread filling her chest. This had all the hallmarks of a conspiracy and she suspected Meredith was at the center of it. Damn that woman! Couldn't she understand that Cady didn't want to meet anyone? This was a small town, everybody would know about Cady's humiliation and she wasn't up to being the brunt of their well-meaning, but unwanted, sympathy and curiosity.

Churchill whined softly and scratched at the door, but Cady avoided looking at him and fell back on the bed, picking up her book with a huff of exasperation. Why wouldn't Meredith accept that she wasn't going to become involved in this town? Cady wished she'd stop being so nice and leave her alone. Didn't she understand that Cady could look after herself, had been doing so for years now? Not only herself, but her two younger sisters. She didn't need anyone else. In fact, she didn't *want* anyone else. She'd let Jameson in, and look where that had gotten her – a one-way ticket to hell. Ignoring her conscience, which was busy suggesting she was chicken, Cady forced her attention back to the book.

After a few minutes, Churchill gave up his vigil at the door and returned to the bed. Instead of jumping up beside her as he usually would, he stood beside the bed with his massive black and brown head resting on Cady's pillow. The reproach in his eyes was burning a hole in her cheek, but Cady ignored him, staring at the book. She wouldn't give in; no matter how pathetic Churchill behaved. He just didn't understand how bad things were, how beaten down

Cady felt. How anxious she was about meeting new people. She couldn't trust anyone, no matter how kind they seemed to be. Jameson had been kind, once upon a time. He'd promised her the world and Cady had willingly been drawn into his web, not understanding that it was all a false front, an illusion he'd created to get Cady into exactly the position he'd wanted her. Then he'd set out to destroy her individuality, take away her freedom until she'd lost all belief in herself.

It wasn't long before the knock she'd been expecting came. Cady rolled over onto her side, putting her back to the door and ignored it. A second knock sounded a few seconds later, a little harder and sharper than the first. Cady continued to ignore it, hoping Meredith would get the message and leave her alone. Churchill – the traitor – ran to the door and started up with a determined whine.

The door opened. "Cady, would you come downstairs, please? John and Nancy Garrison have come over and brought the fixings for a barbecue. Kane is here too; you remember him? He collected you and Sid in Billings when you arrived."

"I remember."

"Come downstairs and say hello, honey."

"No, thank you."

Cady heard Meredith's frustrated sigh. "Cady, you can't hide out in here forever."

"I'm perfectly fine, thank you." Cady turned a page in the book, trying her darndest to make it appear as if she was reading, despite not having focused on a single word in the past ten minutes.

She could hear Meredith's sharp inhalation all the way across the room. What happened next was the unexpected part. "Arcadia Williamina Arabella Caldwell! Get your tush off that bed and come downstairs, right this instant. I don't know how it's done in San Francisco, but here in Garrison, we treat people with respect! My friends have come visiting, and they expect to meet my eldest granddaughter. I will not tolerate you being rude just because you're so busy wallowing in self-pity that you think you can hide out in here and treat other people with disrespect! You will come downstairs, you will be polite to my friends and you will eat barbeque with us. You hear?"

Cady's eyes widened, and she sat up on the bed and stared at Meredith, barely suppressing the urge to stand and salute. "I hate my full name!" she grumbled instead.

Meredith heaved a sigh, brushing her fingers through her hair in frustration. "Well, don't make me use it again. You're right, it's quite the mouthful."

"It's a ridiculous name," Cady muttered.

Meredith strolled across to the bed and sat down beside Cady, patting her shoulder gently. "I'm not going to take back what I said, Cady. Like it or not, I'm your grandmother and I'm trying my best to help you here. Come on downstairs; meet my friends. Please."

It was the please which swayed her decision. Her grandmother had yelled at her, but somehow, she'd managed to do it without making Cady feel like she was two inches tall. She hadn't berated her or belittled her. Meredith was trying her hardest to be nice and Cady was beginning to like her. Another complication she didn't need or want. But she could tell from the determination in Meredith's countenance that she wasn't going to let this one go. "Fine. I'll be down in five minutes."

Without another word, Meredith stood up and left the room, leaving Cady feeling shell-shocked and Churchill chasing his tail in delight. Somehow, the dog knew that

Meredith had won this battle. As Cady got to her feet, she humored herself by deciding that while Meredith might have won this battle, she wouldn't win the war. Cady would go downstairs, but she didn't have to socialize. It would serve Meredith right if Cady just sat in the garden and ignored everyone. That would teach Meredith for thinking she could force Cady into doing something she didn't want to do. Nobody would ever do that to Cady, not ever again.

---

## 4

I t took about fifteen minutes for Cady to realize she might struggle to win this particular war.

The sound of voices reached her when she walked towards the kitchen and she brushed her hands over her Capris nervously, smoothing the white linen material. She hadn't changed, deciding if she was being forced into this, Meredith's friends would have to accept her exactly the way she was. Her personal style had developed long ago, and she wouldn't change to conform to Garrison's standards.

Cady had loved the fashions of the forties and fifties ever since she'd been old enough to take an interest in clothing. She's obsessed over information on the internet, borrowing books from the library to feed her passion and watching old movies until she was old enough to make her own clothes. She loved the femininity of the era, the swirling skirts, the petticoats, and the elegance of a time long since passed. It had caused nothing but trouble, first with her father deriding her choices, then Jameson belittling the differences he'd claimed to love when they'd first met.

Despite it all, Cady's obsession had never weakened, her love for the era growing as time passed.

She was dressed casually tonight, the cotton Capris matched with a checked gingham shirt in red and white, the shirttails tied in a knot at her waist. She'd pulled her hair into a ponytail and wore a red scarf tied neatly around the band. Her feet were encased in soft leather saddle shoes in red and white, which she'd sourced and ordered online.

Meredith's kitchen was one of Cady's favorite rooms, featuring warm honey-brown wooden cabinets, terracotta tiles, and walls painted in a rich pine green. The entire room was welcoming and relaxing, a place to enjoy a coffee or sit quietly and read the newspaper. At least, it normally was. Tonight it was a hubbub of activity, with Meredith and the two women Cady had spied earlier working together at the bench.

Meredith threw Cady a grateful smile when she walked in, and the pleasure in her eyes confirmed her approval. "Cady, come here and meet my friends." Cady stepped in, holding back a much more enthusiastic Churchill, who was interested in both greeting the new people and sniffing out the source of the smells emanating from the kitchen bench. "This is my good friend, Nancy Garrison and her daughter-in-law, Hallie. Girls, this is my granddaughter, Cady."

Nancy immediately stepped away from the bench and embraced Cady warmly. "Aren't you just the sweetest little thing? It's wonderful to meet you. We've heard such a lot about you from Sid and Harry, but they didn't tell us how pretty you were!"

"Mom, you'll embarrass her," Hallie said, putting down the knife she'd been using to slice tomatoes. "Hi, Cady, good to meet you."

Cady offered her a little half-wave and a smile.

"This must be Churchill. He's enormous, Meredith! How are you coping with this great big adorable dog in the house?"

Meredith chuckled. "He might be a big fellow, but Cady's got him well-trained. Hasn't she, Churchill?" She scratched Churchill under the chin and Cady smiled at the interaction. Meredith had taken the arrival of a massive black and brown ball of fluff in her stride; although she'd admitted to never owning a dog before, she'd accepted Churchill's arrival in her house with good grace and a significant amount of affection.

"Now you girls head outside, I'm sure Tyler and Thomas will get a kick out of meeting this big fella, and Mer and I can finish up the salads. Hallie, introduce Cady to John; he's been looking forward to meeting her," Nancy announced.

"Sounds good to me. C'mon, Cady."

Against her better judgement, Cady followed the young woman out into the garden, which was an oasis of cool greenery in the heat of a late summer evening in Montana. A paved area was set down along the back of the patio with a barbeque and outdoor setting, shaded by spreading oaks. Kane looked up from the barbeque when the door opened and grinned at Cady, offering her a wink. "Hey, Ms. Caldwell. How're you doing?"

Cady offered him a weak smile. "Call me Cady, please."

"Alright then. Cady." He waved towards the older man who stood beside him, nursing a longneck in one hand, a spatula in the other. "This is my father, John Garrison. Dad, this is Cady."

The older Garrison put down his beer and offered Cady a firm handshake, his piercing blue eyes assessing. "Pleasure to meet you, Cady."

"And this is Churchill," Kane added.

John Garrison crouched beside Churchill, holding his hand up in front of Churchill's nose to allow the dog to catch his scent. "You're a mighty fine-looking dog, Churchill." He glanced up at Cady. "Mastiff?"

Cady nodded shyly. "Tibetan. My sisters brought him for me."

"After your ex-husband killed your other dog, I hear. It's a terrible thing when a man can harm an animal."

Cady blinked, stunned by his candor. "Yes," she muttered.

John straightened up, eyeing her kindly. "You're going to be safe here, Cady. Garrison looks after its own, none more so than anyone related to Meredith. She's well respected around these parts and loved. Her kin are important to us too."

Cady blushed and looked away. She wasn't sure what she'd been expecting from these people, but John Garrison's direct manner of speaking and kindness touched her deeply. He wasn't offering sympathy, instead he was using a no-nonsense, direct approach to acknowledge her problems and treat them naturally. A little of the tightness in her shoulders eased.

"Wow!"

The adults turned as one to see twin boys come running from the back of the yard, their eyes zoned in on Churchill who easily outreached them for height. Cady ordered Churchill to sit and he instantly obeyed the command, watching the two little boys running towards him with his tongue lolling from the side of his mouth, and his tail wagging.

Kane dropped a hand onto each of the boys' shoulders before they could launch themselves at Churchill and knelt between them. "Listen up, you little tearaways. This is Cady Caldwell, and her dog, Churchill. Cady, these are my sons, Thomas, and Tyler." Kane offered Cady a bright smile before he turned his attention to the two boys. "What do you have to do when you meet a new dog?"

"Slow down, Daddy, and let him get used to us."

"That's right, Tyler." Kane brushed his hand across the little boy's dark hair affectionately. "What else, Thomas?"

The second little boy, identical in every way to his brother, pursed his lips and considered the question thoughtfully. "Hold your hand out for the dog to get used to you."

"Good answer, son," Kane agreed with a warm smile. "Now, how do we know if a dog is going to be friendly?"

Tyler giggled, his big brown eyes filled with knowledge. "You can tell if he's happy to meet you because his tail will be wagging." He pointed in delight at Churchill's rapidly swaying tail. "Look, he's happy!"

"Yes, he is, Tyler. But what else do you have to watch for?" Hallie questioned, joining the lesson.

The little boy frowned deeply, his thought processes easily visible crossing his little face. Both boys were the spitting image of their father and had their mother's dark brown eyes. "I don't know, Dad."

Kane ruffled his son's hair and scooped him into his arms for a hug. "Never be ashamed of telling people you don't know an answer, son. That's how we learn new things, by having other people help us out when we're stuck."

Thomas turned to glance up at his mother. "He'll look happy?" He posed his answer as a question, his eyes upturned to watch his mother carefully.

"That's exactly right," John lowered himself to one knee next to his grandson. "See how Churchill is sitting there so nicely, his tail wagging and he looks happy, almost like he's smiling at you, doesn't he?"

Thomas nodded agreement, his little fingers clenching and unclenching as if he couldn't wait to throw his arms around Churchill's neck.

"When a dog is looking happy and relaxed like that, he's comfortable about being around you and doesn't feel threatened. You can go on now and hold your hand out, like this," he demonstrated for them, "and let him sniff your hand and get a handle on your scent, just like we do with the horses out on the ranch."

Both little boys followed his lead and held their small hands out for Churchill to sniff. The dog completed this action with a great amount of gusto, no doubt helped along by the crumbs of potato chips the boys had recently been eating. They both giggled when he licked furiously at their fingers.

"Okay, boys, looks like he's accepted you just fine, so you can go ahead and pat him now," Kane instructed them, with a grin at Cady. Much to her surprise, she found herself grinning back at the antics of two little boys and a huge Tibetan Mastiff, enjoying the boys' delighted smiles and laughter. This was what family was all about – this was what Cady had never had, and she found herself envious of their easy rapport as the two boys played with Churchill and Kane and John returned to cooking the barbeque.

"C'mon, Cady, let's sit down and get to know one another while Kane and Dad finish cooking."

"Would you like a drink, Cady?" Kane offered.

"A juice please."

Hallie grabbed Cady's arm and drew her towards the outdoor setting, settling down on one of the comfortable wicker chairs. "How're you enjoying Garrison so far?"

Cady shrugged, her barricades automatically slamming back into place. "I haven't been going out much."

Hallie chuckled. "So I've heard. You take Churchill out walking and spend most of your time in your room."

Cady bristled. "I hardly think that's any of your business."

"Cady, I'm not trying to upset you, or hurt your feelings. But you've got to admit since your ex-husband attacked you, you've kind of withdrawn from the whole world."

Cady lifted her head to look at Hallie's eyes, seeing nothing but sincerity looking back at her, but the knowledge did nothing to dampen down her anger. "Still none of your business."

"No, it's not, that's certainly true. But your grandmother is worried sick about you, and she's a great friend of the Garrison family. If Meredith Caldwell is hurting – well, the town tries to help. We try to help anyone who's hurting."

"I'm not hurting. I'm fine." Cady mentally cringed at the stubborn tone in her voice, but she couldn't give in to this woman, didn't want anyone trying to help her. It was bad enough that Sid and Harry were stressing themselves into early strokes about her, and now Meredith had joined in. Why didn't they get it? Why couldn't they understand that Cady needed to work through this at her own pace? Why didn't they understand that she was to blame for what Jameson had done?

"Okay." Hallie held her hands up in surrender. "Kane'll tell you I have a bad habit of butting into other people's business," she grinned self-consciously, "and he's right."

Cady turned her attention to where the boys were still playing with Churchill. The dog was laying on his back, four outrageously fluffy legs sticking up in the air, whilst the boys rubbed his tummy gently, laughing and chattering to one another.

"A juice for you and a white wine for my lovely wife," Kane announced, placing glasses in front of the two women with a warm smile. "Everything okay?" he questioned, eyeing Hallie with a raised eyebrow.

Hallie grimaced and squirmed in the seat and Cady found herself answering. "We're fine. Thank you."

The two women lapsed into silence and Cady considered her reaction to Hallie's forthright comments. Despite her qualms, she kind of liked the woman, wished she could be as strong and candid as Hallie seemed to be. From beneath her lowered gaze, she saw an interaction between Kane and Hallie – saw their silent communication and the smile they shared when their gazes turned towards their sons, their eyes lit with delight. Was this what life was like for married couples who loved each other? She had no parameters to judge it by; not her own parents for sure, and her marriage to Jameson had never been a bed of roses, not after the first couple of months.

"Cady?" Hallie's voice interrupted Cady's musings and she raised her gaze to meet the other woman's. Hallie offered her a grimaced smile. "I really am sorry, you know."

Cady smiled weakly. "It's okay, you didn't mean any harm."

"Tell me, what sort of things do you like to do? Did you have a job in San Francisco?"

Cady nodded. "I worked at a bakery."

Hallie straightened, her eyes shining with interest. "You're a baker? Kane'd love it if I could bake – I can't make a cake to save my life." She chuckled.

"I can bake a little, but I mainly do decorating," Cady explained.

"Cake decorating? Like, wedding cakes and stuff?" Hallie grinned. "That must be amazing fun."

Cady nodded, sipping her juice. "It is fun. I enjoy it."

"The only person around here who decorates cakes is old Mrs. Knightley. I swear, every wedding cake she's produced has been the exact same design for at least fifty years. Poor Mrs. Knightley, she doesn't have a lot of imagination."

"Is there a bakery in Garrison?"

"Nah, hasn't been one for getting on for ten years now. Mrs. Knightley does wedding cakes, but she's getting past it. Most of the local girls end up ordering what they want from Billings."

"I wouldn't think there'd be much business in Garrison for a baker." Cady's knowledge wasn't extensive, but the sign they'd passed when they drove into the town limits suggested the population was only about fifteen hundred.

Hallie chuckled. "You'd be surprised. The town might be small, but in a rural area like this, there are a lot of ranches outside of town." She shrugged her slender shoulders. "Lots of cowboys, lots of young women. There's always some sort of celebration going on."

Their conversation was interrupted when Meredith and Nancy appeared; carrying bowls of salad and Nancy had a basket of bread rolls hooked over one arm. Minutes afterwards, Kane laid a big tray of hamburgers and hot dogs on the table. "Dig in, ladies."

Cady settled back as Hallie started to fill plates for Thomas and Tyler, and then called them to the table. The two little boys came running, with Churchill following closely behind and while the boys wriggled up onto chairs, Cady spoke a quiet command to Churchill, who bounded across the patio and settled on the stone pavers beside the door.

John whistled through his teeth. "That's some well-trained dog you've got there, Cady. Did you do the training?" While he spoke, he was filling a plate with meat and salad, adding a crusty bread roll.

"Harry and Sid bought him from Roberto Huerta, a breeder in St. Louis. He was responsible for a good part of the training, and then I took over. I can't take sole responsibility for how obedient he is, Churchill and I have only been together for a few weeks."

John glanced towards Churchill. "You're doing something right; he obviously respects you. It takes giving respect to earn it." Cady suspected there was a hidden message in John's words, but his face remained carefully neutral. He passed the plate he'd been filling across the table, placing it in front of Cady and she paused to stare at the heavily-laden plate with wide eyes.

"Um, thank you?"

Nancy slipped onto the wooden bench beside Cady and chuckled. "John thinks everyone eats the same amount as he and our boys do. Just eat what you'd like, honey, and leave the rest."

"The girl looks like she needs some weight on those bones," John protested with a warm smile.

Cady picked up her knife and fork and began picking at the meal, listening shyly to the conversation going on around the table. It was apparent the Garrisons were a warm and loving family and she was surprised by the amount of good-natured teasing which went on among them. It was a stark contrast to her own family life and Cady felt a twinge of envy towards Kane, knowing he'd grown up in a household filled with respect and love. So different to her own childhood, with Mark Caldwell and Lisa Drummond. The two people who had given life to her had never done anything to deserve being called Mom and Dad. From the time she'd become cognizant of their drug and alcohol use, when she'd realized the strange men coming into their ratty apartment were having sex with Lisa for cash, Cady had thought of them as Mark and Lisa. Or more often than not, 'those scumbags' who had spawned her and her sisters. She was slightly more forgiving of Lisa than she could ever be of Mark. In her lucid moments, Lisa had tried to be a mother, though her efforts were sporadic and ineffective.

Mark Caldwell, however, had never done a thing to deserve her love. In fact, during the last few months when Cady, Harry, and Sid lived with him after Lisa's death, the only thing he'd earned was loathing and hatred. Losing Lisa had barely dented his usual routine of drinks and drugs, but it had certainly curtailed his sexual activity. Without Lisa, his attention had turned to his sixteen-year-old daughter.

The descent into true hell had been gradual – sometimes her father would 'accidentally' walk in on her in the shower. He would brush against her in the small confines of the apartment, making contact with her breast or her bottom. Cady had been terrified and repulsed, and life became a constant battle to keep away from Mark. Worse, she feared for her sisters – with Harry blossoming into teenage curves at the age of thirteen, Cady worried Mark would tire of her efforts to evade him and turn to Harry to get what he wanted. She tried to keep the nightmare from affecting Sid, who at ten, still believed in knights in shining armor and fairy tales. Cady had seen enough at sixteen to know there was no such thing, but she refused to allow Sid's innocence to be destroyed.

She'd struggled to keep the family together for nearly two years, until her eighteenth birthday. Evading Mark's attention as much as possible, she'd gone so far as visiting a hardware store, shoplifting a couple of locks to put on the bathroom door and the small bedroom she shared with her sisters. Buying them had been impossible, most of the time there was barely any money to buy groceries, and they'd long ago learned to hide when the landlord came around looking for the rent. They'd moved half a dozen times in the two years after Lisa's death, and each apartment was worse than the last.

An elderly neighbor, Mr. Kornberg, had fitted the locks for Cady and thankfully, hadn't asked questions. She would have been too embarrassed, to be truthful with the white-haired, stoop-backed gentleman, but his dark brown eyes had been filled with sympathy as he carefully screwed the locks into place. He'd left the apartment with an offer for Cady and the girls to call on him, any time, day or night if they needed him. Cady had been grateful for the offer, but what help could Mr. Kornberg provide? And she couldn't put him in a situation where Mark might get angry and hurt the old man.

"Cady? You've hardly eaten a bite, honey." Hearing her grandmother's voice brought her attention back to the barbeque, and Cady glanced up at Meredith and offered her a tiny smile. "I'm sorry, I wasn't very hungry."

"Are you feeling okay?" Meredith studied her with worry in her blue eyes and Cady squirmed on the spot.

"My back's a little achy," she admitted quietly. It wasn't as bad as it had been straight after the surgery, but the air was cooling down as night fell and it affected the area where her ruptured kidney had been removed.

Meredith patted her shoulder. "I'll run and get you a jacket."

"It's okay...," Cady stumbled over saying 'Gran'. She was trying hard to keep her distance from Meredith, usually referring to her by her given name, but the older woman didn't make it easy. She'd offered nothing but kindness since Cady's arrival in Garrison, but Cady didn't know how she could develop a relationship with Meredith without revealing the truth. She'd do anything to keep the past in the past and certainly didn't want to hurt Meredith with the sordid truth about her son.

"It's no bother, Cady. I'll grab a heat pack for you, as well." Before Cady could protest further, Meredith slipped into the house, leaving her alone with the Garrisons.

"Did you know Cady does cake decorating?" Hallie asked her mother-in-law.

"Meredith mentioned it; she's very proud of the work you do, Cady," Nancy said. She sipped her wine, offering Cady a heartfelt smile.

"We've got Granny Benton's birthday coming up," Kane announced. "Has anyone organized her cake yet? Maybe Cady could rustle up something."

Before Cady could protest, Hallie clapped her hands in delight. "That's a wonderful idea! We'd love you to make Granny Benton's cake. She's Kane's paternal grandmother, Nancy's mother."

"Oh, I don't know," Cady began, but she'd barely gotten the words out before Meredith appeared, handing Cady a heat pack and draping a jacket around her shoulders.

"I think that's a great idea, I'm sure Cady would love to help out, wouldn't you? It would give you something to sink your teeth into while you're recuperating."

"What sort of cake decorating do you do?" Nancy asked.

Cady took a moment to lean forward in her chair and pressed the heat pack against her lower back. "I've done quite a few designs, a lot of traditional cakes, but sometimes customers want something a little more unique. I've done everything from cakes shaped like pregnant bellies, through to giraffes and trucks."

"Wow, really?" Hallie's enthusiasm was contagious, and Cady nodded and smiled.

"Have you got any photos of the cakes you've decorated?" John questioned.

Cady shrugged, a small frown marring her pretty features for a moment. "I only have a few." She was too embarrassed to admit that Jamison had destroyed her display album, burning the photographs in a fit of jealous rage. The only photos left were a few Mario and her friends at the bakery had rustled up before she'd been spirited out of San Francisco.

Before Cady knew what was happening, Meredith and Hallie had disappeared inside again to collect the photographs, after gaining instructions from Cady about where to find them.

Watching as the two women disappeared into the house, Cady suspected this was all happening much faster than she felt able to deal with, and she was swiftly realizing the truth. The Garrison family was a force to be reckoned with.

## 5

C ady stood in the kitchen, humming softly to herself as she put the finishing touches on the cake she'd promised for the birthday celebrations of Nancy's mother.

"How's it going, honey?" Meredith walked in through the back door, hanging her slicker on a hook in the mudroom. "It's pouring out there; seems we've seen the end of summer." The past few days had been wet, and the leaves on the soaring trees in Meredith's yard had begun to turn, their glossy green giving way to yellowing as fall began.

"Nearly finished," Cady announced. It felt good to be working on her craft, although it hadn't been easy without her regular tools. She'd brought nothing from San Francisco, hadn't replaced her decorating equipment after Jameson destroyed everything she'd owned. Consequently, after consultation with Nancy and Hallie about Mrs. Benton's interests and likes, Cady had needed to think on her feet to come up with regular kitchen utensils which could produce the decorations in a professional manner. Fortunately for her, Nancy's elderly mother was a great lover of roses, a relatively simple item to create from icing, and she'd designed a two-tiered cake which had turned out rather nicely, given what she had to work with. Wiping her hands on a towel, Cady adjusted a couple of rosebuds and then stood back with her head dipped to one side, evaluating her efforts.

Both cakes had been covered in creamy ivory fondant, and she'd created an intricate lacework pattern which resembled an elegant tablecloth on each tier. A fondant bow concealed the join between the two cakes and tiny rosebuds in shades from the palest tangerine through to a deep apricot nestled against the ribbons' folds. The entire top of the second, smaller cake was covered in a half circle bouquet, made up of dozens of the same tiny, simple rosebuds, interspersed with green fondant shaped to resemble leaves. All she needed to do now was create a pattern of dots over the fondant bow with royal icing, and the cake would be ready. Mrs. Benton's party was being held at the Garrison's ranch tonight and despite her qualms, Cady was pleased she'd agreed to do the cake. It was therapeutic to work on something requiring her total concentration and now that it was almost complete, Cady had to admit she'd had fun.

"That's so beautiful, Cady, you have an incredible talent."

Cady demurred, turning back to stir the royal icing she'd made earlier, before scooping spoonful's into a piping bag to complete the bow. "It's really no big deal."

Meredith patted her shoulder. "On the contrary – it's a talent, Cady. I certainly couldn't do it."

Cady leaned over the cake and started dobbing tiny icing dots on the bow at precisely spaced intervals. "Honestly, it's just icing. I can't make the cakes, if you hadn't baked them, this would never have happened."

Meredith picked up the kettle and placed it beneath the faucet, filling it with water before returning it to the stove-top. "Either way, I think Granny Benton is going to be delighted. She's really looking forward to meeting you."

Cady straightened up abruptly, twisting to stare at Meredith in dismay. This hadn't been part of the arrange-ment; she'd planned to make the cake, hand it over to Kane this afternoon and stay home tonight. Meredith was welcome to attend the party – Cady didn't intend to go with her. "Oh, no. I'm not going."

"Of course you are," Meredith announced calmly, placing coffee mugs on the counter. She measured out teaspoons of instant coffee and placed them into the mugs. "It's the social event of the year. Surely you realized you've been invited when you've been talking with Nancy and Hallie?"

It was true; Nancy and Hallie had talked endlessly about the party when they'd dropped by in the past two weeks. Ostensibly, they'd been visiting to see how the cake was coming along, but Cady knew they'd also been part of Meredith's plan to coax Cady into becoming more involved in the town's residents. Meredith Caldwell seemed to be waging war by stealth, with visitors regularly 'popping' into the house to meet Cady. It seemed that as far as Meredith was concerned, if Cady wouldn't visit the people of Garri-son, she'd bring Garrison home to visit with Cady. Every other day, they seemed to be hosting an unexpected visitor who had 'dropped by' for a coffee and a piece of Meredith's lemon layer cake, which she seemed to perpetually have ready at a moment's notice.

Well, she'd just show Meredith, Nancy *and* Hallie that they couldn't force her into doing something she didn't want to do. "I won't be attending. I keep warning you – I'm going back to San Francisco, as soon as Sheriff Davis gives me the all clear."

"Now, Cady..." Meredith began, but Cady wasn't having any of it.

"There's no 'now Cady'," she announced, bending back over the cake to continue work. "I'm not going to the party. I won't know anyone, and besides, I've got no intentions of getting to know anyone in Garrison any better." The town was lovely, from what little Cady had seen, and the residents were friendly and warm-hearted, but Cady couldn't afford to stay here any longer than necessary. The fees for Sid's tuition were due, and she needed to get back to work to pay for them. She was already stressed; knowing that Jameson continued to elude capture – in fact, there'd been no sightings of him in the past ten weeks. But he had to be out there somewhere. Sheriff Davis had confirmed Jameson hadn't left the country, so he had to be hiding under a rock somewhere in the States. And Cady had no doubt, given the opportunity, he would finish what he'd started. Despite the warmth in the bright kitchen, she shivered.

"Granny Benton will be terribly disappointed—" Meredith started a new tack in her campaign, reaching into the refrigerator for the milk.

"She doesn't even know me; so how could she possibly be disappointed?" Cady countered.

"*I'll* be disappointed if you don't come along," Meredith retorted.

"Well, you'd better prepare yourself for disappointment. I'm not going," Cady stated, sounding just as determined.

"Damn it. Of course you're going, Cady."

Cady jumped when she heard Kane Garrison's deep voice from the doorway and she rested a hand on her chest, waiting for her heart's tempo to settle before she spoke. "I don't want to go to your grandmother's party."

Kane stepped into the kitchen, his height and size overwhelming the room and behind him; a second man, equally as tall, followed. "This is my brother, Josh. Josh, this is Cady Caldwell."

The man stepped forward, removing his hat and holding out his hand. "Ma'am, it's a pleasure to meet you. Welcome to Garrison."

Cady hastily wiped her fingers on her dungarees and held her hand out to Josh. A family resemblance was visible between Kane and his brother; they both had the same chestnut hair and dark eyes. Both men had broad shoulders, narrow waists, and long, muscled legs, and wore dark Wranglers, well-worn boots, and t-shirts.

Josh stepped back after shaking Cady's hand and wrapped his arms around Meredith, planting a kiss on her cheek. "Meredith, it's good to see you."

Meredith smiled coquettishly, and Cady glimpsed what a beauty her grandmother must have been in her younger years. She was still a beauty, at the age of sixty-four and her high cheekbones and bright blue eyes made her face light up when she smiled. "You too, Josh, it's been a while."

"Yes Ma'am, breeding season is always busy around Garrison. I've been on the road for nearly a month."

"All finished up now, though, I assume?" Meredith turned back to the counter and drew another two mugs from the overhead cupboard. "Cady, Josh is the Garrison vet; he looks after everyone's animals and does a damn fine job of it. I was just saying to Cady; I think we've seen the last of summer by the look of that rain out there."

"Yes, ma'am, but I hope the rain clears a little before Granny's party tonight," Josh said.

"Now what's this I hear about you not coming to the party? You just know Mom is going to insist on you being there, 'specially since you made the cake and all," Kane announced, leaning up against the counter beside Cady.

"I won't know anyone, and I'd really prefer to stay home and paint my toenails."

Kane glanced down at Cady's bare feet and perfectly painted toenails and grinned. "They don't look like they need paintin' to me, Cady. That's just an excuse and you know it."

Cady ignored the indelicate snort of amusement that came from her grandmother and turned back to the cake, picking up the icing bag with a sigh.

"Besides, you can't say you won't know anyone. Hallie, the boys and I'll be there, Mom, Dad, and your Gran. And most of the town is wantin' to meet you. They keep seeing this little sprite running around town, being dragged along the streets by an enormous fluffy mutt..."

Cady spun on her heels, reacting to Kane's well-aimed barb. "I've met *most* of the town already; they seem to turn up here at Meredith's with alarming regularity. And I don't get dragged around the streets by Churchill. And he is not a mutt!"

Kane chuckled. "I notice you're not arguing with the enormous or fluffy."

Josh settled down on his haunches next to the dog in question, who was happily watching Cady work, and rubbed his fur affectionately. "That's some dog, Ms. Caldwell..."

Cady puffed out a breath of exasperated air, watching as Churchill rolled himself belly up to allow Josh to rub his tummy. The damn dog was a traitor, an attention seeker to the worst degree. And were *all* the men so amazingly polite in this little town? "Please, call me Cady."

"Okay, Cady. He's a beautiful dog, how old is he?"

"Nine months," Cady responded, leaning over again to finish decorating the bow.

"I told you he was a good-looking dog," Kane leaned against the bench next to Cady and grinned down at her. "Now about tonight..."

Cady rolled her eyes. "Honestly, Kane, no offense to you or your family, but I don't want to attend a party. I won't be here for all that long – as soon as I can, I'll be heading back to San Francisco, I've got to get back to work. There's no point in making friends when I won't be staying."

"There's always a point to making new friends," Meredith announced. "And honey, there's no rush. You've suffered some extensive injuries; you don't want to overdo it by going back to work too quickly. Besides, where would you live? Until they have that man behind bars, I think you should stay here in Garrison, where you're safe." Meredith spooned sugar into the mugs. "Now, I didn't want to do this, but I'm going to pull the 'good manners' card again. You've been invited to Granny Benton's party, and you'll be attending. Unless you suddenly take ill between now and tonight, I won't take no for an answer, and believe me, I'll recognize if you're faking or not. I've had years of experience around here, not only with my own boys but also with most of the other kids in Garrison when I was working at the high school. And if necessary, I'll have George or Kane turn up and arrest you, to get you out there."

With a satisfied smile, Meredith turned back to the kettle and began to pour hot water into the mugs, leaving Cady to stare at her, her mouth gaping open.

Quinn Garrison hadn't been certain he'd make it back in time for Granny Benton's birthday party – in fact, up until this morning, he'd been convinced he wouldn't. Tasked by his father with heading out to the northernmost reaches of the ranch, to bring in the last of the calves before autumn's cool nights got a grip on the plains, he and Matt had gotten caught up with retrieving a stray group of cattle who'd climbed high into the Beartooth Mountains surrounding the Silver Peaks Ranch. It was remote, inaccessible country and they'd cussed out the cattle who'd taken it on themselves to get stuck in such an isolated area. Getting them down from the ranges proved difficult, especially with the downpours they'd had this morning. Quinn had suspected, up until late this afternoon, they wouldn't make it back in time.

While his mother was usually far too impatient for her own good, in this situation it had proven to be a blessing. She'd sent a couple of the ranch hands to meet up with them in Springwater Gully, and arranged for Quinn and Matt to leave their horses and come back the rest of the way by four-wheel drive. Consequently, they'd managed to shave a good eight hours off their journey and gotten back to Silver Peaks in time to take a long, hot shower and gussy up for Granny's birthday party.

Which, by the looks of it, was going to be quite the shindig. His Mom had outdone herself, cleaning out and decorating the old barn and in the early evening, it was already jam-packed with a noisy throng of people. The pungent aroma of fresh hay filled the air, along with the sound of crackling wood from the fire Josh and Kane had prepared in a pit just outside the barn doors. Even the rain was holding off – probably too frightened to disrupt his mother's plans.

"D'you wanna beer, Quinn?" Without waiting for a response, Matt handed Quinn a longneck, the top already removed. Quinn took a long swig, enjoying the cool bitter taste as it slipped down his throat.

He stood to one side, watching the partygoers who'd already settled into dancing and drinking. Granny Benton had taken up residence in the northernmost corner of the barn; settled in a comfortable armchair, she was holding court with a group of other elderly women. For a lady who'd just turned ninety, she was remarkably spry. Quinn caught sight of his Mom, flitting back and forth, checking on the food that filled four long narrow tables along the wide side of the barn. The aroma of spit-roasted beef drifted across and Quinn realized how hungry he was. He hadn't eaten since breakfast when they'd broken camp this morning, and his stomach rumbled, reminding him of the fact.

"I'm gonna eat," Quinn announced, leaving Matt and striding towards the trestle tables. He stopped to talk to a couple of his friends and avoided one or two women along the way. He caught sight of Marcie Beauchamp and adjusted his direction marginally. She was definitely someone he wanted to avoid, having made it clear she was interested in him after he and Julia divorced. Marcie had been trying to tie him down to a date for months, almost since he'd returned home from Iraq and Afghanistan, finishing his final tour of duty with the 75th Rangers two years ago.

His tour had ended, ironically, on the same day as his marriage, after he'd received a 'Dear John' letter from Julia while he was battling through daily skirmishes with the enemy in Kabul. He'd flown home to the States on the same day as the divorce finalized and returned to Garrison as a newly single man.

Being one of the four Garrison brothers – and now one of the three *single* Garrison brothers, Quinn was in hot demand among the women in the area. He used the situation to his advantage, indulging in a few hot and heavy relationships with some of the local women, although he made it clear to every one of them that he wasn't looking for anything serious. He'd been burned, badly, by Julia's betrayal, and he didn't intend on getting seriously involved with anyone again.

Despite his best efforts to avoid her, Marcie was gaining ground – and apparently intended to cut Quinn off before he reached the food. Scanning the barn, Quinn caught sight of a red-headed beauty standing at one side, engaged in conversation with Meredith Caldwell. He turned on the spot and strode across to them.

"Meredith, good to see you," Quinn said, leaning forward to kiss his mother's friend on the cheek and placing his beer on a nearby table. "I saw you here with this lovely young lady and thought I might come and ask her to dance."

The woman was even more gorgeous close-up, although a second, longer glance confirmed she had unusual tastes in clothes. He couldn't pick for certain, but thought she looked like some of the women he'd seen in movies from the fifties. Her dress fitted her figure perfectly; enhancing pert little breasts and a narrow waist, and her lustrous red hair curled and hung down across one fair shoulder.

Meredith chuckled. "You're a liar, Quinn Garrison. I saw Marcie headed your way."

He rolled his eyes, amused by the sparkle in Meredith's bright blue gaze. He lowered his gaze to Meredith's companion and offered her his most charming smile.

"Please, I'm begging you. Dance with me and save me from a fate worse than death."

The little redhead shook her head vehemently. "Oh, no..."

"Go on, Cady, live a little. Quinn's a nice man." Meredith shoved Cady forward before she could protest further, and Quinn took her hand in his. He was surprised by the tingle he experienced when their skin touched.

She obviously wasn't thrilled with the idea of dancing with him, and he had to admit to being curious. Usually, women threw themselves at the Garrison men, but this little filly didn't seem impressed in the slightest. In fact, one look at her face suggested she would bolt if he let go of her hand. He drew her across to the makeshift dance floor in the center of the barn and wrapped his arm around her back, drawing her closer before he began to sway to the music.

Quinn glanced around the crowded barn, across the top of Cady's head, and located the source of the music. Tommy Heywood, a high school senior and Garrison's only DJ, was set up in one corner, under the watchful eye of the elderly A.J. Harper, who would no doubt be ensuring Tommy played less of his type of music and more of Granny Benton's favorites. Hence, the slow tune he found himself dancing to, enjoying the soft material of Cady's dress brushing against his palm.

"How long have you been in Garrison, Cady?"

"Four weeks or so. I'll be heading back to California soon." She kept her gaze lowered, and Quinn could smell the soft scent of roses drifting up from her glorious mane of red hair.

"California, huh? Never been there myself." A lot of other places around the world, but he'd never stepped foot in California. The idea of busy Los Angeles and San Francisco gave him the heebie-jeebies, but if this woman lived there, he might have to reconsider and make a visit.

Quinn mentally shook himself. Where did that notion come from? He'd known this woman for thirty seconds and knew absolutely nothing about her. Other than the fact that she was one of the most beautiful women, he'd ever met.

"You're not missing all that much. It's busy, crowded. Not like Montana."

"Yeah, I imagine it would be. You're Meredith's eldest granddaughter, aren't you? I've met Sid and Harry. What name did your parents stick you with?"

She stiffened a little in his arms. "Arcadia."

Quinn grinned and whistled. "I like Cady much better."

His words had the desired effect and she looked up, fixing him with a pair of beautiful, baby blue eyes. "So do I."

"Are you enjoying your stay in Montana?"

She shrugged, the movement drawing his attention to the smooth, pale skin on her bare shoulders, skin that he'd like to kiss his way across as his lips found their way to those pert little breasts... Quinn felt himself harden as he inhaled another hint of roses, and he drew back a little, creating a respectable distance between himself and the young woman in his arms. He was intrigued and wanted to know more about her. Having been away for weeks, he hadn't heard much about Cady Caldwell's arrival in town and wondered what had brought her to stay. He intended to find out. He glanced up and saw Marcie standing with some of her friends at the edge of the dance floor, and deliberately turned Cady in the opposite direction.

"Is that the girl you're avoiding?"

He lowered his gaze to Cady's and amended his earlier description. He'd thought her eyes were baby blue, but on closer inspection, they were the color of Forget-Me-Nots. He made an immediate decision that this was his new favorite flower. "Yep, Marcie Beauchamp."

"I'm assuming the Garrison men are hot tickets?"

He laughed aloud. "So I've heard. Where did you hear that?"

"My grandmother told me." She eyed Marcie with undisguised interest. "So what's wrong with Marcie Beauchamp?"

"She's looking to get a ring on her finger."

"And you're not interested in marriage?"

For a moment, he wondered if that was what Cady Caldwell was looking for, but she certainly didn't appear to be angling particularly for his attention, and he dismissed the idea. "Nope. Tried it once. Not gonna do it again."

"I see."

The music stopped and Cady stepped away, offering him a warm smile. "Thanks for the dance."

"Thanks for rescuing me." He glanced across to see Marcie headed his way and turned his attention back to Cady. "Uh, I don't suppose..."

Cady laughed and shook her head. "I'm afraid not. You're on your own." With a warm smile, she sashayed away from him and Quinn was left with the distinct impression he'd just been shut down.

_____

## 6

Cady returned to Meredith's side, and ignored the delight she saw reflected in the older woman's eyes. Sheriff Davis had joined her grandmother while she'd been dancing with Quinn and he looked particularly spiffy in what seemed to be the standard Montana uniform of Wranglers and cowboy boots, which he'd paired with a navy-blue shirt, crisply ironed with sharp creases along the sleeves. He wore a dark brown Stetson on his head, which he tipped in Cady's direction when she arrived.

"Hi Sheriff," Cady greeted him with a little wave.

"Cady, how are you?"

Cady nodded, picking up the glass of wine she'd left sitting on the table and sipping from it. "No news from San Francisco?" She wasn't certain what she wanted most – to hear that Jameson had been captured – or hear that he hadn't been found. When Jameson was apprehended, she'd have to face him again in court, when he stood trial for what he'd done. She'd started divorce proceedings, but Cady was completely terrified of being in the same room with him.

She took a hasty sip from her wine, aware of the trembling that started up in her fingers.

In hindsight, she couldn't understand why she'd put up with Jameson's abuse for so long – but to a certain extent, she also knew that what had happened was her fault. She'd loved Jameson, but she'd also known by marrying him, she'd have the means to support her sisters. The price she'd paid for that support had been incredibly high; in hindsight, too high. She'd fallen out of love with Jameson long ago, but she couldn't help thinking that she'd been wrong to use him the way she had. His money had supported Harry and Sid through college – without his help, Harry wouldn't have been able to finish nursing school, and Sid certainly wouldn't have had the opportunity to follow her dreams and become a doctor. And while Cady was incredibly proud of her sisters and what they'd achieved – she often wondered if she hadn't whored herself out so they could achieve it.

Sheriff Davis' voice drew her back to their conversation. "Nothing, I'm afraid. Wherever Le Batelier is, he's lying low. The SFPD think he's got to be getting help from someone."

"You don't think I could go back yet?" The idea of staying in Garrison long term was inconceivable; Cady had no income, no money, and no way of paying for Sid's final semester. She'd considered seeking a job here in Garrison, but honestly, in a town this size and with the downturn in the economy, she doubted she'd find anything that paid well enough to make it worthwhile. And the truth was, she missed city life. Garrison was so quiet; she sometimes sat out on the porch in the evenings and listened to the silence. It was a tangible thing, something she wouldn't have believed until she'd come to stay with Meredith. She'd never thought silence would have a noise of its own, but it did – it was the sound of her heart beating in her chest, the whisper of the breeze blowing through the trees, the slight flutter of the leaves and flowers in the garden as wind blew them gently across the lawn. No cars, no buses or trains, not a single human element broke the stillness. In some ways, she enjoyed the change from the hustle and bustle of San Francisco, but she couldn't imagine staying here longer than a few more weeks at most.

"Sorry, Cady, but it's not advisable yet. We have to assume that he intended to kill you – and would take the opportunity if it presented in the future."

A chill ran up Cady's spine and Meredith wrapped an arm protectively around her shoulders. "George! Don't frighten her; Cady's had more than enough to deal with from that no-good husband of hers. Now this is a party – Cady, honey, what did you think of Quinn Garrison? Don't you think he's just about the most handsome young man at the party?"

Cady smiled despite herself. "He seems nice. And I'm not in the slightest bit interested." Cady glanced across to where Quinn stood with his brother Josh, and had to admit to herself - if not her grandmother - that he was an extremely handsome man. His dark hair was a little longer than Josh's and touched the collar of the white shirt he wore. His jeans (Wranglers', naturally) sat low on his lean hips and his legs were well developed and muscled. In fact, judging by his lower back, where her hand had rested while they danced, he was well muscled from top to bottom. She tore her gaze away from him and avoided the knowledge-able smirk on Sheriff Davis's lips.

"You say that now, honey, but maybe later when your divorce comes through," Meredith said hopefully.

Cady put her hands up to stop her grandmother.

Despite her best efforts to avoid it, she'd grown to like Meredith Caldwell in the past few weeks, but she wasn't about to let the woman start matchmaking. "Don't you start. Anyway, he told me he's not interested. In fact, his exact words regarding marriage were, 'Tried it once, not gonna do it again'." Cady drained her wineglass. "And I'm of the same opinion."

"Aw, Cady, just because you've had one bad experience—"

Cady held up a hand in protest. "I'm serious. If you don't stop this... I'll leave the party right this minute and walk back to San Francisco."

George laughed, running his hand over his smooth jawline. "Can't say that you can blame the girl, Mer. Seems she's been taking lessons from her grandmother in bribery and corruption."

---

Quinn found himself searching for Cady in the crowded party throughout the evening, keeping an eye on where the little redhead was and who she was spending her time with. For the most part, she remained with her grandmother, keeping to herself and not socializing with the other party-goers. At one stage, he saw her talking with Hallie and some of Hallie's friends, and he was enchanted by her smile. For a long time, she'd settled on a chair by the wall, watching the party activities and keeping herself distanced.

The more Quinn saw, the more he wanted to know. His opportunity came when he grabbed a fresh beer and met up with Kane and Hallie at the front of the barn.

"What's up, brother? How was the trip?" Kane asked with an easy smile. His arm was wrapped protectively around Hallie's shoulders, and they stood in front of the fire pit with a group of the younger attendees. Tyler and Thomas had fallen asleep hours ago, and they were under the watchful eye of some of the teenagers, who'd taken on babysitting duties for the evening. Of course, babysitting duties in this instance meant the benefits of the Garrison family living room, which came complete with a huge, flat screen television, cable TV and an impressive range of computer games. Quinn didn't imagine they were finding it too much of a hardship.

"Long," Quinn grunted. He was rapidly running out of energy; after a 4am start this morning, he was more than ready for his bed, but knew he had an hour or two to go before he'd get the opportunity to slip away. Garrison family parties weren't something you escaped from, especially not when they were in honor of your grandmother.

"You look tired, man." Kane pointed out the obvious.

"Yeah, I'm ready for some shut eye." Quinn caught movement at the entrance of the barn and watched as Meredith and Cady made their way outside. Cady seemed tired, her shoulders drooping a little and she'd wrapped a soft shawl around her shoulders to guard against the late-night chill. Meredith wrapped her arm around her grand-daughter and he watched his dad escort them to where the guests' cars were parked further down the hill.

"I see you've met Cady Caldwell."

Quinn had to forcibly draw his gaze away from Meredith and Cady. "Yeah, we danced."

Hallie punched his shoulder. "Only so you could avoid Marcie, you big goof. Why don't you just tell Marcie you're not interested?"

Quinn rolled his eyes. "You think I haven't already tried that? Marcie's like a freaking piranha." He inclined his head towards Cady. "What's the story? I thought this was the one who refused to come to Garrison?"

"Wow, you really have been out of the loop, haven't you?" Hallie countered, raising her eyebrows. "Kane, honey, perhaps you better catch your brother up on what's been happening in his absence."

"Now I just know you're bustin' a gut to tell him the story yourself, darlin'," Kane smirked and lowered his head to brush Hallie's lips with a kiss.

Quinn suffered a pang of jealousy. He wanted what Kane and Hallie had, even though he was careful to keep the thought to himself and never share it with anyone. After Julia's betrayal he'd sworn to never marry again, but he had to admit he yearned for the closeness Kane and Hallie shared, the palpable love between them. He wanted that affection with a woman of his own.

*Hell, he needed to tamp that thought down, right now.* He would never put himself in a position where he'd get hurt again, not the way Julia had wounded him. His marriage had been a farce from the beginning, when he'd been charmed by Julia's exterior package and hadn't realized the bitter woman who lay underneath. They'd been childhood sweethearts, and marriage had been a natural stepping stone after graduation. He still wasn't certain if they'd married because they'd wanted it, or if it had been what the townsfolk expected. Either way, it had been a terrible, terrible mistake and Julia started fooling around not long after he'd joined the army. The culmination had been her affair with one of his football buddies, whom she'd married about five minutes after their divorce got finalized.

He inclined his head towards Cady's departing figure. "So what's her story?"

"She's gorgeous, isn't she? I just love that fifties thing

she's got going on, she's so comfortable in her own skin, being her own person," Hallie began enthusiastically.

Quinn was quietly pleased to know he'd picked the era correctly, although he still found it strange that Cady wanted to dress that way. Despite his doubts, he had to admit, it was top-of-the-shelf sexy, and she was incredibly feminine. He mentally shook himself, returning his attention to what Hallie was saying.

"… so anyway, her husband is Jameson Le Batelier, you know, one of those fancy-schmancy chefs in San Francisco. They've been married for about seven years, but—"

"Wait, she's married?" Quinn wasn't certain why he cared, but he did.

Hallie rolled her eyes and put a hand on her hip. "Where have you been? Under a rock? How could you not have known that?"

"Unlike you, Hals, I don't listen to all the gossip which gets passed around this little town. Where's her husband?"

"Hiding out somewhere," Kane responded, and Quinn caught the coldness in his tone. "The bastard is a wife beater; beat the crap out of Cady and that's how she ended up here in Garrison. He's on the run; George is running a permanent 'Be On the Look Out' in case he turns up in town, but I doubt he'd show his ugly mug around here. He's got about two dozen charges waiting on him when we catch the bastard."

Quinn watched as Cady and her grandmother climbed into Meredith's sporty little convertible. She might look like a sweet little thing, but he decided there and then that Cady Caldwell obviously had far too much going on in her life to be considered a possible relationship prospect.

And besides – hadn't he just finished telling himself he wasn't interested in a relationship?

7

---

"It's for you."

Cady lifted an enquiring eyebrow. "Again?"

Meredith laughed. "Yep. When you decorated Granny Benton's cake, I knew the residents of Garrison would jump on your services. And when I saw Dotty Knightley at church on Sunday, she was tickled to think she might finally get to retire. She'd be pleased to hand the reins over to someone else." Meredith handed Cady the telephone receiver. "It's Lorna Mendez; she runs the gift store on Main Street. She wants to talk to you about decorating a cake for her son Rory's eighteenth birthday on the fourth of October."

Cady shook her head. "I'm not going to do this." The idea that Dotty Knightley thought Cady was going to take over Garrison's cake decorating requirements sent a swirl of panic through her chest. "I'm not staying here!"

"Of course you can help, honey. I'm glad to make the cakes, and it's providing you with some income. Plus, it's helping the locals at the same time."

Cady shook her head. "I have *no* intentions of living in

65

Garrison. I need to go back."

"You know you can't go back to San Francisco right now! It's too dangerous," Meredith protested. "Anyway, talk to Lorna about what she'd like for Rory's birthday, it's only a couple of weeks until then, and we can discuss your plans when you finish your phone call."

With a sigh, Cady took the phone and found herself agreeing to help Lorna Mendez with a cake. It was already mid-September and now she'd tied herself into staying until the first week of October by agreeing to this order. Even though the people asking for her help paid well and seemed so grateful, it wasn't going to be anywhere near enough to cover Sid's tuition costs. With a sigh, Cady disconnected the call and turned to stare out of the window. This was one of her favorite spots in the house; the reading nook, Meredith called it. Situated underneath the stairs, it featured a large ninety-degree window which looked out over the yard, and a long, comfortable couch, which was fitted in snugly beneath the stairs, making it the perfect spot to lay and read on a cool autumn day. A pile of cushions in shades of pink, raspberry and fuchsia were piled at one end and Cady slumped back onto them, dropping her hand to scratch Churchill, who was lying in a fluffy pile next to the couch to snooze.

She chewed nervously on a fingernail. She didn't really know what to do. Despite her best efforts, she was beginning to form relationships here in Garrison, especially with Meredith. She'd been doing her best to remain distanced, but the older woman worked hard to break down Cady's barriers. There was no way she would stay in this small country town – her life, such as it was, was in San Francisco. Mario was still holding her job, and she needed the income. She'd been here for five weeks already, and it was almost three months since Jameson's attack. She was running out of time.

As if Meredith had overheard her thoughts, she appeared with a mug of coffee and a warm smile. "All sorted?" She handed the mug to Cady and settled beside her on the couch.

"I've agreed to decorate a cake for her, yes," Cady sipped her coffee, chewing her lower lip pensively, "but after that, I really need to go back to San Francisco. There are things I can't avoid any longer."

"I don't think that's wise; George says you'll be in danger until they capture Jameson."

Cady huffed out a frustrated sigh. "There doesn't seem to be any sign of him and it's been eleven weeks! And I can't put my life on hold forever. I'll stay until after I've done the cake for Lorna, and then I'm going back. I'll ask Harry if I can stay with her and Scott for a while."

Meredith remained silent for a few seconds before she spoke again. "Cady, I wish you'd talk to me about what happened. We've been living together here for over a month and yet you won't talk to me at all."

Cady squirmed uncomfortably. "We do talk."

"Not about anything important," Meredith disagreed quietly. "You do your level best to keep our discussions on neutral subjects. You won't talk about your husband. You don't talk about your parents."

Cady turned to stare at the garden outside, stubbornly avoiding Meredith's gaze. "There's nothing to say."

"I've got no doubt you had a difficult childhood, Cady," Meredith began in a low voice. "Lord knows, Mark was no angel, and the private detective said that more than once, you and your sisters were put into the foster system. I'm sure that had a terrible effect on the three of you."

Cady wrapped her arms around her waist and stared resolutely out the window. There was no way she'd discuss Mark with this woman; she had no intentions of shattering whatever illusions Meredith held regarding her son. How could she? There was no way to explain the hell she and her sisters had lived in, until Cady had taken the girls and run away from their father when she was barely eighteen.

Meredith tried again. "Cady, I want to help you, I really do. But I can't help if you won't let me know what you're thinking, how you're feeling."

"I'm feeling fine, and honestly, none of this is your business. I appreciate you letting me stay here, but this is only temporary. I'm going back to San Francisco," Cady said stiffly.

"I think that's a terrible mistake," Meredith started, but Cady held up a hand in warning.

"Please. I can't stay here forever. There are things I have to do back in San Francisco."

Meredith inhaled heavily. "Do you realize you never, ever call it home?"

Cady stared at Meredith. "What?"

"You never say, 'I want to go home'. You always refer to it as 'San Francisco'."

Cady shrugged, her frustration growing. "What does that have to do with anything? It's where I live, where I belong."

"Is it? I know from the private detective I hired that your parents dragged you all around the country, from place to place, from one disgusting apartment to another. They only ever stayed until they got into trouble with the law or had to run off in the middle of the night because they owed money on the rent and couldn't pay it. Or they were going to be arrested for drug use or robbery..." Meredith drew in a sharp breath, "...or prostitution."

Cady shook her head impatiently. "What's your point?"

"San Francisco isn't your home, Cady. I don't think you've ever had somewhere you could put down roots." Meredith took another deep breath as if mentally preparing herself for an attack. "I think you're going back to San Francisco because that man you worked for is holding your job. I think you're in such a hurry because you're worried about Sid's fees for her final semester at college and your hospital costs." Meredith leaned forward, placing a hand on Cady's shoulder. "You don't have to worry about it, I've already paid those bills. You have nothing to rush back to San Francisco for."

Cady stared at Meredith, unable to believe what she was hearing. "Why would you do that?"

"Because I could. And because I didn't want you to be worrying about either of those things while you're recuperating."

"And because you thought you could take over my life?" Cady demanded. "What right do you have to interfere? Neither of those things was your responsibility!"

"Cady, I just wanted to help—"

Cady threw her book to the floor and hastily got to her feet, spilling coffee all over the couch in the process. Churchill nudged Cady's fingers with his nose and Cady ignored him. "I didn't ask for your help! I didn't want your help! Sid and Harry are my responsibility, not yours!"

Meredith stood up. "They're *my* granddaughters!"

"They're *my sisters*! I kept us together, I kept them safe! I got us a place to live when we left that shithole and ran away! I got a job and kept them in school! Don't think you can take over our lives now!"

Meredith looked horrified. "Cady, that was never my intention—"

In a temper, Cady threw the mug to the floor, the last of the coffee splashing across the tiles when the mug smashed. "We don't need you! Sid, Harry and I have done just fine without your help!"

"By marrying Jameson Le Batelier? Yes, that worked out beautifully! You nearly got yourself killed by him, to support your sisters!" Meredith snapped.

For a tense minute, silence descended between the two women, and Cady stared at Meredith, breathing heavily.

"Cady—" Meredith's face fell and she stepped forward to comfort her granddaughter, but Cady took a swift step backward, shaking her head.

Without another word, she turned and walked to the front door, wrenching it open and snatching Churchill's lead from the small hallstand. She whistled, and Churchill bounded out beside her before Cady slammed the door, barreling down the stairs in a fury.

---

CADY STOMPED ALONG THE STREET, barely aware of the beauty of her surroundings as she dwelled on Meredith's words. She couldn't have hurt Cady more if she'd taken a knife and stabbed her in the chest.

Cady was only too aware of the mistakes she'd made – painfully aware of what a blunder it had been to marry Jameson. Older than Cady by a decade, he'd pursued her from the moment he first met her. Cady had been working in a diner near his restaurant when he'd stopped in for a coffee one morning. That first morning had led to Jameson visiting the diner regularly, but it had taken a while for a naïve Cady to realize he was coming because of her, not for the diner's somewhat ordinary coffee.

Jameson had bedazzled her from the very beginning; with charm, a warm smile and what seemed to be genuine interest in the quirky twenty-year-old, who was barely keeping her family together with three minimum wage jobs. She'd been fortunate, because they found a safe, warm home with Mr. Kornberg's widowed sister. Mr. Kornberg had been a lifesaver – he'd kept a solicitous eye on Cady and her sisters after the lock incident, and often met Cady at the door to his apartment when she walked past. Sometimes he'd give Cady a couple of dollars to buy some bread and milk; or hand over a pot of soup, which Mrs. Kornberg had made for the girls to survive on for a couple of days. When things deteriorated still further, and Mark had begun to threaten Cady with the prospect of prostituting herself to pay for his drugs and drinking, Mr. Kornberg stepped in. When Mark was out buying drugs one night, Mr. Kornberg appeared at their apartment door with his wife. Between them, they'd packed up a couple of battered bags with Cady, Harry, and Sid's meager possessions, and given the girls money to buy bus tickets out of Detroit. Mr. Kornberg handed Cady a slip of paper with a San Francisco address written on it and told Cady to take her sisters and run.

Cady had thanked the elderly couple and done exactly what they'd suggested. She still remembered the terror of that trip – the rush to the bus station, buying the tickets, trying to make it seem as if she was confident and wasn't stealing her underage sisters away from their abusive father. Cady knew that at eighteen, if they were caught and the girls were sent into the foster system again, she wouldn't be going with them, and might lose contact with them forever. More than once, the three girls had been split up for placement, and after the last time, she'd sworn to Sid and Harry she would never let it happen again.

Arriving in San Francisco, Cady had been overwhelmed and uncertain if this was the right thing to do. Could they be leaving the horror of one dire situation, only to fall into an even worse one?

Fortunately, that hadn't been the case. Sylvia Olszewska, Mr. Kornberg's widowed sister, was their salvation. Seventy-two years old, the elderly woman had taken the three girls in, giving them a place to stay and providing them with love and acceptance. She'd made sure Harry and Sid got off to school each day and been there when they got home, while Cady worked to provide them with what they needed.

But Jameson had swooped in, like a knight in shining armor, and taken over fiscal responsibility for Harry and Sid after he'd convinced Cady to marry him. Mrs. Olszewska had regarded Jameson with skepticism, and a healthy dose of warnings about him 'not being everything he seemed', but Cady was already certain she loved him and believed everything he told her about how wonderful their life would be together.

It had all been a ruse. Cady had no doubt Jameson did love her, in his own twisted way. But now, she was certain he'd looked upon her as a project, someone he could shape to his very specific ideas on how a wife should behave and act. It hadn't taken long for Cady to realize she couldn't reach his high ideals – that she was destined to be a continual disappointment to Jameson. Nor had she allowed for the abuse she would suffer when she failed to meet his standards. It hadn't taken long to realize that what she'd believed was love, was, in fact, a form of hero worship for someone she'd thought could keep her safe. But she'd remained with Jameson, long after she should have because he'd provided the means for Harry and Sid to follow their dreams, to build the lives they deserved. The lives they wouldn't have had if Cady hadn't used Jameson and access to his money.

Glancing up, Cady realized she'd left Hillman Street and they were walking along Polson, which led on to Main Street. With a wry smile, Cady considered the possibility of every small town in America having a Main Street. Perhaps she'd Google the question later, see if she could find the statistics. Meredith had been letting Cady use her computer since she'd been in Garrison, a novelty because Jameson had refused to allow Cady to have one, part of his methods for keeping her under control. Without a computer, she had limited access to the outside world, other than what Jameson provided. He had a laptop, a top of the range, expensive one which he used all the time, but he refused to allow Cady to access it. She wasn't allowed to have a cell phone either. It had been the story of her life after their marriage – being told what she could and couldn't do; and what she did and didn't need. Where she could and couldn't go. Jameson had only agreed to Cady enrolling in a cake decorating course because he'd gotten talked into it by a business associate, whose wife wanted to do the same course. She suspected Jameson thought it was harmless and wouldn't take Cady away from meeting his constant demands.

The problem with that theory happened when Cady discovered she had a natural aptitude. In fact, she mused as she turned onto Main Street – it was something she'd proven to have a real talent for. She had a natural flair for creating something special from a cake and some icing, an ability she'd never been aware of until she started classes.

The desire to create new and more complex cakes grew, and she'd wanted to find a job where she could continue expanding her skills.

Getting a job was another stroke of good luck because Jameson had refused to consider Cady working until one of his associates celebrated a birthday. Cady decorated the cake for the occasion and overwhelmed by the number of compliments she received, Jameson had been at a loss for words when another associate suggested Cady follow her dreams and start decorating cakes – and said he knew someone who would be happy to have Cady join his team. Reluctant to let his friends discover their marriage was a sham and he controlled every minute of Cady's life, Jameson agreed, assuming Cady would follow his orders, delivered through a meaningful glare, and refuse the offer.

To his disgust – and Cady's shock – she'd thanked Jameson's associate and presented herself at Mario's Bakery the following Monday morning. From that point on, their marriage had deteriorated rapidly, culminating in Jameson's jealous rage after she won the award.

Cady mentally shook herself, drawing away from the memories. Thinking about it wouldn't change anything. If she had the opportunity to do it over, she'd probably still make the same decisions, even knowing in hindsight how bad they'd been. But what she'd done had improved Harry and Sid's lives, and that's all she'd ever wanted. Even if it did leave her consumed with guilt for using Jameson the way she had. But when she considered the cost she'd paid, Cady thought they might be a little more even. Jameson had supported her sisters' – but Cady had paid for that support in blood and misery.

Churchill was sniffing the sidewalk, lifting his nose to trace the source of the many scents wafting from the stores.

Pausing at the corner, Cady glanced around. She had to admit Garrison was a pretty town, although like most of rural America there were signs of the recession. A few stores were boarded up, and in between some of the modern buildings were a couple that had probably been built before the turn of the century and long ago abandoned. One had an old ice cream sign hanging from its second story, the plastic cone and ice cream faded and the wording indistinguishable. Against the row of buildings, the majestic Beartooth Mountains created a picturesque snow-covered backdrop.

Some older buildings had been renovated and across the road, Cady saw what she now knew to be Lorna Mendez's gift store, brightly painted in pale green with dusky pink and white trim, big pots of brightly colored flowers lining the windowsills. The town was still bustling with activity in the late afternoon, the road on either side lined with cars parallel parked to the curb. Next to the gift store, Cady saw the hardware store, and a little way up, past one of the abandoned stores, people were still darting in and out of the grocery. She started walking again, Churchill happy to wander further. Usually, she would stick to the back streets, but today Cady needed a good long walk to clear her heart and mind of the anger that had built up.

She could hardly blame Meredith for what she'd done – in any other circumstances, Cady probably would have been grateful. But Meredith had hit her squarely in the solar plexus with first, the revelation that she'd so easily paid what would have taken Cady months to deal with, and second; her point, so close to the mark, about how much of a disaster Cady's marriage had been. And Cady had only herself to blame.

## 8

Cady arrived home well after darkness fell, to find the detritus of her temper tantrum cleared up, and a fresh cover on the couch under the stairs. Offering a polite apology for breaking the mug, Cady managed to reach a truce, of sorts, with Meredith in the following days. Cady reverted to her usual strategy, remaining well-mannered, but distant, and for now, Meredith seemed happy to accept her reticence. There'd been no more mention of Jameson Le Batelier or Mark Caldwell since their fight and both women were keeping the subjects pushed firmly into the background.

"Your sisters are coming to visit this weekend," Meredith announced the following Friday after they'd eaten sandwiches for lunch. "I thought you'd like to spend some time with them after being here for so long. They'll be arriving tonight, a little after supper."

Cady lifted her head, surprised to hear her sisters would be visiting and wondering if this was a ploy on Meredith's part, to force her into talking about her ex-husband or her dead father. She met Meredith's steady gaze with the question in her eyes and Meredith smiled and shook her head. "They want to see you, to confirm for themselves that you're recovering well. You can hardly blame them for being worried."

"Are Scott and Dylan coming with them?" Scott was Harry's husband of two years, an electrician, fanatical football fan, and all-around nice guy who adored his wife and was protective of his sisters-in-law. Dylan was Sid's boyfriend, a fellow med school student who intended to specialize in emergency medicine. Dylan and Sid shared an apartment near their college with two other med students, all of them working part-time jobs to cover their living costs. Dylan worked at a nearby Cheesecake Factory as a server, and Sid had picked up some tuition work for nearby high school students and worked at a supermarket most weekends.

"Nope, just the girls. They seemed to think a girls' weekend without Scott and Dylan would be fun."

Cady suspected this visit had been orchestrated by Meredith, part of her efforts to thwart Cady's plans of returning to San Francisco. There was still no sign of the elusive Jameson Le Batelier, but to Cady's disgust his restaurants were reportedly doing huge business, Jameson's fame only increasing with his status as a fugitive.

With a sigh, Cady turned from filling the kitchen sink and met Meredith's gaze. "It'll be good to see them."

Meredith grinned. "I think so too, Cady. Telephone calls just aren't the same as a visit." The blue in Meredith's eyes sparkled – it was apparent she adored her two younger granddaughters. "And I've heard from your Uncle David, he and his wife are visiting the following weekend." She hesitated, eyeing Cady cautiously. "You'll still be here, won't you?"

"Yeah. That's the weekend of Rory Mendez's eighteenth birthday. I'll finish up his cake and head back to San Fra—... *home*, on Monday," Cady responded, turning back to washing up the lunch dishes. She was determined to leave Garrison before she got more firmly entrenched and carefully avoided further eye contact with Meredith, evading the hurt she was sure would be revealed in the older woman's expression.

---

"You're looking so much better, Cades, country life seems to be agreeing with you." Sid slumped into a corner booth at Grizzlies, the only bar in Garrison, and flipped the cap from her beer before she glanced around the busy venue. "Oooh, look – they have karaoke on Saturday nights – we should come along for the heck of it, before Harry and I head home on Sunday!"

Cady slipped into the booth beside her sister, picking up Sid's beer cap and flicking it neatly into a nearby trash-can. "I think one visit will probably be enough," she announced, sipping from the glass of white wine she'd been talked into ordering. Coming to the bar had been Sid and Harry's idea – Cady would quite happily have remained at the house, but the two girls had joined forces and insisted she needed to get out. Grizzlies appeared to be the only form of social life available in Garrison, and on a Friday night, the stone building was bursting at the seams. Up at the bar, patrons stood three deep waiting to place their orders, and four servers were rushing around the vast room, struggling to keep up with demand. The servers balanced their trays high over their heads, to avoid being jostled by the nearly wall-to-wall mass of customers vying for positions near the half-dozen pool tables, or dancing to music being pumped from the jukebox in the corner. Much to Cady's amusement, Wranglers and Levi 501's once again seemed to be the standard uniform for everyone, including the waitresses and the bartenders who were rushing back and forth, supplying their patrons with booze. Everyone who worked here wore a white t-shirt with 'Grizzlies' written across the chest, a bear face superimposed into the capital 'G'.

In direct contrast, Cady wore a red checked shirt with a white collar, the sleeves rolled up to her elbows, and rocka-billy-style denim overalls, with big white buttons on the side pockets. The wide cuffs at her ankles revealed patent red sandals with wedge heels and peep-toes. She'd pulled her hair up and curled it in a style reminiscent of the early forties. With matching nail polish and lipstick, she was pleased with the overall effect and had applied a small spray of her favorite rose-scented perfume.

"It might be fun Cades." Harry slipped into the seat opposite Sid and Cady and touched her hair self-consciously. Since Cady had seen her last, Harry had cut her hair into a cute, chin-length bob, and the gorgeous red tresses hung softly about her face, enhancing her elfin features and big hazel eyes.

Cady smiled at her middle sister. "Stop fussing. It looks amazing, Harry. Gorgeous. Does Scott like the new style?"

Harry smiled and reached for her wine. "Yeah. He says he does, but you know Scott. If I shaved my head, eyebrows *and* my eyelashes, and finished off by piercing my lip fifteen times, he'd still tell me I looked amazing."

"And he'd be right," Sid agreed, sipping her beer. "So Cades, how are things going with Gran?"

Trust Sid to cut straight to the chase. No beating around

the bush with the future Dr. Caldwell, pediatric specialist. "It's been okay, but I'm coming back to San Francisco in a few weeks."

"Is that a good idea?" Harry asked. "They haven't found that asshole yet."

"I can't stay here indefinitely," Cady pointed out. She glared at Harry, annoyed that her sister was spouting the same concerns as Meredith had, and she suspected it was beginning to sound like the party line. Didn't anyone realize her situation out here in the boondocks was untenable?

Sid grinned, indicating a group of beautifully muscled, Wrangler-clad butts near the bar. Cady followed her gaze and then hurriedly glanced away with a blush. "I don't know, Cades, the scenery is great out here, and I'm not talking about the Beartooth Mountains."

Cady chuckled, despite her annoyance. "Does Dylan know how bad you are?"

"Dylan knows I'm an independent, free-spirited woman, who appreciates the finer things in life," Sid retorted. She eyed the group of men admiringly. "And as long as I only look and don't touch, he's fine with that arrangement."

"We're getting off track here," Harry pointed out, offering Cady a worried smile. "Cades, until Jameson is arrested, it'll be dangerous for you to be in San Francisco."

Cady gulped down some of her wine; probably a little faster than she should, but her anxiety levels were high and Sid and Harry seemingly siding with Meredith didn't reduce her unease. "I've got to earn some money." She glanced from Sid to Harry and back. "Did you know that Meredith paid my medical bills, and Sid's tuition for this last semester?" she demanded.

Harry averted her gaze, a tactic she'd used since childhood when she'd been caught out keeping a secret. "Well, yeah. But Cades, she wanted to do it. And when are you going to start calling her Gran, like the rest of us?"

"Yeah, and you've taken responsibility for us for far too long," Sid agreed, tipping her beer from side to side and watching the liquid sway.

Cady downed the rest of her wine. "But you *are* my responsibility."

Sid drew closer to Cady and squeezed her hand. "No, Cades. We were never meant to be your responsibility. Those assholes we managed to score as parents were supposed to be responsible for us, and a fat lot of good they were. Gran can afford this, and she wants to help."

Cady huffed out an impatient breath. "Am I the only one who thinks this isn't her problem?"

A server arrived at their table and snagged Cady's empty wineglass, smiling brightly at the three women. "Anything else?"

"Yeah," Cady grumbled. "A scotch on the rocks. Make it a double."

---

By eleven pm, Cady was happily drunk. Not fall-off-your-chair, outrageously smashed, but certainly the type of drunk that meant for the moment, her worries had fallen by the wayside. She'd given up fretting over Jameson; she'd stopped worrying about the money Meredith had forked out. She wasn't even considering how uncomfortable she was, staying in the same house her father had grown up in. She was relaxed and enjoying watching the spectacle that was Garrison on a Friday night. Sipping her third scotch, Cady was comfortably settled in the booth, watching Sid and Harry whoopin' it up on the dance floor with a couple of cowboys. They were having an awesome time, and it was fun to watch. Harry was usually so serious, so to see her boot scooting like a pro was amusing. Even more so was her solemn discussion with the cowboy she was dancing with, before she'd agreed to get up on the floor with him – ensuring he understood completely and thoroughly that she was a happily married woman.

"Hey, honey. Now aren't you just the prettiest little freak of nature I've seen here in Garrison?"

Cady sat up a little straighter, twisting towards the man who'd spoken. He was tall and slender, with bright blue eyes and dirty blonde hair. He licked his lips, studying her lasciviously and Cady shuddered. "Hi."

"That's quite a look you've got going there, little girl. Did you get stuck in a time machine or something? You look like you're in the wrong decade." He laughed and settled into the booth beside her. "Is this some kinda Back to the Future thing? You from another dimension or somethin'?"

Cady slid across to the far end of the booth, out of his reach. "That's another *decade*, not a *dimension*, you tool. Didn't you ever see the movies?"

The man refused to be discouraged. "Whoa there, darlin'. Come a little closer, I want to get a good look at that getup you've got going on—"

Cady shook her head. "I think you should go back to your friends—"

Not taking no for an answer, the blonde man gripped her arm. "Now don't be such a bitch, I just wanna get to know you a little better, that's all—"

"Get the hell out of my seat, you moron." Sid appeared at the end of the table, glaring down at the man, her eyes blazing fire.

Beside her, looking no less fierce, was Harry, who scowled. "Leave my sister alone, you dickwad."

The man's casual countenance disappeared, and his beer-soaked breath wafted over Cady. She wrinkled her nose in disgust. "Why don't you two girls go back to your dancin', while me and this little lady get better acquainted? I ain't doing her no harm—"

"Why don't you go on home to your wife, Earl, and leave these young women alone?" A big man leaned into the booth and grabbed the blonde man by the sleeve, dragging him out forcibly. Cady watched as the newcomer gave the man a good shove, pushing him towards the doors leading outside. "You've had a skin full, and you need to head on home now. Stop being an ass."

Cady watched as Earl stumbled out through the door, and the big man who'd come to their rescue shook his head when he turned back to her. He appeared to be about fifty years old, but his skin was weathered by years of outside work and darkly tanned, so it was difficult to tell. "You alright, Ma'am?"

Cady nodded, abruptly soberer than she had been. She'd been harassed for the way she chose to dress by people before, but it hadn't happened in Garrison until now. "I'm ready to go home," she announced.

"Let me walk you to your car," the big man said, tipping his hat. "The name's Hop Skipton; I work out on the Crazy Horseshoes Ranch."

Sid giggled, staring up at the man with mischief sparking in her eyes. "That's your name? For real?"

Hop grinned, his brown eyes warm. "Yes, ma'am. Of course, Hop is just a nickname. Real name is Ed."

"Thanks for your assistance, Hop," Harry said, helping Cady to her feet. "This is my sister, Cady Caldwell, I'm

Harry, and this is Sid. We can make our own way home, we're just a street away and we walked."

"Cady Caldwell? The cake lady? I've heard about you – you're all Meredith's kin, aren't you?" He doffed his hat and indicated the door. "Let me make sure you ladies get back to Meredith's house safe. Earl's probably well on his way home, but better safe than sorry, I always say."

By the time they reached Meredith's house, Cady was still smarting from the way the blonde man had spoken and using his behavior as further validation for leaving Garrison. Who was he to pick on the way she liked to dress? The sooner she was out of this hick town, the better off she'd be. Obviously, some of the locals were narrow-minded enough to think she should be just like everyone else.

Deep down, Cady knew she was being unfair to Garrison's inhabitants, but she was still smarting from the way her sisters had taken Meredith's side. After an enjoyable couple of hours, she was fast falling into a funk.

"Thank you, Hop," Harry said when they reached the gate.

"My pleasure, ladies." With another flick of his hat, Hop grinned down at the three young women, and then sauntered back along the sidewalk, retracing his steps to Grizzlies.

"Well, that was fun," Cady announced dryly. She slumped onto the porch swing, leaning over to remove her shoes. After the walk back from Main Street her feet ached and all she wanted to do was collapse into bed.

"It was kinda fun to see you standing up for yourself," Harry smiled. "Haven't seen the spirited Cady Caldwell in quite a while."

Cady stopped in the task of undoing one shoe and stared at Harry. Her sister was right – it was a long time since Cady'd had the courage to tell someone to back off. Maybe she was healing and hadn't noticed.

"Aw c'mon, Cades, it was fun, until that fool started annoying you," Sid protested. "Once the locals get to know you, none of them will bother about how you dress."

"They're not *going* to get to know me," Cady muttered. "Haven't I just got through telling you I'm not staying? Three more weeks and then I'm heading back to San Francisco."

"I really think you should stay here," Harry protested.

Cady picked up her shoes and got to her feet. "I am *not* staying here."

"Cades," Sid protested, looping her arm over Cady's shoulder while Harry unlocked the front door. The living room light was still glowing, and upstairs, Meredith's bedroom light was on. "It's nuts to go back now when that bastard is still on the loose."

"Yeah, yeah, I've heard this about a million times," Cady grumbled. "Why don't you two understand – I can't stay here!"

"Because I don't understand *why* you can't stay here," Harry muttered, shoving at the front door with her hip. "Damn it, this door always sticks."

Cady sighed heavily. "You two are driving me nuts. Yes, Meredith is nice, and I get that you both like her so much. But don't you see? I will never, ever be comfortable in this place." The alcohol had loosened Cady's tongue, and she shook her head vehemently when she stepped through the front door.

"Why? It's not like Gran has dozens of photos of Dad all over the house!" Sid grumbled. "There are hardly any reminders of him here at all."

Cady turned on her sister, her voice rising. It had been a

long twelve weeks, and the stress of what Jameson had done, fleeing to Garrison, the uncertainty she was facing – it all came crashing in on her at once. "I can't stay here! Don't you see that? This is the house where *that man* – my so-called *father* lived! The man who wanted to sell my virginity to the highest bidder! The man who wanted to *molest* me! Why do you think I stole those locks at the hardware store and got Mr. Kornberg to put them on the doors? Why do you think I was so grateful when he and Mrs. Kornberg gave us the money for bus tickets? I was saving myself – and *you* – from *him*!"

Harry and Sid stared at Cady, their mouths hanging open, and she watched as the color receded from their cheeks. As fast as her temper had flared, it receded, leaving Cady feeling empty, gutted. She'd kept this information from her sisters for a decade, wanting to protect them from learning what their father had really been like. After his death, she'd continued to keep the secret, not wanting to recall the details and dredge up the past. They'd escaped, the girls were safe, and Mark hadn't gotten his way. What was the point of bringing up the subject and further destroying Sid and Harry's opinion of their father? It would resolve nothing, only make them feel worse about what Cady had done to keep them safe. She'd never wanted to burden anyone with that knowledge.

Cady sniffled, surprised to notice she was crying. She'd held the emotions in for so long, and to admit the truth now, to the two women she was closest to in the world, was crushing.

"Cades..." Sid began, but Cady held up her hand.

"Not tonight. I never meant for you to find out what happened. I'm sorry. I just can't... I can't..." Cady brushed her palms across her face, wiping away the tears. "I can't deal with this tonight, I'm sorry."

She turned away and glanced up the stairwell, her heart coming to a standstill in her chest.

Meredith was on the upstairs landing, her hands clutched to her breast in dismay.

# 9

Cady woke early the following morning and slipped out before anyone else got up. The autumn air was crisp and cool, her breath creating a fine cloud of mist as she walked Churchill around Garrison. Despite being early, many of the residents greeted her with a smile and a wave when she walked past, and Cady admitted to herself she'd judged the town harshly last night, because of one bigot's behavior. Worse still had been her own actions, when she'd lost her temper and opened her big mouth.

Now she'd have to face the fallout. Buying some time when she got back to the house, Cady pulled off her jacket and hung it in the mudroom, then slipped off her boots, leaving them standing neatly by the mudroom bench. Just inside the kitchen, she'd spied Harry and Sid sitting at the table, watching her every move as if they suspected she'd try and escape again.

"You could have told us, Cades," Harry suggested quietly, watching Cady make a cup of coffee after she entered the kitchen.

"What was the point?" Cady asked, when she sat down

opposite her sisters at the table. There was no sign of Meredith; Cady wondered if she was out of bed yet. A pang of guilt twisted her gut – she would never have intentionally hurt the older woman; another reason it had been so hard to live here. She wouldn't have shared this information about Mark with anyone, not if she could help it. Nothing happened, other than some inappropriate touching, and she'd gotten her sisters out before it could amount to anything more awful.

But strangely enough, Cady did feel a little better, knowing she wasn't holding on to such a huge secret any longer. Her steps had been lighter when she'd strode through the streets with Churchill, a weight lifted off her shoulders had made her greetings to the Garrison towns-folk a little more enthusiastic, her smile a little brighter. Cady suddenly realized she was coming to like the place. Weird.

Her attention was drawn back to Harry and Sid, who were both staring at her as if expecting a response. "I'm sorry, what?"

Harry looked exasperated. She wrapped her fingers around her coffee mug, leaning it against her chin. "The point is, we're your sisters! You should have told us about this, from the very beginning!" She shook her head indignantly. "We already knew Dad was an asshole—"

"Shhh! Keep your voice down! I don't want Meredith to hear you talking like that about him," Cady warned.

Sid laughed dryly. "Cady, you think Gran doesn't already know this? You've been living here for six weeks – haven't you talked to her about Dad at all?" Sid paused, observing Cady and when no response was forthcoming, she continued. "Cades, Gran knows *exactly* what Dad was like. He was in trouble with drugs and alcohol before he ever left Garrison. If you'd talked to Gran, you'd know that she holds no illusions over his character."

Cady stared silently at Sid. Harry lowered her coffee mug onto the table and reached across, grasping Cady's hands in hers. "So much more makes sense now. I think, deep down, I always knew there was something hinky about Dad's behavior after Mom died. And remembering you getting Mr. Kornberg to fit those locks— well, I should have realized. But I was just a kid, Cades. God, I'm so sorry." Harry tucked her hair behind her ear. "Did he... well, did it..."

Cady rushed to reassure her sister, shaking her head vehemently. "No! No." Just the memory was enough to send a shiver racing down her spine.

"Just another reason to be glad he's dead," Sid added bitterly.

Cady stared at her in surprise. While she hadn't been able to protect her sisters from everything their parents had done, she'd tried her best. It was a shock to consider she might not be the only one harboring secrets. "He didn't... do anything..." She found she couldn't finish the sentence.

Harry screwed up her nose. "Ew! No." Wrapping her arms around herself, Harry brushed at her skin as if trying to get rid of an errant cobweb. "I don't know how you stayed so strong for so long, Cades."

"Neither do I," Sid agreed. "But don't you think it's time you let us look after you?" Sid's expression softened, her green eyes luminous as she watched Cady. "Stay here in Garrison. Please. There's no reason for you to leave right now and Harry and I will both feel better, knowing you're safe here with Gran."

"I know you hate the thought of living in the same house as Dad did, but honestly, Cades, there's very little evidence of him ever being here. It's years since he ran away from home."

Cady nodded, sipping her coffee thoughtfully. "I know that, but it's hard, you know?"

It was true, there were very few mementos of Mark Caldwell in this house, but there were a couple of photos on the mantel, and some in the study, which Cady avoided whenever possible. She hated being faced with the reminders. Glancing around the kitchen, Cady turned back to Harry. "Where's Meredith?"

Harry rolled her eyes. "*Gran*, Cady. For God's sake, call her Gran! She's gone to visit with Sheriff Davis. She left not long after I got up."

Cady chewed her bottom lip, worried that she'd hurt Meredith's feelings. "Was she okay?"

"She's fine. Cades, she doesn't blame you for any of this. And to be honest, I think it was a relief for her to get a little understanding about why you were so determined not to talk about Dad. But you forget we've been visiting with Gran for a while now. I don't think there's much that Sid and I haven't told her about the nightmare that was 'growing up Caldwell'."

Cady stared at Harry for a moment, then smiled weakly. "'Growing up Caldwell'? Really? That's what you're calling it?"

Sid chuckled. "Yeah, it's like our own sick, twisted and perverted little reality show." She winked at Cady. "Besides, Cades, you've had enough sadness and drama in your life – if we don't try and laugh about this stuff, and move on – what's the point in surviving it?"

MEREDITH WAS SITTING in George's kitchen, an unusual occurrence on a Saturday morning. George knew she had something on her mind – he just wasn't certain what it was. She'd arrived a little after eight, with a wan smile and tired eyes, asking if she could share breakfast with him.

Hiding his surprise, George had ushered her inside, settling her at the breakfast bar while he got the coffee pot running and hustled to find something he could offer Meredith for breakfast. Usually, he grabbed a bite on the way to work, and he hadn't been grocery shopping this week, but if Meredith was here and wanting breakfast, well, he'd damn well make certain he gave the lady breakfast.

"I've got some puffed wheat, or I can cook some toast," he announced after a fruitless search of the freezer. Hell, he didn't even have any eggs.

"Toast is fine," Meredith responded quietly. She was staring out of the window, her thoughts apparently a hundred miles away. George guessed it had something to do with Cady – he just wasn't certain what. All he did know was that Meredith was here, with him, and this was a step forward in their relationship. He didn't want to blow it now.

For as long as he could remember, George had been friends with Meredith. They'd both grown up in Garrison, attended school together. He'd always suspected he would marry her until she'd up and married Jim Caldwell. Not that George held a grudge – Jim had been a good man, and Meredith had adored him – but he'd loved her from afar and never gotten over her. Hell, he'd never married because of her. When Jim died, George had been there, the good friend Meredith needed as she recovered from her husband's death. He'd been a shoulder to cry on, a friend to attend functions with, when either of them required a partner. Now he wanted to be more. Lord, how he wanted to be more to Meredith.

George took some bread from the freezer and placed it in the toaster, pulling some plates out of one cupboard, and mugs from another. "Coffee?"

"Please." She continued staring out the window, picking at one fingernail inattentively.

George poured coffee, buttered a couple of slices of toast and placed the plate and mug in front of Meredith before his impatience got the better of him. He considered it some sort of record that he'd managed to last this long. "Eat. And for Christ's sake, tell me what's going on with you."

Meredith drew her attention away from the window and offered him a drawn smile. "I thought I'd heard the very worst of what my son did to his family. Until last night." She lowered the mug to the table and shook her head. "The private detective I hired, he told me about Mark's arrests for drugs, being drunk and disorderly, the prostitution charges – and I thought I could eventually come to terms with everything he'd done." She stopped speaking, dropping her head into her hands. "Did you know he attempted to molest Cady? Intended to prostitute her – sell her to the highest bidder?"

*Well, shit.* George settled into a chair opposite Meredith and reached across to place his hand over hers. "I've seen his rap sheet, Mer. There's nothing to suggest he was sexually assaulting the girls. Abusing drugs, petty theft, check fraud, prostitution, selling drugs, credit card fraud..." George listed off everything he could recall, from what he'd seen after the PI located Mark. "With regards to the girls, there was reckless endangerment, abandonment, any number of charges of the girls being left to fend for themselves at odd hours. I didn't see any evidence to suggest he was sexually assaulting Cady."

Meredith looked up at him, and he was stunned by the anger in her expression. "You don't believe what Cady says is true?"

George shook his head and held up his hands in protest. "Now hang on a minute. That's not what I said, Mer. I said there weren't any *charges* of molestation. That doesn't mean it didn't happen."

Meredith's shoulder slumped. "It happened after their mother died."

George clenched his jaw, thinking over his response. If Mark Caldwell had still been alive George would have killed him with his own bare hands, for the pain he'd put Meredith through. "Cady told you this?"

"I overheard her when the girls came back from Grizzlies last night." Meredith dropped her head back into her hands. "I want to help Cady so badly, but I just don't know how! And now she's threatening to go back to San Francisco—"

"What?" George rubbed his hand across his jaw. "She can't go back to San Francisco."

"I know that. You know that. But convincing Cady is going to be the difficult part. She's resentful because I paid the fees for Sid's final semester and covered her medical bills. She doesn't think she belongs here. She doesn't like living at my house, and I can hardly blame her, she must feel as if her father is all around her."

George didn't respond, thinking furiously about what to do to convince Cady to stay. "The problem is; the girl is directionless. She's lost her husband, the need to help her sisters – her whole life. She's got nothing to plan for, nothing to look forward to…"

"She's only twenty-eight, George – she's got her whole life ahead of her!" Meredith protested.

"I know that," George responded gently. "But she's had a tough time of it, Mer. She's only had herself to rely on, and she's been responsible for Sid and Harry – for years. Now she needs to refocus on her own future, and that's not going to be easy."

Meredith sipped her coffee and picked up a slice of toast, biting into it as she considered his words.

"Maybe it's time to give the girl a reason to stay in Garrison," George said, snagging a piece of the toast.

"What would you suggest?"

"From what I hear, she's getting regular orders for those cakes she decorates. Why not help her set up a business here in town? You've got the property up on Main Street – let Cady do something with it. It's her inheritance, after all."

Meredith shook her head. "Oh, no, George. I don't think that would be a good idea."

George lifted a eyebrow. "Why not?"

"You know why – she'd never accept it."

George shook his head. "Mer, what the girl doesn't know won't hurt her. Let Cady see the place, make up her own mind. Offer it to her. You might be surprised."

———

"CADY, can I talk to you please?" Meredith stood in the doorway to Cady's bedroom, patting Churchill when he bounced across the room to stand beside her.

Cady nodded. "I'm sorry about last night. I never intended—"

Meredith held up her hand, halting Cady's protest.

"Don't apologize, Cady. It isn't necessary." She walked into the room, settling next to Cady on the bed.

"Cady, I know my son was no good; I've known for a long time." Meredith paused, clasping her fingers together tightly. "He got in with the wrong crowd, started drinking, and then came the drugs. He barely came home, dropped out of school, and caused your grandfather and me endless worry. I can't tell you how many times George brought him home in the back of a squad car because Mark had been up to no good. He vandalized things, he stole." Meredith brushed an errant tear away, when it rolled slowly down her cheek. "To be honest, in some ways it was a relief when he ran away from home. Your granddaddy and I had been desperately worried about him, but we were also concerned about the influence he was having on David. He was four years younger and adored his older brother. If Mark had stayed here in Garrison... well, I always worried about him drawing David into his schemes."

"I've never met Uncle David, but Harry and Sid speak highly of him."

Meredith smiled. "David loves the girls." She crossed her legs taking a moment to compose her next words. "Cady... what you said last night, did Mark— did your father do anything... untoward... to you?"

Cady inhaled sharply, rubbing her hands up and down her arms as if to warm herself. "No. It never got that far. Most of the time, he was drunk, or drugged, or both." Goosebumps swelled on her arms, and Cady shivered.

Meredith offered her a relieved smile. "I wish I could have saved you from going through such a terrible childhood. If I'd known—"

Cady shook her head vehemently. "You couldn't have known. And it's been tough, but we were fortunate that our neighbor helped us out when things got really bad." She smiled, flicking through the pages of her book thoughtfully.

"Sid and Harry told me about Mr. Kornberg, and his sister, the one you lived with, in San Francisco."

"Without them, I think we would have ended up in the foster system permanently, and probably split up forever," Cady responded.

"I've been talking to George. He strongly advises that you stay here in Garrison, and I have to agree with him."

Cady started to protest, but Meredith held up a hand. "Please, let me finish. Cady, you've got nothing to go back to San Francisco for. Your marriage is over; you told me yourself you've started divorce proceedings. Sid and Harry have lives of their own now, and you don't have to financially help them any longer. It's time to start thinking about yourself. Why don't you consider opening a cake store, here in Garrison?"

Cady's mouth dropped open, her eyes growing wide, and then she snapped her mouth shut again while she considered Meredith's suggestion. Was her grandmother out of her mind? How could Cady possibly do that? "I can't open a store."

"Why not?" Meredith questioned smoothly. "I think you'd enjoy it. And lord knows we need something new in Garrison. All our cakes are shipped in from Billings, they're practically stale before they get here, and you've already seen how keen people are to have you do their cake decorating. And Dotty is practically beside herself, with the prospect of stepping down.

Cady shook her head, scarcely able to believe what she was hearing. "I can't do that. I'd need someone to do the baking..."

"I'm sure that could be arranged—"

"...and I don't have the money to start up a business..."

"I can help you—"

"You've done more than enough to help already—"

Meredith held up a hand. "Please, Cady. Hear me out. I never thought I would say this, but I hate my son. Not only for what he did by abandoning his family but for what he did to you girls. I want you to have the opportunity to succeed at something you do so very well. I have the property; I own a couple of buildings on Main Street, and they've sat empty for years. Just come with me, take a look, and see what you think once you've had a few days to think it over."

"I can't do this—" Cady began, but Meredith held up a hand.

"Cady, listen to me. You've got nothing to go back to San Francisco for. Your abusive husband is out there somewhere, and he hasn't been arrested yet. Your sisters don't need you any longer. It's time you did something for yourself."

---

"I'm not certain this is going to work," Meredith said doubtfully, studying the empty store a few hours later. The building had been vacant for a long time, but she hadn't allowed for how run down the interior had gotten. At some stage, local kids must have gotten inside and spray-painted graffiti on the walls, and damaged most of the fittings. A heavy layer of dust coated everything. She'd considered selling the building over the years, but she'd stubbornly held onto it, hoping one day to bring it back to life.

"It's amazing," Cady breathed. She was enchanted by the old building, which she'd passed dozens of times since she'd been walking Churchill around town. It was a two-story clapboard, the one with the faded ice-cream sign hanging out the front. The windows were covered over with boarding, leaving the interior dimly lit, dust mites wafting through the still air. The linoleum on the floor was chipped and cracked, the walls damaged, the stairs leading to the second level had collapsed, but Cady could imagine how it would look if she put in a little hard work and elbow grease. The idea of owning a cake shop was growing on her, the possibility of having something of her own enticing.

"You really think so, Cades?" Sid began doubtfully. "There's a heck of a lot of work to be done."

"And remember you can't bake," Harry added. She wrinkled her nose at the stale smells pervading the store. "A cake store needs a *baker*."

Meredith was watching Cady surreptitiously; pleased with the excitement she could see in her eyes. "I like to bake," she announced.

Harry lifted an eyebrow, fisting one hand onto her hip. "Gran, how would you fit that in? Between your historical society meetings, the gardening club, and the patchwork quilters' society, I thought your life was fairly full."

"Well, that's certainly true," Meredith conceded. "But I'm certain we could find someone to hire, someone who would do the baking."

"And who's going to pay them?" Cady questioned. "You've already done more than enough to help me." Although the idea of owning her own business was exciting, Cady was suddenly overwhelmed by the prospect. She had no money to do this, and the building alone would need a ton of work before it would be usable.

"I will, of course." Seeing Cady about to argue, Meredith held up a hand. "Now just hang on. I'm not going to give you the money, Cady. We'll consider it a loan. I'll provide the finance to prepare the building, and get you set up. Once you start making a profit, in a year or so, once you're established – you can start paying me back. I'm considering it an invest-ment, and I expect to see a healthy return on my outlay."

"In Garrison?" Sid questioned. "I doubt that's possible."

"You've seen the number of people who visit Grizzlies – that's because it's the only place in town to socialize. The local women need to come in to town for groceries, to collect their mail, and to buy fuel. There isn't one place on Main Street where they can go to buy something to eat and grab a cup of coffee. I was thinking maybe Cady could run a coffee shop, in tandem with the bakery side of things and if she was to hire someone to do the baking, she could concentrate on cake decorating. Cady, honey, you've only been here for a few weeks and you know as well as I do, you've gotten orders for cakes without even trying. It can only grow."

Sid pursed her lips, running a finger across an abandoned countertop. "It would be good for you, Cades, to have something to focus on."

Cady chuckled. "Now I'm not certain if you think a bakery is a good idea, or a bad one."

Sid shook her head, bracing her hands against her slim hips. "I'm not certain either. On the one hand, I think it would be great for you to have something just for you, Cades. But on the other hand, a bakery, here in Garrison? You know how the economy is right now; small businesses are failing all over America."

"Sidonia Marigold Beatrice Caldwell! You be supportive of your sister, and listen to your grandmother," Meredith ordered brusquely. "I've lived in Garrison all my life, and I think the cake shop is a sound idea."

Harry laughed and slapped Sid on the back. "Look out, Gran's on the warpath – it's always bad when she uses our full names."

Cady found herself chuckling along with Harry and when she turned to look at Meredith, she found her eyes sparkling with amusement. "I'll give it some thought... Gran. I'm not promising anything, but I'll think about it."

---

QUINN WALKED into Grizzlies on Saturday night and glanced around, catching sight of Hop standing by one of the pool tables. He greeted his friend with a slap on the back. "Ready to get your ass kicked?"

"Bullshit, Quinn. You haven't been at Grizzlies for nigh on a month – you ain't possibly gonna beat me at pool tonight."

"Because naturally, you've been practicing every Saturday night in the meantime, right?" Quinn questioned with a grin. He grabbed a cue from the holder on the wall and held it up to his eye, checking for straightness. "You'd probably do better, Hop, with fewer beers under your belt and more dedicated practice."

"With or without the beer, Quinn, I can kick your ass," Hop retorted with a grin.

Quinn chuckled. "You're on." He pulled a twenty-dollar bill from his pocket and laid it on the edge of the table. "Let's play."

Sometime later, Quinn was about to sink a ball when he glanced up and caught sight of Cady Caldwell. She was standing at a booth with her sisters, both of whom he'd met during one of their previous visits to Garrison. The three girls shared the same fiery auburn hair; although he thought Cady's might be a shade or two redder than her sisters'. He smiled when he caught sight of tonight's outfit; she was wearing a soft pink sweater and a full, belted skirt, which swayed around her knees in a gentle motion. By the looks of it, she had some type of petticoat underneath the skirt, making it sit out in a bell shape.

She was simply the most beautiful woman he'd ever seen.

His attention was pulled back to the game by Hop, who nudged him none-too-softly in the ribs. "She's a looker, ain't she? That's Meredith's eldest granddaughter—"

"Cady Caldwell," Quinn finished the sentence.

"You've met, I assume," Hop smirked. "Trust you to have met the new filly in town already."

"She was at Gran's birthday party," Quinn replied, still watching Cady as she laughed in reaction to something Sid said.

"Yeah, well, she caught the attention of that bastard, Earl Henderson, last night," Hop said, giving Quinn's ball a subtle nudge with his cue while Quinn wasn't looking.

Quinn scowled. "What was that asshole doing?"

Hop shrugged. "He was drunk, got a little too mouthy, and too friendly with her. I sorted him out."

"Bastard," Quinn grumbled. He turned his attention back to the table and lifted an eyebrow. "Are you cheatin', Hop?"

Hop grinned and shrugged. "Hit the damn ball already."

Quinn leaned over the table, and much to Hop's obvious disgust, pocketed the ball anyway, just hitting it into a different pocket than the one he'd originally intended. Ultimately, he was the better pool player, but the two men enjoyed these pool competitions regularly, and Hop occasionally surprised Quinn by beating him.

"Uh oh," Hop announced, just as Quinn was lining up his next shot.

"Not gonna work, Hop, I won't fall for that old trick again."

"No, man, not that 'uh oh'." Hop inclined his head towards the other side of the bar. "*That* 'uh oh'."

Quinn straightened up and sighed heavily. His ex-wife, along with a few of her she-devil friends, were marching towards Cady, and Julia looked fit to blow. No doubt, this had something to do with Julia's drunken husband trying one on with Cady last night.

Quinn handed the pool cue to Hop and strode across the room towards Cady's booth, determined to head off Julia before she could do any damage.

---

Cady was having a good time. Admittedly, she hadn't wanted to come along tonight, but after the day's events, it felt good to visit Grizzlies and enjoy a glass of wine before bedtime. And with any luck, she could escape before karaoke started. According to the poster out front, she had half an hour before she needed to vamoose.

She'd spent nearly all afternoon contemplating Meredith's offer. While she didn't see herself as a country girl at heart, the thought of having her own store was tempting. Very tempting. For the first time in Cady's life, she would have something of her own, something she could be proud of, a business she could grow and develop exactly the way she wanted it to. It seemed as if her luck might finally be turning around, but Cady wasn't entirely certain she could trust it. What if she failed? What if she couldn't make it work? Garrison wasn't a huge place; could the small population support a cake store? Cady wasn't afraid of the hard work involved, but she was terrified of failing.

"What sort of weirdo are you?"

Cady turned to discover a woman striding towards her, along with three others. The speaker was about Cady's age, wearing tight blue jeans, a red tank top, and boots. Her brown eyes flashed as she glared at Cady, and much to Cady's shock, the woman shoved her. "How dare you flirt with my husband?"

"Excuse me?"

"You, you crazy bitch! My Earl says you made a play for him last night, you freak! What the hell is up with the way you dress?"

Cady shook her head in disbelief. "*Your* Earl? You mean the big blonde guy, the one who was bothering me when I was minding my own business?" She nearly added 'the one who was dumber than a bag of bricks' but bit her tongue at the last minute.

"Julia, knock it off. Why don't you and your friends go back to your table and leave us alone," Harry growled. "We don't want any trouble."

Julia ignored Harry, continuing her tirade at Cady. "Earl wouldn't be interested in a itty bitty freak like you – what do you wanna dress like that for, anyway? Have you got your granny panties on underneath that ridiculous skirt?"

Much to Cady's chagrin, the patrons nearby had stopped what they were doing and focused on the altercation. What was it with this bar, which meant two nights in a row she was copping abuse? "If you must know, the outer layers are authentic nineteen fifties," Cady announced, stepping closer to the woman. "But underneath? I'm wearing a very pretty lace bra and matching thong, which are *quite definitely* twenty-first century."

Cady heard several wolf whistles from nearby and

wished she'd kept her mouth shut. What was it about Grizzlies that got her all hotheaded and shooting off her mouth? Just as she turned to tell Sid and Harry she was going home, Quinn Garrison appeared in her peripheral vision, grabbing Julia's wrist before her hand connected with Cady's cheek.

"Julia! That's enough. You and your friends are drunk. Go home, to your *husband*," Quinn growled.

Julia's smile was brittle. "Quinn. I heard you were sniffing around this bitch at your gran's birthday party. Did you know she was fooling around with Earl behind your back? Don't tell me you're shagging this little freak?" Julia announced. "Wow, you've really sunk to a whole new level."

Cady stepped forward, prepared to stand up for herself, but Quinn placed a warning hand on her arm. "Julia, that was uncalled for. You owe Cady an apology."

"And then you can damn well leave my bar," another voice announced.

If Cady had thought the bar quiet before, it was nothing compared to now. An African American woman, perhaps Meredith's age had appeared, giving Julia such an icy look, Cady expected to see frost spreading across her cheeks. "Julia Henderson, you need to get out of Grizzlies, and take your friends with you." The three women who'd stood with Julia visibly deflated, and with muttered complaints, they stumbled out of the bar.

Julia remained, her mouth set in a defiant line. "You can't throw me out, I've got a right to visit Grizzlies, just like every other loser in this podunk town."

"I *own* Grizzlies, you little bitch. And if I say you get out, you'd best do it. Take your trailer trash ass and go on home to your husband. I have a good mind to ban you both."

Julia threw the older woman a sour look and then glared at Cady. "This isn't over."

"Oh, yeah, it most certainly is!" The older woman shoved Julia. "Now go on, get out."

With one last, sullen look, Julia turned and stalked towards the door, pushing it open with both hands so the door slammed against the outside wall. There was a smattering of applause and cheers from the patrons after she left.

"Okay everyone, get back to enjoying yourselves, and karaoke starts in about fifteen minutes, so get your drinks refilled in plenty of time," the older woman announced before she turned and held her hand out to Cady. "Luanne Mulroney," she proclaimed with a crooked smile. "And judging by that pretty little getup – you'll be Mer's eldest grandbaby."

Cady took the woman's proffered hand and shook it. "Cady Caldwell."

The older woman looked up at Quinn and offered him a warm smile, her brown eyes twinkling. "You were lucky to escape from that one, Quinn, you mark my words."

Cady saw Quinn swallow heavily before he responded. "Yes ma'am."

Luanne brushed her hands down her jeans and straightened her shirt. She was a heavyset woman, perhaps five feet ten inches tall and nearly as wide. "Now that drama is over, I'm going to get back to my tallying." She eyed Cady thoughtfully. "I saw you and your family over at that old building Meredith owns this mornin'. You thinkin' about doing something with it?"

"Cady might open a bakery," Sid announced gleefully.

Luanne nodded. "This town could do with somethin' new; it's been far too long since any new businesses have started up."

"You're thinking of staying in Garrison?" Quinn questioned. He glanced down at Cady, and she noticed again how tall he was, and what a clear blue his eyes were. A lock of his hair fell boyishly across his forehead, and she couldn't help but notice how well his sweater fit across his leanly muscled shoulders.

She stared up into his eyes for a moment before responding. "Maybe. Although the welcome from some of the locals hasn't been particularly warm."

Luanne chuckled. "Don't you be worrying your head about those losers." With a wink and a smile, she turned and ambled back through Grizzlies, disappearing behind a door at the back of the bar. Once she'd gone, the noise level increased as everyone went back to what they'd been doing.

"I'm sorry about Julia's behavior," Quinn announced quietly. "Can I buy you a drink?"

Cady shook her head and smiled. "Thanks, but no thanks. Karaoke isn't my style, I'm heading home." She drained the wine from her glass and set it down on the table. "And you're not responsible for some crazy woman's behavior."

"She's my ex-wife," Quinn announced, offering Cady a chagrinned smile.

Cady smiled up at him. "And still not responsible, whether she's your ex-wife or not."

"Can I walk you home?"

Cady hesitated for a moment before she shook her head. "Thanks, but I'll be fine, it's not far."

"Awww, Cades, why don't you stay for karaoke?" Sid questioned with a pout.

Cady smiled. "You know I hate karaoke."

"Hmmm. I have to agree with you there," Quinn smiled.

Harry smiled slyly. "I think you should have an escort home, Cady," she announced. "Those girls could be hanging around outside."

Before she could argue, Quinn surprised her by grasping her hand and placing it on his arm. "It'd be a pleasure to walk you home, Ms. Caldwell. And your sister's right, you can't be too careful when it comes to my ex and her buddies."

## 11

"I think I could have managed this on my own," Cady commented when they left Grizzlies car park. "There's no sign of Julia or her friends."

"I was happy enough to get out before the karaoke starts," Quinn commented. He glanced across the dimly lit street to where the building Meredith owned stood. "You really thinking about doing it? Opening a store?"

Cady shrugged. Quinn still had her hand wrapped around his arm, and he was resting his other hand on hers. His skin was warm, comforting in the cool evening air and she was relaxed, despite his close proximity. "Maybe. I don't know." She smiled, glancing up at him. "I don't know if I want to stay in Garrison permanently."

"Where's home?"

Cady chuckled softly. "If you asked Meredith that question, she'd say I didn't know. But San Francisco, to all intents and purposes is home. Sid and Harry both live there – it's where we settled after we left Mark's."

"Your Dad?"

"Yeah. The guy who spawned me," she announced bitterly.

"Hmmm. Touchy subject."

Cady lifted her gaze to meet his. "Less than it used to be. Meredith is wearing me down."

It was Quinn's turn to laugh. "She has that effect on people." They reached Polson Street and turned the corner.

"So Julia is your ex-wife?" Cady questioned a minute later.

Quinn sighed heavily. "Yeah. We divorced two years ago."

"I'm assuming it wasn't amicable?" she probed softly. She was intrigued, couldn't figure out why the woman would have dumped a seemingly nice guy like Quinn Garrison, for the moronic Earl. Sure, Earl was okay to look at, but from what little Cady had seen, he didn't have many other redeeming features.

"She told me our marriage was over while I was in Afghanistan. I was pissed," Quinn admitted.

Somehow, Quinn had slid his hand down and clasped Cady's fingers in his own, and Cady wasn't certain if she was comfortable or not. She was still a married woman, and she certainly didn't intend on getting involved with another man. Ever, probably. Yet she didn't feel inclined to pull away. "Tough break."

"Yeah, I thought so at the time – but now, I'm kinda glad we split."

Cady wondered about his reasoning, but didn't want to probe too deeply, given the way he was gripping her hand. "You were in the military?"

"Yeah. Texas Rangers for a decade."

Cady paused mid-step and stared at Quinn. "Wow. That's impressive."

Quinn shrugged. "Not so much."

Cady got the distinct impression he didn't want to talk about it, so she changed subjects. "You work on your family's ranch?"

"Yeah. When I discharged from the Rangers, I came home to the Silver Peaks." He glanced up, his gaze encompassing the darkened mountains in the distance. "There isn't anywhere on earth like Montana."

"I have to admit; it's a pretty state. I imagine it's a wee bit chilly in winter, though."

Quinn laughed, his deep baritone breaking through the mid-evening silence. "If you count blizzards, a few feet of snow, and below zero temperatures for weeks on end as chilly, then yeah. I guess you could call Garrison chilly." He smiled down at Cady and she returned the smile. "If you open that cake store, I bet you'll be inundated with people, just because you've got an oven turned on."

"Hmmm. There's a sound reason to go ahead," Cady grinned.

"There are a lot of hungry ranchers around Garrison. I think you could make it work."

"You don't even know me," Cady protested.

It was Quinn's turn to stop walking and she turned to face him, a question in her eyes. "I'd like to get to know you," Quinn said quietly.

He aligned himself in front of Cady, mere inches from her and she shifted anxiously, uncomfortable with his proximity. She was aware of energy, a tangible heat which was resonating between their bodies, and she didn't like it. It was too much, too soon; she didn't know this man, didn't want to put herself in a position where he could hurt her, in a position where she might get hurt again. He studied her eyes, frowned and took a step back, giving her some space and Cady took the opportunity to snatch her hand from his.

"I'm sorry," Quinn stated. "I didn't mean to pressure you."

Cady didn't respond, instead turning tail and hurrying towards Meredith's street. Her mind was awash with anxious thoughts and an undercurrent of panic. What the hell was wrong with her, freezing up like that? And what sort of a fool was she, allowing him to hold her hand, prob-ably think she was interested? She couldn't trust a man ever again, wouldn't allow any man to get close enough to beat on her like Jameson had.

She'd only taken a couple of steps when Quinn caught up and wisely, he kept a cautious distance between them. "Hey. Please, let me walk you home, no pressure. Just friendship. Okay?"

Cady inhaled sharply, contemplating whether to blow him off, tell Quinn to leave her alone. She dismissed the thought almost instantly. He hadn't suggested anything untoward and he'd backed off the second she made her anxiety clear. "Sure."

They started walking again, a companionable silence building between them for a few minutes. "You're going to think about the bakery?" Quinn questioned.

Cady nodded. "I'm definitely going to think about it."

But honestly, she couldn't see how she could make it work.

And she still wasn't convinced she wanted to.

---

On Monday morning, Cady was sitting in the kitchen drinking coffee with Meredith and Nancy Garrison when they heard a knock on the front door. "I'll get it," she offered, pushing away from the table and hurrying through the hallway to the entrance. Through the stained glass in the door, she could see the shadow of someone waiting on the porch.

Cady pulled the door open and found herself face-to-face with a middle-aged woman, perhaps in her early fifties. "Can I help you?"

The woman swallowed hard and shuffled on the spot. "Luanne Mulroney suggested I come and see you, Ms. Caldwell."

"Oh – please, call me Cady."

The woman smiled shyly and nodded her agreement. "My name is Paulette Shelby, and I'm looking for work. I'm a very good cook, and I can make just about any cake you might be wantin' for your new store—"

"Paulette? Is that you? Come on through to the kitchen and have a coffee with us," Meredith called.

Cady inhaled sharply and pasted on a bright smile. "Please, come in... Mrs..."

"Oh, you can call me Paulette, honey. Everyone around here does." The woman smoothed her hands down over her faded jeans and stepped through the doorway. Cady led her to the kitchen and filled the kettle with fresh water while Paulette settled at the table with Meredith and Nancy. "Is Luanne right? You're thinkin' about opening a cake store?"

"Thinking about it," Cady agreed cautiously. "No decisions have been made yet."

Meredith wasn't nearly as reticent. "I just knew you'd be interested, Paulette! And you'll be perfect for the position, you need some extra income with that grandbaby on the way. Tell me, how is Jenny doing; how far along is she now?"

Paulette smiled happily, and Cady took a moment to assess the newcomer while her attention was focused on Meredith. The woman appeared tired and worn, as though she'd spent a great deal of her life with a heavy weight on her shoulders. Her hair was pulled back in a loose bun, lines of gray streaking through the faded brown and her hazel eyes were careworn, as if she had suffered some great toll in her life. She'd teamed washed-out blue jeans with a worn green button-down shirt and wore minimal makeup and jewelry. A plain gold wedding band resided on her finger, a simple silver watch on her wrist. Lines etched her eyes and marred the skin beside her mouth, and Cady reassessed her age estimate, pegging Paulette at closer to sixty. "She's coming up to six months and looking as pretty as a picture. I'm so excited about the baby arriving – did you hear she's having a boy?"

Meredith smiled and reached across the table to pat Paulette's hand. "I had heard – that's wonderful news. She and Rick will be so excited."

"And it's even better, with Rick picking up some extra work over on the Mackenzie's ranch, they're hoping they'll be able to move into a little place of their own before the baby arrives."

"Well, that's just wonderful news," Nancy declared, sipping her coffee. "And how are you and Dan doing?"

The smile on Paulette's lips faltered a little. "We're doing okay, although money is tight now that Dan's insurance has stopped."

Meredith frowned. "I'd heard a rumor about it. That's too bad." She turned to Cady, who'd gotten another cup out of the cupboard. "Dan is Paulette's husband, he was involved in an accident on their ranch about eighteen months ago and lost the use of his legs."

"I'm so sorry," Cady responded quietly.

Paulette offered her a weak smile, intertwining her fingers together anxiously. "It could have been much worse, I'm lucky my Dan is still alive. It was a terrible accident with the harvester, could have killed him." She turned her attention to Cady. "I really need some work, Ms. Caldwell. I don't have many skills to speak of, but I do bake a fine cake, and I'm willing to learn anything you'd need me to do."

Cady began to shake her head, but before she could respond, Meredith spoke up.

"I think that's a wonderful idea!" She turned to Cady and smiled brightly. "Paulette would have to be just about the best cook here in Garrison; she's taken out any number of prizes at the annual Garrison Fair with her baking, and I just know she'd be perfect to work with you."

Paulette nodded shyly. "Luanne called me this morning, told me that she'd heard that there was a possibility Cady was going to open a store. I thought I'd come by and see if there was a chance I could get some work; we could certainly use the money."

Cady shook her head, pouring hot water into the mug she'd prepared. "Oh, I'm not sure yet that I'll be employing anyone," she warned. "Nothing has been decided yet—"

"But I'm certain if the cake shop gets off the ground, Cady will consider you," Meredith interjected smoothly. "We can certainly keep you informed about when the shop opens and there really isn't anyone in Garrison that I could recommend more highly than you, Paulette."

Paulette blushed and smiled gratefully when Cady set the mug of coffee down in front of her. "Thank you, Cady."

"Please, help yourself to milk and sugar," Cady said, resuming her position at the table. "But I should warn you,

I'm not certain I'll be opening the store. It's an idea I need to give serious consideration to."

"But you'll keep me in mind?" Paulette prodded hopefully.

Cady sighed heavily and offered the woman a tight smile. "Of course."

"Cady just has a few things to work through, and I'm sure as soon as she's made a decision, she'll let you know, won't you Cady?" Meredith asked.

"Yes, of course." Cady lowered her gaze to her mug, keeping one ear on the conversation while her thoughts returned to the idea of the bakery. Harry and Sid had done nothing but talk about the concept before they caught their flight back to San Francisco late on Sunday afternoon, and Cady was finding that the more she considered the prospect, the more she liked it. What they'd said was true – she had no reason to return to San Francisco, and the idea of a business of her own grew more appealing with every passing hour. Of course, there was a veritable motherlode of subtle pressure being placed on her by Meredith and Nancy, and now with Paulette Shelby added to the mix, Cady was beginning to think she should take Churchill out for a walk to escape.

She was drawn from her musings by the telephone ringing and watched as Meredith got up to answer it. "Hello?" She lapsed into silence for a few seconds, before she turned to Cady with a coy grin. "It's for you, honey. It's Quinn."

Cady's eyes rounded in surprise. "Quinn Garrison?"

"He's the only Quinn in town," Nancy confirmed with a laugh.

With a blush spreading across her cheeks, Cady took the receiver from Meredith. "Hello?"

"Hi, Cady. I've got a couple of free hours and wondered if you'd like to head out to the lake for a walk? It's a beautiful day out, and it won't be long before days like this are buried under six feet of snow."

Cady turned away from the three intrigued faces watching her avidly and stood up, slipping out through the back door and onto the porch. She ignored the catcalls and whistles emitted by the women as she left and shook her head when she responded to Quinn. "Sounds good. Can I bring my dog?" Cady surprised herself by agreeing, but she figured she could use a break from Meredith's gang and their plotting, and she found herself drawn to Quinn Garrison. Nothing would come from it, she'd made sure on Saturday night that he was aware she wasn't looking for a romantic relationship, and Quinn had agreed. But he seemed like a nice guy, and he'd offered her friendship.

And if she was intending on staying in Garrison, Cady figured she could use all the friends she could get.

## 12

Quinn arrived at Meredith's house half an hour later and stopped in front of the neat picket fence bordering Meredith's garden. The fact that his mother was visiting Meredith brought a wry smile to his lips; word would soon spread around town that he was calling on Cady Caldwell, and there was no getting around it.

The grounds surrounding the house were a picture this time of the year, with the bright golds and reds of fall creating a vibrant splash of color around the Victorian house. He turned off the engine and unclipped his seatbelt, but he'd only just gotten out of the car when Cady appeared, coming down the porch steps with the biggest mountain of dog he'd ever seen in his life. He'd heard about the dog from Kane and his Dad, but he'd never expected such huge animal. "Well, I'll be damned," he muttered, hiding a grin.

Cady met him at the sidewalk, commanding the dog to sit down at her side. Seated, the dog reached her elbows – granted, she wasn't a big woman, but... *man*, that was a dog and a half. Quinn hunkered down and held his hand, palm down out towards the big mutt. "Hey there, what's your name?"

"Churchill," Cady supplied as the dog licked Quinn's hand and wagged his tail so hard that his whole backside wobbled from side to side.

"As in 'We shall fight on the beaches; we shall fight on the landing grounds' Churchill?"

Cady grinned and patted Churchill's head. "Very good. Not everyone gets the connection."

Quinn straightened up and smiled warmly. "I studied English history in high school, thought Churchill was a pretty cool guy." Quinn looked away into the distance for a moment or two, and then quoted the pertinent part of Winston Churchill's speech. *"We shall go on to the end. We shall fight in France, we shall fight on the seas and oceans, we shall fight with growing confidence and growing strength in the air, we shall defend our island, whatever the cost may be. We shall fight on the beaches, we shall fight on the landing grounds, we shall fight in the fields and in the streets, we shall fight in the hills; we shall never surrender".*"

Cady clapped her hands in delight.

Quinn let his gaze slide down Cady's body, taking in today's outfit. She was pretty as a picture, in dark gray trousers and a red sweater, which had white trim around the neck and sleeves. Her feet were encased in shoes resembling ones Quinn had seen in old movies, and once again, he found himself drawn to her beauty. She was certainly unique; he'd never met anyone quite like her. "I'm guessing you kinda like the forties?"

Cady smiled a little self-consciously, following Quinn as he walked around to the back of the pickup. "The forties and fifties."

Quinn pulled down the back of the truck and patted it. "Will he jump?"

"Churchill – up," Cady commanded, and he obediently leaped up on the flatbed of the pickup. Cady eyed the space doubtfully. "Will he be safe? He's never ridden in the back of a pickup before."

Quinn laughed. "We have limited choices; he's certainly not going to fit in the cab with us." He grabbed hold of Churchill's lead and drew him closer to the front of the truck. "See, here? I'll tie his lead to the back of the cab, I do the same with my own dog."

"You have a dog?" Cady questioned, watching him cautiously as he tied Churchill's lead securely to a pole which ran the length of the back of the cab.

"Yeah, an Australian Cattle Dog. His name is Moose." Tugging on the lead to confirm Churchill wouldn't be jumping out during the ride, he strode back around the truck to the passenger side and held open the door for Cady. She was so tiny, she nearly needed a boost to get up into the seat, and Quinn grinned, making sure Cady was still turned away so she wouldn't see it. He got the feeling this little spit-fire wouldn't like him laughing at her size... or anything else, for that matter.

The drive out to Garrison Lake took about forty-five minutes – to the east of the town, the lake had been the first thing Quinn's Great-Great-Great-Grandfather had discovered when he and a group of fellow newcomers to the Americas had set out across the country, searching for good land to settle on and create a life for themselves. Charles Garrison had been twenty-five years old when he settled on the land which later became the Silver Peaks Ranch, and he'd been the first mayor of the town he'd founded in 1872. The lake was nestled at the foot of the Beartooth Mountains, and the Silver Peaks land followed along its western side. On the eastern edge, Quinn explained to Cady, were cabins and camping sites popular with tourists. The shores of the lake were bordered by towering pine trees, and as Quinn drove down the gravel road towards the edge of the lake, he glanced across and saw that Cady seemed totally enchanted by the view. He loved it too and had built his own home on the shoreline of the lake, enjoying the opportunity of gazing out across the water from his porch whenever the mood hit him.

For a guy who never intended on getting seriously involved with another woman, he was rapidly discovering Cady Caldwell had gotten under his skin. She'd captured his attention at Granny Benton's birthday, and again on Saturday night at Grizzlies. He found himself hiding a grin when he recalled her smartass retort about wearing twenty-first-century underwear below her twentieth-century clothing. The thought aroused him, and he shifted uncomfortably, willing the burgeoning erection away and hoping Cady wouldn't notice. She'd experienced some tough times from what he'd heard, and he didn't want to frighten her off. She'd told him she was only looking for friendship, and she was still married to her louse of a husband or so he'd heard, so he could understand her reticence. And, he reminded himself firmly, he wasn't interested. He loved women, enjoyed their company immensely, but he had no intentions of getting into a serious relationship again.

And Cady Caldwell was the wrong type of woman to indulge in a casual fling with – she was fragile, wounded by her past. Still, he couldn't help noticing the curve of her hips, the way she'd painted her nails a shade of red which matched her sweater. She wasn't wearing a wedding ring, but he could see the mark on her finger where it had once been. She was off-limits in every possible way, but he couldn't seem to stop thinking about Cady Caldwell.

Quinn brought the truck to a stop and turned to Cady with a warm smile. "Well, here we are."

"It's beautiful."

He watched Cady as she observed their surroundings. With winter approaching, the lake water had darkened, the sunlight overhead no longer keeping it bright with its reflection. It was fun to see the interest in her eyes, he'd lived here nearly all his life and living by the lake was second nature, something he enjoyed but didn't think about much. Watching Cady, he could appreciate how beautiful it was all over again, seeing it through her eyes. The pines were intermingled with patches of deciduous trees, which had turned in the cooler weather and exhibited a lively display of scarlet, gold, and yellow leaves as winter approached.

A bark from Churchill brought his attention back to the present and Quinn got out of the cab, hurrying around to open the passenger door for Cady. She slid down from the seat and onto her feet, still absorbing the breathtaking beauty of a Montana fall. Quinn undid the knot holding Churchill's leash and opened the back of the truck, letting the big dog jump to the ground.

"Is it alright to let him run without his leash?" Cady enquired.

"Sure. There aren't any rules about letting dogs loose here." He glanced around, confirming there was no one in the vicinity. "I doubt he's going to cause any trouble."

He watched Cady unclip Churchill's leash and then she rolled it into a neat circle, leaving it in the back of the truck. "He'll love having a run, I take him out twice a day, but what dog doesn't love being off the leash?"

123

Quinn glanced down at her. "He does look like he's having fun."

Churchill had bounded off towards the water, sniffing the ground along the way, his tail high in the air and wagging furiously. The dog caught sight of some ducks further along the shoreline and barked, setting off at a run to chase them into the water.

Cady laughed, and the sound made Quinn's heart sing. "Shall we follow Churchill's lead?" he suggested.

With a nod, Cady set off along the edge of the lake, keeping an eye on her dog as he bounded in front of them, intent on chasing two ducks who hadn't bothered diving into the water yet. Quinn matched his pace to Cady's shorter legs and they walked in companionable silence for a few minutes.

"I thought working on a ranch, you'd be busy from dawn until dusk," Cady pointed out.

Quinn surveyed the lake, his gaze skimming over the Garrison's land. "It's always busy on a ranch, but we've got plenty of hands available to share the workload. We've been fixing fences today, so it was easy to slip away for a while."

"How much land does your family own?"

"Ten thousand acres," Quinn responded. He glanced down at Cady, forcing back a desire to take her hand. *Friends, Quinn – she just wants to be friends*, he reminded himself. "When Charles Garrison settled here, he purchased five hundred acres, but over the years, we've expanded and diversified."

"You run cattle on the ranch?" Cady asked.

"Yeah, that's our main source of income, but we're also growing durum wheat, corn, flaxseed, and canola."

"How many cows do you have?"

"We run a steady herd of about two and a half thousand

cattle on the property, a mixture of Angus and Hereford. That jumps up by about three hundred in the spring when calving happens."

Cady glanced up at him and he found himself captivated by the color of her eyes. "Wow. That's a lot of cows," she remarked. "Do you have to milk them all?"

Quinn grinned. "They aren't milking cows – they're beef cattle."

Cady screwed up her nose. "You eat your cows?"

This time, Quinn couldn't rein back the chuckle which escaped his lips when he saw the consternation on Cady's face. "Of course we do, Cady. Why? Are you a vegetarian or something?"

"Well, no – but I saw some of the cows when we came out to the ranch last week, and they look so... cute."

"I don't know that I'd ever call a fifteen-hundred-pound bull cute," Quinn suggested. "And I'm fairly certain Matt would assure you there's nothing cute about them when he's sitting up on the back of one at a rodeo."

"Matt?" Cady questioned.

"Yeah, another one of my brothers. You probably met him at Granny's birthday party."

Cady looked thoughtful for a moment and then nodded. "I remember now, Meredith introduced us."

"Matt's the quietest of the four of us, but he rides a mean bull."

"Isn't that dangerous?"

Quinn grinned. "Of course, but Matt loves it. Mom hates it of course, but there's no way Matt wouldn't bull ride. He loves the adrenaline fix it gives him."

"What about you?" Cady asked. "Do you ride rodeo?"

Quinn shook his head. "No, not anymore. I used to when I was younger, but after I got back from Afghanistan

—" He broke off, not wanting to bring the subject around to his service. It wasn't something he liked to think about, and after two years at home, he'd laid most of his ghosts to rest.

Cady studiously turned her attention towards the lake, and Quinn appreciated her not commenting on his military service. They walked in silence for a little while, and Quinn satisfied himself with surreptitious glances at Cady from time to time, admiring her beauty. "So, have you thought any more about the bakery?"

She screwed up her nose, an endearing gesture which had Quinn wanting to pull her into his arms and kiss her. *Jesus, get a hold of yourself, Quinn.* He focused on Cady's response, pushing the errant thought away. "I haven't thought about much else, to be honest. I love the idea of having something of my own, a way of creating a future for myself."

"I sense a 'but'," Quinn prodded.

"It's a huge risk. I don't know the first thing about running a business, Meredith wants to finance it and I'm terrified of losing all her money." The words left Cady's lips in a rush, and she lowered her gaze, running her fingers anxiously through her hair. "Sorry, you probably don't want to hear this."

"I don't mind. If it helps you to make up your mind about what you should do, I don't mind acting as a sounding board."

Cady remained silent for a time, and Quinn thought perhaps she wanted to let the subject drop. He was about to move them onto a safer, neutral subject when she spoke again.

"The building Meredith offered me – the one opposite Grizzlies—" She stopped abruptly, as if she needed to gather her thoughts before she went on. "It's a great place, much like Lorna Mendez's building, but it needs so much work. Are there people in Garrison who can do carpentry work, plumbing?"

"Sure there are," Quinn replied readily. *Almost too readily,* he thought and wondered if he was getting carried away in his enthusiasm because he wanted Cady to stay. "Walt Whitney is a good carpenter, and Paul Compton is handy with plumbing. Griss Peters lives a little way out of town, he's a qualified electrician." He whistled to Churchill, who'd gotten a little too far in front of them, thinking Cady would be pissed if the giant dog went missing. "Most of the men in town are reasonably handy when push comes to shove."

"I guess," Cady said doubtfully.

"I think you could make it work," Quinn added. He stopped walking, turning to look down at Cady. "What have you got to lose?"

She wrinkled her nose again, in that delightful way which had him wanting to reach out to touch her, but he clenched his hands into fists, determined to keep things on friendly terms. "Nothing, I suppose."

Quinn shrugged. "So go ahead – give it a whirl."

"I don't know that I want to be indebted to Meredith."

Quinn glanced away, shaking his head at the way Cady kept referring to Meredith by her first name. "I thought you might have gotten comfortable with the idea of calling Meredith 'Gran' by now," he suggested gently.

"I've been avoiding getting too involved," Cady admitted with a shrug. "Calling her Gran... the prospect of doing it makes me uncomfortable." She lapsed into another bout of silence, and Quinn decided to wait her out, see what else might be admitted if he let her gather her thoughts. "I know what *he* did has nothing to do with her, but it's hard, you know? Hard to be living in the house where he grew up. And David is coming to visit this weekend – I saw some photos of him when he was younger, and he looks so much like... Mark." She gripped her hands together anxiously. "I worry it's going to bring back some memories I'd rather forget."

"Your Dad was an asshole," Quinn admitted. "He was ten years older than me, David is six. I know they were alike when they were young, but David turned out more like Meredith's side of the family, Mark took after his father's side. I don't think you'll see any great resemblance between the two now."

He saw surprise flicker across Cady's face, but she didn't comment on the age difference between them. He knew from Hallie that Cady was twenty-eight, a full fourteen years younger than he was, but he didn't give a damn. *Wait, what? Where did that thought come from? It didn't matter whether Cady Caldwell thought he was acceptable to date!* "Besides," he added hastily, "Meredith is a wonderful person, and she loves you, I'm certain of it. It would please her no end if you'd call her Gran."

Cady glanced away, gathering her thoughts before she spoke. "I'll think about it," she agreed quietly.

Churchill came bounding back towards them, his tongue lolling out and Quinn would have sworn the dog was grinning, he looked so pleased with himself. "It seems Churchill is making himself at home here in Garrison, Cady. Maybe you should do the same, too."

13

Cady woke the following morning, deeply discomfited by the dream she'd experienced.

She'd dreamed about Quinn Garrison. Worse, she'd dreamed about making love with Quinn Garrison.

Where on earth had that come from? Sure, they'd spent an enjoyable afternoon together at the lake, and Quinn had proven himself a great sounding board – in fact, Cady had found herself telling him more about herself in a couple of hours than she had told Meredith... *Gran* in weeks. And he was an attractive man, absolutely. Tall, lean, well-muscled and tanned, he could have his pick of company and for some reason, he'd chosen to spend time with her and Cady had enjoyed herself. But she wasn't even divorced yet, and Quinn had made it clear, several times, that he was only interested in casual affairs. Inhaling heavily, Cady rolled over in bed and found herself face to face with Churchill, who was lying beside her, his head on the pillow, his tail thumping out a steady rhythm on the comforter. "I don't need a man in my life. And I need to stop dreaming," she muttered, reaching out to brush her fingers over Churchill's massive head. "And I definitely need to stop dreaming about Quinn Garrison."

Pulling back the covers, Cady slipped out of bed and pushed her feet into her slippers. There was a decided chill in the air this morning, and a glance at the window confirmed condensation had built up overnight, as the outside temperatures dropped. Cady pushed the thought of Quinn Garrison firmly to the back of her mind and wandered downstairs, finding Meredith seated in the kitchen with the morning newspaper spread out across the table, and a mug of steaming coffee grasped between her hands.

"Morning, Cady. How did you sleep?"

Cady nodded, rubbing her eyes and turning on the kettle. "Okay. How are you?"

"Just fine, honey. What are you planning on doing today?"

Cady busied herself putting cereal in a bowl, taking her time while she gathered her thoughts. Long after Quinn had dropped her back at the house yesterday, she'd considered his advice about the store. He was right about one thing – what did she have to lose? What did she have in San Francisco that was worth going back for? Besides a few friendships with people she'd worked with, and Sid and Harry, she didn't really have any reason to return to San Francisco and now, after thinking about it for most of the night, she'd made up her mind. Pouring a cup of coffee, she settled into the chair opposite Meredith before she spoke again. "Actually, I was wondering if we could go and have another look at the store."

Meredith lifted her gaze from the newspaper, her expression hopeful. "Sure we can."

Cady smiled. "I'm not saying I'm doing it. But I'd like to take another look."

"That's wonderful! I'd be happy to come with you. We should take a notepad and pen, so we can take notes about what needs to be done."

"Quinn recommended some people around Garrison who might be able to help out with the work."

Meredith nodded enthusiastically. "There's a lot that needs to be done. We should make a list and organize some quotes."

"It might be too expensive," Cady warned. She'd already spent the evening working out rough estimates in her head, trying to guesstimate what was needed to make the building serviceable. Without even including the expense of an industrial oven, display cases, and shelving, she was already fretting over the costs.

"Oh, honey, you'll be surprised how much gets done around a country town with the goodwill of the residents. I'm sure we'll get plenty of help once they figure out there's going to be a new place to socialize in town," Meredith responded with a grin.

———

"We'll need to purchase a reasonable sized refrigerator, and you'll want one of those fancy coffee machines if you're going to serve hot drinks to your customers." Meredith was leaning on the rickety benchtop in the store, making copious notes on the clipboard she'd brought along. "And I think you'd need one of those glass-fronted coolers, to store soda and the like – we can check with Neil over at the grocery – he's got one out front of the registers. I have in mind that the soda company provides one for free, or at a minimal rent if you sell their drinks exclusively."

Cady stood in the kitchen area, arms crossed, studying the worn cabinets, the peeling paint on the walls and the inches of grime covering every surface. Some of the cladding on the exterior walls had rotted away, leaving gaping holes and weeds were growing through the gaps. "I'm not sure... Gran." Cady forced herself to say the word, even though it sounded so strange on her tongue. She ploughed on, pushing the discomfort to one side. "Maybe there's too much work to cope with. Even if we get it started, it might be better to concentrate on baking, and leave the coffee shop idea to one side for now."

There was a protracted silence before Meredith appeared in the doorway, her smile brilliant when she joined Cady in the kitchen. "Why honey, I think that's the first time you've ever willingly called me Gran."

Cady smiled shyly but remained quiet, not certain how to respond.

Fortunately, Meredith filled the void, not allowing the silence to stretch. "I think it's more than possible to fix up the place. Of course, there's a little work to be done to make it useable," she began, glancing around the room before she settled on Cady's incredulous expression, "okay – quite a bit of work to be done – but I'm certain these older wooden buildings can't be all that expensive to fix, and I'm sure Walt will give you a fair estimate. I'm certain he could prob-ably shingle the roof, too." She glanced meaningfully at the big damp spot on the ceiling overhead. "You could start with the downstairs and leave the upper area until you've started turning a profit. I'm not even certain what you'd do with the space. Traditionally, the shopkeeper lived upstairs in these old buildings."

Cady followed Meredith's line of sight, to where the ramshackle remains of the staircase leading upstairs were lying in a pile on the floor. "Maybe Lorna could let us have a look at the space in her shop?" The prospect of living above the store hadn't occurred to Cady before now, but hearing Mer— *Gran* mention it, the prospect of a home of her own was the kernel of an idea she'd like to consider in the future.

"That's a good idea, honey. And then we should head home and make some phone calls, ask Walt to meet us down here to look over the place, provide some estimates."

"Sounds like a plan," Cady agreed. If she was honest with herself, Cady was excited about the prospect of the bakery. She'd even allowed herself to fantasize about what the store might look like, the kind of cakes they'd sell... and she already had a name picked out. It was a name she'd come up with a few years back, when she'd dreamed of having something of her own.

When she'd first started cake decorating, Cady had deluded herself into thinking Jameson might see how much she loved it and cut her some slack, give his approval of her taking the job. She'd planned to save up and start a little business of her own, fund it from the money she'd earned. Jameson put a stop to that dream, demanding her paycheck be placed into his account and withholding it from her. He'd said it was repayment for what he'd paid out, and Cady hadn't had the courage to argue with him. And deep down she suspected Jameson was right. He'd treated her badly, and she could never forgive him, but she owed him for what he'd provided to her sisters.

Mentally shaking herself, Cady reminded herself that she'd paid – many times over – for Jameson's generosity. He'd taken it out of her flesh, both verbally and physically, for several years. He would have killed her that final night, *had* intended to kill her. Surely, she'd paid the price for his support and should be allowed a life of her own now? She wanted to believe it, she truly did, but something held her back. A fear that Jameson would find her here, in the wilds of Montana, and finish what he'd begun. A fear that no matter what good came her way – from Mer— *Gran's* generosity and support, to the good people of Garrison, who had offered her no-strings-attached friendship – something would go wrong. It was a worry, buried deep in her heart, which she couldn't seem to dismiss.

Inhaling deeply, she forced a smile for Meredith, who was watching her with a worried frown. "Are you alright, honey?" Meredith asked.

"I'm fine. Just fine." Cady forced another smile. "Let's start making plans."

---

MEREDITH WAS NEARLY at the end of her tether by the end of the afternoon. She'd been so enthusiastic about Cady's plans, thinking it was something which might bring them closer together, and she'd become too enthusiastic. Her good sense had gotten lost somewhere in the mix, and she had to admit, she'd badly underestimated the costs.

Sitting across from Walt, her heart sank with each new number he scribbled on his notepad. The stump of a pencil he perpetually carried around on top of his ear was currently clenched tightly between his stubby fingers and he was muttering aloud in his Texan drawl as he made notes. Whether the mutterings were directed towards her and Cady, or they were merely Walt working out numbers in his head, Meredith didn't know. But she could see the numbers on his slip of paper had worked their way up to five figures and her heart sank with every new strike of Walt's pencil.

"That entire roof is gonna need replacin'; no way around it, Missy."

Meredith hid a smile, despite her disappointment. Walt was at least a decade younger than she was, but he referred to every woman in Garrison as 'Missy', regardless of their current time of life. She glanced across at Cady, eyeing the worried frown etched on her pale forehead and resisted the urge to reach across and squeeze her fingers in reassurance. Cady had yet to reach a stage where she'd allow such physical contact. Meredith had initially found Cady's reticence deeply disturbing; she herself was a demonstrative woman who enjoyed hugging and kissing, but Cady had made it clear she wasn't open with her affections. The more Meredith learned about her granddaughter, the more she could understand her reserve. Even with Sid and Harry, Cady shunned overt displays of affection. Meredith had been thrilled earlier when Cady referred to her as Gran, and each time she'd repeated the word with a little more confidence, Meredith's joy had increased. It was progress, real progress, after weeks in which Meredith thought she'd never make a real connection with Cady. It might not be a hug, but hearing 'Gran' leave Cady's lips sure felt like one.

Walt scribbled another number on the paper, and Meredith cringed at the zeroes punctuating the end of the digits. Damn. She'd expected it to be moderately expensive to fix up the building, but never considered as much as Walt was suggesting. Inwardly, she cursed herself for getting Cady's hopes up, when it was swiftly becoming apparent she just couldn't afford the work needed. Not do that and get the bakery up and running.

Paying Cady's hospital account and Sid's tuition had made a hole in the tidy nest egg Jim left when he died. Her beloved husband had always been frugal, careful with his investments and made sure both he and Meredith had been insured in case of 'anything unfortunate happening' as Jim worded it when he was alive. It turned out his careful planning had been fortuitous because he'd died of a heart attack, a few years after Mark ran away. The strain of dealing with their son's troubles had been difficult for them both, but Jim had always suffered more, convinced he'd done something which set Mark on the path to disaster. Even now, Meredith could remember sitting out in the garden with her husband, trying to reassure him that Mark had made his own choices, and nothing he nor Meredith could have done would have changed the outcome. She'd been devastated when Jim died, and now, having located their three granddaughters, she often wished he was still around because he'd have loved being a granddaddy. She was fortunate Jim had been so careful and left her with a home to live in and investments to keep her so comfortable. This house had been the dream home she and Jim coveted when they first married. One of the few Victorians remaining in Garrison, she and Jim had spent months restoring the old house to its former glory. She fondly recalled the weeks when they'd eaten nothing but tinned beans, so they could pay for the renovations as they went along. They'd snapped up the house for peanuts and thought themselves so darn clever – until they'd started the renovation. Then it had come down to a matter of saving every penny, putting each one towards the next room needing restoration. Her own family thought she and Jim were crazy at the time, indeed, a lot of the locals had shaken their heads dolefully whenever they walked past, but Meredith and Jim had been determined, knowing this would be the house of their dreams. Glancing around the kitchen, Meredith knew it had been worth every single dime. Jim had loved this house as much as she did, and the rooms held joyful memories, alongside the darker ones.

Drawing back from reminiscing, Meredith turned to Walt's incessant scribbling, hoping he was getting towards the end of his lengthy calculations. Even if he wasn't, it would probably be better to be honest now, tell Cady and Walt that she couldn't afford to go ahead with the plan. She had more than enough money to live comfortably for the rest of her life, but no matter how much she wanted to help Cady, she couldn't afford to spend all that money on renovations and opening the store. She could hear Jim's calm voice in the back of her mind, warning against overextending.

Before Meredith could blurt out her apologies, Cady beat her to the punch. "Thank you, Mr. Whitney; Gran and I appreciate you taking time out of your day to give us a quote, but I can see from the numbers you're writing down that it's going to be too expensive."

Walt dropped his pencil stub onto the sheet of paper, his faded green eyes revealing genuine distress. "Now hang on a minute, Missy. These here are rough figures, and I always aim to overestimate, rather than underestimate, to be certain the folk around here don't get any nasty surprises."

Meredith watched Cady as the younger woman studied the sheet of paper in front of Walt. "Even with the possibility of you overestimating, I'm afraid those sorts of figures are just too much." She glanced up, meeting Meredith's steady gaze. "I can't do it... Gran. I can't let you risk all that money on something that might not work out."

Meredith crossed her arms on the kitchen table, chewing on her lower lip for a second or two before she responded. Oh, how she wished she could tell Cady they could go ahead! She wanted her to stay here, more than anything in the world. She loved all her granddaughters', but her heart wept for Cady's past and her soul wanted nothing more than to make things right, maybe in some small way make up for what Mark had put this lovely young woman through. Still, Jim's warnings to be cautious with money continued to echo in her mind and she nodded. "I'm afraid it's true, Walt. I never dreamed it would be so expensive."

"Well, it's a mite difficult nowadays, the price of timber has gone through the roof with every passing year, and these old timber buildings – if they haven't been properly looked after – they soon fall into disrepair."

Meredith nodded. "I see that now." She kept her gaze fixed on Walt, trying to avoid the disappointment she was certain would be visible in Cady's eyes. "If you wouldn't mind providing a final quote when you have the opportunity, I'd still like to check it over."

"I don't think it's worth taking up any more of Mr. Whitney's time," Cady began, but Walt held up his hand.

"Now hold it right there. I know it's a big expense, but some of this work, I'm almost certain you ladies could manage yerselves. Get those other two granddaughters and their fellas up here from San Francisco, and I wouldn't mind betting we could get this price dropped quite a bit."

"Even so," Cady started, but Meredith quickly interrupted.

"I think Walt's right. Let's see what the final figure is before we make any firm decisions. What work do you think we could do ourselves?"

For the next half hour, Meredith listened as Walt patiently went through the list with her, suggesting areas they might be able to cut corners on cost. It wasn't going to cause a massive drop in the overall price, but left Meredith feeling a little more confident that they didn't need to throw the entire idea on the scrapheap just yet. When Walt finally left for the evening, taking his sheet of paper and pencil stub with him, Meredith poured herself and Cady a glass of wine and they flopped down into the armchairs in front of the fireplace in the living room. Cady looked almost as exhausted as Meredith felt.

"I'm thinking I might pop into the store tomorrow and buy Walt a new pencil. I swear he's been using that itty-bitty stub of a pencil for as long as I've known him, and given he was born and bred here in Garrison, that's quite a while." Meredith smiled but got no response from Cady. "What do you think about ordering a pizza in for supper?" she added, sipping her wine. "What sort of pizza do you like?"

Cady was absently rubbing her fingertip over the top of her wineglass, her focus fixed on the glowing coals in the hearth. The flames colored her hair, burnishing it with hints of gold and amber, and Meredith watched transfixed for a moment, relishing the opportunity she'd received, in getting to know Cady. She might not like the circumstances which brought her to Garrison, but she was thankful that from something so terrible, something good had come and she was being given the opportunity to spend time with her granddaughter.

As though she'd been thinking for a while and gathering the courage, Cady took a deep breath and spoke up. "About the store—"

Meredith held up a hand. "No. I refuse to consider closing down the idea altogether – not until we've seen the final quote from Walt."

She expected Cady to grouse, to argue the point, so it

came as somewhat of a surprise when Cady merely smiled and sipped her own wine. "I wish I could have your confidence, but I've got some big doubts about the prospect."

"We need to work on your ability to find the bright side."

Cady laughed, but the sound was bitter, mirthless. "I haven't had much opportunity to look at bright sides."

Meredith held her breath, wondering if Cady would shut down like she usually did when the subject of her past was raised. When Cady didn't continue, instead staring complacently at the fire, Meredith found the nerve to speak. "If you go through life without finding a bright side, there isn't much to look forward to."

She watched as Cady's gaze shifted upwards, towards the mantelpiece. For a minute, the younger woman didn't respond, and Meredith thought she was going to lapse back into the silence which had become so much a part of their daily routine. Thoughtfully, Cady rubbed her fingers through Churchill's fur. The dog was settled by her side, his heavy head resting on the arm of Cady's chair. "You put the photos away. The ones of—" Cady stopped abruptly, and Meredith saw her swallow deeply before she dropped her gaze to the fireplace again.

"Yes, I did. After hearing what Mark did, I decided I didn't want them on display any longer."

"You didn't have to do that."

Meredith nodded. "Yes, I did. I didn't think my respect for Mark could drop any lower until I overheard you talking to Sid and Harry. What I heard then, it confirmed that I didn't know my son at all."

Cady was silent for a long time, and Meredith thought she'd shut down, but she suddenly spoke again. "I'm glad you put them away."

"I can understand that, honey."

Another long pause. And then, "I can't bear to call him Dad. He was never a father to us, not once in eighteen years. I was glad when he died."

The weight of bitterness in Cady's voice was tangible, and Meredith worked hard to keep her expression neutral. "How did you learn he'd passed?"

Cady snorted derisively. "He died, Gran. I'm under no illusions that heaven was his destination." She hesitated, sipping her wine reflectively. "'Passed' is such a polite term, don't you think? Nothing that man did would have earned him a spot anywhere but in hell, and that's the truth." Cady inhaled sharply and twirled the stem of her glass between her thumb and forefinger. "I'm sorry. He was your son. I shouldn't say such things."

"Honey, I'm just glad to hear you saying anything at all about the subject. It's been worrying me, you so closed off like you have been. I know you haven't had it easy, but I've always found it was better to talk things through. Bottling it up isn't helping to heal the wounds of the past."

Cady huffed in a sharp breath. "I wanted to save you from hearing what an asshole he was."

Meredith was stunned by the ferocity in Cady's words, but she remained still and quiet, waiting to see if Cady would at last open up.

The younger woman continued to stare into the fire, but from where she was sitting, Meredith could see the shimmer of tears brimming against Cady's eyelashes, the firelight making them glisten. "Living with them – it was a living hell. My earliest recollections include Mark ushering strange men into his bedroom – *their* bedroom – for Lisa to screw, to pay for their next fix." She shook her head forlornly, clutching the wine glass a little more firmly. "He

141

would sell anything; didn't care if we girls had nothing to eat, no money for school books or clothes, or shoes – nothing mattered to him, or her when they were jonesing for a fix. I suppose I should be thankful he took off into the streets to whore himself out, didn't do *that* with strange men in the apartment – but the things that went on were bad enough. Dealers banging on the door day and night, demanding payment for drugs. Landlords bashing on the door, wanting the rent. Debt collectors, social services – you name it, we were always running and hiding from someone."

When Cady lapsed into silence, Meredith waited for a long, agonizing minute before she dared to speak, frightened that any response would shut Cady down again. "I heard social services took you a few times."

Cady nodded infinitesimally, and if Meredith hadn't been watching her so closely, she would have missed the minute movement. "The school reported us for being absent too often, for arriving without lunch, or books." She laughed, but again the sound was so desolate, so mirthless, Meredith's heart ached. "Sometimes we would turn up without shoes. And more than once, neighbors reported our situation to social services, and then they'd turn up, take us away for a while and put us into foster homes."

"I haven't been able to figure out why social services would keep returning you to your parents when things were so bad."

Cady glanced up, and Meredith watched a lone tear slipping down her cheek, leaving a fine line of dampness across her porcelain skin. "Social services are overworked, underpaid and have dozens – hundreds of cases to deal with every day. *They* would clean themselves up for a while, turn up, and petition to get us back. A couple of times, they turned up at the school and just snatched us, took us away to a new town, started the whole cycle again."

"When they treated you so badly, I can't imagine why they kept coming to take you back?" Meredith asked carefully.

Cady shook her head. "You have no idea. They used us, we were pawns to beg for money, for food, to try and convince a landlord to give them an extra few days to come up with rent, because wouldn't the landlord feel terrible if he pushed those three little girls out into the streets?" She lifted her gaze and focused on Meredith, and the depth of pain in her eyes, the agony of eighteen years of living with Mark, was leveled at Meredith when she spoke again – and it took Meredith's breath away. "We were belongings. Three items that could be used to his benefit. I don't think he ever loved us. We were just a means to an end, and when Lisa died, if we'd stayed any longer he would have prostituted us out to pay for his next fix. He would have done things to me that I still can't bear to think about, even a decade after the fact. I'm sorry to tell you these things about your son. But he was a worthless, no-good bastard and I hope he's still burning in the flames of hell for what he did."

14

---

Meredith suffered a disappointment on Friday when David telephoned to say he wouldn't be able to make it to Garrison for the planned weekend. In some ways, Cady was relieved – she was still haunted by the prospect of meeting a man who might resemble her father in some way, despite the years that had passed. But she was sorry for Meredith, who seemed to be suffering a week of disappointments.

Walt had provided the final estimate for the carpentry and roofing, and as Cady suspected all along, it was far too expensive to contemplate. It didn't matter how many ways Meredith broke down the estimate, nor how much Walt suggested they could do themselves, the final figure was too prohibitive.

The disappointments had been tempered by an invitation from Nancy Garrison, asking Meredith and Cady out to the ranch on Saturday night for a cookout before the weather precluded outdoor events. Even now it was cool enough to need a coat, Cady thought as she dressed. She'd settled on modern jeans and a sweater for the evening, forgoing her fifties fashions. Summer was Cady's favorite time of the year, when she could wear her favorite clothing every day, but winter always found her swapping into modern clothing to avoid freezing to death. She smiled as she pulled a knitted cap over her hair and wrapped a scarf around her neck; now that she was living in deepest, darkest Montana, the likelihood of freezing to death seemed a distinct possibility. Although it was too early for snow, the crisp air when she walked Churchill in the mornings confirmed winter wasn't too far away.

Cady studied her reflection in the mirror, satisfied by what she saw. She'd put on a couple of pounds since arriving at Gran's, and her jeans fit a little more snugly than last year. She turned to one side and had to admit to being pleased with the curves she saw in the mirror. Her hair was loose, and she put a dab of mascara on her eyelashes before she stepped back, pulling the woolen cap a little more securely onto her head. Pulling on boots, she called to Churchill and he leaped down from his location on the bed, following Cady obediently down the stairs.

"You look as pretty as a picture," Meredith announced from the bottom of the stairs. She too had dressed for the weather, wearing blue jeans and a bright red cashmere sweater beneath a hound's tooth jacket. Her feet were covered in sturdy black boots, and Cady spied a scarf wound around the strap of her purse. Meredith's eyes twinkled. "If you're trying to impress a certain young man, I think you'll succeed."

Cady rolled her eyes. "Seriously, Gran. There's nothing going on with Quinn and me. I haven't heard from him since he took me up to the lake, and I'm not expecting to."

"He might be there tonight."

Cady glanced suspiciously at her grandmother,

suspecting she knew more than she was letting on, but Meredith gazed back at her without a hint of complicity in her blue eyes.

Meredith laughed. "C'mon, let's go and enjoy the last cookout of the season. Another few weeks and we'll have to dig the car out of the garage before we can go anywhere."

Sitting in Meredith's sporty little car, with Churchill taking up the entirety of the tiny back seat, Cady admitted she was secretly hoping Quinn *would* be there tonight. It was a ridiculous desire, given her current situation, and yet, there it was. She wanted to see him again and if she was honest, she'd been disappointed when he hadn't contacted her again. Maybe he'd decided he didn't want to pursue a friendship? Or maybe he'd been considering her as a possible conquest, and backed off when Cady made it clear she wasn't interested in casual sex?

She took a deep breath. The idea of sex with Quinn Garrison had crossed her own mind more than once during this past week. Damn, the man had gotten into her head, and she didn't seem able to shift him. She spent the drive out to Silver Peaks alternating between a desire to discover Quinn at the cookout, and silently hoping he wasn't invited.

She wasn't certain whether she was disappointed or relieved when Meredith parked in front of John and Nancy's beautiful timber home, and she spied Quinn's truck parked a few feet away. She also noticed Kane's truck and realized the whole Garrison family must have been invited. Nancy had told her that all four of their sons had left home and settled into places of their own, but nobody lived far away – in fact, Kane, Matt, and Josh had built their homes on Silver Peaks land. Only Quinn had moved a little further away, buying his own land and building on it.

They made their way up the stairs to the front door, and

Cady admired the beauty of the Garrison home. She'd only had a brief glimpse last time they visited Silver Peaks, when the party was held in the barn, quite a distance from the main house. But now, Cady could see how beautiful the house was and appreciated how wonderful it must be to live out here in the Montana countryside. The house was nestled in the fork of a valley, and the Beartooth Mountains stretched up behind the house, creating a glorious vista which would never get boring. It was breathtaking, there was no other word for it. The house was built from logs, but it was the most opulent log cabin Cady had ever seen. Gran had explained on the drive out that John had built much of the house himself, with help from his own father and brothers when he and Nancy first married.

The door got pulled open and Nancy appeared, her cheeks flushed with color and a bright smile on her lips. "Mer, Cady! Come on in. Let me take your coats and we'll head out – everyone else is here, and John's ready to start cooking. Given that we're only in the first week of October, I swear we're headed for a long frigid winter."

Cady shyly followed the two women through the house, craning her neck to take in the beauty. It was amazing – so completely different to Gran's Victorian, but still lovely. The living room ceilings were high – so high in fact, the windows looking out over the mountains seemed to stretch up to the clouds. They were unadorned by fixtures, no curtains to impede the breathtaking view from either side of the vast fireplace. The living room was larger than anything Cady had seen and decorated in muted browns, creams and greens which blended with nature's palette outside. It was, quite simply, the most gorgeous room Cady had seen, and she complimented Nancy.

"I must admit, I love it myself. The house is too big for

John and me now, but when we're gone, the boys will inherit the ranch and the house, and no doubt they'll make their own changes to the place, just like we've done, and all John's ancestors have done throughout the decades. Would you believe, this house started as a little one room shack when the area was first settled by John's Great-Great-Great Grandfather? Each new generation adds, subtracts, builds a little more, adds something else so that now, it's such a unique house I couldn't imagine living anywhere else. Ol' Grandpappy Garrison certainly picked a magnificent spot to stake his claim."

"He certainly did," Cady agreed as Nancy led them through a double doorway and into the enormous kitchen.

"The kitchen was our addition. I love to cook, but the old kitchen hadn't been updated since the nineteen thirties, so we ripped out the entire thing and modernized." Nancy pointed to the black granite countertops, and the dark wood fixtures. "My favorite room in the house – we used to eat all our meals in here, at that big old table over there. If I'd had my way, we'd be eating inside tonight, but John insists a cookout needs to be eaten outside." She laughed. "Given the temperature has dropped so low, I did convince him we should eat up in the old barn – Quinn and Kane have started a fire in the pit outside, so it'll be a mite warmer than we'd have been on the patio."

"Sounds good," Meredith agreed, handing a dish to Nancy. "Blueberry Cobbler for dessert. I'm glad I made an extra-large one, seeing how everyone is here."

"Yeah, it's always tough filling these boys, especially when they've been busy branding all day. The last of the stock is heading off to the sale yards on Monday, so things should settle down a little and we can get the preparations for winter finished off. Seems to have been a real rush this year, with one thing and another." Nancy placed the dish into the oven on a low temperature and turned back to Meredith. "C'mon out and say hello to everyone."

———

Quinn was standing at the fire pit when his mother appeared with Meredith and Cady in tow. He'd had a hell of a day and almost blew off the idea of coming to the cook-out, but one thing kept him from turning his truck towards home.

Cady Caldwell.

And here she was, and she took his breath away. He'd only ever seen her in those fancy clothes she loved to wear, but tonight, in tight fitting blue jeans and a sweater which followed every luscious curve... man, was he glad he'd succumbed to temptation. His eyes grazed over the gentle curve of her hips, the narrow waist, and upwards to... Catching himself, he forced his gaze up... up... to where a pair of beautiful blue eyes were twinkling mischievously at him while he tried to keep his mouth from dropping open.

Her reaction surprised and pleased him. Surprised, because given her background, he wasn't too certain that a woman such as Cady would appreciate a man ogling her the way he'd been doing. And pleased, because she seemed to like the idea that he'd been caught out staring at her. "Evenin', Cady," he said, certain there was a twinkle in his own eye and sure Cady would catch it. "How are you?"

Cady smiled shyly and took the wine glass his father handed her. "Fine, thank you."

"Come sit over here, Cady," Hallie called from the table where she was sitting with the twins. The boys had coloring books open in front of them and judging by the way their tongues poked out between their lips, Quinn suspected there was a good deal of concentration going into creating their masterpieces. No doubt those same masterpieces would end up somewhere on the front of his Mom's refrigerator, and Quinn suppressed a grin. He and his brothers kept threatening the need to purchase a much bigger 'fridge if Mom insisted on squeezing more of the twins' artwork onto it. Cady offered him another tiny smile and turned away to join Hallie, affording Quinn a fresh opportunity to study those luscious curves.

"She's a picture, isn't she?" John sidled up beside Quinn, pulling the top from a beer and gulping down a mouthful. "She's just blossoming now she's away from that husband and surrounded by people who care for her."

Quinn shot a sharp glance at his father, not certain if his words held some hidden meaning, but John merely sipped his beer again, his gaze focused on Cady, Hallie, and his grandsons. Quinn's eyes followed the same direction and he watched, fascinated as Cady spoke to each of the boys and then happily accepted a crayon from Tommy and started to help him with the page he was coloring. She'd make a wonderful mother some day.

Quinn squeezed his eyes shut for a moment, blanking out the image of a pregnant Cady, her skin glowing with good health, her body ripe with his child. *Whoa there, fella. What the hell?* Slapping his father on the back, Quinn inclined his head towards the barbecue. "Let's get the food cooked."

"Yeah, wouldn't do to just have you standing here, mooning over that pretty-as-a-picture redhead, would it son?"

"Dad..." Quinn voice held a warning.

Much to Quinn's chagrin, John didn't bother to hide the

shit-eating grin he had plastered across his face when he turned to head over to the grill.

Quinn looked back at Cady for a moment longer, searching his heart for the truth. If he was honest with himself, his father was right. He was mooning over this woman.

Maybe it was time to figure out what was brewing between them.

———

THE BARN WAS a picture in the early evening, and Cady admired the casual chic of the decorations. Nancy had a talent for classy displays, that was for sure.

A long wooden table had been positioned in the center of the barn, the double doors at both ends open to reveal the Beartooth Mountains to the west, the sparks and flames of the fire pit at the east. Although it was cool outside, the hay bales stacked against either wall of the barn created insulation between the guests and the weather outside.

The table was well-worn and used, scarred from years of mealtimes, the wood polished to a shiny patina. A hodge-podge of chairs lined either side, with two at the head of either end. A long white tablecloth ran down the center of the table, a green runner adding a splash of color. Nancy had filled a couple of big vases with slender branches of multicolored leaves, adding a kaleidoscope of Fall colors to the display. The barn was decorated with dozens of fairy lights and they twinkled overhead in the gathering darkness, creating a charming atmosphere. It would be romantic, Cady suspected, if you were in the mood for romance. In this instance, it created a pleasant backdrop for a family cookout and she stopped coloring from time to time to admire her surroundings, much to Tommy's annoyance. The little boy only gave her a few seconds grace when her crayon stopped moving and Cady couldn't remember how many times she'd had to apologize for her tardiness.

"Foods up," Quinn announced, placing an enormous platter of barbecued steak in the center of the table. It smelled delicious, but Cady did briefly ponder whether these were some of the cattle who'd once grazed on the hill beyond the barn. It seemed probable, but she was starving, and it did smell great. Pushing aside any concerns, Cady helped Tommy and Tyler pack up their coloring books and crayons and then waited expectantly as the table filled with members of the Garrison family.

"Steak, Cady?" Kane asked, plonking a large filet onto her plate before she had the opportunity to respond.

"Thanks." One by one, large bowls of mashed potatoes, green beans, coleslaw and honeyed carrots were passed around the table, along with a basket of warm crusty bread rolls.

"Well, it does a heart good to see a young woman enjoying her meal. Bit different to when she first got into town, hey, Mer?" John was eyeing Cady's stacked plate with amusement as he cut a wedge from his own steak and popped it into his mouth.

Cady blushed, while Gran smiled and laughed. "It does indeed. Things are improving."

"It's all this fresh air," Nancy suggested. She sipped her wine, watching Cady over the rim of her glass and Cady smiled bashfully in response.

"So, tell us," Josh prompted, "what's happening with the plans for the bakery?"

Meredith placed the bowl of mashed potato back onto

the table before she responded. "I'm afraid everything is on hold."

John leaned forward, his cutlery poised midair. "Problems?"

Meredith shook her head. "Walt gave us a quote. Renovations would cost far more than I could have possibly imagined. The cost seems too prohibitive to go ahead."

John focused his piercing gaze on Cady. "So, what are you planning on doing now?"

Cady swallowed a bite of steak which suddenly seemed twice as large when she discovered everyone's attention focused on her. "Honestly, I don't know. Gran and Sheriff Davis don't think it would be wise to go back to San Francisco until my husband has been located, so I'm planning on staying here in Garrison through until Christmas at least. Then I'll reconsider my options." *My very limited options,* she admitted to herself as an afterthought.

"There must be something we can do," Nancy suggested. "What about approaching the city commission for help with costs?" She glanced at her husband, seeking his agreement. "John, surely the commission must have some way of helping out a new business in the district? Maybe a grant?"

John shook his head. "It's a possibility, but it'd have to go before the commissioners and mayor to vote. And there isn't a whole lot of spare money around nowadays."

"That's true," Meredith added. "But I guess we could investigate the possibility, see if we can get some help."

From the optimism in Gran's eyes, Cady suspected she was going to grab onto this idea like a lifeline. All Cady could hope was that she wouldn't suffer yet another disappointment. But she had to admit, she'd like to think the bakery idea wasn't dead in the water just yet. She'd go back to San Francisco if she must, but she'd grown accustomed to the idea of staying in Garrison.

With a glance across the table, Cady met the dark eyes of the person most responsible for her desire to stay in town. Quinn was seated opposite Cady, next to Kane and when he caught her looking at him, he winked. With a blush Cady lowered her eyes, concentrating on cutting a perfect square of steak while she tried to straighten out her tangled thoughts.

She had no right to be thinking about another man, not when she was still married. She certainly shouldn't be considering a future in Garrison based on the same said man. And yet, with another sneaky glance in Quinn's direction, she knew she was far more inclined to stay here in Montana because Quinn Garrison might be part of the package.

And hell, if that wasn't really messed up.

---

"I think I'm ready for some of Meredith's dessert," John announced later when everyone had finished supper. He was seated at the head of the table, Nancy tucked under his protective arm.

Gran chuckled. "Now how do you know I brought a dessert with me, John Garrison?"

"Because I just saw George's car arrive, and that man has an inbuilt radar for your home cooking," John announced with a knowledgeable grin.

Cady glanced over at her grandmother, caught the coy blush which rose on her cheeks at the mention of Sheriff Davis. "I didn't know the Sheriff was joining us," she commented with a little smile.

If anything, the heat in Meredith's cheeks grew a little warmer. "He telephoned this afternoon, and I told him we were coming out to Silver Peaks for a cookout. He mentioned that if he finished up early enough at work, he might pop in for a spot of dessert."

John glanced at Nancy, his eyes sparkling with amusement. "Well, let's get these plates cleared away and get the dessert. Seems to me there was never any doubt George would finish in time."

Nancy smiled and slapped him lightly on the arm. "Behave yourself."

John leaned in, catching his wife's mouth in a tender kiss. "Yes, Ma'am."

"I'll clear the table," Cady offered, getting to her feet.

"Quinn honey, it'll be much easier if you grab that big tray laying over there by the hay bales. It'll make it easier to get everything back up to the house," Nancy suggested smoothly.

Quinn got up and collected the tray, holding it while Cady loaded the crockery and flatware to take to the kitchen. When the tray was full, Quinn turned towards the double barn doors and tipped his chin at Cady. "Wanna come and give me a hand?"

It was Cady's turn to blush, and with a tiny nod, she followed Quinn from the barn. George waved to them when he approached. "Am I too late for dessert?"

"No, man, you're fine. We're just taking the supper dishes up to the house and bringing dessert back," Quinn assured the Sheriff.

They walked in amicable silence, the occasional tinkle of the tray's contents the only sound as Quinn strode along the pathway leading to the house. Darkness had fallen, and the way was decorated with a bright string of lights, creating a festive glow over the surrounding area.

"I think Mom's matchmaking," he suddenly announced.

Cady smiled softly. "I think so, too."

He surveyed the horizon for a moment before his gaze swept down onto Cady again. "That's the problem with small towns. There're no secrets. Still, I wouldn't live anywhere else."

"It is beautiful," Cady agreed.

Quinn strode up the stairs and crossed the patio, standing to one side while she pulled open the sliding door.

She followed Quinn into the big kitchen. The smell of blueberry cobbler wafted through the air, and Cady pulled open the oven door to check on dessert while Quinn lifted the tray of dishes onto the bench. When she straightened up, he was watching her, and she lowered her gaze, embarrassed by his scrutiny.

"Is dessert ready?" he asked.

"Not quite, maybe another five minutes." Cady began to remove the dirty plates from the tray, rinsing each one and stacking it in the dishwasher.

Quinn leaned back against the kitchen bench, crossing his legs at the ankle and Cady's eyes were drawn to the long, long length of his limbs, hidden beneath faded blue denim. When she lifted her gaze to his, Quinn was watching her, his expression amused. "How do you feel about it?"

Cady swallowed heavily. "About what?"

"Mom's matchmaking attempts."

Cady's cheeks heated. "I can't... I don't know." She didn't know what to say. She couldn't admit to the fact that she dreamed about this man and certainly wouldn't own up to the wild dream she'd had where she was a willing participant in some of the most mind-blowing sex she'd ever experienced.

Quinn took a different tack. "You don't know how you feel about mom's matchmaking? Or you don't know if you're interested in me?"

She looked up, noticed Quinn had moved a little closer and for a moment, lost herself in the dark honey brown of his eyes. Mentally shaking herself, she resumed stacking dishes. "You told me you didn't want to get involved with anyone."

He smiled. "That's true."

"So, what does it matter what I think about Nancy's matchmaking attempts?"

He took another step and gazed down at her. "Because despite my earlier claim of not wanting to get involved, I find myself wanting to get to know you better." He snagged an apple from a bowl on the counter and bit into it, swallowing down the mouthful before he spoke again. "In fact, I'm considering throwing my hat into the ring, Ms. Caldwell. I enjoy spending time with you. I'd like to do it more often."

Cady tried to ignore the sudden increase in tempo of her heartbeat. "Quinn, I don't even know if I'll be here past December. I need work and jobs seem to be few and far between in Garrison... unless of course, you count ranch hands."

He smiled. "Plenty of work for ranch hands, that's true." He took another step, getting close enough so Cady needed to tilt her head back to see his face. "And this particular ranch hand..." he leaned in closer, brushing his fingers down her arm, "...would very much like it if you hung around for a while, so we could get to know one another a little better."

Cady's heart clenched uncomfortably in her chest and

fear swept over her in a rush of unexpected panic. She took a step back, shaking her head. "Quinn... I don't... I'm not..."

"Shhhh, Cady. I'm not pressuring you, I promise," he said in a husky whisper. "But I've been thinking about you, day and night, since I met you. I'm attracted to you, Cady, that's the truth. I know you aren't anywhere near ready to get into a relationship with a man. I'm not even sure myself what this might be between us. I know you've got a lot of issues to overcome after what your husband did to you. But I think you're beautiful, and sweet and amazing and I'd like to spend some time with you."

When Cady glanced up at him, tears had filled her eyes. "I'm damaged, Quinn. I don't know that I'll ever..." Her words faded off as she struggled to vocalize her thoughts. Jameson had convinced her she was worthy of no man's affection, and after the beatings, the scars she had, both physical and mental – she didn't think she could overcome her fears enough to trust a man again.

Quinn watched her for a long moment, sympathy filling his eyes. "You're not damaged, Cady. You're beaten down, terrorized and hurting. You need time to figure out your life and I can understand that." He took a step closer, placing his hands onto Cady's shoulders but when she flinched, he immediately dropped them back to his sides. "I promise you, Cady. I have never, ever, hit a woman for any reason. I never will."

"I'm... I'm sorry." Cady turned away, embarrassed by her reaction and Quinn gently turned her back to face him.

"Don't be sorry, you have every right to be frightened." His gaze traced her face, from her cheek down to her lips. "I want to kiss you, but I don't want to scare you. Would you let me try, Cady?" The last words were barely more than a whisper, a sweet verbal caress which had Cady's stomach clenching with butterflies.

For more than a minute she stood frozen, like a rabbit being hunted by a fox. The tremble grew more pronounced as Cady considered what Quinn had said. Could she? She barely knew this man – was it wise to even consider this? Was she considering it? One glance at his handsome face confirmed she was. To Cady's surprise, she realized she wanted Quinn to kiss her, wanted to see if his lips were as luscious as she'd imagined. Squeezing her eyes shut, Cady nodded.

She heard Quinn chuckle softly but was too terrified to open her eyes. Slowly, painstakingly, he ran his hands up from her fingertips, up past her wrists to her elbows, before he gently gripped her upper arms.

"Just one little kiss, Cady. I promise you, nothing more than you can handle. Let's see if this attraction between us is something real." He continued to whisper soft endearments as he drew closer, and Cady was aware of his presence as he aligned himself against her. She could feel the heat from his body as he gently pressed closer, could feel the waft of his breath, the scent of apples, as he leaned forward. He brushed his lips over hers, once, twice, before he slowly lifted his hands up to cup her face gently between them. "Open your eyes, Cady."

Cady blinked open her eyes, immediately lost in the gold-flecked brown of his. They were beautiful. He was beautiful. She blinked again, unable to hide the tremor which rippled through her limbs.

"It's me, Cady. Quinn Garrison. Look at me while I kiss you. I want you to know it's me who's here with you and that I'll never hurt you."

He leaned in, his movements cautious until his lips

brushed across Cady's again. She lost herself to sensation, his lips against hers, the tender way he held her face in his hands. He had big hands, work-calloused, and easily large enough to hurt her, and yet the pressure on her cheeks was no more than feather-light. Closing her eyes, Cady leaned in further and surprised herself by lifting one hand to rest against his chest.

Too soon, Quinn broke off the kiss and Cady slowly opened her eyes, finding him looking down on her with a warm smile. "Okay?" he questioned.

She nodded and sucked in a deep breath. Quinn had made her stomach turn somersaults, and her heart was pounding in her chest, but he'd kept his word.

He offered her a lazy smile and a warm wink. "We'd best get back down to the barn before they send out a search party. I don't know about you, Cady, but that kiss makes me suspect that there might be something special between us." He pressed another soft kiss against Cady's forehead and squeezed her fingers. "So now I guess it's up to you – to decide where we go from here."

## 15

Cady must have picked up the telephone receiver fifty times in the following weeks, and each time she prevaricated. Sometimes she got as far as dialing the number Quinn had given her. Other times she picked up the receiver and hung it up again before she'd even managed to punch in the first number.

*What was she doing?* She asked herself the same question for the umpteenth time, as once again, she picked up the phone on a whim and just as quickly, slammed the receiver down again.

"You know, those things tend to work much better if you dial the whole number and let the person at the other end answer."

Cady started when she heard Meredith's voice. Turning around, she discovered Gran was seated at the desk in the study and watching her from over the top of her glasses.

"I didn't realize you were in there," Cady said, a hot blush rising over her skin.

"Just finishing up this application to the city commissioners," Meredith announced, picking up a sheaf of papers and tapping them against the desk to neaten them. She stapled the sheets together at one corner before slipping them into a crisp white envelope. "I'll deliver it to the city offices this afternoon. There's a meeting tomorrow night, so I'm hopeful they'll give us a response quickly."

"Do you think there's hope of a grant being approved?"

Meredith sealed the envelope and placed it neatly on the corner of the desk. "There's always hope, honey." She turned the desk chair around to study Cady. "Why don't you just call him? The longer you put it off, the harder it'll be to do."

"Because I'm not sure it's what I want."

Meredith crossed her legs, slipped her glasses off and studied Cady for so long, she started to feel the urge to squirm. "He's a very nice man, Cady. And you're only telephoning him, not promising to carry his first-born son."

"Gran!"

"And another thing," Meredith continued, completely ignoring Cady's protests. "you keep giving me the 'I'm still married' speech when it comes to seeing Quinn. You're as good as divorced and you know it. So why not go out with Quinn, see what might eventuate?"

"Because I'm not 'as good as divorced'," Cady argued. "Until Jameson is located, I can't move forward with a divorce."

"But you intend to divorce, and your lawyer said that even if that no-good ex of yours doesn't reappear from beneath the rock he's crawled under, after twelve months your divorce can be granted."

"Which means I'm still married for another eight months."

Meredith shook her head, her blue eyes twinkling.

"Which means you've been separated for four months. Plenty of time to have waited before you start dating again."

"You're impossible."

Meredith laughed. "Hardly."

"Well, if it's so easy, why don't you call George and ask him out?" Cady challenged with a triumphant glint in her eye. "You two pussyfoot around one another constantly, and everyone can see he adores you."

Meredith turned back to the desk, hiding her face. "That's nonsense. George and I are good friends. Have been for years."

Cady grinned. "You'd only be telephoning him. Not promising to carry his first-born son."

Meredith swung the chair back around, her eyes narrowed. "Good lord, the thought is enough to give me the heebie-jeebies! My child-bearing days are well and truly behind me."

"So that's a good thing. It means you can go out with George and fool around, without having to worry about getting pregnant."

"Arcadia Williamina Arabella Caldwell!" Meredith's cheeks reddened, and Cady suspected the older woman might need a fan to cool down, she was so agitated.

"Yes, Gran?" Cady asked with an innocent smile.

Meredith opened her mouth to speak, closed it again, and then grinned happily. "It's lovely to see you playing around, Cady. I think you're finally on the road to recovery after everything that's happened."

Cady smiled softly. "I do, too." She stepped further into the study and patted Meredith's shoulder. "So, getting back to the subject at hand... if you call George, I'll call Quinn."

Meredith shook her head, her blue eyes wide. "Oh, I don't know..."

Cady shrugged. "Okay. We'll stay with the status quo then." She turned to go, but Meredith called out before she reached the door.

"You don't play fair, young woman."

Cady turned around and offered her grandmother a brilliant smile. "I think it's very fair – this way, we both have to leap... together."

---

"I'm glad you called," Quinn said on Saturday night when he arrived at Gran's house. He dropped down onto his haunches to give Churchill's head a thorough rub before he straightened up again.

Cady smiled. "Come in."

Quinn brushed the soles of his boots on Meredith's porch mat before he stepped over the threshold and into the house. He glanced around, shrugging off his jacket. "How have you been?"

"Good. Busy." Cady took Quinn's jacket and hung it on the hook by the front door. "Would you like a beer? Or a glass of wine?" She intertwined her fingers, suffering an acute case of butterflies as she gave Quinn a quick once-over. He was wearing dark blue jeans, the denim stretching across well-muscled thighs and lean hips. When he'd taken off the jacket he exposed a gray woolen sweater, the soft material stretching across taut abs and broad shoulders and Cady swallowed deeply.

Quinn hadn't missed her appreciative once-over and grinned. "A beer would be good."

"How about you? Has your week been busy?"

Quinn followed Cady and Churchill down the long hallway and into the kitchen, where Churchill immediately laid out on the tiled floor and watched him with unabashed interest. "Real busy. We've been doing the last of the pre-winter preparations, stuff that needs to be finished off before the first snow falls." He glanced around the empty kitchen and lifted a questioning eyebrow. "Where's Meredith?"

Cady smiled impishly. "She's out on a date."

"A date?" Quinn repeated with a grin. "There's only one person in town I can imagine that would be…"

Cady nodded, turning to the stove to stir the pasta. "Sheriff Davis. We made a deal." She pulled a beer from the refrigerator, removed the cap and handed it to Quinn.

"Oh? What sort of deal?"

Cady pulled the cork from a bottle of wine and poured half a glass. Recorking the bottle, she turned to place it back in the fridge before she spoke. "Gran insisted I should stop being such a chicken and call you. I told her I'd phone you… if she'd phone Sheriff Davis and organize a date."

Quinn grinned. "Hot damn! She and George? Out on a date? It's about time." He sipped from the beer before his gaze settled on Cady again. "And I'm really glad you called. I was beginning to think you wouldn't."

Cady wrinkled her nose. "I almost didn't."

Quinn settled at the breakfast bar, watching Cady place a frying pan on the stovetop. "What made you change your mind?"

She turned and glanced at him before she poured a generous dollop of olive oil into the pan. "I'm not sure I changed my mind, so much as I saw the opportunity to get Gran to see Sheriff Davis as possible dating material," she admitted timidly.

Quinn nearly choked on a mouthful of beer. "So… I'm

only here because you were matchmaking for Meredith and George? Way to deflate my ego."

Cady laughed. "I don't think your ego will suffer too badly, from what I hear."

The dark slash of Quinn's eyebrows arched. "What did you hear?"

Satisfied with the level of heat coming off the frying pan, Cady tipped a bowl of pre-cut onions and diced bacon into the pan and gave it a gentle shake. "I hear that you're quite the man about town and that you've dated pretty much every single woman in Garrison county."

"You've been talking to my beloved sister-in-law," Quinn grumbled good-naturedly. "Hallie's told you my entire history, no doubt."

"Not all of it," Cady admitted. In fact, she suspected there was a lot more to Quinn Garrison than the few snippets of information Hallie had supplied when they had coffee earlier in the week. While Hallie had spoken about Quinn's marriage to Julia, and how it had broken up after Julia indulged in several affairs while Quinn was serving overseas, ending with the Neanderthal-like Earl Henderson, she'd had little to say other than the fact that Quinn dated a lot, but never seemed interested in settling down with anyone. Cady couldn't say she blamed him – after the fiasco of her marriage to Jameson, she wasn't thinking she'd want to settle into marriage again either.

"Good to know," Quinn said with a wry smile. He inclined his head towards the pan. "What's for supper? Smells good."

"Creamy mushroom pappardelle with pistachio gremolata," Cady announced. She gave the fryingpan another shake, before she added mushrooms, garlic, and fresh rosemary.

"I have no idea what any of that is," Quinn said, "but it sure smells good."

Cady wiped her hands on a cloth she had hooked over her shoulder and offered him a wry smile. "Sorry. Old habits die hard. Jameso— my soon to be ex-husband, was a world-class chef. When I met him, I could burn water, but he taught me a lot about cooking during our marriage." *And punished me when I got anything wrong,* she added silently.

"You seem a little more settled now, less anxious than when I first met you," Quinn pointed out.

"I'm beginning to really like it here," Cady admitted. She opened the refrigerator, pulling out a container of cream and tipping the contents into the frying pan, then giving the contents a good stir. She turned and took the saucepan of boiling pasta off the stovetop, draining the contents into a colander in the sink.

"Can I do anything to help?"

"You can put flatware on the table, if you wouldn't mind."

By the time Quinn had prepared the table, Cady had served the pasta onto two plates, sprinkling the mixture with a generous serve of the Pistachio Gremolata she'd prepared earlier. She picked up both plates and brought them over to the table, placing one at each setting. Quinn had set the table so they'd sit opposite one another, and she was surprised that he'd taken two of Gran's candles from the dresser and placed them in the center of the table, creating a romantic setting. She was further astonished when he stood behind her, holding out her chair and settling her into it, placing the linen napkin gently into her lap before he sat down in his place.

She watched as he twisted strands of pasta expertly

onto his fork before he popped it into his mouth and closed his eyes in delight. "This is amazing."

"Thank you." Cady sipped her wine, before tucking into her own supper.

"So, I'm assuming as you and I are dining here at Meredith's, that means George and Meredith are at Grizzlies?" Quinn guessed, with a twinkle in his eye.

Cady nodded. "We drew straws."

"Did you win, or lose?" he asked curiously.

She chuckled. "I'm calling it a win. I didn't want to be out in public. I might have only been here for a couple of months, but it doesn't take long to figure out there are no secrets in a town this size. Which is why Gran ended up at Grizzlies, rather than going to Sheriff Davis's house. She didn't think the locals would think it appropriate for her to be cavorting at the Sheriff's home on their first official date."

Quinn chuckled. "Cavorting? Why, Ms. Caldwell, don't you think that's what people are going to think we're doing?"

The loaded question settled between them for a full minute, and Cady kept her gaze lowered to her plate as she struggled to come up with a response. "I know what we're doing, and that's all that matters," she finally said. "And my track record at Grizzlies isn't good. The first night I visited, I met Earl Henderson, the second time I had an altercation with your ex-wife. I didn't relish the prospect of a third attempt."

Quinn put his fork down and clasped his hands together, resting his elbows on the table. "Julia can be a crazy bitch at times."

"I'm not blaming you for her behavior," Cady responded quickly. "And I'm sure she must have had some redeeming features, for you to have married her." She studied Quinn across the table, saw the way he was wrestling with himself and wondered what he was holding back. She didn't have long to wait.

"We got married straight out of high school. I thought Julia was the most wonderful woman I'd ever met, but things swiftly went downhill."

"Because you were in the Rangers?" Cady questioned.

Quinn shook his head, picking up his beer to sip from it before he continued. "I joined the Army two years out of high school. Back then, I thought I'd outgrown Garrison, and I wanted to see the world, be something more than a rancher. I didn't want to be like my father, and his father before him. I had itchy feet, and a hankerin' to do something with my life." He glanced across at Cady, offering her a rueful smile. "I figured the best way of seeing the world was to join the services." He turned his gaze towards the window, staring out past their reflections, his mind clearly on a distant time and place. "Julia loved the idea of being an Army wife; but our marriage was already in trouble, had been from the very beginning." He glanced up a Cady, offering her a grimace. "Julia struggled to be faithful. My family kept warning me about her shenanigans, but I refused to believe them." He inhaled sharply. "I tend to think part of the reason I joined the Rangers was to get Julia away from Garrison. At the time I figured if there was just her and I, she'd stop fooling around. Even though I denied it was happening, I think in my gut I knew it was true. Anyway, we traveled some, but she soon got tired of the life-style, wanted to come back to Garrison." He turned back to Cady. "I can't blame her, being a military wife is tough, there's a lot of hanging around, traveling from place to place, settling at one base, only to be uprooted and sent to another one a couple of years later. She soon decided it wasn't nearly as romantic as she'd suspected it would be. Things only got worse after September eleven, when I was sent overseas, first to Iraq, then to Afghanistan. I wasn't back home for more than a couple of months at a time, before I'd be heading overseas on another nine or twelve-month tour."

"It must have been difficult for both of you," Cady pointed out softly.

Quinn drained his beer and set the bottle carefully on the table. "Julia was never going to cope." He smiled grimly. "Honestly, Julia was never going to stay faithful. Dad had warned me, right from the beginning that she wasn't the right woman for me, but I was in love and I wouldn't listen to reason. It seemed a natural progression to marry – we'd been together through most of high school – it was what everyone expected."

Cady remained silent, waiting for Quinn to continue. She could see why Quinn would have fallen for a woman who looked like Julia, he was a handsome man and Julia was a very pretty woman. But from her own perspective, Julia's beauty didn't make up for what she suspected was an ugly personality.

It seemed Quinn had been reading her mind because he smiled and nodded. "Yeah, I know. The beautiful outside doesn't make up for a bitchy personality. Dad was right from the very beginning, Julia wasn't the type to settle down and deal with an absentee husband. She needs attention and plenty of it."

Cady indicated towards Quinn's empty beer. "Would you like another?"

He smiled, picking up his fork again. "Yeah, that'd be great."

Slipping from the chair, Cady reached into the refrigerator and grabbed a second beer for Quinn and retrieved the bottle of wine to refresh her own glass. Sitting the beer on the table in front of him, she settled back into her seat and pulled the cork from the bottle.

"Here, let me." Quinn reached across and took the wine bottle, and when he did, his fingers touched Cady's. Rather than moving away, he remained motionless, so that their fingers remained touching for a long moment. A spark of energy seemed to hum between them where their skin touched, and Cady shivered and pulled away. Quinn offered her a tiny smile and refilled her glass before he recorked the bottle and set it down on the table. "So enough about me and my marital woes. The short story is, Julia started an affair with Earl Henderson, whom we'd both known in high school. Earl was fool enough to fall in love with her and told her he wanted to marry her. Right about then, I got served with divorce papers while I was fighting in Kabul." He lifted his beer to his lips and took a long swig. "I knew our marriage was well and truly screwed, and that I'd been a fool to think I could make it work," he added.

"I'm sorry."

Quinn shrugged. "Water under the bridge now. And as you've seen, my ex-wife is gloriously happy with her second husband. So much so that he's wildcatting at Grizzlies, and she's trying to keep him on the straight and narrow by physically threatening anyone he sets his eye on." He grinned, but the gesture didn't reach his eyes. "It's a marriage made in heaven, I guess."

They both lapsed into silence for a few minutes, and Cady finished her pasta beneath the flickering flame of the candles. She honestly didn't know what to say in response to Quinn's words. Fortunately, Quinn took the pressure off.

"You know, I still can't pronounce whatever this is you made, but it's delicious."

"Thank you." Cady wiped her lips with her napkin and draped it across the plate. "Funny thing is, I can cook a supper like this, but I can't bake a cake." She shook her head. "Seems nuts, doesn't it, to think I'm considering opening a bakery?"

Quinn too, had finished his meal and he settled back against the seat, eyeing her curiously. "It does seem a little crazy, but seeing the way you can decorate a cake, I'm sure you could stick to that side of the business. I hear that Paulette is on the shortlist for the baking job."

"Is nothing secret in this town?"

Quinn chuckled. "Nope. Have you made any decisions yet?"

Cady started to gather up the detritus of their meal to place in the dishwasher. "Nope, nothing yet. Gran put a grant application in, so we're waiting to hear on that. I'm not building up my hopes though. While I think it's something I could really be happy doing... if we can't get the building operational, there's no way of going ahead."

Quinn watched while she loaded the dishes into the dishwasher; then he snuffed out the candles and stood up. "Need a hand?"

"You could check the fire in the living room, add some wood if it's started to die down. I've got apple pie for dessert, I'll make coffee and we can eat in there."

"Sounds good. I take my coffee with cream and two sugars."

By the time Cady served up apple pie and made two mugs of coffee, Quinn had the fire built up, and the flames cast a cozy glow over the room. Cady set the tray down on the coffee table and handed Quinn a plate of apple pie. "I can't take the credit for dessert, Gran made it this afternoon."

"Can't beat Meredith Caldwell's desserts," Quinn said with a warm smile. He'd settled onto the couch facing the fire, and for a moment, Cady dithered over where she should sit. Was she brave enough to sit on the couch next to Quinn, or should she sit in one of the armchairs? Would Quinn expect her to sit next to him, or would that be too forward? Was she even considering this as a date? Weren't they just two friends, having supper together?

Quinn resolved her indecision. "Sit down here, next to me. I promise I don't bite."

She settled uncertainly onto the very edge of the couch and Quinn chuckled. "I really won't bite. You can relax. I promise you, there will be no cavorting on our first date."

Cady laughed along with him, realizing how ridiculous she must look. She was a grown woman of twenty-eight – she wasn't some nervous teenager on her first go-round with a man. "I'm sorry, this is all kind of strange."

"I meant what I said a few weeks back; I'm not intending to pressure you into anything." He ate a mouthful of the pie. "Mmmmhmmm. Meredith makes an amazing apple pie." He grinned at Cady. "Wonder how the date with ol' George is going?"

Cady swallowed her own mouthful and grinned. "Poor Gran, she was so nervous before George picked her up, I think for a dime she would have called and canceled – but I wouldn't let her."

"George has carried a flame for Meredith for as long as I can recall, I've always been surprised he hasn't made a move before now."

"I guess he doesn't want to ruin their friendship if things don't work out," Cady suggested. It was a question she'd asked herself and still didn't have an answer for. To all intents and purposes, George and Meredith got on so well that Cady suspected they were perfect for each other – but Gran had loved her husband deeply, and she thought perhaps Gran thought she was being unfaithful to her husband's memory by dating someone new. She explained her suspicions to Quinn and he nodded.

"Meredith and Jim were soulmates. A bit like Mom and Dad." Quinn smiled wistfully. "It's the kind of love that I think everyone wishes they had in their lives, but only a few are lucky enough to find."

The longing in his voice had Cady wondering if Quinn was against settling down as much as he'd claimed. For a moment, she let herself wonder what it would be like to have a man like Quinn Garrison in her life, what it would be like to have him look at her, the way she'd noticed John gazing at Nancy. Mentally shaking herself, she dismissed the idea. She had no business considering that sort of relationship with anyone, not when her own situation was so tenuous. And she'd already proven she was lousy at relationships. With the role models in her background, how could she expect to experience a relationship which was healthy and mutually respectful? She had no parameters to work with, and she'd already made a terrible, terrible mistake by marrying Jameson. It was one she didn't intend to repeat.

Picking up her spoon, Cady warned herself against getting involved with Quinn Garrison. It would be a terrible idea, and if the grant didn't come through, she wouldn't be in Garrison much past Christmas anyway, so there was no point in wishing for something which would never eventuate.

As if he was reading her thoughts, Quinn spoke again. "You sound as though you'll give the bakery plan a green light if the help comes through?"

Cady smiled warmly. "I'd like to. If we can get some financial help, enough to get the building sorted out, it's a possibility."

"I'm glad to hear it." Quinn had finished his dessert and put the plate down onto the tray. "Anything that will keep you here for a while longer, I'm all for investigating."

Cady sipped her coffee, giving herself a minute before she responded. "You don't even know me, Quinn."

Quinn took the mug from her hand and placed it back onto the coffee table before he turned and reached out to capture her fingers in his. "I want to get to know you, Cady Caldwell."

Even as Cady shook her head, her anxiety levels rising, Quinn was releasing her hands, offering her a smile and a reassuring nod of his head. "No pressure. I know. The honest truth is, I'd like to kiss you again right now, but I can see you're not ready for that yet." He got to his feet, leaning over to press a gentle kiss to her forehead. "I'm gonna head out."

Cady shook her head. "Quinn..." she began, but he interrupted before she could continue.

"One day, Cady Caldwell, you're going to feel comfortable enough around me to leap into my arms and kiss me so hard, my boots are going to curl. You mark my words." He winked at her and offered her a lazy smile.

Without another word, Quinn strode to the front door, grabbed his jacket and blew her another kiss. "I think you and I can have somethin' special, Cady. You just need to learn to trust me."

And with that, he opened the door and slipped out, closing the door quietly behind him.

## 16

Quinn rode out across the plain to where his dad and Matt were repairing a fence on the eastern side of the ranch. The morning was crisp and cold, his breath leaving misty pools of vapor in the air.

The top of the mountains was thick with snow, and it was just a matter of time before they'd be hit with the first blizzard of the season. The cattle had been brought down into the paddocks nearest to the house a few days ago, ensuring they'd be secure through winter. But the previous night, a couple of bulls had managed to find their way through a broken string of wiring and headed back up the range, hence the need for repairs this late in the season.

"Mornin' son," John called when he approached. "How'd the trip into town go?"

Quinn nodded, dismounting and gathering the reins in one hand before he approached where John and Matt worked. He'd headed into Billings at the beginning of the week, with a list about a mile long of items they needed for the ranch before the winter blizzards set in. "Yeah, good. I picked up that organic fertilizer sample you wanted and ordered the replacement tires for the tractor. Phil Capshaw says he'll have that engine oil arriving soon, so he'll deliver it all together – should be here in a week or so, hopefully before the first snow. I picked up Mom's new saddle and left it at the stables, she says she'll head out this afternoon and get it on Topaz, see how he adjusts to it. And I picked up the new chainsaw and ordered the lumber you want to expand the work shed."

John wiped sweat from his brow with his shirt sleeve. Despite the icy conditions, the work the two men were doing was intensive and enough to have them perspiring even on such a chilly day. "Sounds good." He glanced at the fence, where Matt was using a tensioner to tighten the wire across the two posts. "We're just about finished up here, we'll ride back with you to the house."

"Sounds good, I'm starving. Mom was making lunch when I headed out," Quinn agreed.

Matt glanced up and lifted an eyebrow at his older brother. "You're always starving."

"And you're not?" Quinn countered.

Matt grinned. "Yeah, but I'm young, I'm supposed to be hungry."

"You're not much younger than I am."

"At least I haven't hit forty yet."

"I swear, you boys can build anything into an argument," John muttered, leaning over to snatch up the bale of fencing wire.

Quinn rubbed his fingers down Tempest's neck, soothing the big horse. The animal had been spirited since the day he'd been born, and Quinn was the only person he'd accept on his back. Tempest was the perfect name, as far as Quinn was concerned; he loved the horse, but he could be a pain in the ass when he was of a mind to act out. "Any news about Meredith's grant application?" he asked.

John straightened up. "City commissioners knocked it back."

Quinn frowned. "Why?"

Matt pulled off his work gloves and rubbed his sleeve across his forehead. "They'd tell you it was because there wasn't enough fundin' available this year."

Quinn stared at Matt. "What's that supposed to mean?"

John clapped his hand on Quinn's shoulder. "It's not being spelled out in so many words, but the fact that Julia's father is mayor might have had something to do with it."

Quinn couldn't believe it. "That has to be bullshit."

John shook his head. "They'll deny it, of course, but the rumor going around is that Julia had a word in her daddy's ear, tellin' him she didn't think the town needed a bakery."

Quinn huffed out a frustrated breath and ran through just about every cuss word he had in his vocabulary. Given that he'd spent years in the military, it was an extensive list.

"Phew-ee! Don't let your Momma hear that potty mouth of yours, son. She'll cane your backside into next week."

"Why the hell would Julia do that?" Quinn groused.

Matt grinned. "Because she was a jealous bitch when you were married, and she's still a jealous bitch now?"

"What the hell has she got against Cady?" Quinn demanded.

John threw the fencing wire into the back of the four-wheeler and whistled to his own mount. "She thinks you're interested in Cady. And she hates Cady because of it."

Quinn scraped his fingers through his hair. "She's not even married to me now!"

"I know, son. But Matt's right. Julia was jealous when

you were married, she's still jealous now. And despite her many faults, she's Floyd Capwell's baby girl. He's too much of a pussy not to give in to her demands."

Quinn stewed over the situation the whole way back to the ranch house, pissed that despite having been divorced for two years, Julia was still screwing him around.

Nancy greeted him with a sympathetic smile. "I can tell by the look on your face; you've heard the news."

"I don't know what she thinks she's going to achieve," Quinn muttered.

"She's causing trouble. It's what Julia is good at," his mother said. "Sit down, have some lunch; we can talk it through. There must be something we can do."

"Would the building be classed as historic?" Matt questioned. He picked up a bread roll and began to stuff it full of meat and salad. "Maybe something could be done on historical grounds."

Nancy glanced across at John. "It's a possibility," she said. "It's about the same age as Lorna Mendez's building, and I think they dated that back to 1885."

"What are the requirements though?" John questioned. "That would be handled by the State authorities, rather than local. It might be worth investigating."

"How are Cady and Meredith taking the news?" Quinn asked.

Nancy cradled her coffee mug between her hands. "Mer is devastated, she'd really pinned her hopes on keeping Cady here in Garrison. And with the sighting of Cady's louse of a husband—"

Quinn frowned. "He's been seen?"

Nancy nodded. "George says local police sighted him in Texas, but he disappeared again before the authorities could arrest him. It's a relief to know he's miles away from

Montana, but it's still enough to make Mer anxious. She'd been hoping he might have gone, left the country rather than face charges for trying to kill Cady. The fact that he isn't in San Francisco seems to have Cady thinking with the bakery dead in the water, she should probably head back."

Quinn's heart sank. He didn't like the idea of Cady leaving Garrison, but without the bakery, he didn't know how to convince her to stay. Their relationship, such as it was, hadn't had a chance to develop yet, and he wasn't sure if it would or not – but it sure as hell had no hope if Cady left town.

"What about a barn raisin'?" John said suddenly. "We do it for barns, who's to say we couldn't do the same thing to get a small business up and running?"

Quinn's mood lifted. "I've got some leftover timber at my place from when I built the cabin, and I'm sure other families wouldn't mind helping out. We could arrange it for this coming weekend or the one after, before winter sets in. At least we could get the building up to scratch, and that would cut the outlay Meredith's looking at. Might bring it back to a figure she's able to work with."

Nancy clapped her hands and nodded eagerly. "That might work!"

"The Oslows just finished shingling their place, they might have some left over," Matt pointed out.

"I'm sure Walt'd be happy to donate some of his time," John added.

"We could still follow up on the historical aspect," Nancy suggested. "I can speak to Lorna, get a firm idea of the building's age."

"And if this plan goes ahead," Matt added with a cunning smile, "Cady Caldwell is more likely to stay in town, which will make my big brother a very happy man."

"That's got nothin' to do with it," Quinn said.

John laughed. "I think it has a heck of a lot to do with it, son."

"Yeah," Matt laughed. "Seemed like the two of you got a head start on enjoying dessert that night at the cookout, and you had a nice, private supper with her at Meredith's a few weeks later."

"Shut up, Matt," Quinn warned.

This time, he had to put up with both his parents and brother laughing at him, but there was no way he'd rise to the bait. Cady was too fragile, needed time to settle into the idea of spending time with him and he wouldn't let rumors and innuendo spread around town where she was concerned. "Regardless of Cady's involvement, it'd be a shame not to help a small business get started in town. It can only do Garrison good to have something extra to draw people here. Christ knows enough local businesses have closed in the past few years."

John sobered. "That's true, son. The town is dying, bit by bit. The idea is a sound one and we should do as much as we can to help a new business get off the ground."

---

"Let's take Churchill for a walk," Meredith announced a couple of weeks later.

Cady glanced up in surprise. "O-kay. But don't you have gardening club this morning?"

Meredith shook her head, sitting on the mudroom bench to pull on a boot. "Not today, it's been canceled."

Cady raised an eyebrow but remained silent. Gran had attended the gardening club every Saturday morning since

Cady's arrival, without fail. And she'd never volunteered to come walking when Cady took Churchill out.

Not that Cady was complaining about the prospect of a walk. She'd been busy all week working on a cake she'd promised to decorate for one of the local's twenty-first birthday, and Churchill had been reduced to one walk a day while she rushed to finish the job. The cake had turned out well, Toby Thomson was a Star Wars fan, and she'd been able to design a cake which recreated the Death Star. Given that the Death Star was shaped like a planet, it had been quite a feat to get the cake sitting upright and appearing appropriately Death-Star-ish. The work had taken days; when Cady came up with this brilliant idea, she hadn't allowed for the enormous amount of fine detail the cake required. Now though, it had been safely delivered to the birthday boy, and she was looking forward to getting back into twice-daily walks with Churchill. The big dog needed the regular exercise, and with a proliferation of treats from Gran, he was growing a little plumper every day.

"I'll just get my coat."

Cady ran upstairs, taking them two at a time, with Churchill bouncing beside her, his tongue lolling out. When she grabbed her sneakers from the closet, he began to chase his tail in excitement, understanding what Cady was preparing for.

Once outside, the chill of the early November morning against her cheeks had Cady slipping back through the front door to grab a scarf from the coat rack.

"My goodness, it's chilly out here," Meredith announced, slipping her gloves on before she buried her hands deep in her pockets. "You can almost smell snow in the air."

Cady grinned. "I'm looking forward to seeing snow,"

she admitted. She hadn't seen snow since she and her sisters had left Detroit, over a decade ago. Back then, winter had been a miserable experience, with the girls suffering in inappropriate clothing and footwear. But now, when her life had taken a turn for the better, Cady intended to enjoy a snowy white Christmas in Montana before returning to California.

"You won't be saying that when we're digging ourselves out of a four-foot snow drift," Meredith warned with a sunny smile. They'd reached the front gate and Meredith held it open for Cady and Churchill to pass before she slipped through and relatched the gate. "Snow looks beautiful, but it can be a darn nuisance."

"It's a chance I'm willing to take," Cady announced. "It might be my only chance to see it for a while."

Meredith's forehead creased in a tiny frown. "I hope you'll come back for Christmas every year, Cady. I'm going to miss you terribly when you go to California. I wish you'd reconsider."

They turned out of Meredith's street and strode up the moderate hill on Polson, heading towards Main. Churchill bounced happily from one side of the sidewalk to the other, nose down, tail upright as he examined the day's new smells.

"I can't Gran. As much as I've gotten to enjoy living in Garrison, there's nothing here for me. No work, and what I'm making from decorating the occasional cake isn't enough." *Not enough to repay you for everything,* Cady thought.

And of course, Quinn Garrison was the other deciding factor. After their supper together, Cady hadn't seen him again. She couldn't blame him; he'd probably decided she was too much effort to bother with. The way she'd frozen up still embarrassed her and she didn't blame Quinn one little bit for turning tail and giving up on her.

"Let's turn up onto Main Street, I hear Lorna has a lovely Thanksgiving display in her windows this year," Meredith suggested.

Cady shrugged. "Sure."

They turned onto Main Street, and Cady's attention was seized by the display Lorna had arranged in her windows. She'd made a lovely job of it, with lots of bunting in Fall colors of orange, brown and green. A row of comical papier mâché turkeys, dressed in pilgrim outfits, were set up along the sidewalk, making their way inside the store, laden with tiny shopping bags promoting Lorna's gift store. Cady turned to Meredith, ready to comment on the display when she noticed that Main Street was busier than she'd ever seen it before. "What's going on?"

Meredith offered Cady a radiant smile. "Let's go and find out."

Cady remained puzzled until she saw the crowd outside the building Meredith owned. There was a veritable army of men working on the building, and the sound of hammers, saws, and power tools being operated drifted down the street to meet them. Despite the bitter temperature, dozens of people milled around, and out the front of the building a small marquee had been erected. Cady spied Nancy and Hallie Garrison inside, along with a couple of other women, including Paulette Shelby and the elderly Dotty Knightley. Someone had tables and chairs set up outside, which overflowed onto the blacktop outside the building, and with her mouth dropping open in surprise, Cady saw Luanne Mulroney stride across from Grizzlies, pulling a trolley laden with cartons of soda and beer. She waved when she spied Meredith and Cady, beckoning them over with a wide grin.

"What the hell's going on?" Cady demanded.

Meredith practically vibrated with joy when she turned to Cady. "It was Quinn's idea. When he learned the city commission declined the grant, he decided to organize a barn raising."

Cady frowned. "A barn raising?" She had no idea what Meredith was talking about and was struggling to comprehend what she was seeing. It seemed as if the entire population of Garrison had come together, working on the building Gran owned. She'd never seen anything like it before, her association with neighbors had been limited, firstly because of her family's situation, and later, because people... well, they didn't do this sort of thing for one another. She was in such a state of disbelief, Meredith's mention of Quinn didn't compute initially until she glanced up and saw him striding towards her, a big grin on his face. "Mornin' Cady."

Churchill bounced on the spot, clearly delighted to see Quinn again and when he reached them, Quinn crouched to rub Churchill's head fondly. "Hey, big guy."

Cady watched him silently. She hadn't seen Quinn in more than a fortnight, and seeing him now, her heart skipped a beat or two. *Not good, Cady, not good at all.*

*Wait.*

Cady began to put the pieces together. What her grandmother had said... how Quinn had made this event – this barn raising – happen. Did that mean...?

"Quinn, I'm so thrilled that you organized this for us," Meredith gushed, while Cady continued to stare at Quinn in disbelief. "And I'm sure Cady will be very grateful... just as soon as she gets over the shock."

Quinn straightened up, his warm brown eyes on Cady

and a tiny smile played on his lips. "Ms. Caldwell." He tipped his hat, offering her a lazy wink and Cady's heart stumbled again in her chest.

*Damn, but he was handsome.*

"Hey, Cades!"

Cady turned at the sound of her name and saw Harry and Sid rushing towards her, their faces filled with sheer delight. Both girls were dressed in faded jeans and heavy jackets and had clearly been helping with the painting, judging by the amount of paint they had splattered over their hands and faces. Each of them wrapped Cady in a big hug in turn, while she continued to gape at the surrounding activity.

The building already looked different. The faded ice cream sign had been removed, and up on the roof, scaffolding erected and half a dozen men were up there, ripping off the old shingles and replacing them with new. Ladders and more scaffolding had been erected down the side of the building, and volunteers were using crowbars to removed damaged sections of clapboard and replacing them with fresh wood. The broken panes of glass in the front windows had already been taken out, and new ones installed. From here on the sidewalk, Cady could see more people inside, working on the interior. "I don't believe this," she muttered.

"I was keen to get you to stay in Garrison, so I rustled up some friends for a barn raisin'," Quinn announced with a cheerful smile. "Folks have come from miles around to help out, and some local businesses donated equipment, so we can get the buildin' up to scratch."

Cady gazed up into Quinn's attractive face, caught the twinkle in his eyes when he returned her look. "I didn't think... I wasn't sure..." Cady shook her head, frustrated by the way she was stumbling over her words. "You didn't call me again."

Quinn chuckled, glancing back at the building. "I've been kinda busy. Getting this together in less than a fortnight took a bit of work." He lifted an eyebrow. "Did you think I'd lost interest?"

Cady remained mute but was positive her blush answered for her.

Someone shouted Quinn's name, and he turned back towards the building. "Gotta get back to work. We'll talk later." With another wink, he strode away and disappeared into the building, leaving Cady staring after him.

"Shut your mouth, Cades. The flies'll get in." Sid suggested helpfully, a big grin raising her lips.

"I think we can all agree Quinn Garrison has thrown his hat into the ring," Harry agreed with a knowing smile.

"I can't believe you're here!" Cady announced, ignoring her sister's comment. "You knew about this?"

"Yep," Harry agreed. "Gran telephoned us when Quinn started organizing it, and she flew us up here last night. We stayed in Billings and drove to Garrison this morning. She glanced back at the building. "Scott's inside, helping remove the old counters."

"And Dyl is around back; Josh is teaching him to operate a bobcat," Sid added enthusiastically. "Harry and I are helping with painting."

"I can see that," Cady responded with a smile.

"Are you really pleased, Cady?" Meredith questioned. "I've been keeping this secret for more than a week, and I can't tell you how many times I just about chickened out and told you."

Cady reacted in a way nobody could have predicted, wrapping Gran in her arms and hugging her fiercely. "I couldn't be happier, Gran. Really," she whispered in the older woman's ear.

Sid clapped her hand together. "So Cades, now that you'll have your own bakery, you'll need to think of a name for it!"

Cady offered her sister a tiny smile. "I already have a name."

Meredith was still enveloped in Cady's arms, but she pulled back a little to see Cady's face. "You have? What are you going to call it, honey?"

Cady grinned. "'Tokens of my Confection'."

17

---

W hen Quinn knocked at Meredith's door on Sunday
night, he was exhausted, but satisfied. It had been
a long two days, with early starts and late finishes, but the
building was renovated and ready for Cady and Meredith
to begin the next stage.

He'd seen Cady around the work site on and off all
weekend, but the amount of work was so extensive, he
hadn't been able to stop and talk for more than a minute or
two at a time. He'd been pleased to see how Cady had
knuckled under and helped, and immensely proud when
he'd seen the quiet grace and strength she'd displayed and
how she'd been careful to thank everyone involved.

It had been quite a turnout. Given they were a week out
from Thanksgiving, and local ranchers were all deeply
entrenched in prepping for winter, Quinn had expected to
get some help, but nowhere near the amount his Mom and
Hallie had managed to drum up. While they'd been busy
organizing volunteers, Quinn had been on the phone,
begging people to donate what they could to the cause,
letting them know how much Cady would appreciate it and

more importantly, how great it would be for the town to have a new business.

"Hi," Cady said shyly when she pulled the door open. From down the hall, Quinn could hear the excited chatter of Cady's sisters and their partners, along with Meredith's voice.

"Hi yourself," Quinn said. He offered her a warm smile, mesmerized once more by the beautiful blue of her eyes.

"Would you like to come in?"

Quinn grinned. "I wondered if you'd like to go for a walk? We could take Churchill."

Her eyes grew wide. "Um, yeah. That would be good." She beckoned to him. "Would you like to come inside for a minute while I get ready?"

Quinn followed her into the house, wiping his boots on the mat before he snatched the opportunity to watch her curvy hips when she sashayed down the hall in front of him. She was wearing gray trousers which skimmed across her ass and waist, and a pale pink sweater with some kind of fancy neckline, which demurely covered her to the throat. For a minute, Quinn indulged in a little fantasy about lifting that sweater and reaching the treasures he was certain lay beneath before he found himself greeting Cady's family.

Meredith got to her feet and offered Quinn an affectionate hug. "Quinn, once again, I really don't know how we can thank you."

"It was a pleasure, Meredith." Quinn was tickled to see Sheriff Davis included in the group crowded around Meredith's living room. The romance was obviously progressing if George was invited to these family gatherings. He wondered if George had an invite to the Caldwell Thanksgiving next week. The way the Sheriff was settled next to Meredith on the couch, his arm touching hers and his knee pressed against Meredith's denim-clad leg, Quinn suspected the answer to that question was a resounding yes.

"I'll just get my shoes and Churchill's leash," Cady announced quietly before she slipped from the room. Quinn found himself the center of attention with Cady's sisters, and judging by the look in their eyes, he was about to be grilled.

"So," Sid started, her eyes twinkling. "What's the deal, Quinn? I hope your intentions towards my big sister are honorable."

Quinn grinned. He'd met Sid and Harry numerous times since they'd come into Meredith's life and enjoyed Sid's spunky attitude. "Well, Ms. Caldwell, I was wonderin' if I'd be allowed to take your sister out for a stroll around town."

"Hmmmm." Sid held her index finger to her cheek and turned her eyes skyward, seemingly deep in thought. "I guess that would be alright." She made a big show of checking the clock on Meredith's mantelpiece. "Now, I think for a stroll around a town the size of Garrison, a respectable period would be... say... twenty-five minutes."

Quinn chuckled and rested his hands on his hips. "Gee, Ms. Caldwell, I was kinda hopin' I might be allowed a little bit of leeway, given that I've shown my intentions are honorable in the past couple of days."

Meredith laughed out loud. "Given that I'm Cady's grandmamma, don't you think I should be consulted?"

Scott grinned. "I would think so, Meredith. The way these two get into trouble, I don't think either Sid or Harry's opinions should count for much." He stretched out his long legs and lifted his arms, to protect himself from his wife's well-aimed cushion throw. Then he pulled Harry into his arms, kissing her soundly despite her squeaks of annoyance.

Quinn smiled to himself and suffered that same pang he'd been getting ever since Cady walked into town. He wanted this; what Harry and Scott had, what Kane and Hallie had. And he suspected he wanted it with Cady Caldwell.

"I think Cady and Quinn are probably old enough to make up their own minds regarding how long they walk for," Meredith offered with a sunny smile. "They're both intelligent, mature adults. They don't need our interference."

"How about we let Cady decide for herself?"

Quinn twisted around, saw Cady standing in the doorway with Churchill by her side. He was worried she might be offended by the way they'd been discussing her, but judging by the little smile playing on her lips, she was as amused as he was.

"I think Cady's right, you girls," George grumbled. "Let the girl be; she's old enough to lead her own life."

"When do we start calling you our step-granddaddy?" Sid asked sweetly.

Cady rolled her eyes, even as Gran started to splutter denials and George choked on the mouthful of coffee he'd been ready to swallow. She glanced up at Quinn. "Shall we go?"

Quinn nodded and followed her back to the front door, holding it open for Cady and Churchill to step through.

The night air was icy, and Quinn was glad to see Cady had donned a thick jacket and sturdy boots to protect against the chill. She was wearing thick winter gloves, and Quinn reached out, taking her left hand in his. He felt Cady start, was aware of her eyes flashing up to meet his, but he didn't say anything, just kept walking. After a moment or two, she took a deep breath and relaxed, and the pressure of her fingers changed so that she was wrapping them around his, rather than holding them stiffly.

"Thank you. For everything you've done," she said quietly, a minute or two later. "I've never had anyone be so kind to me before."

Quinn glanced down at her, loved the way the streetlights made her blue eyes sparkle in the darkness. "You're welcome. And you deserve to have kind things done for you."

The smile which touched her lips was bittersweet and disappeared as quickly as it had come. "Quinn, I don't know what this is."

Quinn frowned. "You mean this?" He lifted his arm to bring their linked hands up into the light. "I think this is a couple of people who think they might like one another."

"I'm still married, Quinn. I don't want you to think this is something more than what it can be at this stage."

Quinn drew Cady to a stop, turning so that he was facing her. Churchill realized they'd stopped and busied himself sniffing in the hedge outside Mrs. Cornborrow's house, content to wait. Quinn watched Cady, taking in the beauty of her red hair, the way her lips met in a perfect little pout. A pout that he wanted to kiss, so badly, and see if those lips were as soft and velvety smooth as he remembered. "What do you think this can be, at this stage?" he murmured, lifting his free hand to brush his fingers through her long hair. The movement allowed the scent of her shampoo to waft in his direction and he inhaled deeply, enjoying the fresh aroma of peaches.

"I'm... I'm not really sure," Cady admitted quietly. "I... I don't know what you want from me."

Quinn smiled down at her, a gentle smile intended to soothe her anxieties. She was like a captured mustang, trembling and frightened, not quite certain what was expected of her. He knew he needed to tread carefully, not overwhelm her, or spook her so she'd shy away from him. "I think we're becoming good friends. I think we both have things in our past we'd like to forget. I think you're a beautiful woman, and I want to get to know you better." He moved a little closer, aligning his body to Cady's, but leaving enough space between them to let her think she was still in total control.

From Quinn's point of view, he was completely *out* of control. Damn, but she smelled wonderful and looked gorgeous. He wanted her, and he'd been dreaming about her for weeks now. He wanted to kiss her again, but he wasn't certain whether she'd run like the wind if he took things any further. Hell, this hadn't even been his plan in the first place. He'd come to Meredith's tonight intending to take Cady out for a stroll, nothing else. He knew how insecure she was, how she'd flinched when he'd lifted his hands onto her shoulders that night at supper. He never wanted to see that frightened look in those pretty eyes again, but seriously, if he didn't get to taste those lips again soon, he suspected he'd spontaneously combust.

"Quinn?"

The sound of her voice, the uncertain tone pulled him from his internal machinations. When he looked down at her, she was watching him, an unspoken question in her eyes. "Sorry, Cady, I got to thinking and well..." he tapered off, uncertain what to say next. Hell, what could he say? *I was thinking about kissing you, but I'm worried you'll think I'm pushing too hard?*

Her eyes were clear and calm when she looked up at him. "What were you thinking?"

He shook his head, offering her a reassuring smile.

"Nothin' important. C'mon, we'd better get moving or Churchill will complain about the lack of walking in his walk."

For the next few minutes they continued in silence, and Quinn scanned the street ahead. Now he was tongue-tied and couldn't think of what to say to her. *Way to go, Quinn. You're making a great impression. Considering you're usually so smooth with the ladies, what the hell is wrong with you tonight? If your brothers could see you now, they'd laugh their asses off.*

"I'm excited about getting the bakery open, I talked to Walt this afternoon, and he said he'd start work on the cabinets and display cases this week. Gran and I think we might even open before Christmas."

Quinn glanced down at Cady, pleased to see her so animated. "Sounds good. Are you going to stick with the bakery, or try for the coffee shop like you and Meredith originally discussed?"

She grinned. "Now that we don't have a major refurbishment to deal with, I think it might be nice to go with the coffee shop idea. It might bring more people into town and," she glanced around the deserted street, "give people somewhere to take their dates, other than Grizzlies, or out walking on a freezing winter night."

Quinn lifted her arm, tucking it through his, pleased to hear her refer to their walk as a date. "I'll admit, dating options in Garrison are limited. It's better in summer. More possibilities."

"Oh?" Cady said. "Such as?"

Quinn surveyed the street before they turned the corner and walked downhill away from Main Street, towards where the river wound its way along the outskirts of town.

"In summer, there's horse riding, picnics, swimming at the grotto..."

"The grotto?" Cady probed.

"Yeah, it's a rock pool off to the side of Garrison lake. Very popular in summer. The water is incredibly clear, it flows into a natural pool created by volcanic movement of the local granite. When the sun's shining, the water is an amazing color, a really pretty blue-green." He squeezed Cady's fingers. "We should check it out next summer. I'm assuming you intend to stay in Garrison now."

"Maybe."

There was a teasing lilt to her voice and it made Quinn smile. "You mean to say, after all that arduous work we've put in, you might hightail it back to California anyway?" He offered her an artificial pout. "I'm hurt."

"You took quite a risk, thinking that having the building fixed up would make me stay."

Quinn shrugged. "It was a calculated risk. I've seen how your eyes light up when you think about having a little business of your own."

They'd reached the park situated next to the middle school, and Cady tugged on his arm, drawing him through the car park to the playground. She unclipped Churchill's leash, letting him roam as he pleased and tucked it into her pocket.

Quinn inclined his head towards the swings. "Wanna swing?"

"Sure."

Cady settled onto one of the swings and pushed her feet against the ground, setting it into gentle motion. Quinn sat on the swing beside her, twisting the chains so he could watch her.

"When I was younger," Cady said softly, "all I ever

wanted to do was be a normal kid. Visit parks like this, play with my sisters, swing as high as it was possible to go."

"I'm guessing you didn't get to do that much," Quinn responded.

Cady's laughter was dry, the sound hollow in the cool evening air. "Nope. Nothing like it." She continued to swing for a minute or two before she spoke again. "Despite it all, despite everything Mark and Lisa did to us – we turned out okay." She smiled faintly, glancing over at Quinn. "We used to pretend they weren't our real parents; that one day, our actual parents would swoop in, tell us it had all been a terrible mistake and take us to our real home. I used to imagine a place much like Meredith's – warm and cozy, filled with love and laughter. We'd each have our own bedroom, and they'd have matching furniture, and bright curtains hanging at the windows. Our real father would read us stories at bedtime and play board games with us around the dining room table, and our real mom would hug us when we left for school and be there when we got home with cookies baked from scratch. They'd both help with our homework and sit and listen to us when we were scared or needed advice, do their best to help us."

"I can't imagine what it was like, to live with parents like yours. From everything I've heard, you had it tough for a very long time."

Cady let the swing settle and stop before she spoke. "It wasn't great," she laughed dryly, "which is an understatement – but despite everything, we survived it. And I'm proud of how Harry and Sid turned out. They could have taken our parent's example as the way their lives were supposed to be, could have become drug addicts, or alcoholics. I'm quietly pleased, now that I'm having a chance to reflect on things, to know they've taken the life opportunities they started out with and improved on them."

Quinn watched her for a full minute before he spoke. "You were responsible for that, Cady."

She lowered her gaze, stubbing her boot repeatedly into the bark chips beneath the swing. "It wasn't me. My husband..." She turned away, refusing to meet his gaze. "My husband – I used him to make that happen."

Quinn frowned. "I'm not certain I'm following."

A sob burst from Cady's lips, and her shoulders started to tremble. "My husband, Jameson – when I married him, I knew he could help my sisters financially. I knew he could provide what the girls needed to get them through college, that he would give us the stability we needed." She inhaled, the air shuddering down through her chest. "I used him, to ensure Harry and Sid got the lives they deserved."

Quinn got to his feet and drew Cady up from the swing, wrapping his arms around her back. She lost her tenuous control on her emotions and sobbed, her cheek resting against his chest.

"Shhhh. Cady, darlin'. Don't cry. You did what you needed to do."

"It was wrong. I thought I loved him... but now, I don't think I really did. Not really. Not the way he deserved. He was right to be angry with me when I didn't do what he wanted. I was never the right person for him."

Quinn caught Cady's chin with his fingers and lifted her face to meet his. "You listen to me. That man didn't deserve you. You weren't the right person for him – in that regard I think you're right – but only because he didn't treat you right. No man has the right to force you into doing what he wants you to do, to beat on you because you're not following his orders. You are your own person, Cady Caldwell."

"I wasn't a good wife..." Cady pushed against his chest, trying to escape, but Quinn held fast.

"You were in a troubled marriage, that doesn't mean you were a bad wife. Your husband was nasty, from what I've heard, and he treated you bad. It's affected you, and I understand that – I've been there myself. Different circumstances, but still an unhappy marriage. My self-esteem took a shit-kicking when Julia left me, and it got worse when I discovered that all the rumors were true, and she'd been screwing around behind my back."

"It's not the same," Cady sobbed. "My background... it's such a mess. So much crap. I've made so many terrible mistakes."

Quinn hugged her tightly and hesitated for a long moment before he lowered his mouth to hers. It wasn't the right time, God knew it wasn't the right time, but he needed her to see that he cared, that he thought she was worth fighting for.

Damn, but her lips were as soft and welcoming as he'd remembered. For a moment she resisted, but any resistance vanished when Quinn traced his tongue across the seam of her lips, tasting the saltiness of her tears. She opened for him with a breathy little sigh, but Quinn didn't want to take this too far, too fast. He suppressed the urge to ravage her and while he couldn't resist exploring her mouth for a moment or two, his tongue tangling with hers, he used every ounce of willpower he could muster to draw back, pressing a long kiss to her forehead. "I'm sorry, I shouldn't have done that," he murmured against her hair.

"I shouldn't have let you," she whispered.

Quinn caught her chin between his thumb and forefinger and lifted her face so that he could see her eyes. "Cady, there are two of us here in this park, we were both involved in that kiss. You can't take the blame for everything that happens in your life."

"I'm not a good person," she whispered miserably and tried to turn away from Quinn, but he was determined not to let her go. He suspected that Cady had been conditioned to accept blame for everything, that her bastard ex-husband had brainwashed her into believing that she was always in the wrong, and her parents had done it before him. Quinn was determined to get through to her, try and get her to believe that everyone had things in their past they found difficult to live with.

And to do that, he might just have to open up about some of the ghosts in his own past.

## 18

C ady wanted the ground to open and swallow her. She'd been so happy; spending a little time with Quinn had seemed wonderful, but in the space of a few minutes she'd managed to swamp herself in a sea of misery and grief over past mistakes. It would be better if she just grabbed Churchill and ran back to Gran's as fast as she could, and never crossed paths with this man again.

Quinn was making her *feel*. Cady had carefully built up barriers against everyone and everything. Even with Sid and Harry she was distanced, kept herself emotionally disconnected. It was a habit borne through years of practice, from suffering too many disappointments, having too many things go catastrophically wrong. She'd made the mistake of swapping a terrible childhood for an abusive marriage, and over the years, she'd constructed a wide barrier around her heart, keeping everything and everyone at a distance. She loved her sisters dearly, but she preserved an emotional distance from them. It was dangerous to allow people to get close – and from experience, Cady knew it would only lead to heartache. Cady had always been pessimistic, rather than optimistic. It was safer that way. Don't expect praise, don't expect affection, don't expect anything to be good and decent. Always assume the worst. Always assume you're to blame for what goes wrong.

She was drawn back to the present by Quinn's insistent tugging on her arm. "C'mon, Cady."

She shook her head fervently, struggling against his grip. "No, I should go home... this was... is a mistake."

Quinn turned to her, and the determination in his brown eyes softened. "Cady, I'm not going to hurt you. I would never hurt you. But we need to talk, and if I let you go now, you're going to go running back to Meredith's and find some way to convince yourself you and I are a bad idea. I want you to sit and talk with me for a few minutes. If you listen to what I have to say, and still want to go home, I'll take you back, no questions asked. Okay?"

She stared at him suspiciously but dipped her head in agreement.

Quinn drew her away from the swings, leading her to where a wooden bench was positioned for parents to watch children enjoying the playground. He settled down onto the bench, eyeing her silently. With an irritated grumble, Cady settled beside him. Her bad mood worsened when Churchill came bursting out from behind a stand of trees, and ran to Quinn's side for a head scratch, ignoring her.

Quinn leaned forward, using both hands to scratch under Churchill's enormous neck. "Cady, you aren't the only person who's living with mistakes and bad stuff in their past."

Cady remained stubbornly silent, wondering what he could be alluding to. She was determined not to ask though, convinced there was nothing Quinn could say to make her change her mind.

"I was a sniper."

She lifted her chin and stared at him, saw a muscle ticking furiously in his jaw and he'd pulled back from scratching Churchill, his fists clenched tightly against his thighs. "In Iraq?"

"And Afghanistan."

Even by the dim light from the solitary overhead lamp, she could see the way his dark eyes had grown distant, how he held himself stiffly, his entire body buzzing with tension. Whatever was behind his announcement apparently still affected him deeply. Cady thought for a minute, comparing his words with what she knew of the war. She'd seen news reports, of course, it was difficult to avoid them, and she'd shed tears over the coffins returning home, containing men who'd lost their lives in service to their country, but she'd never had a connection with anyone who'd served.

"When our guys were out on routine patrol, walking the streets, my job was to provide support, whenever they got stuck in running battles with the insurgents." Quinn's voice had taken on a distant tone, almost as if he spoke of someone else. "I'd be situated on a nearby rooftop, in a nest, waiting to provide cover fire if they ran into trouble." Quinn's smile was more of a grimace. "And over there – trouble was just around the corner, every damn day."

Cady didn't miss the catch in his voice, the slight tremble underlying the words he spoke, and she reached out instinctively and took his hand in hers. It seemed natural to offer him a modicum of support; physical contact to let him know she wouldn't judge. Quinn gripped her fingers like a lifeline.

"The problem is, you never can tell who the enemy is. It's not cut and dried; the bad guys don't wear uniforms and carry weapons. The enemy can just as easily be that elderly woman, leaning on a walking stick and clutching a parcel under one arm – a parcel which seems innocuous enough, but in reality, it holds a grenade, a grenade she's planning to throw in the midst of our guys. Or it can be a woman, wearing a burqa and looking as if she's walking to the local store, or taking her kids to school. But she's carrying a gun, hidden in the folds of the burqa, and she's going to use it to take out half a dozen men. Or that teenage boy is carrying an IED, and intent on destroying lives in an instant, leaving our guys crippled, blinded, or missing limbs."

"I'm so sorry, Quinn. It must have been awful," Cady said quietly.

Quinn's gaze was focused on a distant point when he spoke. "The thing I'm trying to explain is, you're blaming yourself for the decisions you made, and we all have those situations in our pasts." Quinn swallowed deeply. "My job was to keep an eye on anyone who got too close to our guys on the ground. Make a judgement call on whether they were friend, or foe. For the most part, the locals were okay. They didn't hold harmful intentions toward the American forces, but the risk was always there." He inhaled sharply. "When the situations presented, it was up to me to make a gut call. Was the old lady a friend, or foe? Was her shopping bag filled with food, or a homemade bomb? Was the woman in the burqa genuinely pregnant, or did she have a bucket-load of dynamite strapped to her body? Was she intending to martyr herself in the name of her god?" He inhaled deeply, the sound stuttering up through his chest. "Was the little boy running towards a battalion just a kid begging for a candy bar? Or did he plan to lob a grenade into the patrol and decimate them?" Quinn glanced down at Cady, and she saw equal amounts of pain and horror reflected back from his eyes. "We didn't always know, Cady. We didn't always know if they were harmless, or dangerous, and it was my job to report on what I was seeing and decide. Did I snuff out a life and save a squad of our men patrolling the streets? Or did I kill an innocent, because I got it wrong?" He shook his head. "I didn't always get it right, Cady. Sometimes... I got it wrong. And I'll live with those mistakes, for the rest of my life." He cleared his throat, his Adam's apple bobbing as he struggled with the memories swamping him. "Since I got stateside, I've struggled with nightmares, and sometimes I get caught up in the guilt and what ifs... What if I'd made different choices? Some of their faces have stayed with me, and still haunt me when sleep. I swore after I retired from the Rangers that I'd never pick up a weapon again... and I never have."

"You did the best you could," Cady said, struggling to reassure him. "You did what you had to do, made difficult choices in terrible circumstances, to try and keep those other men alive." She squeezed Quinn's fingers, offering him what little comfort she could.

Quinn shuffled on the bench so that his knee pressed against hers. "Darlin', isn't that exactly what you were doing? Maybe not the same circumstances, but you had to make difficult choices to keep you and your sisters together. To keep them safe. You provided for Sid and Harry and made sure they got what they needed."

Cady lapsed into silence for a minute, realizing what Quinn said was true. She shivered, abruptly aware of how cold the night had become.

"C'mon." Quinn got to his feet and drew Cady up beside him. "It's freezing out here. Let's go." Quinn whistled to Churchill and the dog came running, standing still so Cady could clip his leash back onto his collar.

They walked to Meredith's house in silence, both

deeply enmeshed in their thoughts. Cady considered what Quinn had told her. Had she been too hard on herself? Had she been too acceptant of what Jameson did, because she thought she deserved it? Quinn had given her things to think about, some of which she'd never considered before.

When they reached Meredith's, Quinn gently drew Cady to a halt next to his truck and squeezed her fingers. "It's too cold out here, but I don't relish the idea of heading back inside Meredith's with that crowd."

Cady peeped up at the house; most of the downstairs lights were still casting light across the garden and she knew everyone would still be awake. Sid, Harry, Scott and Dylan would be heading back to San Francisco first thing in the morning, and they'd be enjoying this last night at Meredith's. It was apparent Quinn had had enough for tonight, and after what he'd spoken about, she couldn't blame him. "You're going home then?" She couldn't keep disappointment from coloring her words.

"I wondered if you'd come back to my place for a while? I'll make coffee, we could talk more," Quinn suggested cautiously. "I'd like to spend more time with you, Cady; I just don't want to be surrounded by your family... as much as I like them."

Cady wavered, wondering whether it was a good idea. It probably wasn't... but she was tempted.

With her lack of response, Quinn, sighed heavily. "It's okay, Cady, I don't—"

"I'd like to... I was wondering if it would be okay to take Churchill... I don't want to take him back inside..." Cady's voice tapered off. She suspected if she went inside with Churchill, she'd suffer no end of teasing from Gran and her sisters when she told them she was going out to Quinn's house.

Quinn's expression brightened. "Sure. We can introduce him to Moose; he's good with other dogs."

Not giving herself the opportunity to think too hard, Cady agreed.

---

QUINN'S CABIN WAS ENCHANTING. Nestled on the banks of Garrison Lake, with the moonlight shining overhead, it was a picture. The lights were on inside, and as Cady slipped out of the truck and Quinn untied Churchill's leash from the bar in back, she surveyed the property.

Half a dozen long, wide wooden steps led onto a porch, and rocking chairs were positioned on either side of the front door to take advantage of the glorious views. From what Cady could distinguish in the moonlight, there wasn't a vista which didn't provide a spectacular view. The entire front of the cabin was made of glass, and inside she spied soaring ceilings and stone feature walls.

"It's beautiful," she said when Quinn came to her side and urged her forward with a hand on the small of her back.

"Thanks. I love it."

A dog barked inside, and Cady saw a bundle of fur hurtling towards the front door from around the side of a couch.

"Typical Moose. He's intelligent, but as lazy as they come. Out here there's not much to guard against, so he's gotten a bit slack."

They walked up the stairs, Churchill trotting obediently beside Cady on his leash. "I hope they'll get on okay," Cady fretted as she cautiously watched the barking dog inside the house. "Churchill's been socialized, but he doesn't spend much time with other dogs."

"Don't worry. They'll get along fine. Moose is fairly easy going, and he hangs out with plenty of dogs on the ranch."

Sure enough, Quinn was right, and after a vigorous sniffing and a half dozen laps around the brown leather couch, the two dogs decided they were acceptable to one another.

Cady shyly followed Quinn through the living room, with its soaring ceilings. All the cabin walls were built from long, circular wooden logs, or blocks of warm tan stone, giving it a beautifully rustic atmosphere. A fire burned brightly in the fireplace behind a glass frontage and Quinn smiled when he saw Cady inspecting it. "Gas; it's safer that way. I can leave it burning when I'm out and not worry about the place catching fire."

He led her into a kitchen which took her breath away. "You have a lovely home," she complimented. The kitchen was homely, with black fixtures and grey granite counter-tops. Quinn directed her to a stool at the breakfast bar while he made the coffee.

"I built it after I discharged from the Rangers. Kane, Matt and Josh built their places on Silver Peaks land, but I needed something all my own, especially after my divorce from Julia. Ever since I was a kid, I always had a hankering to live here beside the lake. When I got back from the Middle East, the urge only grew stronger." He offered Cady a tight smile. "I have some demons to deal with, and this place," he waved his hand towards the darkened vista outside, "helps me heal."

"I'm sorry you had to go through that." She'd thought long and hard in the car on the way out here, come to the realization that Quinn had gone out on a limb to share what he'd told her, and she appreciated how much courage it had taken. Her admiration for the man seemed to grow with each passing day.

Quinn shrugged, filling two mugs with coffee. "How do you take it?"

"White, one sugar."

Finishing up the coffee, Quinn inclined his head towards the living room. "Come sit by the fire."

They settled onto the couch together and Cady gripped the mug uncertainly between her hands, sipping the coffee and trying to figure out what to say next. Maybe this had been a mistake; she shouldn't have come out here with him. He'd spilled his innermost thoughts, and she couldn't seem to manage even the most basic of conversations. Years with Jameson had reduced her ability to make small talk, especially with a man, because she feared saying something stupid, or being belittled for her opinion.

Quinn sipped his own coffee, then placed the mug down on the shiny wooden coffee table in front of the couch. "Don't freeze up on me now, Cady."

Startled, she nearly dropped the mug and turned to stare at Quinn, feeling like a deer caught in the headlights of a truck.

Seeming far more relaxed than he should be, he leaned back against the couch and studied her astutely. "Tell me a little bit about yourself."

Cady chewed at her lip, swallowed heavily, then took another gulp from her coffee, nearly scalding her mouth in the process. She put the mug on the coffee table, her hands shaking when she went to stand up. "I think this was a mistake, I should go..."

Quinn reached up, took her hand and gently pulled her back down. "Don't shut me out, Cady. Just tell me a little bit about yourself."

"You know all there is to know..." Cady began, but Quinn shook his head.

"You've told me the Reader's Digest version of Cady Caldwell. The condensed, what-you-obviously-tell-everyone version." He cautiously reached forward and pushed an errant strand of hair back from Cady's face, keeping his movements slow and deliberately measured. "I want to know about the real Cady Caldwell."

"There's nothing to tell—" Cady started, but Quinn shook his head.

"I've opened up to you; told you things I did in the Middle East that I've never told anyone. Admitted to you that I killed innocent people because I had no choice." He leaned forward, his eyes constantly assessing Cady's reactions. She remained frozen in place, squeezing her eyes shut at the last possible minute before his mouth touched hers. She shivered delicately at the pressure of his lips, the tingle of excitement which zinged across her skin with his touch. Just as swiftly, the pressure was gone, and she opened her eyes to discover Quinn watching her, his dark eyes intense. "Tell me something about yourself, Cady. Tell me something that will help me get to know the woman who's hidden herself under so many layers of protection, nobody truly sees her."

Cady swallowed heavily, a fine tremble setting up in her limbs. Could she do what he asked? Could she reveal things about herself that she'd never told anyone? In all her life, there had never been anyone who wanted to listen to Cady's innermost thoughts, nobody who wanted to learn more about who she was. She wasn't sure she could trust this now – Quinn had asked to learn something about her, but surely, he couldn't mean it?

*That wasn't strictly true though.* Gran wanted to know

her. Sid and Harry had tried to get her to talk for years. Cady always shut them down, not believing anyone would be interested in what she had to say. The idea that she could be of interest to someone – anyone – had been beaten out of her by Jameson over a protracted period, until she believed she was worthless.

She glanced into Quinn's eyes again, found he was watching her patiently, applying no pressure, not forcing her into doing anything. She drew her gaze from him and glanced around the room, discovering both Churchill and Moose lying in front of the fire, snoozing.

She could live her life in fear, or she could take a chance. Looking back at the handsome, kind face of Quinn Garrison... she decided to risk it.

## 19

"I don't know what I can tell you," Cady admitted in a small voice.

Quinn watched her carefully for a minute. He'd been observing while she considered and seen the fear, the abject terror which played across her beautiful features. He'd understood her internal turmoil, and to hear her taking the risk, allowing him in, was something he'd suspected wouldn't happen. "Why don't I ask you some questions, and you can answer them?" he suggested gently. "If you find them too uncomfortable, you can tell me you don't want to answer, and we can move on to something else."

She twisted the material of her sweater between her fingers, rubbing back and forth across it while she considered. "All right," she finally whispered.

Quinn picked up his coffee mug, determined to keep things casual and not make Cady think she was part of an inquisition. "Where were you born?"

"Philadelphia. That's where Mark met Lisa."

Quinn sipped his coffee, then leaned forward to pick up

Cady's cup and offered it to her. "Is that where Sid and Harry were born?"

Cady shook her head, grasping the mug between her hands. "We never stayed anywhere long. Harry was born in Indianapolis, Sid was born in Sioux City."

Quinn lifted an eyebrow. "Wow, you really did get around."

Cady shrugged, sipping her own coffee before she responded. "It wasn't by choice."

"Why's that?" Quinn probed gently. He was aware that Cady might shut down at any minute, put those walls of hers back up and shut him out. He wanted to avoid it, learn as much as he could.

There was a long pause before Cady spoke. "They were both junkies, drugs and alcohol the most important things in their lives. We girls were just an inconvenience for the most part. I don't think they ever intended on having kids. We were accidents."

"I can't imagine what that was like." Coming from a strong, loving and protective family, Quinn found it hard to get his head around a background like Cady's.

She shrugged. "It was all we knew. You get to be resourceful; when they were unconscious, or on a binge, I snuck around and grabbed whatever cash I could get my hands on. I used to hide it away for the times when there wasn't any money for food. I got good at shoplifting, I'd steal what we needed from wherever I could get it."

"You did everything you could to protect your sisters."

Cady nodded, her gaze firmly focused on the flames in the fireplace. "I had to do what I could to let them have a childhood. As much of a childhood as I could manage, under the circumstances."

"They've turned out to be strong, intelligent women.

That's down to you." Quinn fought the urge to take Cady into his arms, hold her close. The depth of his feelings had pulled the rug out from under him, and he acknowledged now that he was falling fast for this woman. He wouldn't be able to keep his distance this time, and he realized he didn't want to. He could see a future for himself with Cady, if only she'd let him in.

"It could have turned out so differently. I think it was pure luck that things worked out as they did. We were fortunate that our neighbor helped us to escape."

"What happened, to make you leave your Dad?"

Cady's gaze clouded over, and she wrapped her arms around herself. Quinn noticed a fine trembling had started up in her limbs. Throwing caution to the wind, he eased closer and wrapped his arms around her, relieved when she allowed the action. And pleasantly surprised to discover how right she felt in his arms. He rubbed one hand soothingly across her forearm, giving her time to settle and tell her story when she was ready.

"After Lisa died... things deteriorated fast. For one thing, he couldn't prostitute her out to earn cash for his drugs and booze."

Quinn couldn't hide his shock. "He did that?"

Cady nodded. "Regularly. He used to bring men home to sleep with her in whatever rat-infested apartment we currently lived in. He prostituted himself as well, but he did that away from the house."

Cady's matter-of-fact tone was chilling, but Quinn forced himself to listen calmly, rubbing her arm and hiding any negative reactions to her words. "And when she died?"

"His income was pretty-much halved. And he had no... outlet for his own... urges."

Beneath his hands, her trembling grew, and Quinn's

temper started to grow along with it. "Did he... was he being inappropriate with you?"

Cady shook her head. "It was heading that way, but we got out before it got any worse."

*Any worse than what?* The thought slammed into Quinn's mind, but he took a deep breath. "What did he do?" He managed to utter the question calmly.

Cady shrugged, looking uncomfortable. "Some inappropriate touching. 'Accidentally' brushing up against me or opening the shower door when I was in there. Fortunately, our neighbor Mr. Kornberg helped us get out, and we ran away and went to live in San Francisco with Mr. Kornberg's sister."

"Which is where you met your husband?" Quinn questioned delicately.

There was a long, heavy pause before Cady responded, and Quinn recognized he'd gotten as much from Cady as he was likely to for now. Her walls were slamming back into place.

"So, tell me. What's your favorite movie?"

Her eyes grew wide. "Um, I..."

Quinn took the pressure off. "I like action movies. Anything with Dwayne Johnson is good, or Vin Diesel. I like the Fast and the Furious movies. Do you have any favorites?"

She thought carefully for a moment or two. "I like Disney movies."

Quinn lifted an eyebrow. "Disney movies?"

Cady nodded. "Lady and the Tramp. Lilo and Stitch. Beauty and the Beast."

He grinned. "Can't say that I've seen any of them," he admitted with a smile. "But perhaps we could find a DVD and watch one of them one night."

Cady glanced up, her beautiful blue eyes troubled. "Oh, no, you don't need to watch them, we'll watch something you'd like..."

Quinn took another risk and lowered his mouth to Cady's, brushing his lips over hers. "Cady, there's nothin' I'd like better than to watch something of your choosing with you. I know you haven't had much chance to do things you like in the past and I'm planning on rectifying that situation."

Her eyes were round, and for long seconds she stared up at him, her amazement visible. "You... you would do that? For me?" she questioned.

Quinn nodded, aware that something was happening between them, some change he couldn't explain, but it seemed as if a physical barrier had collapsed between them. For a moment, looking down into Cady's eyes, he could see past the fears, past the anxieties, and caught a glimmer of the real woman beneath it all.

And she was beautiful.

He was further surprised when Cady lifted her hand tentatively, using a fingertip to trace down the side of his cheek, his jaw; her cornflower blue eyes gazing up at him and as he watched, he could almost distinguish the layers of fear and hurt peeling away, layer by layer, as she gathered her confidence. He held his breath when she leaned towards him, in tiny increments of space, keeping her gaze focused on his. Even without touching her, he could imagine how hard her heart was hammering. Still he stayed motionless, waiting patiently, though all he wanted to do was scoop her into his arms and wrap her in a protective embrace, never let her go. But he knew that this time, Cady needed to make this move herself. She was trying hard to open up with him, and he'd be damned if he'd do anything to stop that from happening, no matter how hard it was to sit still and let her make the moves.

Her lips found his, a whisper-like brush of her mouth against his own, and he clenched his hands into fists, fighting against a natural yearning to scoop her into his arms, onto his lap and ravish her the way he wanted. She leaned back infinitesimally, grounding herself again, opening her eyes and looking up into his.

"That was nice, Cady," he whispered softly. "I'd like it if you did it again."

The tiniest glimmer of a smile crossed her lips, and he could see the confidence boost in her eyes before she closed them and leaned forward again. She rested her hands against his chest and pressed her lips to his, the pressure firmer and longer lasting this time. Quinn allowed her to set the pace, her little hands moving restlessly against his chest as she deepened the kiss, experimented a little with opening her mouth against his, her tongue running over the seam of his lips seeking entrance. He did as she wanted, opening his mouth to allow her exploration, but holding back on taking the lead. As much as he wanted to, as much as he liked being in control, in this case it would be detrimental to Cady's confidence, and he wasn't going to destroy the little self-assurance she was managing to build up.

When she leaned back this time, he could see in her expression that she'd reached the end of her tether. While she might have made great inroads and he thought he'd given her the ability to start believing in herself, he knew from the worry in her eyes that she'd reached her limits. He offered her a warm smile, and stood up, taking her hand in his.

"That was real nice, Cady darlin', but I can see that you've had enough for tonight. Let me take you home."

He was pleased when he saw relief blossom in Cady's eyes, and quietly proud of the fact that he was beginning to get a handle on this beautiful girl. She was one gorgeous filly and he was now quite determined to keep her in his life, hopefully forever.

He just had to convince her of how good they could be together.

## 20

Cady balanced on a stepladder behind the store counter, a box of brass tacks in one hand, studying the diagram stuck to the wall. She'd decided against the cost of getting signs made for inside the store, seeking out ideas she could do instead. This concept with brass tacks appealed, so she'd printed the store's name in a font she liked and was using the printout as a guide to recreate the name on the wall.

"You be careful up there," Gran warned. "The last thing we need is you breaking your neck, two days before the grand opening."

"I'm fine, Gran." Cady pushed another couple of tacks into the wall, before she grabbed the hammer hooked in the pocket of her dungarees to drive them firmly into the wood.

Cady glanced around the store with no small amount of satisfaction. It was charming and quaint, and she experienced a deep sense of fulfilment knowing it was all hers, the first thing she'd ever had to call her own. To the right of the front doors, Walt had built display racks into the window, where some of Cady's cakes would be visible from the sidewalk outside along with the fresh bread and cakes Paulette would bake. On the opposite side, Gran was adding final touches to four bistro tables and chairs, somewhere for customers to sit and enjoy a cake or coffee when they visited town. They'd been for sale at a junk store in Billings, and Cady had sanded them back, treated rust and painted them glossy black. Gran had spread an embroidered tablecloth over each one, and now they held menu cards and condiments ready for opening day.

Paulette was busy out back – Cady had gone with her gut instincts and accepted Gran's endorsement, and Paulette had proven to be an excellent baker. Not only did she create cakes in a multitude of varieties for Cady's decorating business, but she'd also proven a dab hand at bread and pastries. The glass fronted display counter would be filled on Saturday with a range of mouthwatering options, and it was all down to Paulette's skills.

The doorbell rang, and Cady twisted on the stepladder to see who it was. With opening only two days away, they'd had no end of interested townsfolk peeking through the windows, but Gran warned everyone they weren't allowed in until Saturday.

A man stood in the doorway, smiling brightly as he surveyed the store. "Well, I'll be damned. Mom, this is wonderful." He glanced up at the stepladder, his gaze meeting Cady's. "And this must be my eldest niece."

Her eyes widened, and she stared at Uncle David. Much to her relief, she couldn't see any resemblance. Mark had had dark hair, pock-marked olive skin and a slight build, Uncle David was more solidly built and had Meredith's fair complexion and blue eyes. A woman stood beside him, wearing a bulky red coat, her neck swallowed up beneath layers of soft white woolen scarf. A matching knitted cap was pulled down over her dark brown hair and red gloves kept her hands warm.

Meredith hurried across and wrapped the man in a welcoming hug. "David! You said you wouldn't get here until Saturday! Come in, come in, it's just bitter outside."

"Thanks, Mom." David pulled off his leather gloves, perusing the store with intelligent eyes. He dropped the gloves onto the counter and began to unbutton his heavy coat. "Thought we'd come a couple of days early, see if we could lend a hand."

Cady climbed down the stepladder, taking the box of brass tacks from the pocket of her dungarees and placing them on the counter beside the cash register. With a second, longer inspection, she established Uncle David didn't look like Mark at all. She could see some of Gran's features, and his eyes were kind and warm when he studied her briefly before turning back to Meredith. "It looks amazing."

Gran completed the introductions. "David, this is Cady. Cady, this is your Uncle David, and this here is his wife, Victoria."

Victoria stepped forward, smiling affectionately. Cady suspected she'd try and draw her into a hug, an exercise which always made Cady uncomfortable, but it seemed Victoria and David had been forewarned of her reticence and merely offered a brief handshake. "Now tell us, what can we do to help?" Victoria asked. She surveyed the interior of Tokens, carefully assessing, and her nod of approval warmed Cady's heart. "This looks wonderful. You all have done a fantastic job."

Meredith nodded, crossing her arms over her chest, satisfaction visible in her eyes. "It certainly is looking good. And I can hardly believe we've only got a couple of days 'til opening! I honestly think the entire town is going to show up at one point or another on Saturday. I've heard from some ranches as far away as Pickens Ridge, who intend on coming along."

David grinned. "That's great, Mom."

Standing to one side, Cady observed as David and Victoria spoke with Gran, her heart still pounding after their sudden entrance. She suspected Meredith was genuinely surprised by their arrival, although Cady wouldn't put it past Gran to orchestrate an early appearance and keep Cady from stressing.

He certainly didn't seem like his older brother; wearing corduroy trousers and a thick Aran sweater in woodsy tones, David was clean-shaven, his skin clear, his hair neatly trimmed. Gran had told her he was a professor at Carleton College in Northfield, Minnesota and looking at him now, Cady thought he looked the archetypal professor.

She experienced a pang of regret and sighed, wondering how different life might have been if Mark had taken a different path. It was a useless question to ask, she knew; the past was gone and couldn't be relived, but she still wasted a moment or two, daydreaming about a father who'd done something positive in life, loved his daughters the way he should.

"Can I help with your sign, Cady?"

David's voice drew her back from her thoughts and she turned to face him. "Um..." Her initial instinct was to say no, to keep away from this man who shared a bloodline with Mark – but seeing his open, friendly expression, she took the risk. "Thank you, I'd appreciate it."

THE DELICIOUS SMELL of roast beef worked its way into Cady's nose. Although the aroma was amazing, her stomach was alternately twisting into knots or feeling like someone had released a bag full of marbles in her gut. She stood by the window in the living room, the position she'd maintained for the past two hours, watching the snow fall steadily outside. Voices from the kitchen reached her ears, where Gran, David and Victoria were preparing supper, but all Cady could focus on was the snow.

This was a disaster. Snow had fallen steadily for five hours, and if it didn't stop soon, she suspected tomorrow's opening would get cancelled. According to the weather report, so much snow had fallen it would be four feet deep by morning – how would anyone get into town? Walt assured her the town had a snow plough, but she couldn't imagine how they'd clear enough streets to make the opening viable.

Gran, bless her, was still positive everything would be fine, but watching the snow falling, along with darkness, Cady suspected it was a disaster.

"Cady? Come on through, honey. David's just about to carve."

Pulling the curtains closed, she shut out the terrible weather, telling herself to stop fretting. What would be, would be. Nothing she could do would change the outcome.

"Still snowing, honey?" Meredith questioned when she walked into the kitchen.

"Yep."

Victoria handed Cady a glass of red wine, offering her a sunny smile. In the few days since their arrival, she'd grown relaxed in David's company and liked Victoria, who was just a few years older than Cady. "Don't worry, Cady. If there's one thing I've discovered since I married my own

Montana man, it's that the locals don't let a little thing like snow stop them from doing stuff."

"I think it's more than a little thing," Cady confessed, watching David carve the roast beef.

"Unless we get a full-out blizzard, they'll come. You mark my words," Gran said. She placed a platter of roast potatoes and another of pumpkin on the table, then added a bowl of collard greens. "And even if we do get a full-out blizzard, most everyone will still come."

"I feel sorry for Paulette," Cady said glumly. "She's worked so hard, preparing for tomorrow. I'd hate to see her efforts go to nothing."

"It won't be to nothing," Gran protested – in Cady's opinion, still blinded to the possibility of anything but success. "It's gonna be fine, I promise."

Cady didn't respond, simply sipping her wine and flopping onto a chair. Gran was overly-optimistic – who in their right mind would come out in weather like this, just to see a bakery opening?

Meredith settled onto the seat beside Cady and set her own wineglass on the table. "You've been antsy all day, honey. I'm sure it's not just the weather, is it?" She patted Cady's hand. "It's nerve-wracking, I know; I'm anxious that it go well myself. But I suspect it's something more that's bothering you."

Cady inhaled heavily and leaned forward to snatch a bread roll from the basket Victoria put on the table. "I wish Sid and Harry were here."

Meredith's face creased into sympathy. "I do too. But Sid's got a terrible cold, and an ear infection stopped her from flying, and Harry and Scott couldn't take vacation days and still get here for Christmas. You know they were desperate to be here."

"I know," Cady agreed. She tore open the bread roll, slathering it with butter. "And I know they've gone out of their way to visit as much as they could..." Cady's voice trailed off. She wasn't sure what was bothering her so much. Something didn't feel right; there was a sense of disquiet in her chest which was pressing on her constantly. She hoped it would disappear after tomorrow's opening, because she was finding it distinctly uncomfortable.

"You just wait and see, Cady, it's all going to work out just fine," David said. He placed a heaping serve of roast beef onto a plate and handed it to her.

Cady offered him a weak smile and tucked into her supper. She could only hope they were right.

***

CADY AND VICTORIA were cleaning up after supper when a knock came at the front door.

"I'll get it!" Gran called from the living room.

"I wonder who that is?" Victoria questioned, handing Cady a plate to be stacked in the dishwasher.

"At this time of night? No doubt it's Sheriff Davis – dropping by in the hopes of scoring leftover dessert... or a kiss from Gran."

Victoria's eyes grew round, and she grinned. "Seriously? Has George finally made a move?"

Cady chuckled. "Not so much a move; but a subtle forward maneuver in his tactical plan to date Gran. Honestly, they're adorable. I think they both care about one another, very much, but they're behaving like kids who've never dated before."

"In George's case, that could be true," Victoria mused. "David says George has had a thing for Meredith for decades, starting way back when they were at school together. That's why he's never married."

Cady arched an eyebrow, one ear on the mumble of voices from the front door. "Surely he's dated?"

Victoria shrugged. "I'm not sure. I imagine so, but I don't think he was ever going to settle for anyone else. Word is, he's loved Meredith for years now."

Their conversation ended when Meredith strolled into the kitchen, closely followed, not by George – but by Quinn.

"You've got a visitor, Cady," Gran announced with a big smile curving her lips. The delight in her eyes was tangible, and Cady squirmed uncomfortably. Churchill bounded up from his mat by the back door and bounced across to Quinn, brushing against his denim-clad leg until Quinn squatted down and scratched his ears.

"Um, hi," Cady said. She was flustered, she hadn't been expecting a visit from Quinn, and certainly not tonight, with the opening tomorrow. Besides, it was snowing buckets outside – what had possessed him to come out on a night like this?

Quinn's eyes gleamed, and he got up onto his feet, offering Cady a warm smile. "Meredith tells me you've finished up supper. I wondered if you'd like to come out with me for a while."

Cady glanced at the kitchen window; snowflakes were clearly visible, flurrying across the glass. "In this?"

Quinn shrugged his broad shoulders, drawing Cady's attention to the thick lambskin jacket he wore. "Got somethin' special planned."

"Go and get rugged up honey," Gran urged. "It's mighty chilly out there, but you're going to love it."

"I'm not sure..." Cady started, but Quinn shook his head.

"C'mon, Cady. I bet you're worrying yourself to death about the opening tomorrow. Instead of sitting here fretting about it, I think we should go take your mind off it for a little while."

Cady stared at him, wondering how he could read her so well. They'd barely spent any time together, yet Quinn instinctively knew she would be fretting over the opening. How did he do that?

By the time she hurried back downstairs, Quinn stood by the front door, and he surveyed her clothes and nodded his approval.

"Can I take Churchill?" she questioned.

Quinn shook his head, a tiny smile playing across his lips. "Not tonight."

"Where are we going?" Cady demanded when she reached the bottom of the stairs.

"You'll see." Quinn held open the door and Cady stepped out, coming to abrupt halt on the porch.

At the end of the front walk, past the gate, a couple of horses stood harnessed to a beautifully carved wooden sleigh. The sleigh was painted red, the carved edges picked out in highlights of gold and green. "Is this yours?" Cady breathed. It was so pretty, it reminded Cady of scenes she'd seen on holiday cards.

"Horses are mine. The sleigh I borrowed from Jimmy Bellefleur. We do have a sleigh out on the ranch, but the weather wasn't conducive to getting it into town tonight." Quinn took Cady's hand, leading her down the snowy walk to the gate.

"Isn't it too cold for the horses?" Cady fretted, reaching

up to touch the grey horse's neck. He snickered and bobbed his head up and down, before rubbing his nose against Cady's arm, seeking more attention. Beside him, a chocolate brown mare snorted, clearly seeking some attention of her own.

"They'll be fine. Besides, this is just a little bit of snow," Quinn reassured her. He held out his hand, offering Cady a warm smile. "Your carriage awaits."

Cady climbed onto the sleigh, and once she was settled, Quinn took a minute to cover her legs in a thick quilt, his protectiveness bringing a lump to Cady's throat. When he was satisfied, he hurried around the back of the sleigh, hauled himself up beside her and casually threw the other end of the quilt over his own legs. The sleigh was narrow, and Cady's eyes widened when Quinn's denim-clad thigh settled against hers. Initially uncomfortable, it didn't take long before she decided she liked the sensation and relaxed.

Quinn clicked his tongue and gave the reins a gentle flick, and the two horses obediently pulled away, tossing their heads up and down as Quinn guided them down the street.

"What are their names?"

"The grey is Cutler; the brown mare is Dixie."

"Do they live on your ranch?"

Quinn shook his head. "I keep them at Mom and Dad's. I'm over there every day anyway, so I figure it's easier." He glanced down at Cady, offered her a sly smile. "Besides, Dad's paying to feed them."

Cady giggled, but her smile faded. "Are you sure they're okay out here? I didn't walk Churchill today because it was too cold."

Quinn lifted an eyebrow. "For that walking fluffball? I'd be more worried about you, than Churchill." Quinn guided the horses into a left turn, leaving Gran's street and entering the next one. "Bet he was unimpressed."

Cady nodded. "He made his unhappiness clear."

Quinn chuckled. "I'm not surprised; he's a mighty clever dog."

Quinn turned again onto Main Street, and Cady was astonished to see other people out in the snow. Some were sledding, and a large group were conducting a rousing snowball fight in the parking lot at Grizzlies. Still others were sliding down a makeshift hill, which had been fashioned out of drifts of snow and as they passed, Cady saw some teenagers sliding down the rise on makeshift sleighs fashioned from cardboard. "I'm surprised so many people are out," she admitted.

"Nobody in Garrison lets a little snowfall get in the way of a good time on a Friday night," Quinn remarked.

They passed the bakery, and Cady experienced a tingle of excitement, quickly swamped by a huge battalion of butterflies which swatted mercilessly at her insides. Quinn noticed and offered her an encouraging smile. "Nervous?"

"Terrified," Cady admitted. Things had happened in such a rush, and now, the night before opening, she'd been left with nothing to do except worry. Right now, the bakery was in darkness, but Paulette would arrive around 4am to get the bread started. Cady intended on being there soon afterwards, and she suffered another frisson of terror over whether this would work out. Could she really run a business? Would the residents of Garrison embrace a bakery? Cady glanced skyward when they passed a street light, watched snow flurry and swirl. Would the snowfall stop in time?

Quinn pulled back on the reins when they reached the end of the shopping precinct, and conducted a neat maneuver, turning the sleigh to head back towards Gran's. Once the horses were facing in the opposite direction, he drew them to a gentle halt and turned towards Cady. By the light of a street lamp, she could make out his features, and saw the desire flare in his eyes when he looked at her. "Cady, the bakery is going to be a success. You've worked hard, and you deserve to have something good."

"I hope so," Cady admitted.

"I know so," Quinn responded firmly. He glanced around the street before returning his attention to her. "Looks like we're alone. I'm wonderin' if I might steal a kiss before we head back?"

Cady smiled, and those anxious butterflies suddenly plunged to a lower part of her anatomy. "I'd like that," she said.

Quinn wrapped an arm around her shoulders and dropping the reins into his lap, lifted his hand to Cady's cheek, brushing across her skin with his glove-covered fingers. "Damn weather," he murmured. "I'd much prefer to be touching skin to skin with you, darlin'." He lowered his head, brushing his lips across Cady's once... twice... then a third time before he gently cradled her face between his gloved hands and kissed her more thoroughly.

Cady inhaled sharply when Quinn deepened the kiss, inhaling the scent of pine, musk and what she was coming to recognize as being uniquely Quinn Garrison. It was a heady aroma, one that left her feeling off kilter, giddy with some emotion she wasn't quite ready to acknowledge.

Somewhere off to their left car doors slammed before a sharp whistle pierced the air, and Quinn drew away. She could feel his heart slamming against his ribs – somehow, during that incredible kiss, she'd ended up working her hands under his thick jacket to rest them against his chest.

Quinn cursed under his breath and offered her a wry smile. "Small towns. Never any privacy."

He took up the reins again, and with a gentle flick Cutler and Dixie started walking back along Main Street.

Cady had to admit she'd been disappointed when the kiss ended, but as she relived those few minutes, she couldn't stop a tremor which travelled along her spine. Annoyed with herself, Cady mentally shook the trepidation away. Everyone else expected the opening to go well, so why shouldn't she?

## 21

"I'll be damned." Quinn slowed when he hit Main Street, joining the line of pickups, trucks and four by fours inching their way into the center of town. Flurries of snow still buffeted the windshield, but it seemed the worst of the storm was over, and the weather had chosen to cooperate for Cady and Meredith's big day. Big drifts had been pushed away from the road, no doubt they'd needed the snow plough out early to prepare.

Travelling at a snail's pace, Quinn watched the almost carnival-like atmosphere outside the bakery. People were lined up in an orderly fashion along the sidewalk and he caught sight of Meredith and Paulette, offering samples from big trays of cupcakes. When he got parallel to the bakery, he discovered why they were serving people outside – inside the little store it was wall-to-wall people. Quinn grinned. He'd been certain things would go well, but this surpassed his expectations. Luanne squeezed out through the bakery door carrying a tray of coffee and started handing out cups to the people waiting outside.

Inching another few feet, he reached his brother – obviously Kane had gotten called in to manage traffic. He pulled up beside him and rolled down the window. "Good turnout."

Kane grinned. "Hopefully this'll put Cady's worries to rest. Seems like everyone from here to Billings've turned up." Kane frowned at a couple of teenage boys who were weaving and dodging through the slow-moving traffic and he held up a finger, waving it from side to side at them. "You know better than that, Billy."

"Aw jeez, Kane, traffic's going so slow, we couldn't possibly get hit! And besides, if we don't hurry, Ms. Cady's gonna run out of cakes."

Quinn grinned when Kane shook his head. "Back to the crossing, Billy. And I have it on good authority that there's plenty of cakes and other goodies to go around." Watching them for a moment to confirm they'd done as they were told, Kane peered in through the window at Quinn. "We've got everyone parking on the side streets; turn left into Dayler and you'll find a space. No doubt you're bustin' a gut to get in there and see your girl."

"She's not my girl yet," Quinn muttered as he inched along the street and took the turn Kane recommended.

Striding back towards the bakery, Quinn surveyed the long line and contemplated his options. He'd love to line jump, see Cady and maybe help out, but judging by the lengthy line, stretched all the way back to Polson Street, he suspected he'd get lynched if he tried. With a sigh, he strode down the sidewalk and took his position at the end.

Surprisingly, the wait didn't seem to take as long as he'd expected, and when he reached the bakery, he discovered why, as his Mom welcomed him to Tokens with a twinkle in her eye. She warned him there was a fifteen-minute limit before he'd be asked to exit through the side door. "When

Cady saw the crowds queuing up, she and Meredith devised this plan to ensure folks didn't wait too long in the cold."

Stepping inside, he inhaled the spectacular blend of spices, coffee and fresh-baked bread which permeated the store. It all looked amazing. He glanced up at the wall behind the counter, impressed by the sign Cady told him about. It was unique, something completely different and thinking about it, he shouldn't be surprised – Cady was as different as night was from day, and he suspected that's what he loved about her.

*Wait.* The concept of loving Cady had come out of the blue, but even as he considered it, he had to admit the truth. He'd fallen fast and hard for the beautiful little free-spirit, and he wanted her in his life on a permanent basis...

"Quinn!"

He turned to find Cady approaching, a dazzling smile on her lips and a tray of baked goods in her hands. She took his breath away, wearing a red checked shirt which showed a little bit of cleavage, and her red hair was curled up and pulled back with bobby pins. She leaned forward and offered him a kiss on the cheek, and he didn't push for anything more – certain she wouldn't appreciate it in front of half the town. "Hey, Cady. Told you the snow wouldn't stop anyone coming out."

She grinned; the smile the biggest and widest he'd ever seen from her. He'd always suspected she was holding herself in check, and seeing that glorious smile, he knew he'd been right. He mentally reminded himself to make her smile like that again... and often. "Would you like to try a cake? These are Mocha Toffee Fudge Cupcakes, and the ones on the right are Spiced Apple Pie Cupcakes with Caramel Buttercream."

Quinn rolled his eyes. "You're making me choose? How can a man make a choice between those two?" He eyed the cakes; both looked wonderful and his mouth watered.

Cady laughed – another sound Quinn suspected he'd like to hear often – and lifted the tray towards him. "Go on, grab one of each. I won't tell."

He did as she'd said and ignored the grumbles from some of the other visitors in the store. In a small town like Garrison nothing was private, and he suspected they would be the main topic of discussion in every home later today. And he realized he didn't give a damn.

He bit into the apple cupcake and wanted to moan his appreciation. It was soft and fluffy, the apple revealing a hint of cinnamon and the caramel buttercream was decadently rich and smooth. He suspected he'd be spending a lot of time in town in the future.

"Mmmm, delicious," he muttered past a mouthful.

Cady beamed under the praise. "I'd better keep circulating," she said.

"Will I see you tonight? We could grab a drink at Grizzlies."

He noticed the slightest hesitation before she responded, her gaze skimming across the nearby crowd, who no doubt shamelessly eavesdropped. "Yes. I'd like that."

Given the way she'd evaluated the crowds the agreement surprised Quinn, but he didn't give her an opportunity to change her mind. "Great. Pick you up about seven?"

She nodded hesitantly, then smiled. "Yes, okay then."

Quinn watched her disappear into the throng of visitors, her magnificent red mane vanishing from view. Turning, his attention was taken by the displays, and he edged through the crowd to view them.

Her talent was unbelievable; even knowing nothing of the craft he realized how clever Cady was. The window display held eight different cakes, each one beautifully designed and decorated. He was amused by one which was decorated in white and pink. On closer inspection, he figured out it was shaped like a pregnant woman's belly and decorated with a variety of baby items fashioned out of icing, the detail incredible. A second cake was decorated for a little girl's birthday, complete with Minnie Mouse sculpted in icing on the top, one layer covered in polka dots, another layer covered in mouse ears. Another one was obviously made for a wedding, one half decorated traditionally with lots of white icing, but the other half looked as if it had been made from Lego bricks, complete with a Lego Batman climbing up the tiers. Quinn had never seen anything quite like it, and it made the cake he and Julia had at their own wedding seem ordinary.

Before he could look at the other cakes, or more importantly, try and snatch another cupcake, he heard Luanne's voice. "Ladies and gentlemen, that's your visit to Tokens at an end; feel free to join the back of the line if you'd like a second chance to tour the bakery." Her tone brooked no argument, but she grinned broadly. "If not, don't forget Grizzlies will open in an hour or so. But I've tasted Cady's cakes and if I was you, I'd be lining up for another tasting."

A cheer erupted from the people in the store, and they cheerfully exited through the side door, allowing the next group to enter.

Quinn slipped out through the door and immediately strode along Main Street to reach the end of the line. Given the deliciousness of those cupcakes, he'd happily spend the rest of the day doing the exact same thing.

QUINN HELD THE DOOR TO GRIZZLIES' open and Cady slipped inside. The bar was, unsurprisingly, filled with people on Saturday night, and Cady found she was subject to plenty of attention after the bakery's successful opening. Quinn took on the role of protector, steering her towards the bar, using the barest trace of pressure against the small of her back and fielding questions and compliments from the bar patrons.

Luanne was working the bar, her solid frame encased in the standard Grizzlies' uniform of t-shirt and blue jeans. "Here she is!" Luanne patted her expansive belly. "I swear, Cady, if I'd eaten one more of those cakes, I would have exploded! I'm gonna want a Caffè Americano and one of them blueberry chiffon cupcakes with vanilla buttercream every single morning the bakery's open, y'hear?"

Cady smiled and slipped onto a barstool, which another patron freed up after receiving a pointed glance from Quinn. "I'm so thrilled you like them."

"Like 'em? Honey, I loved them! I'm already carrying extra pounds; and with that new bakery of yours, I'm gonna be heading towards a diabetic coma before too long."

Cady shook her head. "Oh, Luanne, I hope not! That wouldn't be good for Tokens at all!" Quinn was standing protectively behind her, and she had to admit she liked his presence, felt secure knowing he was there. When he lifted his hands and placed them on her shoulders, she wanted to twist her head to the side and rub up against his skin like a kitten, relishing the sense of security he created.

"What will you fine folks be having?" Luanne questioned.

"I'll have a beer," Quinn said. "Cady? What would you like?"

"A white wine, please."

Luanne served their drinks and then ambled down to the far end of the bar to serve other patrons.

Quinn dropped his hands from Cady's shoulders, leaving her feeling momentarily bereft. He sipped his beer, then placed the longneck down on the bar and leisurely twisted Cady's stool so she faced him.

The tempo of Cady's heart increased when Quinn stared down at her, his gaze intense. When he didn't say anything, she started to squirm a little.

Her discomfort pushed Quinn into action, and he leaned over so he could speak against her ear. "I wanna get a little closer, darlin'. Is that okay with you?"

Cady considered the request for a moment before she responded; she wasn't sure what Quinn was suggesting – but she was grateful for the fact that he wasn't just forcing her into doing what he wanted. She nodded, the motion hesitant.

Quinn stepped forward until his thighs were pressed up against her denim-clad knees. Cady struggled with her anxieties, which were a direct contrast to the way his proximity made other parts of her feel. The heat of his body penetrated her clothing, and she twisted to pick up her wineglass, taking a nervous sip.

She swallowed a second sip – more of a gulp – when Quinn placed his hands on her thighs and using gentle pressure, pried her legs apart. The movement was calculated, completed in careful increments, reassuring Cady that if she put up any resistance, if she showed the slightest signs of discomfort, he would stop. And she knew instinctively, deep in her heart, if she showed the slightest panic Quinn would back off.

The sounds of the crowded bar receded into the distance as she focused on Quinn. It came as a revelation to find she didn't want him to stop. Didn't fear him.

Quinn stepped forward cautiously, his eyes focused on Cady's and she realized he was gauging her reactions. He slipped between her legs, the heat of his thighs searing against hers, and she idly considered the fact that she'd never experienced this sensation before. When he was as close as he could get and remain decent, he leisurely raised his arms and rested them around Cady's neck, leaning down to press a gentle kiss on the top of her head.

When he straightened, she looked up into his face and smiled. Quinn smiled back, lowering his mouth to press a kiss against hers. She fleetingly tasted beer before he straightened, and Cady let her instincts take over, wrapping her arms around Quinn's waist. The texture of his shirt was soft beneath her fingers and hard muscle in his back flexed and stretched beneath her palms.

Quinn lifted an eyebrow, then his lips curled in a lazy smile. "I'm likin' that, Cady Caldwell."

People ebbed and flowed around them, the bar sometimes five deep, and many wanted to congratulate Cady on the opening of Tokens. She was grateful for their kind words, but for the most part she and Quinn were engrossed in one another, and that was the way she wanted it. Quinn Garrison was becoming an addiction, and she was blossoming under his gentle attention.

Someone started a new song playing on the jukebox, a ballad, and Quinn drained his beer before he caught her eye. "Wanna dance?"

She hesitated, questioning how much more attention

she wanted to garner from the Garrison townsfolk. Allowing this to continue, adding to the hotbed of gossip which would no doubt billow through the streets of Garrison tomorrow might not be wise.

She decided she didn't care. People were going to talk no matter what, and she and Quinn had given them plenty of ammunition tonight. What difference would a little dancing make? "Okay."

Quinn grinned, stepping out from between her legs and holding out his hand. Cady took it and he led her out onto the small dance floor, already packed with other couples. He managed to segue into a small opening and held out his arms, allowing Cady to move into his space in her own time. She did so willingly, with no hesitation and Quinn wrapped his arm around her waist.

They started to dance, their movements stilted by the crowded floorspace, but somehow it made the dance more intimate, more special. For the second time that evening; first up at the bar, and now here on the dance floor, Cady suspected if she looked into Quinn's eyes, it would seem as if they were the only two people in the room. He had a way of making her believe she was the most important woman in the world, that nothing else mattered. It was a deeply unsettling sensation, one she wasn't certain she could trust. There'd been a time when Jameson had made her feel this way – admittedly, not to the extent Quinn did – but he'd promised her the world and when she'd given him her trust, he'd betrayed it. A shiver of apprehension snaked up her spine.

"I suspected you were going to say no," Quinn spoke softly against her ear. "You were thinking hard."

"I nearly did," Cady admitted.

"You don't like dancing?"

"I wondered how much more attention I wanted tonight."

Quinn drew her against him, so that her chest was pressed against his, not a sheet of paper's thickness between them. Cady followed her instincts again, forcing back her fears and resting her face against his hard chest. The steady pounding of his heart was detectable beneath her left cheek, and she wished the bar was quieter, so she could hear it. "I think we're already beyond the point of no return," he stated quietly. "Not much else we could do to get more attention. They'll already be taking bets on when we're getting married."

Shocked, Cady pulled away from Quinn and only relaxed incrementally when she saw amusement twinkling in his eyes. "They'd be hedging bets that aren't going to pan out," she announced. "I'm not getting married again, and you said the same thing."

Quinn's smile was enigmatic. "True. But sometimes, circumstances change and——"

"Well, well. Look what we have here. My ex-husband and his weird new girlfriend."

Cady pulled away from Quinn, but he didn't let her move far, keeping a protective hand against her back. "Julia, you're drunk."

Julia was holding onto Earl's arm and judging by the way she wobbled on her stilettos, Quinn was right – she was three sheets to the wind. "That's your problem, Quinn – that's *always* been your problem. You're a bleeding heart." Julie surveyed Cady's fifties-style clothing and sneered. "And you're a hopeless freak. I've heard all about you, how you were too weak to stand up to your husband. How he beat the shit out of your useless ass."

Quinn bristled angrily, and he squeezed Cady a little

tighter, as though he could save her from hearing any more with his proximity. "Julia! Shut the fuck up."

Julia refused to be shut down and she brushed her hair back from her face, spilling some of her drink in the process. The jukebox had shut down, and Cady was agonizingly aware of the fact that everyone in the bar was now listening. "Poor little Cady Caldwell. Gets smacked around by her husband, though frankly, I would have probably put up with it, because wasn't he loaded? Isn't Jameson Le Batelier like a really successful chef who makes a fortune from his swanky restaurants?"

Earl tugged on Julia's arm, and Cady suspected that even he thought Julia had gone too far. Julia wasn't going to be dissuaded and she yanked away from his hold, stumbling forward. Quinn drew Cady closer, wrapping his arms around her protectively.

"I wish someone would give me a little store. I wish this pissant town would get together and hold a huge pity party for me and fix all my shit up. I've lived in this piece of crap town all my life. Guess that sort of thing only happens when yourDaddy owns some property and your Grandma just gives it to you because she thinks your life's such a freaking tragedy..."

Julia continued with her drunken tirade, but all Cady focused on were those last few words, and she clapped her hands to her mouth, stunned by the disclosure. She didn't hear anything else.

*Tokens had belonged to Mark?*

## 22

"Are you sure you're okay?" Quinn asked when he stopped outside Meredith's. Cady had been silent from the minute she'd turned tail and headed for the exit at Grizzlies, and Quinn rushed to follow her, dropping a filthy stare on his ex-wife in the process. He'd had no idea the building belonged to Mark Caldwell; and he had no clue how Julia did. No matter how she'd found out, the fact was Meredith had chosen to keep the news from Cady, and judging by her pale face and big blue eyes, there was a good damn reason for Meredith's reticence. But Quinn didn't want to let Cady just up and hurry into the house without trying to figure out her state of mind. He was worried.

Cady was staring at the house, her reflection visible in the window and he watched her slowly turn to face him, offering him a tremulous smile. "I'm fine."

Quinn recognized it as being the 'fine' that someone offered when they really weren't. He reached out to brush a tendril of scarlet hair back from her cheek. "Darlin', you're Grandmamma probably didn't want to upset you..."

"I know."

"It doesn't make any difference, Cady." He started again, desperate to get her talking. "Your Dad is long gone. The building is just a building. I doubt he ever stepped foot in it."

Cady stayed quiet, refocusing her attention on the window. The lights were on in the living room, and the front porch light was on, making the snowy ground around the house glisten. George's Sierra was parked on verge in front of them, the Sheriff no doubt enjoying another date with Meredith.

"What are you planning to do?" Quinn asked. He dreaded the answer.

Cady didn't respond, simply hugged her arms around herself and Quinn caught the fine shudder which rippled through her limbs.

A sense of desperation rose in his chest. She was going to run, he could practically guarantee it. Thrown by this news about Tokens, she was uncertain, unhappy; and the sense of hopelessness was a tangible barrier growing between them. She was going to run, and Quinn had to do something to stop her. "Darlin', this isn't a big deal."

Cady turned on him. "It is to me! For the first time in my life, I had something that was mine, and now... now I learn that the man I hated my entire life is the only reason I had it! There's nothing here for me without Tokens!"

She was being unreasonable, and Quinn's temper rose along with his frustration. "Cady, you're being ridiculous! This isn't a big deal! Your father's dead; has been dead for years. Why shouldn't you get something out of all the heartache he caused? For Christ's sake, it's just a building, just wood and nails!"

She visibly shrank in on herself, and Quinn cursed himself six ways to Sunday, knowing he'd undone virtually all the progress he'd made so far. She was fragile, beaten down, and he'd just beaten her down some more. Damn it all to hell!

Cady reached for the door handle and shoved the door open, and Quinn further damned himself when he reached across and clutched her upper arm. His grip wasn't harsh, but there was fear in Cady's eyes when she turned back to him... and the terror discernible in her body language made him sick to his stomach. He quickly released his hold, apologizing hurriedly. "Cady, I'm sorry, I didn't mean—"

She shook her head, her eyes round, her face filled with panic. "Goodnight, Quinn."

She leaped down from the seat and hurried up the front walk to the gate, shoving it open and running through the snow to the porch. He watched her twist the key in the lock and rush inside. She didn't look back.

Quinn knew he'd blown it, but right now, there was nothing he could do to fix the situation. Cady was so stressed, she wasn't going to listen to reason tonight.

Still mentally berating himself, Quinn turned the key in the ignition and slowly drove away.

---

Hop Skipton shouted his goodnights to Luanne before he stepped out through the doorway at Grizzlies, yanking his sheepskin collar a little more securely around his ears. It was mighty cold tonight, and the chilly wind lashed across his exposed skin on the walk to his pickup. It had been a good night, all told, except for that catfight between Julia Henderson and little Cady Caldwell. He'd given Julia a piece of his mind, which seemed to be happening on a regular basis. She'd never been the right woman for Quinn, and her recent behavior had only reinforced that opinion in Hop's mind. Luanne threw Julia and Earl out after what she'd done; and Hop hoped that one of these days, Julia would earn herself a permanent eviction. Couldn't happen to a nicer person. Julia was a piece of work; there was no doubt about it.

And after such a great day with the bakery opening and all, it was disappointing to think things had been spoiled by Julia's bad attitude. Hop had taken a liking to Cady, and he'd enjoyed a cake or two at today's tasting. He was unlocking the door of his pickup when he heard a vehicle driving along Main Street behind him. He'd yanked open the door and was about to climb in when the sound of smashing glass caught his attention.

Skip scrutinized Grizzlies, trying to establish if that was where the sound of breaking glass had come from. Nothing out of the ordinary was discernible at the bar, and he watched a couple stumble through the doors, no doubt hurried along by Luanne, who was formidable at the best of times and a force to be reckoned with when it was time to close each night. Most of the surrounding area was in darkness, other than small pools of light thrown by street lamps overhead.

Maybe he'd imagined the noise. He'd only had a couple of beers, but with another scan of the surrounding area, Skip had to admit he couldn't tell where the sound came from. He was about to turn back to the pickup when a tendril of yellow flame caught his attention. He squinted into the darkness, trying to ascertain exactly what it was he was. With a muttered curse, he hurried to unlatch the tonneau cover on the back of the pickup, reaching in to snatch up the fire extinguisher before he ran, stumbling and sliding on the icy ground towards Cady's store. Careering past the couple leaving Grizzlies, he shouted to them. "The bakery's on fire! Call 911!"

Hop ran across the road and almost reached the other side of the blacktop when he lost his footing and slammed down onto his left knee. He struggled back onto his feet and hurried onto the sidewalk outside Tokens. Now he was closer he could clearly smell smoke, the acrid scent wafting out into the night. Overhead, smoke filtered up past the street lamp, creating eerie patterns.

The window on the right of the bakery door was smashed, and peering inside, Hop saw the flames spreading. Two of the tablecloths on the little tables were well alight. He cleared slivers of broken glass using the bottom of the extinguisher as a makeshift hammer, then began to spray the extinguisher's contents over the flames. He heard yelling from somewhere behind, then Luanne joined him with an extinguisher from Grizzlies. Moments later, sirens reverberated along Main Street and vehicles screeched to a halt besides the bakery. Fire Chief Tom Jenkins and members of his crew scrambled out of the cab of the town's solitary fire truck, in readiness to fight the fire.

Hop had almost gotten it under control before they arrived, with Luanne's assistance, but he limped out of the way. George arrived, striding across to where Hop and Luanne watched the firemen work. Judging from his untucked button-down shirt and tousled hair, he'd come straight from home.

George surveyed the activity, his heavy eyebrows drawn down with an intense scowl. "What the hell happened?"

Hop lowered the fire extinguisher to the ground, relieved to see the last of the flames peter out before Tom and his crew poured a load of water over the bakery's interior. In fact, the worst of the damage was contained to the customer seating area, and other than the burnt tablecloths and broken window, Cady's store seemed safe. "I'm not sure," Hop admitted, still assessing the dim interior. The combination of the street lamp overhead and the flashing red and blue lights of Garrison's law enforcement provided just enough light to see. "But I think it mighta been a Molotov cocktail."

George lifted the flashlight clutched in his right hand, switched it on, and flashed the beam across the interior of the store, concentrating on the wooden floor. After a moment or two, he dipped his head towards a section of the floor where the beam focused. "You could be right. That looks like the remains of a bottle." George glanced around the chaotic scene and caught the eye of Tom Jenkins. The burly fire captain hurried over and George indicated the area he'd shown Hop. "Is the fire put out?"

Tom nodded, resting his hands on his hips. "Yep. Hop and Luanne had it about under control before we got here." Tom sounded almost disappointed.

"Good. I need forensics in there as quick as we can organize it. I'll put a call through to Helena, have them send someone down." George lifted his chin towards the young deputy; Hop couldn't recall his name, but he was new, green and eager. "Deputy Reid, I'm leaving you here overnight to guard the store, Kane'll relieve you at 7am. Nobody goes in there until forensics have photographed the scene."

Luanne spoke up for the first time, which, in Hop's opinion, was a miracle of restraint on behalf of Grizzlies' owner. "You can bet your bottom dollar, George; it was that no-good Julia Henderson and that Neolithic oaf she's married to. Julia created a ruckus in Grizzlies tonight, upset Cady, tellin' her that her Daddy used to own Tokens."

George rubbed his forefinger and thumb across his temples, shaking his head tiredly. "Damn. That explains why she was upset when she got home tonight. She told us she wasn't feeling good, but I suspected there was something else going on."

Hop kept his gaze averted, keep the grin he was having trouble hiding from the Sheriff. Vaguely, he wondered if the reason George looked so disheveled was because he'd come straight from Meredith's rather than his own place. "So, what do you think?" Hop questioned. "Could it be Julia and Earl?"

George inhaled sharply, then released the air through his lips in a rush. "Don't know. But they'll be the first people I'll question."

M eredith walked up the stairs carrying a mug of coffee and knocked nervously on Cady's door. Her stomach was knotted in a tight twist of nerves; not only because of the bakery fire, but knowing she needed to speak to Cady about Julia's revelations.

George's return from the bakery had given Meredith plenty to worry over; the damage to the bakery caused by what he suspected was a Molotov cocktail, and the fact that Cady had learned the truth about Mark's ownership of the store. Meredith couldn't predict how Cady would react and she'd decided to leave discussion of either matter until morning.

Cady was upset and unsettled when she returned from Grizzlies last night, and Meredith suspected the best way forward would be to give her granddaughter time to think things through. Now, in the cold light of day, she hoped she'd made the right choice.

Not telling Cady about Mark owning the building had been a mistake, she was certain. Few people knew the truth, and Julia could only have learned of it from one place – her

Daddy being the Garrison Mayor and all. Meredith was going to have a few words with him later today and would be giving Floyd Capwell a piece of her mind.

Cady's voice drew her attention back to the present. "Come in."

Meredith opened the door and stepped inside. A quick glance confirmed everything was where it should be - she'd half expected Cady to be packed and ready to imminently take flight. Instead, she found her sitting in the armchair by the window, gazing out at the snowy scene outside.

Meredith handed the coffee to her granddaughter, before hunching down to give Churchill a good long scratch behind his ears. The dog, shameless attention seeker that he was, immediately flopped onto the floor, twisted onto his back and stuck his legs in the air, giving Meredith access to his tummy. Meredith did as he desired, giving his tummy a good rub while watching her granddaughter from the corner of her eye. Cady's skin was pale and dark circles shadowed her eyes, but she sipped the coffee Meredith had proffered and continued watching the snow fall outside.

Meredith straightened and put a hand on the back of the chair, letting her gaze follow Cady's. There was no point beating about the bush – the cat was out of the bag. "I'm sorry I didn't tell you about the building."

Cady swallowed convulsively and sipped her coffee before she spoke. "I guess you thought I wouldn't accept the offer of the building."

Meredith licked her lips, finding them suddenly dry. "You're right. I didn't think you would."

Cady dipped her head in acknowledgement. "Perhaps I wouldn't." She sipped the coffee again, gripping the mug between her hands. "It was a shock, I'll admit. And I'm not comfortable with it." She glanced up, meeting Meredith's worried gaze. "But I imagine he'd never set foot in the building, so it would be silly to give up everything we've worked so hard for, wouldn't it?"

Meredith's eyes widened. "No, he never did set foot in there. His granddaddy left it to him, along with the old diner, and two other buildings were left to David. David sold his properties once he turned twenty-five, in line with his grandfather's will, but Mark was long gone before then. I doubt he even remembered he owned it."

"He never mentioned property," Cady responded.

"You've surprised me," Meredith pointed out cautiously. "I suspected you'd be running by now."

There was a long pause. "Maybe I'm tired of running. I like it in Garrison. I doubt I'll ever stop hating Mark... but for the first time in my life I have something good, something to look forward to. I don't want to give that up."

Meredith smiled, but the gesture was tempered by the knowledge that she still needed to tell Cady about the fire. "I'm glad to hear it. But honey, I've got something else to tell you and I'm afraid it's not good news..."

---

SNOW WAS AGAIN FALLING outside as Cady watched Walt fixing a sheet of thick black plastic over the broken window, attaching it to the walls with a staple gun. The stub of his pencil was hooked behind his ear as he worked, and she wondered idly how it stayed there without falling.

Overall, they'd been extremely lucky; Hop and Luanne's swift actions had stopped the bakery going up in smoke. They'd been so efficient, in fact, that Tokens would be opening on Monday morning as planned, with only limited disruption to business. Two of the tables had gotten damaged by the fire, but other than a couple of tablecloths which needed to be discarded, and a burnt patch on the wooden floor just behind them, the only other damage was the window. Walt had already quoted on replacing the glass and would order the pane from Billings first thing Monday morning. In the meantime, this plastic would stop the interior being damaged by the weather, and George had reassured them he'd have his men patrolling throughout Sunday and overnight.

Cady wasn't entirely confident about the plan and was considering staying at the store overnight. George had reassured her he'd get to the bottom of who'd thrown the Molotov cocktail, and she hoped he was right. The idea of someone deliberately trying to destroy the store on the day it opened was disquieting, at best. She crossed her arms over her chest, trying to dismiss the chill which had settled into her bones. The events of the past twelve hours had been distressing – the fire, and Julia's revelation about Mark owning the store.

And Quinn. She knew, deep down, he'd had no intentions of hurting her, wasn't truly angry with her. His words had been borne from frustration over her kneejerk reaction to Julia's nasty behavior, but years of cruelty at Jameson's hands had left her gun shy and wary. Jameson had started out getting frustrated, and he used to grab her arm much as Quinn had done, but those instances of trying to control her had morphed into something far more sinister.

Cady liked Quinn – *really* liked Quinn – but she wasn't certain she could risk her heart and sanity by letting him get closer. *What if he ended up being like Jameson?* The warning kept echoing through her brain, but her heart was equally determined he wasn't like Jameson, and she should trust him. But she wasn't certain she could.

"Hop!" Meredith had been standing with George at the counter and she hurried across to greet the lanky cowboy, who was leaning heavily on crutches when he came through the door. "Are you doing okay?"

Cady was rattled by the sight of Quinn coming through the doorway after Hop, almost as though she'd conjured him up by thinking of him. She turned away, focusing on Walt's efforts with the broken window. She could see what was happening in her peripheral vision and was immediately ashamed of her juvenile behavior.

"Yes, Ma'am," Hop said, dropping onto the chair Quinn pulled out from one of the small tables. "Doctor says it's just bruisin', a bit of inflammation around the knee joint. Just gotta rest it for a couple of days and I'll be fine."

Cady gave herself a good mental shake and straightened up, turning back to the men. Hop had been injured saving *her* store – the least she could do was put on her big girl panties and behave like an adult. "Hop, I can't thank you enough for what you did," she said, stepping forward to press a kiss to his cheek. "I appreciate it, more than I can ever say." She straightened up, her gaze getting caught up with Quinn's and she offered him a faint smile, unable to stop herself. Quinn smiled back, and she thought she detected a change in his demeanor, a slight relaxation of his wide shoulders. She wondered if he'd been uncertain about seeing her again too, after last night.

"Weren't just me, Cady, you need to thank Luanne, too. She came rushing over to help," Hop demurred, and Cady suspected she'd caught a slight blush coloring his cheeks.

She offered him a beaming smile and patted his shoulder. "Already done, I went over to see her while Walt's been working to seal up the window until the glass arrives tomorrow sometime."

Meredith offered Hop a happy smile. "Cady and I want to offer you free coffee whenever you're in town, Hop, to thank you for what you did."

Hop shook his head. "That ain't necessary, Ms. Meredith. I'm just happy to know I was around at the right time to hear the glass breaking."

Quinn turned to George. "Rumors are spreadin' all over town. Kane said someone threw a Molotov cocktail?"

George leaned up against the counter, tipping his hat towards the back of his head to scratch at his forehead. "Yep, it was."

"Any suspects?" Quinn asked. Cady heard an icy note in his voice, making her think he already knew about George's suspicions.

George stared at Quinn for long seconds before he responded. "I thought Julia and Earl might have something to do with it, given Julia's... hostility towards Cady, but I've been out to their trailer to question them. They both swear they had nothing to do with it."

"You believe them?" Quinn demanded.

George shrugged. "No reason not to. Hop heard a car, but he didn't see it. We've got no proof either way. Might've been kids. Who knows?"

Quinn didn't look convinced, and Cady eyed him surreptitiously. He seemed tired, dark rings circled his eyes and he was wearing the same clothes he'd been in last night, when she left him in the car. She suspected he'd slept just as badly as she had, and she suffered a wave of remorse.

Quinn glanced over, and even though she'd been trying to be subtle, he obviously knew she'd been watching him. He smiled. "Might go and have a word with Julia and Earl myself," he proposed. He slapped Hop on the back, none-too-gently. "Let's get you home."

Concern drew Meredith's brow into a tiny frown. "Who's going to look after you, Hop? While you're recovering?"

"Not to worry, Ms. Meredith. Quinn's taking me out to the Silver Peaks. Ms. Nancy's gonna keep an eye on me for a couple of days 'til my knee settles."

George crossed his arms over the top of his gun belt. He was in full uniform, the arson serious enough to have him working on a Sunday. "Quinn, don't you go getting all up in Julia and Earl's business. They said they didn't do it, and I'm inclined to believe them, judging by their reactions when I told them about the fire. There's enough animosity between Julia and Cady... I don't want things getting worse."

Cady's lips narrowed into a thin line. "Don't involve me in this mess with Julia. There's no animosity on my part – it's all on her."

Quinn didn't bother hiding a grin when he responded to George, and his eyes twinkled when he looked down at Cady, making her heart skip a beat. "I promise, no trouble. Just want to check for myself whether Julia's telling the truth." He shook his head. "I reckon I'll be able to tell, just by looking at her."

George pursed his lips, considering for a second before he nodded. "Alright, then."

Quinn glanced over at Cady. "Can I have a word? Outside?"

Cady dipped her head and hurried toward the front door, not wanting Meredith and George to see the blush suffusing her cheeks.

Quinn followed along, watching Cady pull her gloves on. Snow was swirling around them, the sidewalk already buried under a few inches of fresh snowfall. Cady pulled the hood of her jacket up over her hair and turned to face Quinn. Before she could speak, Quinn stepped forward, wrapping his arms around her waist and he pressed a gentle kiss to her lips, much to her surprise and pleasure.

"I'm sorry, Cady. Sorry that I got annoyed with you, and sorry that I grabbed you the way I did. Knowin' your background... well, I'm guessin' that frightened you. I want you to know, I understand I did the wrong thing. I don't have any excuse, except to say I was frightened you were gonna run after what Julia said."

Stunned by his declaration, Cady remained immobile in his arms, watching him as he spoke, and when he stopped, she remained silent, staring up at him for a moment or two. "You did frighten me, a little," she finally admitted, "to begin with."

Quinn frowned, searching her eyes for an explanation.

"Coming from... having dealt with... an abusive husband... I'm frightened of getting hurt again," Cady continued, "and to start with, I thought maybe you were like him, that you would hurt me too." She stopped abruptly, tugging her bottom lip into her mouth with her teeth. "But then..."

Quinn continued to watch her, but when no words were forthcoming, he spoke again. "But then?"

"I've thought about it quite a lot, and I think... I know... I think I know..." Cady swallowed convulsively, trying to collect her scattered thoughts and provide Quinn with a cohesive explanation. "I've gotten to know you, and even though I sometimes get frightened, I don't think you'd hurt me. I don't think you're that type of man."

Quinn's lips curved up. "Damn straight, Cady." He brought his hands up from her waist, gently catching her cheeks between his palms. "I will never, ever hurt you. I can't promise that I won't get frustrated with you from time to time, I can't promise I won't yell occasionally if things get worked up between us... but I won't ever hurt you. Not physically, not emotionally, not verbally. Can you believe me about that?"

Cady thought for a second or two, watching Quinn's handsome face. When she spoke, there was a little edge of sadness in her voice, but she had to be honest, needed Quinn to know the truth. "I can't say I totally believe you yet," she responded quietly, and saw hurt blossom in Quinn's eyes. "But I can tell you that I think... with time... I might be able to believe in you."

Quinn lowered his mouth to hers in another gentle kiss, and when he lifted his head again, he offered her a warm smile. "I can live with that."

Quinn drove up to Earl and Julia's trailer and killed the ignition, leaning back to survey the area. He wondered, for what must be the hundredth time, why Julia had given up her life with him to live in this crappy trailer with Earl. He and Earl had been buddies once, long ago, but sleeping with Quinn's wife had put paid to that friendship.

Both their cars – Julia's crappy little Taurus and Earl's pickup were parked outside the trailer, so he knew they were home. Besides, Grizzlies wouldn't open for another few hours, so Earl had nowhere else to be on a Sunday afternoon. He was probably watching football and drinking beer.

The Henderson's trailer was parked by the barn on the Hustlin' Horseshoes Ranch, where Earl had worked for the past decade. How he held down a steady job when he drank so much, Quinn would never know, but he suspected it helped that the Hustlin' was owned by Julia's uncle. Quinn would never trust the guy enough to work with him, but Julia's family had a long history in Garrison, almost as long as his own, and family looked after one another, whether the recipients deserved it or not.

He yanked the keys from the ignition and stepped out of the truck, surveying the deep drifts of snow all around the trailer. Winter had well and truly set in, and he noted that someone had been out shoveling to clear a path from the trailer to the cars, and recently.

Quinn strode up to the trailer door and knocked on the aluminum siding, his gaze skating across the surrounding area. The Hustlin' Horseshoes was a smaller operation than Silver Peaks, but it was always interesting to see what other ranchers were doing.

The door got wrenched open and his ex-wife stood at the top of the steps, her expression colder than the snow at his feet. "What do you want, Quinn?"

Quinn tipped his hat. He'd already decided there was no point in being antagonistic, he just wanted to confirm George's opinion. "Hey Julia."

Julia leaned up against the doorframe, resting her shoulder against it and crossed her arms. "What do you want?"

"Who is it?" Earl's voice came from somewhere inside the trailer, and Quinn could hear a football game playing out on TV.

"It's Quinn."

Indistinct muttering came from inside, before Earl's head appeared over Julia's shoulder. His eyes were bloodshot, and Quinn suspected the guy was already three sheets to the wind. He wondered briefly why Julia had left him for this loser, but he quickly dismissed the thought. Glancing up at Julia, seeing the hard expression in her eyes, the fine wrinkles appearing around her lips, he found he was glad that she'd left him. And besides, if she hadn't left him, he wouldn't have the opportunity to get to know Cady. An image of the beautiful redhead popped into his mind and he banked down a smile which wanted to blossom just at the thought of her. Hell; he had it bad.

"Whaddaya want?" Earl asked. He lifted a can of Budweiser to his mouth and guzzled down a mouthful, using the back of his sleeve to wipe his mouth when he'd finished.

"Just wanted to confirm that you two didn't have anything to do with the fire at the bakery," Quinn announced. He'd decided on the way out here to launch into the question without warning, so he could see Julia's reaction, judge whether she told the truth or not.

"Is that what the bitch told you?" Julia screeched. "What the hell would I do something like that for? I don't give a damn about that freaky little bitch, but I wouldn't do somethin' like that to Meredith! While I don't much care for that little waste of space, I wouldn't cause Meredith any trouble, and you should know that!"

Quinn knew instantly Julia was telling the truth. If she'd been lying he'd have seen it in her eyes, the way she always looked to the left if she was trying to get away with somethin'. In this case, her gaze held steadily on his, hers filled with the fire and brimstone of someone who thought they were being unjustly accused. Julia might lie about a lot of things, but she wasn't lying about this.

Earl took another slug from his beer while Quinn was subjected to Julia's tirade, and after wiping his mouth with his sleeve a second time, he placed his hand over his heart. "I know you and me don't see eye to eye nowadays, but we're telling the truth. We didn't set fire to the bakery."

"I CAN'T IMAGINE who else would have done it," Cady admitted, an anxious frown creasing her forehead.

"Maybe George is right; could be it was kids pulling a prank," Meredith proposed. She wrapped a blanket more firmly around her legs, trying unsuccessfully to mask a shiver as the temperature in the bakery continued to plummet. The pot-bellied stove Walt installed was doing its best, but the plastic stapled over the window couldn't stop the arctic-like winds slipping through the gaps.

"You should go home, Gran. It's much too cold for you to stay," Cady protested, and not for the first time.

Meredith wrapped her gloved hands around the mug of hot chocolate Cady had prepared and shook her head. "Absolutely not. If you're staying, I'm staying."

"But Gran..."

Meredith shook her head for a second time. "Don't even try it, Arcadia—"

Cady held up a gloved finger and waggled it, shaking her own head and grinning. "Don't you dare. I've heard my full name more times since I moved to Garrison than I've ever heard it before – and trust me, that isn't something I look forward to."

Meredith returned the smile and adjusted a heavy blanket around her shoulders. "I guess I do tend to use it when I'm frustrated with you."

Cady chuckled, pulling her own blanket tightly around her knees with one hand, and balancing a mug of hot chocolate in the other. "And I'll admit, I've probably frustrated the heck out of you."

Meredith sipped her chocolate. "You do have a way of riling me up at times."

The two women laughed and settled into companionable silence, broken only by the rattling of the heavy black plastic against the window frame. Cady surveyed the store, a sense of pride welling in her chest. She'd never imagined this – having something of her own – a chance to build her self-esteem and sense of self-worth. It was a dream come true, and after so many weeks spent trying to escape Garrison, now she was a little more settled with each passing day.

The thought of someone attacking the bakery was shocking, a worry she couldn't shake off, but she'd considered every possibility and disregarded them all. She figured she'd just have to take George's guidance and consider it a random act of violence, maybe local kids acting out. She was trying hard to believe it, but at the back of her mind, Cady couldn't quite dismiss the prospect of something more sinister. But who? George and Quinn believed Julia and Earl had nothing to do with it, and Cady hadn't experienced any problems with anyone else. Maybe it was a random act, but she couldn't shift the sensation of a target on her back.

"Is everything alright between you and Quinn?"

Gran's question came out of the blue, startling Cady. She stared down into the mug, watching steam rising from the hot liquid. "Yeah, we're okay."

Gran wasn't going to be dissuaded so easily and she reached over, patting Cady's shoulder. "I heard you slam the door on Quinn's truck last night. I know you were upset about Julia, but a girl doesn't slam a truck door unless she's got good reason."

Cady smiled faintly, surprised by how intuitive Meredith had become regarding her moods. "When Quinn bought me home, he was worried that I was going to run, and I couldn't tell him I wouldn't, because I was still coming to terms with what Julia had said. Things got heated between us… and I freaked out. He grabbed my arm, and got a little angry, and… it frightened me."

Meredith's face was masked in sympathy. "And it reminded you..."

"... of what Jameson did," Cady admitted forlornly. She put her mug on the table and intertwined her fingers, gripping them tightly when a tremble erupted across her body.

Meredith hurriedly left her seat, kneeling next to Cady and wrapping her arms around the younger woman's waist. She stayed silent, allowing Cady to decide the way forward. The air was thick with tension, ripe with emotion, while she struggled to control her visceral reaction to recalling Jameson's brutality.

"I know Quinn didn't mean anything by it, but he grabbed my arm. He didn't hurt me, but it's what Jameson did, a means of controlling me. We'd be out at a dinner party, and Jameson would grip my upper arm," Cady repeated the action she'd been subjected to so frequently, unconsciously clutching at her own arm while she stared into the distance, "and I could tell, by how hard he squeezed... it was practically a barometer of how badly I'd misbehaved. A quick, sharp squeeze usually meant I'd disobeyed him, and he was warning me not to do it again. A longer, more forceful squeeze meant he was annoyed about something I'd said, and I could expect a verbal assault after we left the party." Cady's limbs shook, her gaze focused somewhere far in the distance when she recalled Jameson's brutality. "If he squeezed especially hard – hard enough to leave bruises, I knew I was in for a beating when we got home." She forced herself to meet Meredith's eyes, expecting to see horror in the older woman's gaze, or disbelief, or pity, but Gran's clear blue eyes were focused on her, and the only thing Cady could distinguish in her expression was love. It gave her the confidence to continue. "It was a living nightmare, one I never expected to escape from. I assumed that one day, Jameson would be angry enough that he'd kill me."

"He almost did," Meredith pointed out quietly.

Cady rubbed absently at the scar where her kidney had been removed. "But he didn't. And," she smiled tremulously, "it brought me to you." She waved a hand to encompass the bakery. "And this. I'm trying to think more positively, and I think without my past, I wouldn't have reached the point where I'm at now." The smile morphed into a weak grin. "In this freezing little wooden store in the middle of a snowstorm."

Meredith laughed. "If George could see me now, he'd—"

They both jumped when someone banged on the glass door, and Meredith hurriedly straightened up. "It's George," she announced in surprise. She glanced down at Cady, rolling her eyes. "Now we're in for it."

"*You* are," Cady retorted. Personally, she suspected she could manage George just fine.

"So are you," Meredith countered. "He's brought Quinn." She rushed across and unlocked the door, pulling it open to reveal George, and behind him, Quinn. Both men wore heavy coats and hats, and a light dusting of snow fell from their shoulders and onto the wooden floor when they stamped their feet on the welcome mat in the doorway.

"Fine guard dog you are," Cady grumbled, watching Churchill roll over and get more comfortable in front of the fire.

"What in hell's name are you doing down here?" George demanded, eyeing the piles of blankets, the cooling mugs of chocolate and the blazing fire before he turned his piercing gaze on Meredith.

Cady was impressed by Gran's tenacity; Meredith stood

her ground in the face of George's disbelief, holding her head high and wrapping the blanket more tightly around her shoulders. "Cady wasn't comfortable with leaving the bakery, with just that piece of plastic up against the window. She decided to stay overnight, and I couldn't just let her stay alone now, could I?"

George crossed his arms over his chest, narrowing his eyes as he considered. "Did I not tell you... *both* of you... that I'd have the on-duty deputy patrolling overnight, keeping an eye on the place?"

Cady bit back a smile when Meredith looked up at George... and batted her eyelashes. "Now George, you know as well as I do that Deputy Reid can't be watching the building all night long. And what happens if whoever set the fire comes back?"

Now George's eyes widened, and he stared at Meredith in disbelief. "They're gonna find two defenseless women on the premises! What good's that gonna do?"

"And Churchill," Cady piped up. She felt Quinn's eyes on her and peeked up, saw his eyes twinkle with amusement.

George threw his hands in the air. "Look at the damn dog! What good is he going to do? He didn't bother getting up to investigate who was knocking at the door!"

Cady couldn't help herself; George's frustration was amusing, and she piped up again. "Obviously, he didn't bark at you – he knows who you are. It would have been a different story if you'd been a stranger."

Churchill didn't bother lifting his head; merely opened his eyes, heaved out a loud sigh, licked his lips and settled back to sleep.

Quinn stepped in. "George, take Meredith home. I'll stay here with Cady."

Cady swung her attention back to Quinn and started to protest, even as Meredith added a protest of her own. "Oh, no, you don't have—"

"Cady and me are just fine —"

"Sounds good," George interrupted. "Meredith, grab your things... *please*." The word was added as an afterthought when he saw the glare Gran directed at him, and Cady suspected there was every possibility George would spontaneously combust under the pinpoint accuracy of that gaze. "I don't want you catching your death of cold, Mer. Come on home, and let Quinn and Cady keep an eye on things here."

Cady threw George a bone, feeling a little sorry for him. "George is right. It's much too cold for you, and as much as I appreciate the help, maybe you would be better off at home."

Gran shrugged. "Alright then. Quinn, you'll stay with Cady? Keep her safe?"

Quinn dipped his head in agreement. "Yes, Ma'am. I give you my word."

Meredith stepped over to where Cady stood and wrapped her in a hug. "If I was you, honey, I'd jump his bones – y'hear? Quinn Garrison is quite the catch, and he's obviously smitten with you," she whispered against Cady's ear.

And with one last wave and a little chuckle, Meredith followed George out into the snowy night, leaving a startled Cady in her wake.

C ady pulled herself together and relocked the door, and when she turned back Quinn was crouched in front of the potbelly stove, adding another log of wood and stoking the embers.

"Would you like a hot chocolate?" Cady questioned nervously, tugging at the blanket over her shoulders.

"I'd much prefer a coffee."

Cady busied herself making coffee with the new machine, pleased with the result. Along with Gran and Paulette, she'd taken lessons in operating the coffee maker, but she wasn't certain she'd mastered the process. Quinn's coffee seemed okay though, and she carried it across to the table.

Quinn had pulled the table and chairs closer to the potbelly stove, and he offered her an encouraging smile when she put the coffee mug down on the table. "Might be better closer to the fire – these things pack plenty of heat, but when it's competing against a broken window, it's not as efficient as it would be normally."

Cady settled onto the chair to the left of the table, picking up her mug. "Thanks for staying."

Quinn grinned. "It's a pleasure."

For a few minutes, Cady lapsed into silence, and then turned back to Quinn. "You spoke to Julia?"

Quinn nodded, sipping his coffee before he responded. "Yeah, went out to their trailer this afternoon. She didn't do this." He indicated the broken window with a dip of his head.

"I guess George is right," Cady mused. She suppressed a shiver and finished the last of her hot chocolate. "Maybe it was just kids."

Cady found herself lost for something to say and silence descended between them. Quinn's presence was tangible, a sensation floating in the air which encircled her in a sense of security, a security she couldn't recall experiencing before. Despite that, she found she was uncomfortable; the prospect of spending the night with this man disconcerting. Of course, they weren't *spending* the night together – she'd needed help and Quinn had offered it. Nevertheless, the air between them was fraught with tension, and she was acutely aware of his handsome features and his strong body, just feet away. To her chagrin her mind was working over-time, and she experienced glimpses of what Quinn might do to her with that strong body of his. Her own body tingled with anticipation.

Quinn drained his coffee mug and stood up, pushing the chair back against the wall before he lifted the table out of the way, leaving an empty area in front of the potbelly stove. "It's late, Cady. Let me sort out these blankets and we can make a bit of a nest here in front of the stove. You look half-frozen to death."

"Oh, I'm perfectly okay," Cady protested, thoughts of being held in Quinn's arms hijacking her brain.

Quinn fluffed out a blanket and lay it on the wooden floor, then hurried towards the door. "Even Churchill looks a mite cold, and given he's a Mastiff, that's saying something. I'll be back in just a minute."

He disappeared into the darkness and returned moments later, carrying a couple of pillows under one arm, and hugging a big quilt to his chest. "Mom sent the quilt, it's nice and thick, perfect for this sort of weather." He dropped the pillows down onto the blanket and then unfolded the quilt, laying it across the top. Once he was satisfied, he shucked off his boots, placing them to one side and settled cross-legged on the quilt. "C'mon, Cady."

She remained rooted to the spot, watching Quinn and hearing Gran's advice about jumping Quinn's bones echo through her mind. "I think... um, I'm okay here."

Quinn laughed, the sound echoing around the room. "I promise, all I'm offerin' tonight is body heat. Nothin' more." Churchill got up from beside the stove and flopped down by Quinn's side, begging for attention. Quinn laughed again. "See, even Churchill is clever enough to realize there's warmth in numbers. C'mon. I promise, nothing underhanded. Just shared warmth, straight up."

Convinced, Cady got up and pushed her chair out of the way and cautiously dropped down onto the blanket next to Quinn. She felt awkward and shy, but Quinn was matter-of-fact in his approach, and once she'd joined him, he made a fuss of making sure she was completely covered by the quilt, hemmed in on one side by Churchill, and on the other side by Quinn himself.

Self-conscious, she wriggled down until the quilt covered her all the way to her nose, turning to face

Churchill. Quinn shuffled around behind her, and she was shocked when he snuggled down and wrapped her in his arms, her back and buttocks spooned against his front. Holding herself rigidly, Cady wasn't certain how to react, but Quinn's body was so warm, she found after a minute or two that she couldn't help but relax against him.

"Okay?" Quinn murmured. His arms were wrapped around her, but he was carefully keeping his hands on neutral ground. Even so, Cady's skin was literally humming, every nerve, every cell totally aware of the sensation of Quinn Garrison pressed against her. And she liked it. She'd rarely felt more alive, and having Quinn hold her, his body pressed against hers, created a delicious sense of contentment previously unknown.

"Okay," Cady agreed quietly. The only sound in the room was the popping and hissing of wood burning in the stove, and outside, the wind whistled and swept through the town as snow continued to fall.

Churchill inhaled, the sound momentarily interrupting the silence and the huge dog licked his lips before he settled back to sleep with a contented groan. Cady couldn't help but smile and she felt, rather than saw Quinn's matching smile. "That's some dog, Cady Caldwell."

"Yes, he is."

Quinn's breathing was regular, his chest lifting and dropping rhythmically against her back before he spoke again. "I should warn you, Cady, I'm not certain I can stop myself from gettin' aroused with you so close. But I'll keep my hands to myself."

Cady considered for a moment, surprised firstly, by Quinn's admission, but also amazed to find she was disappointed. When had she gotten so comfortable with him that she was considering a more physical relationship? When had she reached the stage when she'd be disappointed because he wasn't taking things further? She didn't know, but she turned in his arms, wanting to see his face in the soft light cast by the soda fridge. She gazed up into his eyes, offering him a careful smile. "What if I don't want you to keep your hands to yourself?"

Quinn's eyebrows met in a dark slash. "Aw, Cady, I wish I thought you meant that. But I don't think you do." He rubbed his hands across her back, skimming over the top of her buttocks. "But I certainly wouldn't object to a bit of kissin' and cuddlin'." He dropped his mouth over hers, pressing a gentle kiss to Cady's lips, and she lifted her arms to wrap them around Quinn's neck. The kiss expanded and grew, Cady experimenting, learning Quinn's likes and dislikes, even while his hands roamed restlessly over her back and hips, keeping to his word. Cady could tell from the tremble in his fingers that he was fighting against his baser instincts.

"I want to touch you," Cady demanded, tugging at the waist of Quinn's shirt, almost delirious with need. She couldn't remember experiencing this level of desire before now – certainly not with Jameson – she couldn't recall ever being so aroused. Quinn was doing things to her, making her feel things... for the first time in years, she felt alive.

"I'll take off my shirt," Quinn agreed, tugging at the garment haphazardly, "but will you do me the honor of taking yours off, Darlin'?"

Cady had been pulling at his shirt, her fingers working of their own accord to unfasten the buttons, but now she came to a standstill, staring up at Quinn before she reacted. "Quinn... there's something you should know..." Her cheeks heated, and she inhaled suddenly, the breath stuttering up through her chest. "My ex... he..."

Quinn's hands stopped, and he placed his fingers under Cady's chin, gently lifting her face to meet his. "Whatever it is, Cady, it doesn't matter. I'm going to accept whatever it is, because it's part of you."

Cady wrestled for a moment or two, trying to decide how to move forward, whether she could do what Quinn had asked and reveal her scars to him, when she hadn't exposed them to anyone else. Even Sid and Harry hadn't seen them, had only heard about them from staff at the hospital. Taking a deep breath, centering herself, Cady tried to swallow back the shame, the disgust she'd experienced since Jameson's attack. Glancing up into Quinn's eyes, she was surprised when he sat up and pulled off his shirt, leaving her faced with an expanse of gorgeous, golden, muscled flesh.

When he spoke his tone was even, his expression carefully smoothed into neutrality. "It's okay, Cady. I'm happy enough being here, with you. Holding you is enough. Being in your company is enough." Quinn settled back down beside her, putting his arms up behind his head and depicting a complete lack of threat. "It's all up to you, how we proceed from here."

Cady drew herself up, resting her head against her fist while she gazed down at Quinn. He returned her gaze, his handsome features serene, although the spark of desire was visible in his eyes, the heat which couldn't be suppressed. She was excited about being desired by this man and that knowledge came as a surprise. He'd stolen her heart, and she hadn't even realized it was happening. Cady sat up and pulled her sweater over her head, shivering not only from the cool air but terror over how Quinn would react.

"When my ex... when he was beating me up that last time..." She spoke as she began to undo the buttons on her blouse, each one a lesson in effort as she battled against shaking fingers, and trembling nerves. "He was... he wanted..."

Quinn's relaxed stance disappeared, and he sat up, cross-legged opposite Cady. "You don't have to explain," he offered quietly, "and you don't have to show me. Not now, not until you're comfortable with me."

"That's just the thing," Cady admitted. "I am comfortable with you. I'm more comfortable with you than just about anyone, besides Gran, Sid and Harry." Cady worked on the buttons on her shirt, undoing one after the other with dogged determination. "He... he burned me... with a cigarette."

She pulled the sides of the silk blouse apart, revealing her breasts encased in a lacy bra and she was surprised when Quinn forcibly kept his gaze focused on her eyes, although his Adam's apple bobbed as he swallowed, gulping down air. Cady touched the edge of the bra cups, using her fingers to push the material down from her breast, knowing exactly how far to go to reveal the cigarette burns. "This. This is what he did to me."

Quinn's gaze traced down over her cheek, her jaw, and along her neck in a slow, cautious exploration until the moment his gaze reached the scars, and she saw anger blossom in his eyes. But she didn't see pity, didn't see disgust, and for that she was grateful.

"May I?" he questioned, lifting his hand.

Cady swallowed heavily, managing a faint, single nod.

And she thought her heart would burst to overflowing when Quinn, rather than reaching over to touch the scar, instead touched his fingertip to his lips. And then he pressed that kissed fingertip to each of the scars, one after the other, letting Cady know they didn't matter. Her past didn't matter. All that mattered was Cady herself.

When he'd finished he carefully drew Cady into his arms, her bra-clad back against his bare chest, wrapped his arms around her securely, and Cady experienced the joy of falling asleep in Quinn's arms, content in the knowledge he'd accepted her exactly as she was.

"Wake up sleepy head!"

Grumbling, Cady rolled over and wrapped the covers more closely around her neck. Gran had the heat on, but there was still a distinct chill to the air and the skin on her nose and cheeks were aware of it.

"Cades! C'mon! You promised to take us to the bakery as soon as we got here!" Sid's enthusiasm was apparent as she strode across to Cady's bed and bounced her hands up and down on the mattress a couple of times, jiggling Cady none-too-gently.

Cady lifted her head, squinting at the clock on the nightstand. "Yeah... I did. But not at 7am on a Sunday morning!"

When Sid spoke, there was a distinct whine to her voice, one which Cady was all too familiar with. Sid had put Cady's teeth on edge with that whine when she was a little girl, and things hadn't changed. "Please, Cades! C'mon! Tomorrow is Christmas, and the next day we've got to head back to California. This is my only chance!"

Cady heaved out a breath. "The bakery will still be

there, exactly where we left it, in another hour or two. Come back then."

Sid started to pound on the mattress with her fists, making the bed rock as if Cady was floating across a choppy ocean. "Aw, c'mon Cades! Times a wastin', and later we've got to help Gran with preparations for tomorrow! Let's go! My time is limited!"

"Your time is gonna be really limited, if I end up strangling you," Cady warned, but she threw back the covers and twisted to sit on the edge of the bed. "Harry probably isn't even awake yet."

"Trust me, I'm awake," Harry announced as she stumbled into Cady's room, pulling a robe over her pajamas. "I got the first wake up call."

"Lucky you." Cady got to her feet and walked over to the window to pull the curtains back, revealing the snowy scene outside. Despite her annoyance at being woken early, Cady had to admit the view was never going to grow old. The sparkling snow, the banks of trees, bereft of leaves in the chilly winter air, the festive decorations the people of Garrison had decorated with for the Christmas season – it was a picture-perfect view. And one she had grown quite fond of.

Churchill trotted to her side and rubbed his head up against her hand, eliciting a head scratch for himself as Cady admired the neighborhood. A month or so ago she wouldn't have believed it, but Garrison seemed more like home with each passing day. And it wasn't only the bakery or Gran's presence... it was Quinn.

The man had gotten under her skin and was working his way into her heart. In the fortnight since their stay at the bakery, Quinn had been a regular visitor at Meredith's, stealing his way into her life. And he was good at it; reading

Cady perhaps better than anyone before. He seemed to gauge exactly how much she could cope with, giving her time and space to adjust. He would visit, but didn't stay too long. He'd kiss her – boy, how he would kiss her – but didn't ask for more. He accepted her limitations and her fears, and pressed gently against them, stretching her boundaries. For the first time in years Cady was starting to think she was capable of being part of a healthy relationship, one not based on control and abuse.

Sid's voice drew her back from her musings. "C'mon, let's go. Get dressed. Gran's got breakfast ready, she's made waffles, and then we can go to the bakery. After-wards, we'll come back to the house and finish prepara-tions for tomorrow's supper, and then we can decorate the tree! Don't you just love the scent of a real tree, it makes the whole house seem so Christmassy. This is going to be a great Christmas, all of us together with Gran, and George of course—"

Cady threw her hands in the air. "Stop! I promise, I'll get ready, but Sid, please... could you stop talking? For five minutes?"

Sid sniffed disdainfully, at odds with the sparkle of mischief in her eyes. "Hmmmph! If that's your attitude, I'm going downstairs with Churchill. We just might eat all the waffles without you."

"Do not feed him waffles! D'you hear me?" Cady called after Sid's retreating back.

Harry chuckled, wrapping Cady in a heartfelt hug. "Relax. You know she's only messing with you."

Cady sighed, turning back to make the bed. "I know. But she's so good at it."

Harry grinned. "She's had years of practice. She was a pain in the ass as a kid, and she's still a pain in the ass now."

"I heard that!" Sid shot back indignantly, and the two women laughed.

---

"LET'S BUILD A SNOWMAN," Sid announced on their way back to Gran's.

The visit to the bakery had been a resounding success, both Harry and Sid declaring their pleasure over how great it had turned out. Sid had studied every little detail of the building, 'oohing' and 'aahing' over every feature while Harry sat with Cady at one of the tables, drinking coffee and catching up on each other's news. She'd avoided telling them about the Molotov cocktail, not wanting either of them to worry. Besides, nothing else had happened, so Cady suspected George was right and it was a random act of vandalism.

"A snowman?" Cady repeated.

"Sure," Sid announced diverting towards Garrison Park with Churchill in tow. "It'll be fun."

"I'm not sure about that," Harry said doubtfully. She dug her hands deeper into her coat pockets and glanced at Cady. "It's freezing out here."

Sid wasn't going to be dissuaded though, and the two women followed as she led them further into the park, past the rotunda and coming to a stop by the children's play area. The swings were covered in a good two inches of snow, and the top of the slide also held a good covering – confirming, in Cady's mind, that they were the only crazy people out on Christmas Eve in Garrison. Sid dropped Churchill's leash, leaving him to his own devices and he happily began to sniff the ground, no doubt finding a scent or two to trace near the swings. Churchill wouldn't stray far, and Cady watched Sid start to mound piles of snow onto a park bench beside the playground.

"Sid, what are you doing?" Harry questioned.

"Making a snowman." Sid deposited another pile of snow on to the bench, then started to collect up snow from the ground, scraping it up between her mitten-clad hands.

Harry chuckled. "We obviously failed as older sisters," she remarked, glancing at Cady. "She doesn't know how to make a snowman."

"Of course I do," Sid retorted scornfully. "But I'm making a *Quinn* snowman, sitting on the bench!" She grinned at Cady, batting her eyelashes flirtatiously. "Gran seems to think there's quite a thing going on between you and a certain rancher."

"We're friends," Cady stated guardedly.

Harry smiled, crouching down to collect up another pile of snow. "More than friends, I hear."

Churchill bounded through the snow to Cady and she squatted down to pat him, buying herself a little time before she replied. The snow was so deep, Churchill's chest and the length of his legs were wet, and snow was starting to collect in his fur, but judging by his tongue hanging out of his mouth, and the big soppy grin on his lips, he was having a grand time. "Good friends," Cady responded.

"Aw, c'mon Cades," Sid admonished. She'd gathered up a big armful of snow and started fashioning it into a torso, while Harry had gotten into the spirit of things and was creating legs. "Be honest. Why are you always so restrained! From what Gran told us last night, it's more than friendship."

Cady rubbed Churchill's ears, then bent down to start collecting snow in her gloved hands. It was icy cold through the leather gloves, and she shivered despite wearing a thick coat and scarf. "This is crazy. No sane person is out in this weather."

"Crazy," Sid agreed, "but fun. I can't recall ever building a snowman when we were kids."

"We lived in California for a good part of it," Cady pointed out. "No snow in San Francisco."

"But what about before California?" Sid demanded.

Cady straightened up and plonked the mound of snow onto the top of the section Sid had fashioned. "There wasn't much fun when we were kids, Sid. Didn't matter where we happened to be living." Her mood darkened a little, remembering so many Christmas pasts when they'd had nothing but each other.

"Exactly." Sid threw her hands in the air, in a gesture matching the tone of her voice. "So why not have a little fun now? And who cares that nobody else is outside? We Caldwell girls are made of tougher stuff."

"Except I'm likely to freeze my ass off," Harry countered.

"You're not going to freeze your ass off. Not while you keep active, anyway. And you can trust me - I'm a doctor."

"Almost a doctor," Harry retorted.

"Regardless," Sid continued, rolling her eyes, "let's get back to the point at hand." She dumped a big heap of snow onto the bench and patted it between her gloved hands, shaping the upper section of the snowman's torso, then focused on Cady. "Spill. What's the deal with you and Quinn Garrison?"

Cady ran her finger through the snow on the right-hand side of the snowman's torso, fashioning an arm. "I like him," she admitted quietly. "I like him very much."

Harry paused, crouched beside the snowman and brushing snow from her gloves. She looked up at her older sister and grinned, pleasure radiating in her tone when she spoke. "Oh, Cades, I'm delighted to hear that. Quinn is such a wonderful guy, he'll be so good for you!"

Cady held up a hand in warning. "Whoa there. It's early days, I hardly know him yet—" She was stunned when a snowball slammed into her cheek and turned to stare at her youngest sister in disbelief. "Did you just throw a snowball at me?"

Sid giggled, and backed away, fashioning another one. "Maybe."

"Right. This means war." Cady knelt and began to scrape up a big pile of snow, laughing when Sid slipped and fell on her ass in the snow. "I'd get up, if I were you, Sid Caldwell. Because I'm about to whoop your ass."

"Now children," Harry began with a giggle. "Let's not get out of hand—" Her words broke off abruptly when a snowball hit her upper shoulder and she shrieked. "Cady! I was going to be on your side!"

Cady got to her feet and laughed, turning tail and running towards the playground to seek some cover. "No sides – it's every woman for herself!"

And with a whoop of excitement, Cady ran across the park, experiencing more unadulterated joy than she could ever recall experiencing before.

"**A**m I too late?" Mr. Harper came through the front door of Tokens, leaning heavily on his cane. He stopped beside the coat stand, dropping his hat onto one of the hooks and hobbled closer to the counter. "I had an appointment with Doc Ogilvie, and he insisted on doing every darn test he could think of, made me late getting back here. Are there any left?"

Cady grinned and reached into the display case, retrieving a plate with a solitary cupcake at its center. "Now Mr. Harper, would I forget it's Thursday afternoon? One lemon cupcake with fresh blueberry buttercream, and if you take a seat, I'll be across with your coffee in a minute."

"You're a treasure, Ms. Caldwell. Fancy you keeping one of my favorites for me! I love this bakery of yours, and that's the truth." He hobbled towards one of the tables and slowly sank onto the seat, hooking his cane over the back-rest. "The fine weather looks like it's bringing everyone out today. And please, you need to call me A.J., like everyone else."

Cady grinned at Paulette who appeared in the kitchen

doorway. "Only if you call me Cady," she insisted, repeating the same discussion they conducted every week when the elderly man visited for cake and coffee. He'd been a regular since their first week.

"Hiya A.J. Snow's not too deep out at your place then?" Paulette enquired. She took the plate from Cady and made her way around the counter to deliver the treat. Mr. Harper lived a few miles out of town, on the same small ranch he'd bought forty years before when he'd arrived in Garrison. Now his two sons ran the place for him, keeping an eye on their elderly father – who from all accounts, had been quite the charmer in his day. Cady could believe that, because he came in here once a week and charmed her every time.

"Nah, not too bad. Only about three feet sittin' on the ground. Nowhere near as much as we had back in '73," he announced.

Paulette put the plate down in front of him. "1873?" she enquired innocently. In the weeks since Paulette started working for Cady, the older woman had blossomed, revealing a mischievous streak and a wicked sense of humor.

Mr. Harper cackled, revealing a gap-toothed smile. "Aw gee, you're a hoot, Paulette. 1873! I'm getting on, but I'd be some kinda miracle worker if I was still around back then!" Cady watched the man's faded blue eyes light up after he ran his finger through the blueberry icing and sucked it from his finger. "Delicious," he declared with another smile.

Paulette hurried around the counter and flicked her gaze over the small group still waiting at the counter. "Do you want me to stay?" she asked.

Cady checked the clock; it was nearing two, already an hour past Paulette's official shift finish. "No, you go home. I can call Gran if it gets too busy, but things should slow down soon." In the weeks since the bakery opened, they'd gone from strength to strength, gathering new clientele as Garrison residents embraced the new business. Cady had expected the initial interest to die down after a week or two, and worried if there would be enough custom to keep her afloat – instead, the opposite had happened, and her customer base improved with each passing week. It meant Cady was enduring a steep learning curve, and she sometimes stopped for a second and wished the whirlwind would slow down and give her a little time to breathe, but she was grateful, so grateful for the way Garrison had adopted her little bakery. Now her problem was the opposite of what she'd expected; with so much custom, she and Paulette were run off their feet.

"Let me stay an extra half hour, help you with service."

Cady shook her head, knowing Paulette's husband was home alone. "No, really, Paulette. Go home to Dan. And drop in and see your daughter... how much longer does she have?" Paulette's daughter was heavily pregnant, and Paulette was excited about the imminent arrival of her first grandchild.

"A week, the Doc says, but I suspect she'll go over. She's not looking ready to pop just yet."

Cady grinned, handing a take-out coffee to one of the men standing by the counter, and simultaneously ringing up another sale on the register. "Go. You work too much overtime. I was talking to Gran last night, about hiring someone part time to serve behind the counter. We both think it's feasible, given how well things are going."

One of the customers immediately waved her hand. "If you're looking for staff, my Neeta needs a part-time job."

Cady grinned, and handed a cup of coffee to Paulette. "Can you give that to Mr. Harper on your way out?" To the customer who'd questioned the job, she nodded. "Once I have the details settled, I'll let you know."

Paulette shared a knowing look with Cady. She should really have learned after living in Garrison for a few months – keep your mouth shut until your plans are figured out, because once the other inhabitants learn about them, news spreads like a wildfire.

"I'll see you tomorrow," Paulette said. "And enjoy your date with Quinn!"

Cady rolled her eyes at Paulette, knowing she'd mentioned Cady's date deliberately. Talk about fanning the flames of gossip – Paulette's mischievous nature had just thrown gas on top and set a match to it.

---

QUINN STEPPED up onto the porch at Meredith's. With one thing and another, he hadn't seen Cady for more than a week, and although he made time to call her each day, he was craving seeing his little redhead in the flesh. Since the bakery opened, time with Cady had been a rare commodity, and though he was grateful for everyone making an effort to support Tokens, he didn't like that it kept them apart. He craved holding her in his arms, kissing that pert little nose... and other things.

He'd been counting down the days impatiently, knowing they were meeting up tonight. Initially, he'd planned to take Cady to Bertram, some eighty kilometers away, for a romantic supper at Bertram's one and only restaurant. It would have given them more privacy than supper at Grizzlies, but he'd changed his mind. Cady was dead on her feet most nights, and he didn't think she'd appreciate the lengthy drive, even if it did afford them some privacy. Besides, she needed to be up early in the morning to open the store, so Bertram was a non-starter.

Grizzlies was out. Every time Cady entered the bar the fates collided, creating an altercation between her and Julia or her and Earl, and he wasn't willing to chance it. So he'd come up with a Plan B, and hoped to hell he could pull it all together. His cooking wasn't great; at the best of times his abilities were limited, but he wanted to wine and dine Cady with as much privacy as they could get, and this seemed like his best option.

He knocked at the screen door and heard Churchill bark. The knowledge elicited a smile, especially when the big dog reached the front door and somehow figured it was Quinn standing outside and not some stranger. The big goof stopped barking and started whining instead, as though urging Cady to hurry and open the door.

Cady pulled open the door as Quinn pulled on the screen door, leaving them standing staring at one another. Cady was a picture; despite the icy Montana winter she'd gone with her favored look tonight and wore a get-up which Quinn could only resoundingly approve of. Navy blue pants with a high waist skimmed closely over her waist and hips, before flaring wide at the ankles, and she'd teamed them with a sailor-style top in white and navy, which fitted closely to her chest and waist affording him an unobstructed view of her gorgeous curves. And thanks to a steady diet of love and affection from Meredith, those curves had blossomed during her time in Garrison.

And Quinn was a man who loved curves.

"Hey, Cady, how are you?" Without giving her a chance to think about it, he leaned forward, gently gripping the back of her neck and pressing a kiss to her glossy red lips. Inhaling deeply, he enjoyed the aroma of rose-scented skin and breathed in again, brushing his lips over hers once more before he released her. He was pleased, when he stepped back to see a dreamy look in Cady's eyes, and he hoped to duplicate that look with her again, and soon.

"Hi Quinn. Did you want to come in?"

Quinn rubbed his hands together. "How about we head out, while the going is good?" He glanced back, to where burgeoning dark clouds threatened more snowfall.

Cady turned in the path of his gaze and a worried frown creased her pale forehead. "Do you think we'll get more snow? Maybe we should stay here…"

Quinn caught her hand, simultaneously giving Churchill a good scratch on the top of his head while he drew Cady out through the doorway. "Nope, I've got plans for us tonight, Ms. Caldwell." He reached inside and took Cady's coat, scarf and gloves from an amused Meredith's hands.

Meredith grabbed hold of Churchill's collar, stopping the dog before he tried to join them. "I'll see you later," she called, closing the door swiftly.

Quinn had expected a little anxiety from Cady, but a casual glance found her seemingly calm. He handed her coat and gloves to her, before wrapping her scarf gently around her neck himself. It gave him the opportunity to steal another kiss, this one lasting a little longer, and when he pulled back, Cady's eyes sparkled. "I thought you wanted to avoid the bad weather?" she pointed out, indicating flakes which were beginning to flurry across the landscape around them.

"Not avoid it. Miss the worst of it," Quinn retorted, taking her hand and leading her down the front walk. "This is Montana, there's no avoiding the bad weather."

Cady settled into the truck's cab and leaned down to

place her purse on the floor at her feet before she settled back, turning in his direction. "I've missed you."

Judging by the stunned expression in her eyes, those words had slipped out before she'd had the opportunity to think on them, and he watched her cheeks color. He moved quickly to defuse the situation, leaning across to press another kiss to her mouth. If he got his way, he'd have that rich red lipstick worn off those pretty lips by the end of the night. "I missed you too, Darlin'."

Watching the expression in her eyes was magic, and he saw relief blossom before pleasure rapidly overtook it, along with a healthy dose of disbelief – as if she couldn't trust that he might feel the same way she did. Quinn lifted his hand slowly, brushing his knuckles gently over her silky cheek. "Believe it, Cady. I like being with you."

The drive to his cabin passed pleasantly enough, easy conversation passing between them as they recounted their activities in the past few weeks. Quinn wanted them to spend more time together, but didn't want to press too hard, knowing Cady could panic. If he'd learned nothing else, it was the importance of taking things slowly, giving her time to make up her mind. He sure as hell wouldn't force her into anything, not after seeing the way her ex-husband had destroyed her confidence, but he found himself chomping at the bit, wanting more than Cady could give right now.

Usually, Quinn never had to wait with women he dated – most of them were more than happy to enjoy a supper, followed by a mutually satisfactory roll in the hay. Cady was a different kettle of fish, and he'd settled into the idea of it being a long time before they'd be intimate. He suspected it would be worth the wait, and he'd do anything – *anything* – to make her comfortable and feel secure.

Once again, the word 'love' reared its head and Quinn

studied the road ahead, allowing the word to reverberate through his mind. A few months ago, he'd have run a million miles from the concept of loving someone, of allowing himself to be vulnerable again – but this time, with Cady – he suspected it was worth the risk.

---

"MAKE YOURSELF AT HOME," Quinn said, shutting the front door and dropped his keys onto the hall stand. "I've got a couple of things to do for supper. Would you like a wine?"

Cady nodded, brushing her fingertips over the black enamel frame on a painting, which took up a significant area of wall space in the entrance. The painting appeared to capture the view from the edge of the lake Quinn's cabin sat on, looking out over the water to the mountains beyond. The painting depicted the area in the summer, judging by the lush green of the surrounding land, and the reduction of snow on the high peaks beyond. "A red wine, please. I didn't know you could cook." She followed Quinn through to the well-appointed kitchen, found him pouring red wine into two long-stemmed glasses before he handed her one.

"'Cook' might be an exaggeration," he admitted with a bashful grin. "I'm good at heating stuff up." He leaned over to turn on the oven, affording Cady an excellent view of his denim-encased backside, and she experienced a thrum of desire which created butterflies in her tummy. When he straightened up, she quickly averted her eyes and swallowed down a mouthful of wine, instantly regretting the decision when she choked and started to cough wildly.

Quinn took the glass, patting her back until she

regained control. "I hope you're not choking to death over the idea of me cooking supper."

His mouth said one thing, but his eyes, and the way he looked so knowingly at her, suggested something very different. Cady's face heated when she realized he'd probably guessed she'd been ogling him. She was relieved when Quinn threw her a reprieve and smiled, picking up her wineglass and handing it back to her. "Leave your purse there, I've got a surprise for you."

Cady immediately tensed, worried what this surprise could be, but after a moment of indecision, she followed him.

Quinn led the way through the living room with its soaring windows looking over the lake and down a wide hallway on the other side. A quick glance revealed a couple of bedrooms, a bathroom, Quinn's laundry room and another room which held a pool table. None of the bedrooms appeared to be the main bedroom, however, which Cady suspected must be upstairs. The last room revealed a jacuzzi, unlike any Cady had seen before. Stone walls rose from floor to ceiling, and on one side, clear glass revealed a vast outdoor patio. The jacuzzi was constructed from the same brown stone, perhaps granite, and was the size of a small swimming pool. Lights built into the sides of the jacuzzi created a soft glow, and steam rose from the heated water. All around the edges, candles in all shapes and sizes flickered and Cady noticed a cheese platter sitting by the edge, accompanied by crackers, bunches of grapes and slices of fresh cantaloupe.

She stood, mutely watching the water bubbling and tried to catch a cohesive thought. "You left the candles burning?" She cringed, knowing it was probably the stupidest comment she could have made. Between that and the choking incident, Cady wished she could sink to the bottom of the jacuzzi and drown herself.

To her shock, Quinn chuckled, drawing her cautiously into his arms. "It was a calculated risk," he admitted. "With the stone walls, and the door shut, I was reasonably certain the house would stay in one piece." He lowered his head, capturing her bottom lip between his, suckling it gently before he released it and kissed her mouth. "Besides, I wanted it to be pretty when you arrived. Would you like to climb in?"

Cady didn't know what to think, wasn't sure if she should agree or decline. This was a different Quinn to the one she'd gotten used to; a Quinn skilled in the art of seduction, and to her mind, he was clearly angling for sex. She wasn't ready, and even as Quinn lowered his mouth towards hers again, Cady squirmed, the edges of a panic beginning to creep into her heart, making the tempo increase.

Quinn released her immediately, taking a step back to give Cady a chance to breathe. "Cady? What's the matter?"

Cady intertwined her fingers, clasping them together until her knuckles whitened and she stepped back, almost falling over a chair. Quinn reached out to grab her, but Cady shook her head, her eyes wide. "No, uh, no, this is... I don't..."

"Shhhh," Quinn said softly. "Shhhh, darlin'. Calm down. Take it easy." He took a step toward her, came to a halt, then took another cautious step. "Cady, I don't know what's going on in that head of yours, but I don't—" He stopped abruptly, squeezing his eyes shut and cursing under his breath. "Damn it, Cady. I'm not trying to seduce you."

Cady found her voice. "But..."

Quinn shook his head. "No, I'm sorry. You're right." He glanced across at the jacuzzi ruefully. "I was goin' for tranquil and relaxing, I swear to God, Cady, that's what I was aimin' for. But I can see how you could look at this and think..." He inhaled deeply and chewed on his lip for a minute. "I swear, I wasn't tryin' anything with you. I just thought, you'd been so damn busy with the bakery, and I assumed you might need to relax, so while I prepared supper, I thought you could sit in the jacuzzi and unwind."

Cady tugged self-consciously at her clothing. "I... Quinn... I don't feel comfortable being naked—"

"Aw hell, I really have made a mess of this." Quinn scraped his fingers through his dark hair, before he took to rubbing the back of his neck sounding completely forlorn. "It was part of the surprise," he finally said. "I dropped by Meredith's earlier in the week and she put together a bag for me to bring out here, with some of your stuff, so you could go in the jacuzzi and be totally comfortable." He shook his head. "I've made a disaster of this whole thing."

It was Cady's turn to step forward and she reached out to pat Quinn's arm, wanting to wipe the pitiful expression from his eyes. "Oh, Quinn, thank you. And I'm sorry, I shouldn't have jumped to conclusions about your intentions."

Quinn's expression brightened, and he stared down into her eyes, searching them. "You're sure now?"

Cady nodded, her heartbeat slowing now she wasn't so panicked. "I'm sorry too, for being such a goose."

Quinn grinned, and lowered his head to press a gentle kiss on Cady's lips. "You're a cute little goose, I'll give you that much."

---

Cady rolled over, opening one eye to check the alarm clock. Seeing the time, she threw the covers back, swinging her legs off the side of the bed and coming to her feet in one motion, immediately regretting the undertaking when she tripped over a slipper, and stumbled past the bedside cabinet, stubbing her toe. "Oh, for goodness sake!"

Churchill glanced up, opening his mouth wide and yawning heavily before he settled his head back onto his paws.

"Fat lot of good you are," Cady grumbled, sitting on the edge of the bed to rub her throbbing toe. "Our first day without Paulette and I'm late, and Gran's at the bakery alone. We're due to open in a half hour!" She got up and hobbled into the bathroom, intent on snatching a quick shower before she dressed and hurried to the store.

Paulette's new grandson had made his arrival the previous day. As agreed when Paulette took the job, she was taking a few days off to spend with her daughter and new grandson. Meredith had taken up the slack, insisting early mornings didn't worry her, so she'd started at four am this morning, getting the bread baked for opening at eight. Washing her hair, Cady cursed about sleeping through her alarm, worrying about Meredith coping alone with the day's preparations. While Gran was capable of a great many things, Cady worried she worked too hard in her efforts to help Cady with Tokens. And typically, she'd left Cady to sleep in, rather than calling to remind her when she was late arriving.

Minutes later, Cady arrived at the bakery, hurrying through the door to help with icing cupcakes and stocking shelves ready for the day's trade. "Gran!" she called, hanging up her coat and stuffing her gloves into the pockets, before unwinding the scarf from her neck and hanging it with her coat. "You should have called! Now we're running late..."

Cady would normally have brought Churchill along, but in a hurry, she'd left him at home, leaving him with a treat and a promise that she'd come and pick him up during the first lull in the day. Not surprisingly, Churchill had whined, even scratched a little at the door when Cady shut it behind her. She mentally promised him an extra-long walk when she got home that afternoon. Churchill went to work with her most days, perfectly content to sit on a mat outside the store greeting customers, or when the weather was icy and cold, lying on a blanket beside the stove, warming himself and being patted by most everyone who came in. He'd swiftly become a part of Tokens charm.

Cady stopped abruptly, suddenly alert to the silence in the store. Paulette and Gran usually had the radio on, listening to music while they worked, and by now, the whole bakery would smell heavenly as the day's bread supply filled the air with warm yeasty goodness and the cupcakes cooled in preparation for icing. It was always a conglomeration of pleasant aromas, one that Cady would breathe in deeply and experience a great sense of satisfaction from but today, those smells were missing. Her nose detected the rich aroma of risen yeasty bread, but not the smell which resulted from baking. "Gran?" she called and heard the hesitation in her voice.

Cady walked towards the counter cautiously, eyes roaming across every inch of the shiny top, taking in each detail, searching for what was creating the sizzle of electricity up her spine, the hairs on her neck to stand on end. "Gran?" she repeated, her voice barely above a whisper.

Nothing seemed out of place but trailing her fingers across the top of the register, her over-wrought senses were ringing. There was no sound coming from the kitchen at all and her sense of dread grew, creating a tangible sensation in the store. Gran hadn't responded to anything she'd said, and the trepidation increased, pressing against her chest like a heavy weight.

She wanted to turn tail and run, get out of the store, escape whatever might be waiting for her in the kitchen, but Gran was in there, she was certain. She couldn't leave her. Cady reached for the phone on the wall but before her fingers reached the handset she hesitated, dropping her hand back to her side. She needed to find out what happened to Gran before she called anyone. Maybe she'd fallen and hit her head, or perhaps something else had happened. Maybe she'd slipped out of the store for a minute or two, and Cady was worrying over nothing. "Gran, I wish you'd answer," she muttered, turning the corner and entering the kitchen. "Oh! Gran!"

Meredith lay on her left side in the middle of the tiled floor, both legs bent at the knee. Her left arm was twisted up behind her, and her right arm flopped at an unnatural angle in front of her body. A circle of crimson created a sizeable pool around her head.

Cady shrieked, running across the floor, and dropping to her knees. She reached for Meredith, intent on trying to stem the flow of blood, trying to figure out what had happened. Meredith's skin was deathly pale, her eyes closed; but before Cady could reach for her neck and check for a pulse, she heard a voice which brought her heart to a standstill.

"It's about time."

———

LUANNE SHUT the door to Grizzlies and locked it, dropping the key fob into her pocket before she began a careful walk across the icy carpark, intent on collecting her morning pleasure. Wasn't doing her figure an ounce of good, but an espresso and one of them blueberry chiffon cupcakes with vanilla buttercream had become an addiction. Every morning Luanne came into the bar, checked over the work the cleaner had completed the night before, settled into her stock take and ordering and then headed over to Tokens about five minutes before opening time, to collect her daily fix.

Treading carefully across the road and stepping up over the curb on the other side, Luanne noticed the front door of Tokens was open. It struck her as odd, given how cool the weather was still. While the bakery got quite warm with the ovens going, it was never hot enough that Cady and Paulette would leave the door open. And today, Luanne reminded herself, it would be Meredith, since Paulette's daughter had delivered her baby just the day before. She stepped over the threshold, brushing her feet carefully on the mat, and glanced around. Strangely, there were no cakes in the display cabinet yet; usually by now, Cady had everything tiptop and shipshape in preparation for opening. In fact, most mornings, she was to be found standing behind that fancy coffee making machine, prepping Luanne's coffee ready for her arrival.

There was no one to be seen, and a glance confirmed the fire burning in the stove was down to embers, emitting very little heat to keep the store warm. Cady's outerwear was hanging on a hook by the door, and next to it, she recognized Meredith's thick navy coat and checked scarf.

Where were they?

With worry rising rapidly in her chest, Luanne hurried around behind the counter. Usually, she wouldn't dream of entering the Caldwell women's domain – just like she wouldn't expect them behind the bar at Grizzlies. Today, however, was not a normal day.

"Oh, sweet lord Jesus," Luanne muttered, rushing across the floor to where Meredith was, a pool of blood surrounding her head. She suspected the older woman was dead, and lowered her bulk carefully onto one knee, groaning when it cracked as she landed heavily against the tiles. She reached out to touch Meredith but found herself terrified of doing so. What if Mer's skin was cold to touch? Luanne and Meredith had known one another for years, were firm friends, and Luanne couldn't bear the prospect of Meredith being dead. What had happened? Was it a robbery? A quick scan revealed no sign of Cady in the small kitchen, and a dreadful thought dawned on Luanne. Had Cady been snatched by someone? Was Meredith the victim of a murderer? Luanne knew enough to know she shouldn't touch anything and she struggled back onto her feet. Hurrying out into the shop, she snatched up the phone to call for help. She didn't know nothing about first aid, and it was obvious from the pool of blood that Meredith needed help just as soon as she could get it.

She waited only a second or two before she was put through to the Sheriff's office and recognized Kane's voice when he answered the phone. "Garrison Sheriff's office."

"Kane, oh, good lord, Kane..." Luanne was flustered, couldn't seem to string a sentence together and she rubbed a hand over her brow, trying to settle her nerves. She glanced into the kitchen and the sight of Meredith's prone body brought tears welling up in her eyes.

"Luanne? Is that you?" Kane's deep voice was calm, his tone filled with authority as he automatically seemed to switch into investigative mode. "What's wrong?"

"It's Meredith, she's— well, I don't know what, but it's bad, Kane. She's bleeding, bleeding a lot and she looks—" Luanne's voice caught in her throat and she slapped her hand against her chest, as if she could calm the erratic pounding of her heart with the gesture.

She heard Kane talking rapidly to someone in the background, before he came back on the line. "Are you at the bakery? Where's Cady?"

Luanne swallowed heavily against a throat which was abruptly dry and coughed once or twice before she spoke again. "I don't know. Lor' Jesus, I don't know!"

"Alright, the ambulance is on its way, be there in a couple of minutes and I'll be right behind it. Don't touch anything; just wait there until we get there, y'hear?"

---

GEORGE PULLED UP OUTSIDE TOKENS, finding a sizeable crowd already gathered in the early morning. Luanne stood to one side with Kane, watching on as the town's paramedic team rolled Meredith out of the store on a gurney. His heart climbed up through his chest and into his throat at the sight of Mer; lying on her back, she had an oxygen mask over her mouth and nose, and her eyes were closed. Half her face had been swallowed up by a heavy dressing, bandaging wrapped around her head to stem the flow of blood. He pushed his way through the milling crowd to her side, just as the paramedics were preparing to lift her into the ambulance. "Is she okay?"

P.J. Mandrell stopped and turned to George, his dark eyes solemn. "She's taken some substantial blows to the head, at least two, maybe more. Looks like whoever did it used a rolling pin; it was lying on the floor near her body. We need to get on the road, George. Got to get Meredith to Billings for treatment."

George took Meredith's hand and squeezed her fingers, searching her delicate features for any sign of movement, some recognition – but her pale face remained passive, revealing nothing to confirm she was alive. George lifted her fingers, pressed a kiss to her knuckles and tried to bank down the sense of helplessness which had been building in his chest since Kane called him, telling him there was trouble at the bakery. And now he was faced with his beloved Meredith looking so lifeless and so pale, and Cady was nowhere to be found.

P.J. patted George's shoulder, and when he looked up into the paramedic's ruddy face, he could read the sympathy in his eyes. "Her condition is serious, but stable. She's gonna be fine."

To his mortification, tears welled in George's eyes and he turned away, focusing with laser point accuracy on a car parked at the other side of the street until he got himself under control. "I know she's in good hands," he said, when he could be sure his voice wouldn't waver. He wanted to go with her, would have given anything to get in the ambulance with Mer, but he was needed here. His small team had a duty to investigate what happened, figure out where the hell Cady had gone. Pushing his hat back onto his head, he indicated the ambulance with a tip of his chin. "You take care of her, y'hear?"

"Will do," P.J. responded, pushing the stretcher so the legs began to fold under while Allan Drey, the other half of Garrison's paramedic team shoved from the bottom end. P.J. leaped up into the back of the ambulance and settled beside Meredith's body, checking the IV line and strapping the gurney into position. Allan offered George a sympathetic nod before he hurried around to climb into the driver's seat.

"If she wakes up..." George inhaled sharply, bracing his hands against his hips, wondering what he could say in front of this crowd. When he did speak again, he went with his heart, and to hell with the consequences. "You tell Meredith... tell her I love her. And I'll be there, just as soon as I can. You boys can get me on my cell if there's any change in her condition. Y'hear?"

P.J. settled back on his seat, placing the buds of a stethoscope in his ears. "Yes, sir."

George slammed the doors shut and banged twice on the ambulance, letting Allan know he could take off. The paramedic did so, turning the strobe lights on top of the ambulance on and slowly pulling away from the bakery before picking up speed. Once he was a distance away from the crowds, he turned on the siren and George watched as the rig faded from view. Adjusting his hat, he put on his game face, pushing worry about Meredith to the back of his mind. Right now, he needed to figure out who'd done this, and why, and where the heck Cady had disappeared to.

George strode across to Luanne and Kane. Luanne was visibly anxious, a frown creasing her ebony forehead and she rubbed at the side of her face in a nervous motion, back and forth, back and forth as she spoke with Kane. "No sir, I didn't see anyone else in there. Just Mer, lying in the middle of the—" Her breath hitched, and she worked discernibly to calm herself before she continued, "...floor, with all that blood."

Kane turned to George, his face stony. "Luanne found Meredith when she came over to collect her morning coffee, around 8.10 am. She found the door open and the stove banked down, as though it hadn't been tended since Meredith opened early this morning. I've done a preliminary check of the building and determined it's empty. There's no sign of Cady." Kane glanced at his notes. "No sign of forced entry, and I suspect Meredith either let the perpetrator in of her own free will," he swallowed convulsively, "or forgot to lock the doors."

"Wouldn't be the first time," George growled, clenching his teeth hard enough to make his jaw ache. He'd grumbled at the two women numerous times for leaving the door unlocked, and both Meredith and Cady promised they'd remember to lock it. But this was a small town, and he knew they'd grown complacent. He also suspected the women had started to think they had nothing to worry about from Cady's ex-husband after so many weeks without a sighting. Not that he had proof yet that Le Batelier was behind this, but his gut was sending him messages and he was apt to listen. Le Batelier had sworn to finish what he'd started, and George had to wonder if this was his handiwork.

Kane nodded. "Reid's inside taking crime scene photos,

and I've called in reinforcements from Bertram, along with their Crime Investigation Unit. They'll be here within the hour."

George nodded, thinking fast as he surveyed the street, his gaze focusing on Grizzlies and then back on Luanne. "What time did you get in to work this morning?"

Luanne took a moment to think. "Being Wednesday, it's ordering day; I got here about 7am."

"Were the lights on over here?" George questioned. He needed a clue, had to get his head around what the situation was and quickly, if they were going to find Cady and whoever had done this. Another thought crossed his mind and a flicker of hope flared. "Has anyone checked Meredith's house yet?"

Kane inclined his head. "I sent Reid to the house while I made my way straight here after Luanne called. Nobody's home."

"That big ol' mutt?"

"Yep, he was there, got all agitated when he knocked on the door according to Reid. He's inside the house for now, but—"

George took his hat off and wiped his brow, frowning. "Cady doesn't usually leave him there."

Luanne shook her head. "No, she doesn't – that girl adores that dog, he's usually right here, with her, every single day."

George exchanged a sharp glance with Kane. "We need to get in the house, check if there's anything out of the ordinary. Maybe Cady didn't make it to the store."

"I think she did," Luanne pointed out. "Her coat and scarf are here."

George huffed out a breath, his mind working at a million miles an hour. "Luanne, I want you to think carefully. When you arrived this morning, did you see any unfamiliar vehicles in the area? Parked on the street maybe, or even in the Grizzlies car park? I know it's hard to recall every vehicle in town, but if you can remember anything..."

Luanne shook her head, crossing her arms over her expansive bosom. "No, sir, I don't recall anythin' out of the ordinary."

George shifted his attention back to Kane. "We need to get into Meredith's house, check around. If for nothing else, we need to get the big mutt, look after him while this gets sorted out." He paused, considering his next words and brushed his hand over his jaw sheepishly. "I'll take him back to my place, until we've found Cady."

George caught Kane's startled look but chose to ignore it. He always referred to Cady's dog in a derogatory manner, either as the 'big mutt', or 'that walking ball of fluff', but in all honesty, he'd grown fond of the damn thing. Knowing how Cady felt about him, and how the dog felt about Cady, he imagined Churchill would be mighty anxious if she didn't make an appearance soon. "Right," George said, pushing his hat back onto his head firmly. He needed to put worry about Meredith, and his own emotions on the backburner while he dealt with this mess. He needed to locate Cady and solve who'd done this to Meredith. "Let's get to work."

## 29

C ady was frozen.
 The biting cold seeped into her skin, reaching deeper by the minute. She visualized the cold meeting and merging with the icy shock squeezing her heart, a terror which had only grown since Jameson snatched her.

The cabin she was in was isolated, located high in the Beartooth Mountains. The road they'd travelled to get here seemed like a fire track cutting through the woods, unlikely to be well-used. This knowledge frightened her even more, and she made another futile scan of the room, seeking anything to use as a weapon, or as a tool to escape.

The tiny cabin consisted of one room and looked almost uninhabitable. The ramshackle building didn't hold a stick of furniture, other than a rusty, potbelly stove in one corner. The rough wood floor was covered in a thick layer of dirt and grime, and rotten floorboards left gaps where the bitter cold gained easy access. Two small windows had broken glass and wind whistled through the cracks. The door stood open, and for the moment she was alone – but Jameson was just outside. She could hear him trudging back and forth around the black pickup he'd driven them up here in. The vehicle was parked right outside the cabin door – and even if she'd been brave enough to attempt an escape, where would she go?

Cady was sitting on the floor in one corner of the room, where Jameson had dumped her after their arrival. She had her knees drawn up to her chest and her arms wrapped around her legs; trying desperately to retain some body heat. Snow lay deep on the ground outside, and Cady only wore denim overalls with a light woolen sweater underneath. Her warm coat, gloves and scarf had all been left behind at the store.

A wave of misery swamped her when she considered Gran's situation, worried the older woman was dead. Jameson had gripped her arm and hustled her out of the store before she could check, but she couldn't erase the memory of all the blood surrounding Gran's head, or how dreadfully pale she'd been. Cady's heart ached when she thought of Gran, and her teeth chattered in a combination of cold and shock.

Other than the few sentences he'd spoken in Tokens, Jameson hadn't uttered another word. During the drive out of town, he hadn't even looked at her and Cady suspected it was part of his plan to throw her off-balance, keep her second-guessing. These were tactics he'd used in the past, threatening behavior to keep Cady anxious about his intentions. She lifted her chin defiantly and inhaled, the icy air chilling her throat. She wouldn't let him do this to her again. He wouldn't get to play his sick mind games this time. Cady was stronger now, owned her own business, was becoming a respected member of the Garrison community. Jameson Le Batelier couldn't take any of that away from her.

But her limbs continued to shake, and her teeth

continued to chatter. And it wasn't all due to the bitter cold in the cabin.

Heavy footfalls sounded outside and despite her best intentions, Cady shrank up against the wall, making herself as small as possible. She peeked up at Jameson as he dropped a box of supplies onto the floor and turned to go back out. Not for the first time, Cady tried to guess what he might be planning. She watched his departing back and shuddered, seeing the gun he'd tucked into the back of his jeans for the first time.

His appearance had changed; he'd disguised himself, no doubt, so he could make his way into Garrison unrecognized. His dark hair had been dyed blonde, and he'd changed the style. His short, stylishly cut hair had been left to grow and fluffed around his face in loose waves. She suspected he was wearing colored contacts, changing his eyes from their usual green to dark brown. He'd grown a beard, and this too had been dyed blonde to match his hair. Peeking at him, she despaired. Unless you truly knew him, nobody would guess this man was Jameson Le Batelier, world-renowned chef. She doubted anyone in or around Garrison had given him a second glance, and nobody would have recognized him for who he truly was.

Cady chewed anxiously at her cheek, wondering how to get out of this mess. She cursed herself for being so scared, for letting him make her feel this way. For sitting here, not doing anything but wait for Jameson to make his first move. Memories of their marriage crowded her mind; the way he'd broken her spirit, taken her free-will, made her too frightened to speak out. Now, all these months later, being in his presence had brought those ingrained behaviors rushing back to the forefront. She despaired, knowing the progress she'd made in Garrison was being eroded by fear and intimidation.

Jameson came back inside, closing the door behind him. Unlike Cady, he was dressed suitably for the weather, with jeans, heavy boots and socks, and layers of sweaters, a thick jacket and gloves. He caught Cady's gaze for a moment and smirked, maintaining the oppressive silence. The intimidation tactics wore at Cady's nerves until her heart began to flutter uncomfortably in her chest and she thought she'd be sick. She lowered her gaze, adopting the submissive gesture which had been second nature when they'd lived together. Now, that same gesture grated, but she was terrified of what Jameson would do.

What *was* his plan? The question had tumbled through her thoughts from the moment she first heard his voice in Tokens. This cabin sat high on the mountain, right on the edge of a sheer cliff face. Although they'd travelled through heavily wooded areas as Jameson drove along the fire track, the area surrounding the cottage was barren, devoid of any vegetation. When he escorted her up the stairs into the cabin, Cady wondered why he'd choose a place which was so exposed. Now, with nothing to do but think, she'd concluded that Jameson didn't want anyone getting close enough to rescue her. The cabin was likely only ever used for emergencies – although given the state of the structure, it had probably been abandoned for years. It was well out of Garrison, on the other side of the Beartooth Mountains. Nobody was likely to come up here searching for her. Why would they? This was miles away from everything, and nobody knew she was gone.

She hoped they'd found Gran by now. Luanne must have come in for her coffee and cupcake by now, and Cady could only hope she'd figured out something was wrong, found Gran in the kitchen and called for help. Cady's teeth chattered so badly, she couldn't stop them, and she wondered how long it took to die from hypothermia. She was so cold now, her toes were numb in her shoes, and she couldn't feel her fingers.

She shook even more when Jameson crouched beside her, reaching out to run one finger down her cheek. Cady forced herself to remain immobile, even as inside, every instinct urged her to run.

But she had nowhere to go.

---

"We'll find her, son."

Quinn stared out of the passenger window, listening to the same words his father had repeated since they left the Silver Peaks to hurry into town. He wasn't sure he believed them, still hadn't come to terms with what had happened. Meredith seriously injured, Cady missing... as far as Quinn could tell, there was only one person to blame – Cady's husband. How he could have gotten into Garrison unnoticed was anyone's guess, but Quinn's gut told him Jameson Le Batelier had done this. Who else would want to take Cady? He was heartsick over Meredith getting hurt, but terrified about Cady's fate. Where could she be?

Jesus, from the chatter they'd heard, she'd been missing for at least an hour or two, possibly more. Kane had told him as much as he could when he called, but he was swamped with the search preparations and told Quinn to get into town as soon as he could. Both his cell and his father's had been ringing constantly since, as news spread through town.

Thankfully, John Garrison had taken the lead, guiding Quinn out to his truck and driving them into town, because

.S. WILLIAMS

one glance down at his hands confirmed they were shaking, and his mind was so blanked out with worry, Quinn knew he'd be a danger on the road. Fear was creating a tight clamp around his heart, and terror gnawed at his gut. He hadn't endured anything like it since his time overseas. He'd believed he had his demons under control, but this situation, knowing Cady was missing – possibly dead – was churning everything up, reminding him of times he'd sooner forget. He'd struggled with PTSD since he'd revealed details about his time in the Rangers to Cady, enduring sleepless nights – but he'd kept the fact from Cady. She was quick to blame herself for so many things; his relapse wasn't going to be one of them. But now, he had to get his head in the game, and bank down the gut-curling stress which was threatening his self-control.

"We'll find her, Quinn." John Garrison clapped his hand on Quinn's shoulder, drawing him back to the present. "She hasn't been gone long – I doubt whoever has her has gotten far. If her ex-husband snatched her, he wouldn't want to stay in the open for long. He'll go to ground, somewhere nearby." John leaned forward, casting a worried glance over the ominous clouds overhead. "Let's hope this storm holds off."

Quinn nodded, leaned his elbow on the windowsill, and rested his head against his fist. He needed to bring his 'A' game to the search for Cady, and with effort, he focused on pushing the other crap into the background.

When they arrived in Main Street they found it crowded with vehicles, and dozens of men and women stood together in the cold January air, waiting outside the bakery for news. Quinn was heartened by their presence; in a time of crisis, the people of Garrison would always come together to help one of their own.

He stepped out of the pickup, shrugging his jacket a little closer around his body before he shoved his hat on his head and strode across the road to the bakery. Flurries of snow began to fall, and the bitter chill in the air promised the upcoming storm would quickly turn into a blizzard.

He caught a glimpse of the crime scene tape around the outside of the shop. Strung up from the side entrance of Tokens, it looped around a light pole at the front of the building and then back to the other side, effectively cutting off access to the bakery. A couple of guys milled around inside – men he didn't recognize – and he guessed they must be crime investigators, called in from Bertram to assist.

Quinn spotted Kane and George with two rangers from the National Park Service; they had a map spread over the hood of Kane's cruiser and the NPS men were pointing at something. George listened carefully to what they were telling him, as he scrutinized the map with a frown creasing his forehead. Kane's expression was grim, the set of his jaw and the tension in his shoulders revealing the pressure he was under.

Quinn estimated the crowd was upwards of one hundred and fifty to two hundred people, and they all huddled together, waiting for instructions about where to search. More pickups, trucks and cars were appearing, seeking somewhere to park so they could join the rest of the searchers. The question was, did anyone know where to start looking? And how long would they be able to search before the weather shut them down? Eyeing the dark grey, almost black nimbostratus clouds overhead, he figured they wouldn't have long before the weather shut down any hope of finding Cady. He resisted the urge to march over to George and demand they start searching immediately. It chafed to wait, but he was as aware as anyone that they needed an idea of where to start, and George and Kane were clearly trying to figure it out.

His Dad came and stood beside him, wearing a thick lambskin jacket. He had his hands balled up in the pockets of his jacket and his shoulders hunched against the icy cold wind gusts. "Your Mom and Hallie are on their way, they're going to help out with catering," he murmured.

George caught sight of Quinn and John and waved them over, his face a mask of cold indifference, totally professional. Quinn knew it to be a mask, he could see from George's eyes that the man was hurting and imagined his own face looked mighty similar. He dipped his head in acknowledgement. "How's Meredith?"

"Unconscious. Severe head wound, but P.J. says she'll be okay."

"Thank God," John said.

"Is it Cady's ex-husband who's done this?" Quinn asked impatiently.

George put his fists on his hips, the composed mask slipping for just a moment and revealing his fury. "We can't be sure... but he's certainly top of the list—"

"Sheriff! Sheriff Davis!" Quinn's head snapped around at the sound of a wavering voice. The elderly Martha Law stood beside her daughter Joanie, at the yellow tape delineating the crime scene. Joanie had a hand wrapped around her mother's waist, steadying her in the icy conditions and the elderly woman appeared to be wearing about ten layers of clothing, from what he could judge.

"Mrs. Law, what the heck are you doing out here?" George questioned. "You'll catch your death."

Martha Law had been born in Garrison some ninety-five years earlier, and her wizened features and faded blue eyes were testament to her longevity. Nearly hidden beneath a fluffy black hat and matching coat, the tiny woman peered up at George with steely determination.

"I did tell her I'd pass on any message, Sheriff," Joanie announced. She rolled her eyes, giving the impression she'd tried, and failed, to thwart her mother's determination to visit the bakery. "But she insisted on coming herself, to talk to you."

"What did you want to tell me, Mrs. Law?" George asked, and Quinn noticed how attentive he was towards the older woman. Martha Law was well known in town for her acerbic wit and intolerance of fools, and that trait was revealed when she spoke. "George, I'd expected you would have called on me before now, with regards to this morning's events. But when you didn't come, I asked Joanie here to bring me to see you. I have important information, which you'll need if you want to find that young woman."

George caught Quinn's eye and he could read the older man's thoughts. Mrs. Law was afflicted with dementia and had been for the past few years, often getting confused and disorientated. The last time she'd had important information to report, she'd been complaining about the fairies who'd taken up residence in her yard and wanted the Sheriff to investigate. It had turned out to be a few scraps of aluminum foil, which had blown into her yard. When the breeze blew across them, they'd caught the light and reflected it back, making Mrs. Law think it was fairies communicating with little, tiny flashlights. Another time, she'd called to report her husband was missing… and he'd been dead for more than two decades. From what Quinn heard, Martha Law was in touch with the Sheriff's Department at least once or twice a month with a problem, and Quinn didn't hold out any hope for whatever information she thought she held now.

George was more solicitous. "What did you have to report, Ma'am?"

"That young woman was kidnapped by the CIA," Martha Law announced, her voice firm. "I seen them outside Meredith's house, more than once." She waved her cane in emphasis, nearly slipping on the icy ground and George reached forward to grip her arm until she found her feet again.

Quinn wanted to roll his eyes but avoided giving in to the urge. Over the top of Mrs. Law's head, he met Joanie's eyes and offered her a sympathetic smile, knowing she had a lot to deal with as Mrs. Law's mental health deteriorated. He was holding onto the last of his patience with a fine thread though, and he wanted to shout and start demanding they start doing something to find Cady.

George took a calmer approach to Martha Law's announcement. Keeping his attention focused on the elderly woman, he reached out and took one of her hands in his. "Now Mrs. Law – why would you think that?"

"Because when Theodore took me out for ice-cream last Tuesday night, we saw a black vehicle parked along the street outside Meredith's house and he remarked on it."

Quinn squeezed his eyes shut, and sucked in a deep breath, wanting to put an end to this ridiculous story. Martha Law's husband had been dead for twenty-five years – he most certainly hadn't taken his wife out for ice-cream last Tuesday night.

George rubbed his gloved hand over the top of Mrs. Laws. "What sort of car was it, ma'am?"

Martha Laws nodded vigorously. "Oh, yes. A black CIA one." She glanced around the street, her faded blue eyes tracing over the vehicles in the immediate vicinity.

"Kind of like that," she pointed to Lorna Mendez's black SUV, parked outside the gift store, "but a little larger."

George pursed his lips. "Did you see it again?"

Joanie spoke up, sounding anxious. "Please, Mama, I'm not sure you really saw it at all," she began, wrapping her arm a little more tightly around Martha's waist. "You don't want to be wastin' George's time – not when Cady—"

Martha's eyes hardened, the pale blue appearing to freeze as hard as the icy ground under their feet. "I am not wasting the Sheriff's time, Joanie. I did see a CIA vehicle parked outside Meredith's house. It was there last Tuesday, and then again on Friday night, and it was there the past two nights. And that was after they changed vehicles; before then, the man was driving a different vehicle, a silver one. And I don't like your tone, young lady. I might be getting a little older, but it doesn't mean I've lost my marbles! Besides," she announced triumphantly and reached into the pocket of her coat, "I got the license plate details and I remembered to write them down!"

---

## 30

Cady glanced at her watch. The face had been partially obscured by the zip ties Jameson used to bind her hands together, but the small hand revealed it was a little after ten in the morning, more than two hours since Jameson snatched her. Had anyone found Gran? Luanne always popped in to Tokens a little after eight, and Cady hoped the Grizzlies owner had figured out something was wrong. Would she have found Gran? For what must be the hundredth time, Cady offered up a fervent hope that her grandmother wasn't dead – that Jameson had only knocked her out and not killed her.

And as a nagging afterthought to fretting over Gran; how would anyone find Cady?

She cast another furtive glance at Jameson, who'd settled on a foldup stool by the empty hearth. When he first sat down, she'd assumed he was going to light a fire and silently rejoiced at the prospect of a little warmth. She wasn't sure if the temperature had dropped, or if she was experiencing the beginnings of hypothermia in the freezing conditions – but she grew colder by the minute and despaired of ever being warm again.

Jameson hadn't lit the fire though; all he'd done was sat and drunk coffee from a thermos and stared at her with his strange dark eyes. It had taken her a while to realize that he wouldn't light the fire, didn't want the smoke to reveal to any searchers where they were.

Jameson's eyes were still on her now – staring, calculating – his expression not giving anything away. It had been one of his favorite tactics during their marriage – a strategy designed to make her squirm, have her second guessing his intentions. Now, it only served to feed her anger.

She'd expected she wasn't going to get out of this alive from the beginning. All these months in Garrison, Cady had waited for the other shoe to drop, suspected Jameson would eventually find her. Deep down, she'd anticipated this would be the end game, knew if Jameson found her, he would kill her. The question was, how he intended to do it... and why was he waiting?

Thoughts of Quinn rose unbidden, and she ached for the loss of his gentle touch, mourned the knowledge she might never see him again. He'd become important to her, and Cady admitted the truth to herself, a truth she'd been avoiding for a while now. She'd fallen in love.

Quinn treated her with respect, challenged her to escape the shackles she'd placed on herself due to her past, and he's only ever shown her kindness. She replayed some of their dates in her mind and recalled the ride in the sleigh just a few weeks ago, which had been magical. Quinn never gave up on her, even when she'd given up on herself, and along with Gran, and nearly everyone in Garrison, he'd worked to build up Cady's self-respect and pride to a point where she could see a path forward.

She would be sorry to lose the friendship of the Garrison family. Nancy, and Hallie had become good friends, people Cady could care about and rely on. John Garrison's down-to-Earth advice and support had been something Cady cherished and more than once, Cady had secretly wished he'd been her own father, the one she'd never truly had. Quinn's brothers – all of them had been respectful and pleasant, offered friendship. She hadn't had time to get to know them and mourned the lost opportunity.

Luanne. Lorna. Old Mr. Harper. Dotty Knightley, who'd been so thrilled when Cady took over creating cakes for the townsfolk. Sheriff Davis. Paulette. Uncle David and Victoria. Each had touched her life in the past months.

And Sid and Harry. The relationship between the sisters, since Cady came to Garrison had strengthened, grown better than before. For the first time, they'd been equals – sisters. The way sisters should be.

And she'd loved it.

She quickly realized the anger – which she needed to feed, allowing it to grow and spread –was being swamped by fear. The same fear which Jameson nurtured, using the emotion to suppress her self-belief, her confidence – her ability to be the woman she was capable of becoming. The woman she *wanted* to be.

She had reasons to live. Lots of them. Gritting her teeth to force them to stop chattering, she made a silent pact. She wouldn't sit back passively and allow Jameson to control her again. If he intended to kill her, she'd go down fighting. He wasn't going to make her cower on the floor, here in the corner of this dilapidated shack. She'd survived everything thrown at her up until now, and Quinn – and Gran, Sid and

Harry – none of them would want to see her cowering in the corner, too frightened to fight.

Squaring her shoulders, she lifted her gaze, forced herself to meet Jameson's dark brown eyes. "Well, you've kidnapped me. Now what are you going to do?"

———

GEORGE STOOD before the large map on his office wall, his eyes raking over Garrison and the surrounding area. *Cady, where the hell are you?* He and his men had retreated to the Sheriff's Office, to coordinate the search and investigate Martha Laws claims regarding a vehicle keeping surveillance on Meredith's place.

George was in turmoil; even though he'd received word confirming Meredith made it to Billings, and that her condition was serious but stable, he was still worried. Every time the phone rang he started, expecting news about Meredith's condition, or Cady's whereabouts. He scanned the map again, surveying possible search parameters. If he didn't find Cady, Meredith would have his guts for garters when she learned her granddaughter had been snatched on his watch.

The folk of Garrison had pulled together in this crisis, as they had time and time again during George's tenure as Sheriff. Search teams had been organized up around the lake, Bertram officers had been pulled in to set up road blocks in and out of town, and George was following up every lead, every piece of information, no matter how small. Some of the townsfolk had taken on conducting a street-by-street search of the small town. He had a call in to Billings for extra officers, and men were on their way now, willing to risk travelling in the increasingly treacherous conditions to help with the search.

Kane stalked in to the office, his expression thunderous, notebook clutched in his fist. "Martha Laws got it partly right," he announced. "She definitely saw a couple of vehicles, but obviously they weren't CIA – that part was imagination. Alamo car rentals in Billings confirm that an 'Alain Mercier' hired two cars from them; a silver SUV initially, and then he came back and swapped it out with a black pickup. He provided an address in Billings which is fake, but they've got a copy of his license and they're emailing it through. I did a little digging around – Alain Mercier just happens to be the name of Jameson Le Batelier's business partner."

"Have you spoken to him?" George snapped. He took a deep breath, realizing he was pushing too hard. Kane was a better investigator than that, and George squeezed his eyes shut, squeezing the bridge of his nose between his thumb and forefinger.

"Yes, sir. He admits to providing Le Batelier with his credentials and cash, says he just wanted to 'help out a friend'." Kane's voice was cold, giving George a clear indication of his opinion regarding Mercier's behavior. "He wasn't keen on helping out, but after a reminder that he's been aiding and abetting a wanted criminal, he 'fessed up with some further information. Le Batelier has colored his hair blonde, and grown a beard that he's also dyed blonde. He's wearing colored contact lenses... I've got an updated description, and it's being promulgated out to the search teams along with a BOLO on the make and model of the vehicle."

"Thank you, Kane." George slumped down into his chair, gaze lingering on the map. "How's Quinn doing?"

"He's out with the search teams at the lake. Calls me about once every ten minutes for an update."

George smirked. "He's got it bad, doesn't he?"

Kane nodded. "Any update on Meredith?"

George sighed, shaking his head. "Nothing since she reached the hospital, but I've got to hope she'll be okay. I know she's in good hands, but I'd rather be with her." It was a huge admission for George, who had tried to keep his relationship with Meredith under wraps up until now. But silently, he offered up a little prayer, a deal to be more open about their relationship, if God just let her live.

"She's a strong woman," Kane offered after a moment's silence. "She'll survive."

"In the meantime, we've got to find her granddaughter," George added. "Otherwise *I* might not survive."

---

"You've ruined my life."

Cady watched a variety of emotions flicker across Jameson's eyes, the only discernable signals he ever exposed. Over the years, she'd learned to read the emotion in those eyes, and today was no different, despite the colored contacts. Anger kept his irises stony, and steely determination was revealed in the way he watched her, the minute flicker of his pupils when his focus flicked from her left eye to her right, constantly on alert for any movement she might make. There was no doubt that in his mind, Cady was the source of everything that had gone wrong in his life and must be punished for her transgressions.

Cady straightened her back, gritting her teeth together to keep them from chattering. She tipped her chin defiantly. "You did that, Jameson, not me. You made the decisions which have brought you to this point."

She expected him to throw the chair to one side, get to

his feet, slap her across the cheek as he'd done so many times before. She'd never had the courage to stand up to him, and even now, her stomach heaved and her heart beat swiftly and erratically as terror threatened to swamp her.

But she wasn't the old Cady – the abused and belittled Cady. Damn it, for the first time she had something good in her life, something wonderful, and she wasn't going to allow him to make her cower again.

She'd go down fighting. And to her astonishment, Jameson was staring at her with what looked like... *disbelief* in his eyes.

"How did you find me?" she questioned.

He recovered his equilibrium and smirked. "I knew those two little cows and you couldn't keep away from one another. I just waited, and watched, until your sisters travelled to this god-forsaken shithole to visit with you."

"You've been around Garrison since Christmas?" Cady asked.

"Longer," Jameson announced, draining the last of his coffee. "I've been here for weeks, but I had to wait for an opportunity to snatch you when you were alone." He huffed out an impatient breath. "In this ridiculous little town, it seems as if you never are."

Realization dawned on Cady, knowledge that the sense of being watched that she'd endured for weeks had an explanation. "You've been following me?"

"Yeah." Jameson made a show of carefully resealing the thermos of coffee.

"The fire? At Tokens? That was you?"

Jameson got to his feet, walking over to peer out through one of the windows. "If those two fools had left well enough alone, the place would have burned to the ground. That's what I'd hoped for – it was no more than you deserve after what you've done to me." He turned back to Cady, waving a hand to encompass the interior of the cabin. "I don't get to stay in fancy houses, or hotels anymore. No, I've got to hide out in these deplorable, shitty cabins, and ratty small-town motels, and hide who I am to keep from being arrested. And in the meantime, you're starting up a little business and hanging out with your new boyfriend; enjoying fancy sleigh rides and romantic suppers. You haven't got a care in the world, while my entire life falls apart. This is all your fault, Cady – everything that's gone wrong in my life is because of you."

Cady shook her head. "No, Jameson. You're in this mess because of what *you* did. You nearly killed me. I lost a kidney after that last beating, I was black and blue for weeks."

"You ruined my life," Jameson repeated, his voice cold and calculating, as if Cady hadn't spoken at all. "You owe me, Cady. You used me to pay for your sisters' education, to cover the costs of raising those bitches."

Cady nodded. "You're right. I did rely on you for financial help bringing the girls up. But you knew, before we got married, that I was responsible for them. You said you were willing to help out."

Jameson's eyes rounded. "If you *behaved*! If you did as you were asked!" The volume of his voice increased with each word, anger tarnishing the edge of every syllable.

Cady swallowed convulsively. "No, Jameson. You didn't want me to do as I was asked. You wanted me to do as I was *told*."

He stormed across the tiny cabin and loomed over her, his size and proximity intimidating. "*You* are my wife! You're *meant* to do as you're told!"

Cady shook her head. Despite her best efforts to appear

brave, she automatically shied away, her back scraping across the rough timber wall. "No. I'm not your wife any longer. I've filed for divorce. You don't get to tell me what to do."

The first open-handed blow across her cheek had Cady seeing stars; pain exploded in her jaw and her ear began to ring. Distantly, she heard Jameson's voice. "You are mine, and once I've finished teaching you a lesson, I'm going to throw what's left of you over that cliff outside. They'll *never* find you."

---

"SHERIFF!" Deputy Reid practically ran across the floor and into George's office, his pale skin flushed with excitement. "We've got a sighting! Carmona Aguilar from the Big Wheel Ranch saw a black pickup, travelling north out of town," he glanced at his notepad, "about thirty-five miles away. He said there was a woman in the front seat who matched Cady's description, and the man driving sounds like Jameson Le Batelier. The description matches the updated BOLO."

George and Kane exchanged a worried glance.

"That's well outside of the roadblocks," Kane admitted.

George got to his feet and hurried over to the map, eyeing it while he tried to figure out what to do next, anticipate where Le Batelier might be heading. The Big Wheel Ranch was nearly fifty miles out of town, and Carmona must have seen the pickup as he travelled south towards Garrison. He pushed a pin into the map. "What time did he see them?"

Reid glanced down at his notepad again. "Around 8.45 am."

George snatched up a marker and made a note on the map beside the pin, noting the time.

Kane came to stand beside him and pointed to a break in the mountains. "My guess is that he'll plan on cutting through the mountains at this point, probably heading further north. He could be intent on crossing the border into Canada."

George considered for a moment or two, studying the options and trying to put himself in Le Batelier's head. What would he do, if he was in the same circumstances? Le Batelier had gone out of his way to find his ex-wife, and in George's experience, there was only one reason a man who was on the run would do that.

This was Le Batelier's end game, he realized with a sinking heart. He didn't intend to survive this – and fully intended on taking Cady with him.

"Get onto the men on the northern roadblock, ask them to check with every car that comes through, see if there's been any other sightings. Pull the men on the southern roadblock back to town. We need to rethink."

31

---

Quinn grew more frantic with each passing minute. He'd joined one of the search teams combing the area around Lake Garrison, if only to give himself something substantial to do; but his frustration grew as each minute passed with no news.

He refused to believe Cady could already be dead. Even though the thought kept edging its way into his thoughts, he pushed it back, refused to consider it. She was going to be found alive, damn it, and he wouldn't accept anything else. He loved her. He needed her.

The thought of love no longer sent a shudder of anxiety through his chest. Sure, he'd insisted he was never going to get involved with anyone seriously again, but that little redhead – that frustrating little redhead who had twisted him every which way but up – had worked her way into his heart and mind.

Quinn tugged at a large branch which had fallen from one of the snow-laden trees, sighing in relief when shifting it didn't reveal anything untoward. Everything they came across, every branch, every rock, every miniscule piece of detritus which might hide a clue had to be checked. And with every item, Quinn experienced the same twisting of his heart, the same gut-wrenching terror that this would be the place where they'd find something of Cady's, proof that she'd been hurt – or killed. *Or worse, they were going to be snowed out of searching,* he thought grimly as he surveyed the heavy snow falling on the search area. It was dropping swiftly, and the conditions were worsening by the minute.

Shouts caught his attention, and Quinn turned back with the other three men in his search group. One of them was Hop Skipton, and his friend placed a sympathetic hand on Quinn's shoulder when the search organizer shouted out to them. The portly man was trudging as quickly as he could through the heavy snow, but it was evident from his ruddy cheeks and breathless speech that the effort had cost him.

"Quinn! Kane's on his way out to collect you."

"What's wrong? Have they found her?" Quinn demanded. He was experiencing a surge of emotions too fast to cope with, and for the first time in months, he could tell from the tight sensation in his chest and the squeezing pressure in his throat that he was close to a full-blown panic attack.

The ruddy-faced man mopped at his perspiring face with a handkerchief. "I don't know the whole story, but they've located where she's being held. It's her ex-husband who's got her, he's holding her up in that old mining cabin, near Clawtooth Point."

Quinn didn't wait to hear any more, turning to run back to the car park near the lake. He lifted his feet high to fight through the thick drifts of snow, Hop right on his heels.

One glance at Kane's face confirmed things were about

as serious as they could possibly be. "What's happening?" he demanded. "Is Cady okay?"

"For now," Kane admitted grimly. "But we need your help."

"Anything," Quinn agreed.

"We need a sniper."

Quinn stopped walking and stared at his brother. "What?"

Kane turned back to Quinn. His expression was a mixture of fierce determination and undiluted sympathy. "Le Batelier is holding her in an abandoned cabin near the top of the mountain. It's isolated, and he couldn't have picked a more difficult place to deal with, because it's in an opening, right on the edge of the cliff. We've got no way to approach the cabin, no way to rescue Cady because we can't get close without Le Batelier knowing about it. We think this is his end-game. He's not intending for either of them to come out alive."

Quinn thought for a minute. "Get a shooter in from Billings."

Kane shook his head. "Nope; don't have time. The nearest SWAT team is Billings. The situation has escalated so quickly, we don't have time to get them out here, and the weather has closed in. Can't risk bringing them in by air because there's no guarantee of landing them; as it is, we're not far off this turning into a blizzard. You're our best hope."

Quinn ran the palm of his hand roughly across his fore-head. His heart raced and sweat began to bead under his arms and across his brow, despite the icy conditions.

He couldn't do this. The things he'd done— He'd sworn he'd never again lift a gun against another man and he couldn't do it now. "Kane..."

They were approaching Kane's cruiser, and Quinn was

stunned to discover both his parents standing nearby, wrapped in heavy jackets, their hands gloved. They were both watching him cautiously, and he could easily read the sympathy in their eyes.

John Garrison stepped forward, wrapping Quinn in a hug which brought tears to his eyes. It had been years since he'd felt this helpless, so frightened, and these emotions, this gut-wrenching fear was exactly why he couldn't do what Kane was asking of him.

"She needs you," John whispered against his ear, keeping Quinn wrapped in an embrace which made him feel like a little boy again. John stepped back to look Quinn in the eyes. "We know you can do this, son. Even if it's the last thing you wanna do."

Nancy Garrison took her husband's place, and Quinn wrapped his arms around his mother. The smooth, slippery material of her red coat was an odd sensation beneath his gloved hands, and he concentrated on the feel of it while he tried to pull his chaotic thoughts into order. He was ashamed to admit his hands were shaking, trembling like they'd done in those first few months back from the Middle East, a time when he'd been haunted by almost constant nightmares regarding what he'd done, the people he'd killed. Standing here with his mom, those faces swam through his mind's eye and he tamped them down, gripping his mother closer while he fought back tears.

Making a conscious effort at pulling himself together, he turned to Kane. "What do you want from me?" He heard the snarl in his voice, expected he was coming across as an uncaring bastard in his desire to avoid what was being asked of him. What they didn't realize was the price he'd pay, for what they were asking him to do. The cost would be so high he wasn't certain he could come back from it.

"We need you further up the mountain from the cabin and above the tree line – George thinks he knows of a good position, but we're certainly open to your professional input. George intends to draw Le Batelier out of the cabin, get him into a position where you'll be able to take a shot."

Kane's voice was cold, about as unemotional as Quinn had ever heard it and he recognized that Kane too had pulled back, was hiding his emotions behind his uniform. It was something Quinn had done himself, when he'd been in the Rangers. But he didn't have that comfort now; he had nowhere to hide, no way of excising the pain which would come from killing another man. He hated Jameson Le Batelier, but faced with this impossible situation – could he kill the man if it would save Cady's life?

"Legally— Jesus, Kane! Do you know what you're asking me to do?" Quinn asked, rubbing the back of his neck mechanically. "I can't just go out there and shoot someone."

"George is planning to deputize you." Kane snapped. He yanked opened the passenger door of the cruiser, and indicated with a bob of his head that Quinn should get in. Quinn hesitated, and Kane let some of that calm exterior slip. "For fuck's sake, Quinn! This might be our only chance to save Cady. They're watching the cabin from the tree line, and they can hear—" He broke off abruptly, avoiding Quinn's gaze.

Quinn didn't miss the worried expressions which passed between his parents, and turned from them to Kane, and back again, searching their faces. "What? What can they hear?"

"He's beating on her," Kane admitted quietly. "He's beating her, and George is frightened he'll kill her, if we don't do something soon."

Long seconds passed while Quinn stared at his brother,

and he swallowed heavily once or twice before he straightened his shoulders. There was no choice. "Let's go," he said, and got into the car.

———

KANE DROVE BACK to where a group of cars had congregated, hidden in the tree line just a few feet from the open area which revealed the solitary, ramshackle cabin. Quinn found himself deputized before he had an opportunity to argue, and then stood with George, surveying the map the Sheriff had spread across the hood of his car. George was pointing out the available options, and Quinn tamped down on his emotions, trying to get a handle on a situation which seemed to be barreling out of control, quicker than he could have believed.

"I've got a couple of choices for you – I'm going to draw him out of the building, but I don't doubt he'll bring Cady with him, use her as a human shield. We don't know what sort of state she's in, but we have to assume it's not good."

Whether he'd heard Quinn's sharp intake of breath, or noticed his shaking hands, Quinn didn't know, but George paused for a few seconds and once again, Quinn found himself questioning if he was capable of this.

"There's this spot, up to the north, there are some patches of trees up there that would give you some cover, but the terrain is difficult. The only way in or out is on foot. This other place," he used an index finger to point to it, "might be the better option, although there's a strong possibility you'll have a crosswind to contend with, because of the way the terrain dips and rises in the area." George inhaled heavily. "What sort of range could you take a shot from?"

Quinn swallowed heavily, his throat arid dry. "Fuck, I don't know. I don't even know what you're expecting me to shoot with!"

George nodded to a heavyset man who'd been standing to one side, his face completely concealed by a thick black scarf. He pulled the knitted material away from his face to speak, and Quinn realized it was Earl Henderson.

Earl handed the weapon he'd been gripping over to Quinn, who recognized it as a Remington 700. "You can use this," Earl offered gruffly. "The scope's definitely good to about seven hundred yards, but I can't guarantee what she'd do over a longer distance."

Quinn stared at his ex-wife's husband for a couple of seconds before he took the Remington. "Why would you help?" he demanded. "You've caused nothing but trouble for Cady since she arrived in Garrison."

"Quinn..." George warned, but Earl held up a hand.

"It's a fair question, Sheriff." He pursed his lips, considering his response. "I'm helping because it's the right thing to do. Because I think what Julia did, forcing her Daddy's hand to stop the bakery from going ahead..." he squirmed on the spot, "it was wrong. Don't think there'll ever be any love lost between Julia and Cady, nor you and me for that matter, but I can't let what's happenin' now go on without trying to help out." He dipped his head towards the rifle in Quinn's hand. "She's a good'un, shoots straight, and true. Little bit more kickback than you might expect, which you need to watch out for, and it'd probably be best if you could get a couple of practice shots in before you do anything else."

Quinn lifted the Remington to his shoulder, turning away from the group of men surrounding him. It felt familiar, a gesture he'd repeated so many times before, but he was still aware of the fine tremor in his hands as he focused down the scope.

"Right. As I was saying, we're going to draw Le Batelier out of the cabin, if it's possible. I'll move out into the opening, try to get him talking," George announced, shrugging out of his heavy jacket to pull on the bullet-proof vest Deputy Reid handed him.

Kane handed George a wireless earpiece, which he slotted over his ear and Quinn took the one Reid offered him, the action achingly familiar, and almost mechanical, something he'd repeated hundreds of times before.

"If we can talk him down, we will. We're running with two scenarios, and we don't know which one his end game is. One is that he'll shoot Cady, but given that he's obviously searched for a while to find this cabin, and its vicinity to the edge of the cliff, I'm suspecting he's plannin' on throwing her over if he thinks he's been backed into a corner…"

Quinn swallowed heavily, mentally beginning to push his emotions down, his fears away. If he was going to do this, he had to be completely focused on the job at hand, not thinking about Cady as the victim. If he thought about Cady… shit, he'd never manage to do this. Forcefully, he drew his attention back to George.

"… if you get a clear shot, take it. As much as I hate this bastard, it'd be better for everyone if you can wing him, bring him down. My boys'll be down here, ready to rush in if we can get him unarmed and Cady out of danger." George's expression hardened. "If you think it's the only way… take the kill shot. I'd rather see this guy rotting in jail for the rest of his life, but if that's not possible, killing him would be the next best thing."

CADY SQUEEZED HER EYES SHUT, waiting for the flashing stars to stop spinning through her brain. She wasn't certain how much more she could suffer through, before she'd give in and bow down to what Jameson demanded, tell him that everything was her fault. But damn if she wasn't still determined to remain stubbornly mute.

Somehow, in the months since she'd separated from him, Cady had developed a backbone.

Not much of one, she admitted, opening her eyes slowly and keeping her gaze lowered to buy a couple of minutes before Jameson hit her again, but enough to have brought his temper to a head. For the past hour or two, Jameson had been screaming at her, shrieking, and yes, he'd been hitting her – but good deal of his anger had been directed at the cabin itself. He'd kicked and punched and thrown his belongings until the room looked like a war zone.

Her left eye felt weird, and wasn't opening as it normally would, the skin around it puffy and hot. She'd lost a tooth, maybe two, and each time she swallowed, she could taste blood. But he'd kept his beating to the use of hands and fists – so far. Cady suspected that would change, particularly if she goaded him too much. But she was heartened by the knowledge that somewhere nearby, George – and presumably, some of his men – had taken up a position to try and help her. Even now, she could hear George's voice; he was talking to Jameson, trying to coax him into responding. So far, other than checking out the window every few seconds to make sure they hadn't moved closer, he'd ignored them.

*"Look at me!"* Jameson raged, when she hadn't lifted her head after another minute.

Cady licked her lips, ran her tongue over a deep split in her lower lip. "Why? So you can hit me again?"

*Whack!* Her neck crashed to the left, and bright white pain exploded in her jaw, tendrils of agony working their way down into her neck and shoulders as she squeezed her eyes shut again.

*You should have expected that,* Cady thought. She was pushing her luck, probably way too far, but what did she have to lose? Jameson was going to kill her. If he didn't do it here in this cabin, he'd said he was going to throw her over the cliff. So, what did she really have to lose?

And that newly discovered backbone was goading her, digging at her. For the first time in her life, Cady wasn't going to be walked over. She had something now, something of her own – something special. Tokens had become the most important thing in her life... other than Quinn.

Despite the pain she was in, Cady's lips curved into a faint smile at the thought of Quinn. She'd spent weeks telling herself he was a good friend, that she was fond of him, but she'd held back from considering it anything more. Now, sitting in this freezing cold cabin on the side of a mountain, getting the crap beaten out of her by this weak, pathetic little man – and she realized in a flash of clarity that the description was apt – she understood that Jameson had never deserved her. She was better than him, better than her rat-bastard father, better than her drug-addicted mother.

And she loved Quinn Garrison.

And she was sorry that she would never get to tell him that truth.

"Look at me!" Jameson demanded. He'd knelt beside her, his wild eyes revealing the full extent of his fury. "You little bitch! *You are my wife!* If I want to beat the shit out of you for being so weak, and so fucking useless, I will!"

Cady swallowed hard, cleared her throat, and brought

her gaze up to meet her ex-husband's. "I am *not* your wife. You never deserved me."

She caught the movement of Jameson's arm, the way he lifted it, squeezing his hand into a fist. Cady closed her eyes, swiftly turning to one side, not wanting to see the coming punch.

But the hit never came. Instead, she heard George's voice, and this time it wasn't coming over a loudspeaker. He was calling, from somewhere outside. Judging by the level of the sound, he was close.

"Jameson Le Batelier! I'm unarmed! I want to talk to you, son. Come on out here, and let's figure this mess out! This doesn't need to end in bloodshed!"

Quinn lay on his stomach, on a tarpaulin laid over the snowy ground. He'd settled on the second nest George had nominated. The wind up here was a little trickier, but regarding line-of-sight and the ability to get off a clear shot, it was his best option.

Hop had driven him out here, and now, while Quinn prepared, his friend had stepped away, leaving him alone on this rocky outcrop high above the cabin to get his thoughts together, prepare himself for this shot that would bring this nightmare to an end.

On the way up here, Hop had stopped for a few minutes and Quinn had taken a quick practice run with the Remington, firing off half a dozen shots to get a feel for it before he'd risk shooting at someone. Internally, he'd already filed away doubts about shooting Jameson Le Batelier, mentally preparing himself for the prospect of killing the man if he needed to. He'd pay for it afterwards – no doubt his demons would come to roost and he'd spend months working through nightmares and insomnia – but for now, Jameson Le Batelier was the enemy and Quinn was responsible for Cady's safety.

His biggest fear was the prospect of not having enough feel for the damn weapon, and accidentally shooting Cady. *Don't think that way,* he warned himself for about the hundredth time. Emotion had no place in the equation, all he needed to focus on was the weapon, the scope and the view of the group standing further down the mountain-side. For the first few minutes after he'd gotten in position, he'd spent the time shutting down outside influences – even now, despite the bitter northerly wind, the constant flurries of snowfall, he was no longer aware of the cold on his face, or the iciness of his fingers. He silently counted backwards from ten, mentally working on his breathing, slowing down his heart rate, becoming one with the weapon, his whole attention on the bodies he had sighted through the scope. The shot was longer than he would've liked, nearly eight hundred yards, but this was definitely the better nest. The other one was too visible; although he doubted Le Batelier would be able to pick him out on the mountain, it was a risk he wouldn't take. This nest was better, hidden, invisible from down below. He'd briefly scouted over Cady's injuries through the scope, and then pushed his horror to the back of his mind. All that mattered, here and now, was keeping the sight focused on Jameson Le Batelier.

The man hadn't stopped moving yet, dragging Cady back and forth, getting closer to the edge of the cliff... then stepping back, just as Quinn was putting pressure on the trigger. If he attempted to throw Cady over the side, Quinn would put a bullet in his head...

Quinn realized he was tightening up and reverted to his customary routine of slowing his breathing, calming his thoughts, refocusing on the target. He needed to de-personalize the situation, focus on the job at hand.

The continual chatter in his ear confirmed George was still working hard, but not having any success in talking Le Batelier down. The guy was agitated, stomping back and forth in the snow and dragging Cady – the victim - along with him. Quinn couldn't think of her as Cady, or he'd screw this up, he was certain of it. Fear and panic were the last thing he needed to be thinking about, and with Le Batelier constantly on the move, Quinn wasn't certain he could take the shot and hit the right person. Or even worse, miss, and have Le Batelier shoot Cady with the handgun he was waving around.

The chatter further down the hill grew more impassioned, voices rising and falling swiftly. Quinn wasn't focusing on the words, only the nuances of the voices, and he realized that while George remained outwardly calm, Le Batelier grew increasingly erratic as the minutes passed.

Watching through the scope, he counted Le Batelier's steps, back and forth, back and forth from the edge of the cliff, and then suddenly, his gut instinct kicked in. Le Batelier's tone of voice changed, growing harsher, and Quinn knew the shit was hitting the fan.

With infinite care, he squeezed the trigger.

He took the shot.

---

"IF YOU JUST PUT THE gun down, give yourself up, we can resolve this," George said, something he'd repeated, to Cady's fuzzy thoughts, continually since this standoff began. She was cold, freezing cold, and the weather was worsening, the sky darker as heavy flurries of snow fell all around them. The wind was getting up, and without gloves and a coat, Cady suspected she'd freeze to death before Jameson killed her. She hurt – oh, how she hurt – but there were so many different aches, pains and throbs, she was starting to think it might be better to go over the cliff and be done with it.

"How can we resolve this?" Jameson shouted, squeezing her more tightly against him, and Cady struggled against the chokehold he maintained around her neck. He was holding her against him, ensuring he was covered as much as possible by her slight body and each time he yanked against her neck, she struggled to draw breath. "I need a helicopter, or I'm going to kill her!"

"There isn't going to be a helicopter, son," George responded calmly. Cady wondered vaguely if he should be lying about that, give her at least a fighting chance of living for another few minutes. Would it really hurt to tell Jameson he'd get a helicopter? George's voice drew her back to the here and now. "The weather's closed in, we're expecting this to turn into a blizzard, in the next half hour or so. Just let Cady go, and we can talk like civilized—"

"No! She's my *wife*! She comes with me!"

Jameson yanked her in the direction of the cliff, dragging her numb body across the snow and darkness began to close in as she struggled to draw breath.

She heard something strange, a sound she didn't recognize, and then the side of her face suddenly got warm; warm and damp. Cady couldn't understand what it was, where it might be coming from.

She heard shouts from the group she'd noticed by the treeline, and in the same instant she realized Jameson had released his grip on her neck but had caught hold of the sleeve of her shirt. There was madness in his dark eyes as he established a better grip on Cady's wrist, and she started to scream in earnest. Blood was pouring from a wound in Jameson's left shoulder, seeping into the down jacket he wore, creating a dark stain. He dropped to his knees, a mixture of stunned fascination and crazed fury visible in his expression as he deliberately leaned backwards, his knees starting to slip over the wet snow, leaving him sliding backwards, back towards the edge of the cliff...

...and he was going to take Cady with him.

GEORGE'S RELIEF on hearing through his earpiece that Quinn had taken the shot quickly morphed to the other end of the spectrum, as he watched Le Batelier's next actions. Quinn had shot him in the left shoulder, and thankfully, the shock was enough to have Le Batelier dropping his weapon.

The man dropped to his knees and George had a split-second to realize that while Le Batelier had released his grip on Cady's neck, now he was clutching her wrist in a death grip. George was on the move before he'd fully comprehended what was happening, what Le Batelier intended to do. He forced his way through the snow, struggling against the thick drifts as he tried to stop the inevitable. Cady's screams rang in his ears, she frantically tried to release her wrist from Le Batelier's grasp, and she was scrambling to stay on her feet, even as Le Batelier slipped over the side of the cliff. He saw when she realized she couldn't save herself by standing, and threw herself onto the ground, flat on her stomach, trying to buy herself a few more seconds before she was dragged over the edge by Le Batelier's weight.

"Good girl," he muttered to himself as he threw his body the last few feet, snatching at Cady's dark boots to try and stop her inexorable fall over the cliff. He wrapped his hands firmly around Cady's ankles, and held on for grim death, hoping like hell that the sounds he could hear from behind were the other men making their way across to help. Already he could feel himself sliding towards the edge, the dead weight of Le Batelier and the icy conditions giving him nothing to grip, no traction to stop Cady from going over. And Mer would kill him, if that happened.

It seemed to take forever, but he suspected it was, at most, a minute, before Kane, Earl and Deputy Reid reached his side. Kane immediately added his considerable height and bulk to George's, to keep Cady from slipping over the edge, and George was grateful for the opportunity to rest his head for a few seconds against the snow. All around him there was shouting, and frantic activity amid Cady's terrified screams. He was mighty relieved when the tension against his fingers was reduced, Cady's inevitable plunge over the cliff thwarted when someone managed to release her hand from Le Batelier's grip. It took him a minute or two to realize it was over, and the sound of cheering was foreign to his ears after the tension of the past few hours. For the second time in as many minutes, he dropped his face onto the snowy ground, grateful for the chill against his sweaty cheek and temple.

Damn it, he was getting too old for this.

---

QUINN JUMPED from the truck before Hop had fully stopped, and flew across the open patch of land, hurrying to where the men were congregated.

His heart had been in his mouth for the past fifteen minutes. He'd watched, initially in satisfaction, as his shot found its target. A sense of relief had swept over him, knowing he hadn't needed to kill the guy. He'd battled with himself over the prospect, up there on the hill, but ultimately, he'd avoided the kill shot. He suspected Cady Caldwell would be his wife one day, and he didn't see how that would work out if he'd been the one who killed her ex-husband. Nope, better for the guy to stand trial, Quinn had thought... until he'd understood Le Batelier's end game was to die and take Cady with him. Hell, if Quinn had known that, he'd have put that bullet right in the center of the bastard's forehead.

But George, Kane, and the other men who'd been waiting at the edge of the clearing had leaped into action when Le Batelier slid over the cliff - trying to take Cady with him - and saved her life. And he was grateful, so incredibly grateful for that, but damn if he didn't need to see her for himself after urging Hop to get him down the mountain just as fast as he could.

Cady was lying on a gurney, bundled in a pile of warm blankets and only her face was visible, pinched, badly bruised and worn-out, but Quinn rejoiced at seeing her alive. Ignoring the paramedics protests, he scooped Cady into his arms and kissed her, eliciting whoops and catcalls from the men around them.

"Quinn..." Cady snuggled against his chest, making a little sound of contentment.

Quinn turned his attention to P.J. Mandrell, who threw him an irritated look and made a pointed gesture towards the gurney. Quinn shook his head firmly. "She stays with me."

"We're taking her back to town," Allen announced. "She has mild hypothermia, she's got a lot of bruising, some lacerations and she might need a few stitches on some of those injuries, but overall, she's doing okay." He glanced at the storm clouds overhead. "Too risky to take her to Billings now, the weather's closing in. We'll transfer her to Billings tomorrow if Doc Ogilvie thinks it's necessary."

"Okay, let's go." Quinn was determined to stay with Cady, wouldn't let her out of his sight now she was safe. Every time he looked at her bruised and battered face, he gritted his teeth and reminded himself again why he hadn't taken the kill shot. But looking at her now, he wished he had…

Cady opened one swollen eye when he started striding toward the ambulance and peeked up at him curiously. "George says it was you – you stopped Jameson."

Quinn pressed a gentle kiss to her forehead and continued trudging through the snow. "Yes, Ma'am."

"Thank you. I know how… difficult that must have been for you."

Quinn came to a standstill, staring down at Cady for a couple of seconds before he spoke. "It would have been harder to lose you," he admitted quietly. He began to walk again, leaving the others to follow behind. His only purpose in life was to get Cady down the mountain, warmed up, feeling better and then… well then, he and she were going to talk about a future together. Quinn wasn't pussyfooting around with Cady any longer. He wanted her to know how he felt, and he hoped she felt the same way.

"I love you."

Quinn came to a standstill for a second time, in the middle of all that snow, with the wind whistling around his ears, and snow falling harder by the second. He stared down at Cady, his surprise, he suspected, visible in his expression. "You do?" he asked stupidly.

Cady blinked sluggishly, before her eyes closed, her dark lashes creating tiny fans against her cheeks. "I do."

During the long drive to Garrison, sitting in the back of the ambulance with Cady's hand in his, Quinn thought about what she'd said, and wondered if she really meant it. She'd been through a lot – she was hypothermic, beaten black and blue, and bloodied. He wanted to believe what she'd said, but he wasn't convinced she'd known what she was saying. But he was clinging to what she'd said like a warm blanket wrapped around his heart and savoring it for now.

# EPILOGUE

The bell over the door at Tokens rang and old Mr. Harper came in. "Good afternoon, ladies."

"Hey A.J., how're you doing?" Gran handed a paper bag filled with cupcakes over to one of the ranch hands from the Lazy K and the tall, gangly man tipped his hat in acknowledgement, before he hurried out the door.

Cady glanced over at her grandmother, looking so much better now her injuries had nearly healed. Besides a severe concussion, the wound had needed nearly two dozen stitches and left quite the scar along Meredith's temple. Fortunately, Meredith had already grown adept at curling her grey hair over the scar while it continued to heal.

"I'm doing just fine, Meredith. Those two granddaughters of yours have headed back to California, I hear."

"Yes; it was lovely to have them here for a few days, but Sid needed to get back to finish up school, and Harry's had so many days off since Cady moved to Garrison, she really couldn't stay long. But it was a blessing to have them here, and I think it was a relief for the girls to confirm for themselves that Cady and I are doing okay."

"More than okay," Paulette announced, carrying a tray of fresh stock for the display case and offering Meredith encouraging smile. "Considering what you two gals went through, I would have thought a couple more days off might have been a good idea."

"Get Cady to leave the store? Impossible," Meredith scoffed, turning to the display stand to retrieve A.J.'s usual order before placing it in the center of a small plate and handing it to Cady.

Cady carried the plate around the counter and deposited it in front of A.J. at his usual table. Hearing a low grumble, she walked across to the source of the noise and slowly crouched down beside Churchill, aware of every ache and pain she was still carrying. He was lying beside the stove, enjoying the heat emanating from the wood fire. She rubbed behind his ears before scratching thoroughly under his jaw. "I'm better off here, at Tokens. There's no point sitting at home, I'd only fret over what happened."

"Yer certainly looking a mite better, but yer poor face – it's black and blue," A.J. pointed out.

Cady got to her feet and spent a moment basking in the glorious heat emitted by the stove. In the five days since Jameson took her, Cady still hadn't lost the sensation of being so shockingly cold. Her hands were warm now – psychologically she knew they were warm – but she could still recall that awful stinging, burning sensation she'd suffered in her hands and feet during her captivity. "It'll heal," she reassured the elderly man. "And I survived."

"You certainly did," Gran announced approvingly. The two women shared an affectionate smile and Cady was reassured by Gran's loving presence, her unconditional support, her unwavering belief. It had been part of what allowed Cady to stick up for herself with Jameson, one reason Cady hadn't cowered so badly with his abuse. It still hadn't been easy, she'd still been frightened, but thanks to Gran, and Quinn, and most everyone in the small town of Garrison, Montana, she'd discovered that Cady Caldwell – the girl who'd endured a dreadful childhood, and suffered an abusive marriage – was also Cady Caldwell, a survivor. She'd survived everything life had thrown at her, and come out the other end stronger, braver, and better.

As if he'd been conjured up by her thoughts, the bell tinkled again, and Quinn walked in through the door. His eyes lit up when he saw her, and a lazy smile brightened his features. "Ms. Caldwell. You're looking a bit better—wooohhthhh!"

Cady had run across the small store, surprising Quinn by throwing herself into his arms, wrapping her arms around his neck and kissing him resoundingly on the lips, seemingly oblivious to who was around to see them. She was vaguely aware of a couple of wolf whistles and some cheering, but all she focused on was Quinn's mouth against hers, his lips and tongue seeking, searching restlessly as he demanded entrance to her mouth and she willingly gave it. He wrapped his own arms around her, surrounding Cady with warmth and a deep sense of satisfaction she'd rarely experienced before. This was her man, the man she loved, and she didn't care who knew it.

When she pulled back, Quinn's eyes were glazed, his breathing ragged, and he squeezed her close. "Dammit, Cady. I think the toes of my boots just curled."

Cady laughed. "I think mine did too."

"I love you, my little redhead." The words fell from Quinn's lips and Cady saw the rush of emotion which played across his features, the shock, and the uncertainty.

She stretched up to brush a brief kiss across his lips, speaking to him as she did so. "I love you, too. Always."

## The End

D.S. Williams likes to live in other people's lives, mainly because they are so much more interesting than her own.

There was a time, many years ago, when D.S. thought she might be able to be like 'other' people and hold down a normal job in the normal world. It soon became apparent, to herself (and everyone around her), that this was not a suitable environment for someone with her head in the clouds, and her heart in a novel; but it took nearly ten years of employment, and fifteen years as a full-time parent, before she found her niche and began working from home – where she can go off on those tangents when the pull of an exciting new character pulls her into another adventure.

Employment and family notwithstanding, she's spent forty odd years in make-believe worlds, creating new friends on paper and putting them into impossible situations, to make them both interesting and entertaining, and bringing new settings and situations to life. Her characters are created in the deepest, darkest corners of D.S. Williams' mind and tend to annoy her the most when she's trying to sleep, or has something imperative she should be doing. And they never, ever do as they're told – while D.S. has a plan for their futures... they tend to have plans of their own, which are usually wildly altered from what was prepared for them.

With a love of multiple genres, D.S. will write almost anything, although she especially loves romances, and if you can add some werewolves, vampires or other mythical creatures to the mix, she's in her element. She also loves a spot of suspense, a touch of teasing, and hasn't met a good cliffhanger that she didn't like.

The author of The Nememiah Chronicles, and Protective Hearts, D.S. is currently working on a number of new projects, including the long-awaited final book in The Nememiah Chronicles series. She adores strong male characters, feisty female characters, and developing complex relationships among everyone who turns up in her books.

D.S. is a member of her local writers' group, who she would probably describe as being 'a bunch of social misfits with anxiety issues and a lack of belief in themselves, but a really brilliant bunch of people'. It is through this writers group that D.S. hones her craft, expands her writing abilities, and tends to do her only socializing with 'real' people.

When not writing, D.S. tends to still be completely engrossed in the written word, with Laurell K. Hamilton, Cassandra Clare, Charlaine Harris, Dakota Cassidy, J.K. Rowling and Cherise Sinclair being among her favourite authors. And when not writing, or reading, she is still involved with the written word in her work as an editor, specializing in indie author works.

D.S. loves collecting notebooks and pens, in fact; some would suggest it has become an addiction. It is an addiction that her Darling Husband constantly shakes his head over but lovingly accepts, because although D.S. is always seeking out beautiful new notebooks, she struggles to bring herself to write in them, because, in her words, "It would mess them up". This doesn't stop her from buying them, however and consequently, D.S.'s home is overflowing with bookshelves filled with (mostly empty) notebooks, and she has a pen for every single occasion.

While DS. was born and bred in Australia, her stories are generally set in other countries, and D.S. uses her love of research, and an addiction to 'Google Search' to flesh out the settings she creates. Some of her books are set in the United States, although a current work-in-progress is set in the wine-growing regions of France, and a future book will take place in Scotland. D.S. considers this beautiful country her ancestral home, and with a father born in the northern highlands, her love of the country guarantees that Scotland will appear in more than one future novel.

An extremely reclusive introvert, D.S. lives in Perth, Western Australia with her Darling Husband, the Gang of Four, and the furry residents, Angus and Tuppence. She has travelled around the country as a military wife, but is now settled back in her home state, where she intends to spend the rest of her days writing, reading and meeting new (fictional) friends.

You can find D.S. here:

Facebook:

https://www.facebook.com/D.S.Williams.Author/

Twitter: https://twitter.com/Nememiah

Blog: https://theworldsofdswilliams.com/

Lightning Source UK Ltd.
Milton Keynes UK
UKHW021023161120
373486UK00004B/523

9 781715 770921